Praise for

The Undermining of Twyla and Frank

"One of the coziest, most whimsical fantasy reads I've ever come across! Megan Bannen has created a world that you'll never want to leave and characters that will carve a spot into your heart. This series is playfully unique, delightfully steamy, utterly romantic, and overall unmissable!"

—Ali Hazelwood, *New York Times* bestselling author of *The Love Hypothesis*

"Bannen manages to seamlessly blend fantasy, romance, and modern family dynamics, all while making you laugh until you (literally) cry. I love this book so much that I would bury bodies for Twyla and Frank so deep no one would ever find them."

—Lish McBride, author of the Uncanny Romance series

"Deeply adorable and heartbreakingly hilarious. Life is hard. Do yourself a favor and read this bear hug of a book full of wonders and pink dragons."

—Jayci Lee, author of *Nine Tailed* and *That Prince Is Mine*

"Hilarious, heartfelt, and irresistibly charming."

—Stephanie Burgis, author of *Wooing the Witch Queen*

"Bannen's witty prose and skillful genre blending shine as she seamlessly weaves together elements of romance, mystery, and adventure. The mature protagonists...offer a refreshing perspective on love and self-discovery in midlife....This cozy, humor-filled romp celebrates the enduring magic of love at any age."

—*Publishers Weekly*

"A delightful story worth every minute of [your] time. Fans of cozy fantasy will find a lot to love here, from glitter-breathing, poodle-esque dragons to a down-to-earth romance between two middle-aged heroes on the brink of retirement. Seriously, the dragons breathe glitter. What more could you want?"

—*Kirkus*

Praise for

The Undertaking of Hart and Mercy

"A uniquely charming mixture of whimsy and the macabre that completely won me over. If you ever wished for an adult romance that felt like *Howl's Moving Castle*, THIS IS THAT BOOK."

—Helen Hoang, author of
The Kiss Quotient

"Truly outstanding romantic fantasy. I loved both its kookiness and its deep authenticity. An instant favorite!"

—India Holton, author of
The Wisteria Society of Lady Scoundrels

"If Lewis Carroll and Nora Ephron teamed up to write a magical Western, this would be the result. An unabashedly offbeat adventure, *The Undertaking of Hart and Mercy* oozes romantic fun." —Freya Marske, author of *A Marvellous Light*

"A lovely, macabre fantasy romance about life, death, and Actually Living. I cried twice and smiled plenty."
—Olivia Atwater, author of *Half a Soul*

"This book is a gooey (and hot!) romance immersed in a tasty layer of quirky fantasy, like some decadent chocolate treat. A little sweet, a little spicy, a little sharp, and entirely moreish!"
—Davinia Evans, author of *Notorious Sorcerer*

"Perfect for readers who love enemies-to-lovers mashed up with a touch of secret pen pal romance. I showed up for the fantastic, fun fantasy setting, but it was Hart and Mercy that kept me reading." —Ruby Dixon, author of *Ice Planet Barbarians*

"Full of sizzle and emotional turmoil, as well as plenty of sci-fi adventure and humor. Readers will be captivated."
—*Library Journal*

"Fans of the *Ask a Mortician* webseries and those who love gore and rom-coms in equal measure will find plenty to enjoy in this quirky outing." —*Publishers Weekly*

"A crispy, hot-fried, pastel-dipped piece of delicious fantasy fiction wrapped up in a ravenous rom-com.... This is a unique read!"
—*BuzzFeed*

By Megan Bannen

The Undertaking of Hart and Mercy
The Undermining of Twyla and Frank
The Undercutting of Rosie and Adam

THE
UNDERCUTTING
OF
ROSIE
AND
ADAM

MEGAN BANNEN

Copyright © 2025 by Megan Bannen
Excerpt from *How to Summon a Fairy Godmother* copyright © 2024 by Laura Jean Mayo
Excerpt from *The Last Hour Between Worlds* copyright © 2024 by Melissa Caruso

Cover design by Lisa Marie Pompilio
Cover illustrations by Shutterstock
Cover copyright © 2025 by Hachette Book Group, Inc.
Author photograph by Brian Paulette

Orbit
Hachette Book Group
1290 Avenue of the Americas
New York, NY 10104
orbitbooks.net

First Edition: July 2025
Simultaneously published in Great Britain by Orbit

Orbit is an imprint of Hachette Book Group.
The Orbit name and logo are registered trademarks of Little, Brown Book Group Limited.

The publisher is not responsible for websites (or their content) that are not owned by the publisher.

The Hachette Speakers Bureau provides a wide range of authors for speaking events. To find out more, go to hachettespeakersbureau.com or email HachetteSpeakers@hbgusa.com.

Orbit books may be purchased in bulk for business, educational, or promotional use. For information, please contact your local bookseller or the Hachette Book Group Special Markets Department at special.markets@hbgusa.com.

Library of Congress Cataloging-in-Publication Data
Names: Bannen, Megan, author.
Title: The undercutting of Rosie and Adam / Megan Bannen.
Description: First edition. | New York, NY : Orbit, 2025.
Identifiers: LCCN 2024055072 | ISBN 9780316568272 (trade paperback) |
    ISBN 9780316568302 (ebook)
Subjects: LCGFT: Fantasy fiction. | Romance fiction. | Novels.
Classification: LCC PS3602.A6664 U525 2025 | DDC 813/.6—dc23/eng/20241125
LC record available at https://lccn.loc.gov/2024055072

ISBNs: 9780316568272 (trade paperback), 9780316568302 (ebook)

Printed in the United States of America

LSC-C

Printing 1, 2025

This one's for Amanda—
sings Thank you for being a friend.

ESHIL
CRAIA

PRITEAN CONTINENT

THE WORLD
OF THE
NEW GODS

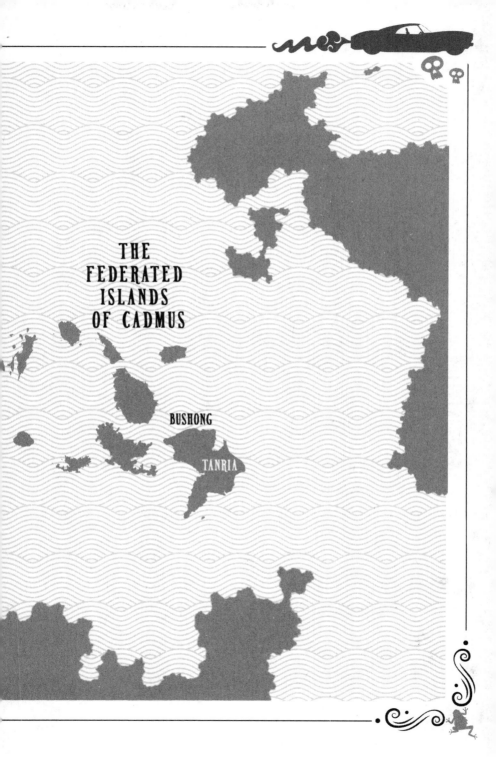

MAP OF TANRIA

NORTH STATION

N-1	N-2	N-3	N-4	N-5	N-6
W-7	N-8	N-9	N-10	N-11	E-12
W-13	W-14 TANRIAN DRAGON PRESERVE	N-15	N-16	E-17	E-18
W-19	W-20	N-21	N-22	E-23	E-24
W-25	W-26	W-27	SECTOR 28	E-29	E-30
W-31	W-32	S-33	S-34	E-35	E-36
W-37	W-38	S-39	S-40	E-41	E-42
W-43	S-44	S-45	S-46	E-47	E-48
S-49	S-50	S-51	S-52	S-53	S-54

WEST STATION

EAST STATION

SOUTH STATION

THE
UNDERCUTTING
OF
ROSIE
AND
ADAM

Chapter One

To Rosie's mind, the word *red* wasn't as cut and dried as most people would have you believe.

If you said someone's hair was red, was it literally red? That primary-color-hanging-out-at-the-top-of-a-prism red? Or was it the kind of red that masqueraded as copper and rust? Rosie Fox's hair was red, but it was the copper and rust kind of red, dangling in a pair of brassy plaits from beneath the wide brim of her flat hat.

Folks usually described the dry, gritty dirt of Bushong as red, the dust of which permanently clung to Rosie's ostrich leather boots like flour on a baker's peel. But it wasn't red. It wasn't even paprika. It was more like cinnamon, although the grit it left in Rosie's mouth on a windy day didn't taste so good.

And what about the red eyes that resulted from too much crying or too little sleep? Were they truly red? Or were the whites simply rendered pink by a body's weariness? Those eyes weren't red, not really.

But Rosie Fox did have red eyes, and that was no lie. Red. The color of apple skins. The color of geranium blooms on a hot summer day. The irises that hugged her black pupils against a field of white were as bright and livid as a vine-ripe tomato.

Those red eyes glinted like a pair of cut rubies as she squinted at the West Station's portal, the befuddlingly complicated archway that was supposed to allow mortals to pass through the Mist, in and out of Tanria. Except it was on the fritz. Again.

"I'm pretty sure whatever you're about to do is a bad idea, RoFo."

Rosie glanced at her partner long enough to give him an insouciant shrug. "What's the worst that could happen?"

"You could break the portal, and I'd get fired from the Tanrian Marshals because of your poor life choices, and then I'd die impoverished and alone?"

The words coming out of Penrose Duckers's mouth were far more alarmist than his demeanor. He looked bored, slouching against the portal's frame, his arms crossed, his *FIC Tanrian Marshals Service* badge glinting on his khaki uniform shirt. For a moment, Duckers's mustache startled Rosie. He was so young when they'd partnered up that he could barely grow peach fuzz on his upper lip. Now he bore an impressive black pelt under his broad, handsome nose. When had that happened?

She shook off the creeping sensation that time was getting away from her again, and faced the portal with its cogs and pistons and pipes. "I can't break something if it's already broken," she reasoned.

"Not sure I agree with that statement."

"I'm not *breaking* it. I'm *fixing* it." She gave the left side a solid *thwack* with her fist.

Louis, the engineer on duty, winced. "I wish you wouldn't."

"Relax, Louis. You know I have a gift."

"Does he know that, though?" asked Duckers. "Do any of us?"

Rosie glared at him, not that her uncanny eyes had any effect on her partner. Never had. It was one of the reasons she loved the kid.

Who is not a kid anymore, she reminded herself. In a way, he was older than she was now.

"Have a little faith, Penny-D," she told him a half second before her fist arced downward, whacking the archway from a different angle. The portal did not whir to life as she had hoped. Instead, a small metal hatch near the main switch went flying off the frame and skittered into the gravel parking lot ten feet away.

"Oh, jeez," said Louis, chasing after it.

Duckers sucked his teeth. "Dang, Foxy, what did I just say?"

"Please. You know the Smack It Method works at least half the time."

"Okay, but the other fifty percent lands both of us in the chief's office. Can we not?"

She pressed her hands together. "Trust."

"Ha! Trusting you is the road to Old Hell. I want to go home."

"I'm not stopping you."

"I drove this time, genius. How else do you plan to get back to Eternity?"

"One more smack, and then we'll go."

"Ugh."

It was autumn, but hanging around in what was essentially a desert with no shade to speak of made Duckers doff his standard-issue flat hat to blot the sweat from his warm brown face. If Rosie took off her hat, she'd burn to a crisp in two seconds flat, even this late in the year. *Red as a lobster* was how people described it, another red that was actually pink. And sunburn red didn't matter a lick to Rosie anyway, since her body would return to its usual ghostly pale existence by morning light.

It wasn't a comforting thought, so she returned her attention to the broken portal, a technical marvel incongruously set into the Mist that shrouded the land of Tanria in a giant, foggy dome. There was a portal at each of the cardinal points of Tanria, the only means by which human beings could enter and exit the former prison of the Old Gods.

Except Rosie and Duckers had been diverted to the North Station's portal when their shift had ended, since this one was down.

Rosie wondered if Chief Maguire would ask the portals' inventor to take a look at it. The engineers were so good at their job these days that Adam Lee almost never came to Bushong anymore. Rosie hadn't seen the man in a good five years, not since the last time he had been called in to fix the West Station's portal when the engineers couldn't figure out what ailed it. Most people found him either boring or intimidating. And yet the last time she had encountered him—

A peculiar spot inside the open hatch caught her attention.

"What is that?" she asked Louis as he positioned the hatch door onto its hinges.

"What is what?" He didn't look at Rosie or even inside the inner mechanism of the portal. He was too busy trying to reattach the door with the smallest screwdriver under the altar of the sky.

Rosie crouched beside him to point at a dark, twisty stain within, lurking behind a pair of tubes and a cluster of wires. "That."

"The tubes?"

"No."

"The wires?"

"No. *That.*"

"There's . . . nothing there?"

"Oh my gods, Louis, look where my finger is pointing."

"Ugh," Duckers moaned again. He shooed Rosie out of the way so that he could have a look.

"Well?" she asked him after he'd squinted inside the hatch for more time than was necessary.

"I see tubes and wires."

"And the thing."

"No thing."

"The shadowy blotch thing in the back."

"Nope. Tubes and wires."

Rosie turned pleading eyes to the engineer. He shook his head and grimaced in apology.

"You guys." She wormed her way between them and reached into the portal to move aside the wires and show them the very obvious spot.

"That's a bad—" began Louis.

And then a jolt shot through Rosie's entire body. She went painfully rigid and her jaw clenched so hard a few of her teeth cracked as wave after wave of pain coursed through her in a matter of seconds. She convulsed with a current so strong it reminded her forcefully of the two times in her life she had been struck by lightning. And then she was hurtling backward, as if she were an ugly rag doll thrown across a room by a petulant child. She landed on the edge of the gravel parking lot in a cloud of not-red dust. She heard and, worse, felt a couple of ribs crack before everything went blank.

Not dark, but empty.

She couldn't hear Louis finish his sentence, uttering the word "idea" in a stunned daze. She couldn't see Duckers rush to her side, cussing his fool head off. She couldn't taste the blood in her mouth. She couldn't smell the smoking mess of her singed hair. She couldn't feel the horrid fracture at the back of her skull. All she could do was *be*, and that was her least favorite thing to do.

Mother of Sorrows, she was dead again.

She hated dying, hated the sickening nothingness inside her rib cage, the eerie silence of death, the freaky way her body stopped hurting. And there wasn't a blessed thing she could do about it but let the burden of her immortality crush her soul while she waited for her body to return to her. Which it inevitably would.

It always did.

The heart always recovered first, then the lungs. After that was anyone's guess. This time, her sense of touch was next in line. She could feel a dull ache at the back of her head and a tightness—stitches, probably, with a thick pillow of gauze over them. Her hearing arrived shortly thereafter, which was unfortunate, since she was now treated to her boss's wrath.

"Salt Sea and all the gods of death! What now?" came the voice of Chief Alma Maguire, ringing through the infirmary. At least, Rosie assumed she was in the station's infirmary. That was usually where she woke up. Ah yes, there was the particular squeak of the infirmary's door swinging closed in Maguire's wake. Someone ought to oil that.

"Hi, Chief," said Duckers.

"Don't *hi* me. How is she?"

"Not dead," muttered Dr. Levinson.

"She's going to wish she was after I'm done with her. I've got a puddle of blood causing a hazmat situation in the parking lot and an engineer who's going to need years of therapy and...Let me think...Oh, that's right. There's a charred hole in the West Station's portal! What happened this time?"

Rosie's hearing was never so acute as when she was half dead. She could actually make out the sound of Duckers's hands nervously bending and unbending the brim of his hat, a habit he had picked up from his mentor when he first joined up twelve years ago.

"So, the portal was down," he began.

"I am aware. Louis was fixing it."

"Fox decided to help."

"And then she touched wires with steam-powered current running through them and got herself killed," Dr. Levinson finished dryly, her mouth a disapproving slash across her face as she lifted Rosie's wrist and took her pulse. So apparently Rosie could see now.

She blinked.

"Well, look who's alive," said Maguire with false joviality. Alma Maguire was the best boss Rosie had ever had, but the woman laid on irony so thick you could prod it with a fork. She glared down at Rosie's prostrate body on the exam table, her own brilliant aquamarine demigod eyes glinting with icy fury. Rosie was jealous of those eyes, so striking in Maguire's deep brown face. Blue-green and red were simply shades on the color wheel, but stick them into a demigod's eye sockets, and one hue became beautiful, while the other became terrifying.

Plus, rumor had it that Alma Maguire's divine mother was nice. Some demigods had all the luck.

"What were you thinking?" Maguire barked, rousing Rosie from her sulk.

Act first, think never, because fifty years from now, no one is going to remember this anyway, Rosie thought in reply, her oft-repeated personal motto. It was probably for the best that her mouth wasn't working yet.

"She kept saying there was something wrong inside the portal." Duckers spoke for her.

"As if she would know." Maguire looked down at Rosie again. "Remind me, Fox: When did you finish that graduate degree in mechanical engineering?"

"I think maybe she really did see something, Chief, something that Louis and I couldn't see. She kept talking about a shadowy...blotch...thing." As Duckers spoke, he slowly withered under Maguire's fierce gaze.

"Of course, a shadowy blotch thing. Clearly a valid reason to go poking around inside a complex and extremely expensive piece of machinery."

Duckers was mangling his hat, but he continued to stand up for Rosie, gods love him. "She was adamant. She definitely saw something in there."

"What are you trying to say?" Maguire asked him, softening. She always showed greater mercy to Duckers than to Rosie, not that Rosie could blame her. Duckers was a human plushie.

He gestured toward Rosie with his hat. "What if this is her demigod gift?"

"I didn't think Fox had a gift."

Gods of creation, it was so weird to have people talking about her as if it were Rosie's dead body in the room rather than the immortal piece of shit she'd been born with.

"Well, maybe she finally found it," said Duckers.

"The ability to see a shadowy blotch thing?"

"The ability to see stuff no one else can see. You know, the way Hart can see souls."

Hart Ralston had been Duckers's mentor, and before that he had been Alma Maguire's partner prior to her promotion to chief marshal. Like Maguire and Rosie, he was a demigod, but unlike anyone walking the earth, he could see the souls of the departed as they floated off to sail the Salt Sea.

Maguire's demigod gift was the ability to light a fire with her bare hands. Again, she was a million times cooler than Rosie would ever be. It was so unfair.

"Whatever it was, she was trying to show Louis. She was trying to be helpful," said Rosie's faithful partner.

Dr. Levinson snorted at this, earning her a baleful look from the chief, a glare the marshals under her command referred to as Maguire's Ire. The doctor cringed in apology and resumed bandaging Rosie's head, even though her skull was likely to be completely healed by morning.

Maguire released a long, gusty breath full of irritation. "Well,

I'm delighted to hear that Fox wants to help out so badly, because she is about to get her wish."

"That doesn't sound good," said Duckers.

"Au contraire, Marshal, I'm sure your partner is going to be thrilled with this assignment. Since fixing the wreckage out there is way outside Louis's pay grade, I've had to call in Dr. Lee, the man himself." Alma smiled sharply at Rosie, who was powerless to respond. "You get to be his escort for the duration of his stay, Marshal Fox, so that you can answer any questions he might have as to how you managed to fry his portal so very, very, very badly." With each *very*, Maguire's face inched closer to Rosie's. Mother of Sorrows, the woman knew how to make a marshal quail.

"Dang." Duckers laughed under his breath.

"You, too, Marshal Duckers."

"Me? What did I do?"

"You partnered up with a loose cannon ten years ago. That's on you. I'm expecting Dr. Lee early next week. You?" Here, she loomed over Rosie like the ancient God of Wrath. "Rest up and be less dead. I need you on your best behavior when Dr. Lee arrives. And don't think I don't see those non-regulation ostrich leather boots you're wearing. Get it together, Fox. And as for you." She turned on Duckers, who visibly shrank. "Keep your partner in line. I'll see you both first thing Sorrowsday morning."

Maguire made to exit the room but paused at the door and addressed Duckers, her demeanor somber.

"Will I see you at the funeral tomorrow?"

He nodded bleakly.

"I know it wasn't unexpected, but it's a sad business all the same," she said. "Till tomorrow, then."

With that, she exited the infirmary, accompanied by the familiar squeak of the door hinge.

Rosie experienced a stab of guilt as she looked at Duckers. She had been so focused on her own problems, she had forgotten that he was dealing with his own. She wished she could offer him a hug or some words of comfort, but all she could manage was a dramatic moan, a sound so pathetic that even Dr. Levinson took pity on her.

"I'll get you an aspirin."

Rosie was still moaning when Dr. Levinson finally released her from the infirmary a half hour later, mostly to cover up the stream of complaints freely flowing from the mouth of Penrose Duckers as he drove them both home.

"This is the third time you've up and died on me!" He shouted to be heard over the powerful engine of his cherry-red muscle duck. "For most people, the average lifespan is, like, eighty years. For you? It's three, maybe four. It's ridiculous! *You're* ridiculous! And it stresses me out! I don't like it when you die! How many times do I have to tell you this?"

He smacked the steering wheel throughout this speech to drive home his point.

"I don't die as often as I did when the drudges were around."

"Exactly! There aren't any murderous undead bodies roaming Tanria now, so you have zero excuses!"

Duckers was being generous. During the years when the drudges had terrorized the former prison of the Old Gods, her many partners had not accepted the undead as an excuse for her propensity to die in the line of duty. She would always contend that she had saved lives by putting herself in harm's way, but she had burned through eighteen partners before she'd found Duckers, the only one who had stuck with her. Of course, the way he was laying into her now made her worry that she had tried his patience too far, too many times.

"And now you've got us both on babysitting duty next week," he said. "I mean, have you met Adam Lee? The guy is boring as shit. I think he might actually be an automaton."

"He's not that bad."

"Yes, he is. He is *that bad*. And now we're going to have to spend quality time with him because of you. You know what that makes you? A ninnyhammer."

"I know. You're right. I'm a . . ." Rosie pulled up short. "What am I?"

"A ninnyhammer."

"What's a ninnyhammer?"

"You. Total ninny. And if anyone could be described as a hammer, it's you, bowling through life like a tornado and whacking anything that looks like a nail. Ninny. Hammer."

She regarded him with profound affection. "Gods, I love you."

"It's a great word, right?" he said with an irrepressible grin.

"So you forgive me?"

"Yes, I forgive you."

"And you won't leave me?"

"Nope. You're stuck with me." He reached across the bench of his autoduck and gave Rosie's knee a reassuring squeeze, revealing the stoppered bottle tattooed on his arm. As a teen, he'd nearly lost his soul when his appendix burst. A temple votary had had to reattach it to his body in permanent ink.

"We're partners, RoFo. I'm not leaving you."

Except he would. Someday. He would leave her the way everyone left her—across the Salt Sea to the House of the Unknown God, and even that tattoo wouldn't be able to hold his soul in this world. But that was a problem for Future Rosie. For now, she'd be contented and grateful to have him by her side.

"What time's the funeral tomorrow?" she asked him.

His face fell. "Ten o'clock."

"I guess Zeddie's going to be there, huh?"

Zeddie Birdsall was Duckers's ex-boyfriend. He'd been so upset when they broke up ten years ago that he'd left the island of Bushong to take a job at an upscale restaurant on Medora. He rarely came home, and when he did, his visits were brief, so it had been easy for Duckers to avoid him—until now.

"Yeah, he'll be there," Duckers said with the same grim resignation he might use to say something like *So I guess I'll stick my head in this noose now*.

"Want me to go with you?"

He shot her a hopeful glance. "Would you?"

"Least I can do after croaking on you today."

"I'd hate to put you out, though. Normally I'd beg Hart and Mercy to go with me, but that's not going to work this time. Obviously."

Hart and Duckers had remained friends after the former had left the Tanrian Marshals, even though Hart was married to Zeddie Birdsall's sister, Mercy. Thanks to Duckers, Rosie was friends with Hart and Mercy, too.

"Seriously, don't sweat it," said Rosie. "I'll go."

"But you hate funerals."

"Everyone hates funerals."

"I know, but..." He weighed his words. "You hate them for your own special Rosie Reasons."

"True, but I love you more than I hate funerals, so I'm going. End of discussion."

"Gods, thank you."

"That's what friends are for, Penny-D. But to be clear, you're not carrying a torch for this Zeddie guy, right?"

"No, of course not."

She gave him a hard side-eye.

"I'm not! That was ten years ago, and I was the one who broke things off."

"When's the last time you went on a date?"

"This again?"

"This again."

"I date."

"Not much."

Duckers scoffed. "Like you have room to talk. I can count on one hand the number of people you've dated since we partnered up. And by *dated*, I mean *went out with one time and decided nah*."

"Fair, but I, unlike you, have all the time in the world to find my one true love."

"Ouch. Cold."

"I'm just worried that it's going to suck for you to see your ex-boyfriend tomorrow." She patted him on the shoulder.

"I'll be fine. I'm bringing a hot date to this funeral, remember?"

"You'll have the hottest date in the temple. I'm a total snack."

He shook his head, smiling. "I fucking love you."

"Aw, I love you, too, hot stuff."

Despite the fact that Rosie had died that day and Duckers was gearing up to go to a funeral tomorrow, they drove the rest of the way home in good spirits.

Chapter Two

Rosie dropped her rucksack on the antique wooden chair beside the front door of her apartment over Wilner's Green Grocer—the one with the fraying cane seat—and turned on the parlor sconce to its lowest setting. Her mother used to hate it when Rosie would crank up the gaslights in their postage-stamp-sized apartment on Seventh Street in Morton City, the slapping of equimaris feet and the rumbling of carriages and the music of buskers and the leering calls of drunks playing on a constant loop outside their windows. *Lamps only, darling. You're killing the mood*, Jocelyn Fox would tell her daughter, and then she would give one of Rosie's coppery braids a playful tug.

Rosie had held on to her mother's lamps for as long as she could, but had had to give them up decades ago when they no longer worked with modern pipe fittings. Her current parlor lamps were in the same style, though—one with a painted porcelain base, another featuring ornate iron scrollwork, both with floral silk scarves draped over the shades. She turned them on now, filling the room with a soft, gauzy light.

The dish on the altar by the front door was dry, so Rosie refilled it with salt water before dipping her fingertips into the bowl and touching her mother's birth key. Jocelyn—who had raised Rosie to call her by her name rather than Mom or Mama or Mother— had died a hundred and twenty-two years ago last month, but

Rosie still missed her. She wondered if that deep sense of loss would fade over time. She hoped not.

The honoring of the dead complete, Rosie began her post-tour routine, the first step of which was the removal of the godsawful Tanrian Marshals uniform. For twenty-seven years, the marshals had been able to wear whatever they wanted on the job. For practicality's sake, this usually involved work shirts and dungarees and sturdy boots, but Rosie had managed to cobble together a decent look for herself while she was on tour. Her hats and neckerchiefs and boots had added style to an otherwise functional work wardrobe. But since the Assembly of the Federated Islands of Cadmus had conferred national park status on Tanria, she'd had to wear a uniform—a short-sleeved khaki shirt cut for a man's torso, canvas pants in a drab olive hue, and a laughable flat hat. She hated it.

Hated. It.

Her friends Lu and Annie Ellis, who worked at the Tanrian Dragon Preserve, got to wear emerald-green polo shirts. Rosie was not a fan of polo shirts as a general rule, but she at least looked good in green. Sadly, the green shirts were for marshals working in the Education Division, whereas Rosie and Duckers had been grandfathered into Park Security, and marshals working in Park Security had to wear the khaki nightmare.

Her one fashionable comfort—when she wasn't trying to sneak non-embarrassing footwear into Tanria—was the fact that no one could control her undergarments. And Rosie Fox excelled at lingerie, as her mother had before her. She could picture Jocelyn sitting sideways in the old armchair in their cramped parlor as she read reviews in the newspaper, her legs hanging over the side, her floral dressing gown riding up, revealing the lace hem of her slip and a peek at her nylons and garter clips. A cigarette would dangle from her lips with a ring of plummy lipstick around the paper wrapper. If she wore her violet satin T-strap pumps, Rosie knew she'd be heading to the theater soon. If she wore her marabou slippers with the kitten heels, she'd be staying in for the evening, probably expecting a gentleman caller.

Take pride in your intimates, Jocelyn had told her regularly. *If you give your buds the best, my darling rose, the rest of you will accept nothing less.* To this day, Rosie was not entirely certain what that meant—especially since Jocelyn had seemed to accept the worst when it came to her paramours—but thanks to her mother's tutelage, Rosie had always taken great pleasure in quality undergarments.

She stripped off the horrid uniform—noting the bloodstain on the collar—as she made her way to her bedroom, where she switched on the kitschy mermaid lamp that sat on her bedside table in a froth of porcelain sea-foam—a lamp she loved from the depths of her soul. She stuffed the hated clothing out of sight in her laundry hamper and, after slipping on a floral silk robe over her pretty pink brassiere with lace cups shaped like seashells and matching panties, she ran a bath. As the tub filled, she put a record full of bittersweet torch songs on the gramophone in the parlor so that the music would filter gently into the bathroom. She lit the two candles she kept on top of the toilet tank and turned down the gas sconce to low. The mood set, she retrieved a bottle of red wine, the expensive kind—gods in the Void, she loved having all the money in the world—and a crystal wineglass from the cupboard. She hung her robe from the hook on the bathroom door, then removed her undergarments and placed them in her mesh lingerie bag to wash by hand later. Wearing nothing but her birth key on a gold chain around her neck, she submerged herself in the tub at last and let the lavender-scented bath salts lift the Bushong dust from her pores while expunging the experience of dying yet again from her heart.

Brigitte Porcel's smoky alto sang to Rosie from the parlor.

Decades after her death, the singer's voice lived on in this glorious, tinny recording.

> *It was just another love song*
> *Like a holiday in spring*
> *A nothing-much, a fling...*

She had seen Brigitte Porcel perform at the Midtown Folly forty years ago. At the time, Rosie had been stuck in an illusionist's show, and even that had been better than working in the traveling circus, the grim fate from which the Tanrian Marshals had saved her.

> *There was no right or wrong*
> *We thought we were so clever*
> *But songs don't last forever*

Brigitte Porcel had sung her heart out when gramophones were a new invention, so her recordings had a scratchy patina that could never capture the depth of the woman's talent in life. People today would never know what Brigitte Porcel truly sounded like, which seemed like a tragedy to Rosie as she let her fingers prune.

The thought of Brigitte Porcel moldering in her funeral boat weighed down Rosie's already heavy heart as she sipped her wine—not that her body would let her get drunk—so she turned her thoughts instead to Adam Lee's impending arrival.

A memory resurfaced, as it had when she had spied the strange spot inside the portal's frame—like a bucket being pulled out of a dark well, that single moment in time when Adam Lee had stood in the same spot beside the portal with a bottomless anguish in his eyes.

For some reason, dread squeezed her at the thought of seeing him again, as if her skin were too tight to hold her body in place. She had accidentally walked off with his handkerchief five years ago—a mix-up that involved her bandaging a cut on his hand with her own linen hankie—and his silk pocket square remained in her possession to this day. She ought to return it to him, but she wondered if she would come across as a creeper if she did. Like *Hey, I stole your hankie and kept it all this time. Here it is. I haven't put it on my Adam Lee shrine and lit candles in your honor or anything.*

Side A of the Brigitte Porcel record came to the end and made that irritating bumping, scratching sound that could be remedied only by getting her ass out of the tub and taking the needle off it. The water had gone cold anyway. Rosie toweled off and padded into her bedroom for her simple yet elegant slip panties in forest-green silk and a negligee covered in a vine pattern, the leaves of which matched the panties to a T. She slipped her dressing gown over top of it, stepped into her embroidered silk slippers, and after putting the gramophone needle out of its misery, set about making pasta to go with what was left of the wine.

As garlic softened in a skillet of butter, she scrounged up a can of tuna from the kitchen cupboards and threw up the window sash over the sink, despite the cruciferous smell from the grocer's dumpster wafting over the faucet. The second she pulled open the utensil drawer where she kept the can opener, she heard the demanding yowl of a rangy black-and-gray-striped tabby.

"Using me for my food again, I see," she told the cat as she set the can on the windowsill and watched him tuck in. At least he had the decency to purr like the oversized engine of Duckers's muscle duck when she stroked the surprisingly soft fur along his spine.

" 'Feed me and give me love, hooman, as is my due,' " she said on the cat's behalf.

Rosie had barely removed the pan from the burner when a

knock sounded at the door. She considered pretending that she wasn't at home, but whoever was out there on the landing could probably see the lights on in her place and had likely heard her doing her awesome cat voice. She got up to peer through the peephole to find a man she had never seen before waving at her.

Rosie knew who it was, though.

She rolled her eyes and opened the door, and her father waltzed into her apartment in the guise of a clean-cut, wholesome dad type in his midfifties wearing khaki pants and a navy sports jacket.

"Hey, kiddo!" he said, leaning in to kiss her on the cheek, which made her cringe.

"Hey," she said unenthusiastically.

Rosie didn't call him the Trickster, because that would be weird, and she definitely didn't call him Dad, so she simply didn't call him anything. She frowned as he took a tour of her parlor, imagining how it must look from his perspective, a room cluttered with over a century and a half of memories: dusty black-and-white photographs of her mother in various stage costumes, paintings and vases and sculptures she had fallen in love with over the years, a clay finger pot she had made when she was seven, a hodgepodge of knickknacks that reminded her of the people who had come and gone from her life, souvenirs from all the places she had been.

"You know what this place needs?" said her father. "More shit. Not enough shit in here."

As if in proof of this assertion, he stumbled over the cat, who had come to rub against his shins.

Rowr, the tabby groused at him in a way that said, *How dare you fail to greet me. But also, don't touch me, or I will kill you. Unless I want you to pet me, in which case, pet me, or I will kill you.*

"Hello there, uh..." The god shifted his gaze from the stray to his offspring. "Does this one have a name?"

"Blammo Tinky Fartface," Rosie answered flatly.

"What do you call it for short?"

"Blammo Tinky Fartface."

In fact, most of the time, she called the cat Tinky, or occasionally Fart, but she wanted to make a bona fide god who had witnessed the creation of the world and the birth of humanity say *Blammo Tinky Fartface*. That was true power.

The Trickster smiled benevolently at the ratty-looking cat and said, "Hello, Blammo Tinky Fartface."

True power, Rosie thought smugly, a smugness that evaporated when her father made himself at home on her vintage sofa with its worn blue velvet upholstery. He squinted critically at the hokey painting of the Briar Thief that hung on the wall. Rosie loved the story of the great tragic hero who had tried to steal immortality from the garden of the Old Gods, only to be caught by the God of Wrath and impaled on the Thorn of Eternal Life. In her little heart of hearts, she imagined a world in which he had succeeded, where everyone lived and lived and could not die, like Rosie. In the painting, even in agony, the Briar Thief was handsome with his flowing chestnut hair and his brawny frame and his stoic suffering on behalf of all mortals, a hero's hero.

"I have never understood your obsession with that guy," said the god with infuriating scorn. "He was a loser. And that doesn't look a thing like him, by the way. He was a pip-squeak. And the plant is all wrong. I should know. I was the one who created it."

Do not let him goad you, Rosie told herself, even as she folded her arms and glowered at him. "I haven't seen you in four years. Why are you here now?"

"I heard you died today," he said as he fiddled with a half-finished puzzle on the coffee table, knocking a few pieces onto the rug in the process.

"Yep."

"I know it's hard, this immortality gig. Believe me; I know."

In a single sentence her father deftly turned a conversation about her into a conversation about himself. Same shit, different day.

"I'm fine," she told him.

"Aren't you going to offer me some snacks?"

"Don't have any."

"Well, something sure smells good," he said with a wink. Did this honestly charm people? It made Rosie want to beat her head against a wall.

"That's my dinner, which I would like to eat now. So can you...leave? Please?"

"Is that any way to treat your dear old dad?"

"I'm sorry that I'm not rolling out the red carpet, 'dear old Dad,' but I just got off work, and I'm tired. I would like to eat my dinner and go to bed. I may be immortal, but I'm still human, okay?"

"Fine. Okay. I get it."

The Trickster stood, bumping into the coffee table and scattering more puzzle pieces onto the floor.

"Good night," Rosie told him as he headed for the door.

When his hand landed on the doorknob, she was foolish enough to think that she was in the clear. But of course, that's when he declared, "Actually, no, it's not fine. It's not okay. I don't get it."

He turned to face her, cloaked in tragedy and grievance, and it was all Rosie could do not to throw back her head and yowl like Blammo Tinky Fartface.

"The God of War was responsible for millions of deaths, and yet people worshipped the guy," whined the Trickster, a speech Rosie knew so well by now she could recite it along with him if she wanted to (which she didn't). "Me? I get nothing. I gave the

21

world humor. I gave the world laughter. I gave the world a little fucking joy."

"And also deception," said Rosie, but the Trickster was on a roll and would not be waylaid.

"I'm the reason the human soul exists. You're welcome, but you know, don't mind me. And this twerp." The Trickster gestured at the painting of the Briar Thief. "Don't even get me started."

"I won't," said Rosie, much good it did her.

"He gets statues and paintings and altars in temples all over the world, people heaping praise upon him, and for what? He tried to steal immortality for humanity. Big deal. He fucking failed. He's a failure. You know what we call that where I come from? Losing. Meanwhile, I'm over here trying to give immortality to people— for free, I might add. And everyone's all, 'That god tried to give us eternal life. What a dick!' Where's my shrine, huh? Where's my altar? Even my own daughter doesn't appreciate me."

"I'm not building a shrine to you in my apartment. Or anywhere else for that matter."

"What about your altar? You honor your mother on your altar."

"Because she's dead."

"Well, I can't die."

"That's not my problem." Except it was. It was Rosie's exact problem.

"Would it be too much to ask for a hug?" her father said with wounded exasperation.

Rosie did not want to hug him, this god in a skin suit she'd never seen before and would never see again. But since it seemed like the most expedient way to get him out of her apartment, she bit her tongue and wrapped her arms around him.

As he held her, he grew several inches so that he was the one holding rather than the one being held. It was so rare for Rosie to feel small in someone's arms. "I was worried about you. That's all," he said softly into her no-longer-singed hair before releasing her abruptly and letting himself out.

And now Rosie felt like a grade A equimaris's ass for booting him out.

Blammo Tinky Fartface had returned to his perch at the kitchen window, and he chirped contentedly as he attacked the can of tuna once more. Rosie wanted to pick him up and bury her face in his floofy tummy and let all that warmth and softness wash over her. But she knew, from personal experience, that Tinky would rather die than be cuddled, and if she were a normal human being, she'd have the scars to show for it. She burst into tears instead and respectfully petted the purring monster on her windowsill and told him what a sweet little dickhead he was. She cried as she shoveled cold spaghetti into her mouth, and she cried while she brushed her teeth, and then she cried until she was exhausted and her body—her traitorous body—let her conk out at last.

Chapter Three

It was raining when Duckers came to pick Rosie up the following morning, but since All Gods Temple was only a few blocks away, they decided to walk, both of them huddled under Rosie's dramatically oversized yellow umbrella.

"Thanks again for coming with me. It would have sucked to face this on my own."

"It's no problem."

This was not entirely true. Funerals made Rosie's skin crawl. And she was not a *rah-rah-gods!* gal in the first place. But Penrose Duckers had been there for her through all her nonsense over the past ten years, so she did not hesitate when he needed her.

Besides, she got to wear her filmy teal dress with periwinkle flowers on it for this occasion and a fresh pair of nylons, her seams straight as pins. Her shoes were brand spanking new, specially ordered from a store on Lyona since she could never find cute shoes her size in regular shops. They were pale blue leather pumps with three-inch heels. She figured that if the gods of creation had seen fit to make her a giant, what was three more inches?

When they arrived at temple, Rosie shook out her umbrella and set it with all the others in the foyer. Both she and Duckers signed the guest book on the podium in the entryway before they walked arm in arm along the main aisle. Gray dreariness trickled through the skylight of the Unknown God overhead, so the gas sconces on the walls had been turned up. They passed by the smaller alcoves for minor gods and made their way toward the larger alcoves for the gods of life and death. A small statue of the Briar Thief sat on a table outside the alcove of the Salt Sea with a few offerings of fruit at its base.

It didn't take long to find the mourners, dressed in the soft blues and greens of the Salt Sea, milling about the alcove of Grandfather Bones, a fitting place for the funeral of an undertaker. The altar had been pushed against the mosaic depiction of the god that covered the far wall to make room for the funeral boat. It was a beautiful wooden sailboat, scaled down in size to contain the body within it.

The family stood in a line to the side of the boat, greeting people in hushed tones as friends and neighbors shuffled forward to pay their respects. Obviously, Rosie knew Mercy Birdsall and Hart Ralston, and she was acquainted with Mercy's sister and brother-in-law, so she could only assume that the tall golden-haired paean to masculine beauty in human form standing to Mercy's left was her brother Zeddie.

"Is that him?" she whispered to Duckers.

"Yeah."

"Fuck me, Grandmother Wisdom. You dumped *that*?"

Duckers turned his head to hide his face from his ex. "RoFo, we're at temple."

"So?"

"So watch your language. There are temple-going old ladies all over the place here."

"They're old. They're not dead. I'm sure they're thinking the same thing I am."

"Rosie." He gave her a warning look, the sort of look her mother would have given her if Jocelyn had been a normal sort of parent.

"Okay, Mom, but good on you, because that is one fine-looking man."

"Yeah, got the memo."

It occurred to Rosie that she was being an insensitive asshole, at a funeral no less. "Sorry. Are we going up to give our condolences?"

"I guess we should." Duckers positioned himself so that he had his back to the Birdsall family. Rosie could tell that he didn't want to face his ex-boyfriend at his ex-boyfriend's father's funeral, and she couldn't fault him for it.

"You know, it's perfectly acceptable to skulk in the back. You've signed the guest book, so they'll know you came. They'll know you care."

"That's weak."

"No, it isn't. Death is weird. You're here, and that's what counts. Come on."

She took him by the arm and led him as far from the altar as they could get.

"Pen, Rosie, over here." Lu Ellis waved to them from the second-to-last row. He was sitting with his sister, Annie, and their dad, Frank. They squeezed together with the Banneker family to make room for two more.

"Thanks," said Duckers as he and Rosie crammed themselves into the end of the pew. Most of the town of Eternity had turned out for Roy Birdsall's funeral, so it was a crush for everyone, but Rosie couldn't help but think that this was yet another reason why funerals sucked.

"How are you doing, sweetie?" Twyla Banneker asked Duckers with a face full of maternal sympathy. She and Frank had briefly worked with him before they opened the Tanrian Dragon Preserve, and they frequently invited him and Rosie over for cookouts.

"I'm all right," Duckers lied.

"Come over for a beer later if you want," Frank offered. "You, too, Fox."

"Thanks, Ellis," said Rosie, after which everyone settled into respectful silence. Duckers kept his head bowed, both out of respect and to hide his face from Zeddie. Rosie was tempted to follow suit, but the sad truth was that she stood out in a crowd, no matter what she did. There were enough demigods working in and around Tanria to render her appearance generally unremarkable in the border towns, but in such close quarters with normal people, she felt like a giraffe at a bunny convention.

She gazed up at the mosaic of the god that expanded across the far wall of the alcove in pearlescent tiles. As in all depictions, Grandfather Bones was so old that his face appeared skeletal, his cheekbones flaring, his eyes so sunken they were black hollows. And yet there was a gentleness to him, a sort of smile hidden in the billows of his beard, a softness in the waves of his long white hair. He held out a lantern, calling to the souls of the dead. Behind him, a boat waited at his dock, ready to carry souls over the Salt Sea to the House of the Unknown God, where the Warden would open the door and welcome them home.

Several candles sat on the altar with flames dancing on their wicks. There were offerings of Roy Birdsall's favorite foods—croissants, snickerdoodles, a three-tiered cake, and a beautifully plated chicken piccata with haricots verts and polenta. Rosie had been to many funerals over the years, but she had never seen a spread this stunning. And then she remembered that Zeddie Birdsall had spent nearly a decade cooking at one of the fanciest restaurants in the Federated Islands of Cadmus.

At the center of the altar sat Roy Birdsall's birth key on a blue velvet cloth and a series of photographs of the man himself—grinning on his wedding day, beaming in a family portrait with his wife and children surrounding him, dancing with his daughter Lilian at her wedding, playfully scrubbing a much-younger Zeddie's curls with a work-hardened hand, building a funeral boat beside Mercy in the boatworks at Mercy's Undertakings (formerly Birdsall & Son, Undertakers), reading a picture book with his two oldest grandkids in his lap, giving a bath to his two youngest grandbabies in the kitchen sink—a handful of good memories in a life filled with many.

An uncomfortable bitterness squeezed Rosie's chest as she regarded Roy Birdsall's kind face smiling benevolently on all who came to grieve him. No one would ever grieve Rosie. It was like that saying about always being a bridesmaid and never a bride, except she was always the mourner, never the mourned.

She heard Duckers sniff beside her, and she took his hand in hers. Her eyes welled up, not for Roy, but for the friend who was sad today, who had loved Roy Birdsall like a father, the friend who would sail the Salt Sea himself at the end of his life and gouge another hole in Rosie's already-bruised heart.

She really did hate funerals.

Once the pews were packed tight, with more people standing along the sides, the family took their seats in the front, and Votary Asebedo began the ceremony.

"On behalf of the Birdsall family, I'd like to thank you all for coming today," she said, holding *The Book of the New Gods* reverently in her arthritic hands. "Mercy tells me that Roy asked to keep these proceedings short and sweet so we can get to the cheesy potatoes—his words, not mine."

Soft laughter rippled through the crowd, those who knew the man well thinking fondly to themselves, *Isn't that just like Roy*.

"As always, we'll begin with a reading from *The Book of the New Gods*. It's the story we share every time we must say goodbye to someone we have loved and cherished. I find there is a comfort in the repetition. The story of the Salt Sea and how our souls came into being reminds us that we will all return to the Unknown God one day. We all return to where we came from."

Not all of us, Rosie thought. *Not me.*

"Roy's daughter Lilian will honor her father by reading the story today. Lilian?"

Roy's second daughter rose from the pew and took the tome from the votary with a nod. She walked it to the podium, opened it to the place marked by a satin ribbon, and began to read.

Here is the story of the Salt Sea's Loss and the Gift of the Soul.

This schlock was always read aloud at funerals, and with each telling, the old-timey language grated more and more on Rosie's nerves. It was the story of a lake god who fell in love with a mortal fisherman and longed to keep the man beside him forever.

There was a time when gods could create gods, but that time had long passed. The New Gods were too weak to make immortals, and so the god of the lake could do nothing to keep his love beside him.

No disrespect to you, Mr. Birdsall, but this story makes me want to barf in my mouth, Rosie thought at Roy's photograph on the altar. And then her father entered the story, because of course he did. She couldn't get away from him, not even at a funeral.

One day, the Trickster came to visit the god of the lake. He should have known better than to trust the Old God, but he was as innocent as his mortal lover and did not understand things like deception and deceit.

"My friend, I can help you," the Trickster told the god of the lake. "You are too young to create immortal life, but I am old and wise. I will plant a tree beside your waters. That tree will give your love comfort and shade, and one day, it will bear

blossoms. If your beloved picks one of these blooms, he will live a thousand thousand years with you."

Even in the stuffy language of a religious text, Rosie's father sounded like a snake oil salesman. Accurate.

And then came the moment when the mortal schmuck picked the flower without knowing how screwed he was.

He plucked the blossom, but there was a thorn hidden beneath the petals, a barb that drew blood. This was in the time before the Old Gods put pain and misery in the world, and the man did not have a word for what he felt. Nothing had ever hurt him before. But the god of the lake was so happy that he did not see his lover's pain. All he could see was his own joy.

At first, the fisherman was thrilled, but when he watched everyone he had ever known and loved die one by one as the Old Gods filled the world with war and disease and misery, he figured out that the "gift" from his lover sucked ass. *Who could have predicted that?* asked Rosie's inner snark. She jiggled her leg with impatience while the story went on and on.

As the long days gnawed at him like a dog on a bone, the tree bent and twisted and became a gnarled, hideous thing, as ugly as the resentment in the man's heart.

"You never asked me if I wanted to live a thousand thousand years," the fisherman cried at the god.

"But you were happy!" the god replied.

"And now I am wretched," said the man.

You've got that right, brother, Rosie thought. The god didn't even give the guy a choice. Such grapshit.

And then the story got barftastically melodramatic.

Because the god could not bear to see his love suffer, he took hold of the thousand thousand years living inside him, and he pulled and pulled until the long years released their hold on the man's heart and came tumbling out.

The fisherman was grateful, but the god howled in anguish, knowing that his love was doomed to die and leave him. He filled the distance between the earth and the Void Beyond the Sky with his tears, an entire ocean containing his love and his sorrow, the Salt Sea that separates the world of the living from the land of the dead.

The Unknown God, the eternal one, the first and greatest of all the gods, took pity on the lovers. They bound a piece of theirself to the fisherman's life, a piece that would live in tranquility, even when his body died, so that the Salt Sea would know that his love lived on, even after they parted.

As his earthly life drew to a close, the fisherman found it in his heart to be happy once more and to love the god again.

Fuck that, thought Rosie.

At least the story was finally coming to an end.

The fisherman eventually reached the end of his life, so Grandfather Bones lit a lantern and called to the guy's brand-new soul and built a boat so that his spirit could sail away. And then the lake god, who had become the Salt Sea, billowed him along the waves of death until his lover arrived at the House of the Unknown God, where the Warden let him in.

And so the immortal world was separated from the land of mortals by the Salt Sea, and the human soul came into being, the piece of the Unknown God that resides in each of us

and lives in peace long after we are gone. To this day, we remem-
ber the sweet-smelling blossom that hid a thorn, a reminder
that while everlasting life may appear tempting, it comes with
pain and tribulation. And that is why death is as precious as
life.

Lilian closed the book and returned to her seat, where her husband put his arm around her and drew her in close.

Votary Asebedo stepped forward once more. "Roy's daughter
Mercy will now give the eulogy."

Rosie was a big fan of Eternity's undertaker. For one thing,
Mercy's fashion sense was always on point. Even today, she looked
sharp in a sea-green fit-and-flare dress and matching pumps. For
another thing, she was tall. It was a ludicrous reason to like someone, but when you were a big girl navigating a world in which
the Old Gods' notions of femininity lingered like Man Smell in
a locker room, you tended to like your fellow women of a certain size. Also, Mercy was smart and nice, and that combination
wasn't always easy to find.

At this moment, Rosie felt a keen sympathy for her friend.
She had barely uttered a few words at Jocelyn's memorial service
before she lost it, and that was a small gathering among friends.
She had no idea how a person managed to get through a eulogy
for a beloved parent in front of a crowd, but if anyone could pull it
off, it was Mercy Birdsall.

Mercy cleared her throat, adjusted her glasses, and began.

"It's amazing how death is always a surprise. Even these past
few months, when Pop wasn't doing so hot, his steady presence
remained the quiet bulwark of our lives. I don't know how to be
in the world without my father. I've never had to try. But that's
what life is, isn't it? Trying every single day, even if it might be
your last.

"And that is how Roy Birdsall lived. When my mother died, he was there for me and Lilian and Zeddie. He had to swallow his own loss to help us handle ours, and to this day, I don't know how he did it without breaking.

"When he suffered a heart attack thirteen years ago, he demonstrated the grace of acceptance, of how to let someone else carry your burdens when you need help. Although he never did let up on the coffee and doughnuts, much to the dismay of Dr. Galdamez."

A smile tugged on Mercy's mouth as a low hum of appreciative laughter filled the alcove.

"When his grandkids came along, he was all in. I'm so glad that Emma Jane, Tony, Bea, and Lottie got to have their grandpa in their lives, however briefly. What a loss to have Roy Birdsall leave us like this, but what a gift to have had his life in ours in the first place.

"My father taught me how to build boats, how to sing the incantations over the dead, how to care for the precious body Grandfather Bones leaves behind, and how to send a life sailing over the Salt Sea with dignity and respect. Like Pop, I have always taken pride in comforting the living with my care for the dead. And so it has been an incredible comfort to me, the living, to build this boat for the man who loved me without limit and made me who I am."

She took a long pause, busying herself with the shuffling of her note cards until she could speak again.

"As you can see, he chose to be buried in a simple sailboat. You'd think an undertaker who loved to build sloops and schooners and cutters would have chosen a more exciting vessel for his final voyage, but last year, he told me, 'I don't want anything fancy, Muffin. Grandfather Bones knows where to find me.' I can't tell you what an honor it has been to make my father the boat he wanted in the end.

"As many of you know, Roy Birdsall was an avid fan of the Bushong Giant Squids."

There was some light clapping and chortling here, and Mercy gave a tearful laugh in response.

"Professional sea polo was as much a religion to the man as his faith in the New Gods. Well, Pop, you have played your last match. The final chukka has run out and the bell has sounded. You have had many a good neck shot in this game, and hardly any fouls to speak of. You have played well—so well—and you deserve to hang up your mallet and rest in the House of the Unknown God. You have had to get by without Mom at your side for the past twenty-five years, so I know you must be happy to go home to her at last. Thank you for the beautiful life you have shared with us. We'll miss you until the Unknown God calls us home to you."

As Mercy returned to her seat, Rosie realized that she was crying. She had barely known Roy Birdsall, and here she was, weeping like a baby at his funeral. And Duckers was crying even harder. Gods, funerals sucked. Except this one was also heartfelt and wonderful. She dabbed her eyes resentfully on one of her sleeve cuffs, leaving a smear of mascara on the pretty fabric.

Once again, the votary stepped forward.

"Each one of us is given a key when we are born," she said, "a reminder that we will always have a home in the House of the Unknown God. As you can see, Roy's birth key is here with us today. For many years, Roy celebrated the lives of his parents and grandparents and great-grandparents and his cherished wife by taking good care of their keys. Today, Mercy and her husband, Hart, and their children, Bea and Lottie, will add Roy's key to their altar, and they will take on the responsibility of honoring those who came before them. But for now, Roy's family invites you to come forward and press salt water to his key. And then, of course, you are all welcome to join us in the temple basement for lunch and an assortment of Roy's favorite desserts, lovingly prepared by his son, Zeddie. Thank you for coming and for celebrating Roy's life with the Birdsall family."

"May the Warden welcome him home," the attendees answered, the traditional funeral blessing that brought the proceedings to a close.

The mourners rose, some to make their way to the temple basement, others to pay their respects to Roy Birdsall's birth key, and many more to offer condolences to the family.

"Well, that was lovely," said Twyla as Frank took a handkerchief from his coat pocket and handed it to her with a fond shake of his head.

"Hush," she told him before discreetly blowing her nose.

"You do this every time."

"I don't need to bring a hankie. I have you."

He put an arm over her shoulder. "That you do, darlin'."

"Those two are adorable," Rosie told Duckers with a jerk of her head toward the world's cutest couple in their sixties.

"For real."

"Hey, there's a mob of people talking to the family. If you wanted to touch salt water to Roy's key, I think you could pull it off without you-know-who seeing you."

"You think?"

"Yeah, but go now."

She shooed him toward the altar and headed for the lobby to wait for him when, to her surprise, Hart Ralston caught up to her in the main aisle of the temple.

"I thought I saw you," he said as she hugged him.

"I'm hard to miss. Sorry for your loss."

He nodded sadly. "I need to get back, but listen: I want to

talk to you about something. Can you stop by this week, maybe Wisdomsday?"

"Sure," she said, but there was a gravity in his words that made her add, "Everything all right?"

"It's nothing bad." He seemed like he might say more, but Hart had always been a man of few words and apparently decided he had said enough. "Thanks again for coming," he told her before stalking off on impossibly long legs to return to his wife and family in the alcove.

"We're heading downstairs. Are you coming?" Lu asked Rosie as the Ellis family passed by her.

"No, I think Duckers wants to head out."

"Too bad. Twyla made cheesy potatoes, and they are amazing."

Duckers was making his way toward them when Lu suddenly wrapped Rosie up in a hug, stood on tiptoes, and whispered in her ear. "Zeddie Birdsall was hired as head chef of the Dragon's Lair. Need you to break it to Pen."

He released her and wished her a cheery "Bye!" before escaping with his sister to the luncheon in the temple basement. Duckers waved at Lu and Annie, completely oblivious, while Rosie mouthed *Chickenshits!* at them.

Rosie had long suspected her partner of harboring dumper's remorse when it came to Zeddie, so she wasn't sure how he was going to take the news of his ex's permanent return to the island of Bushong. But if Zeddie was working at the new restaurant overlooking the Tanrian Dragon Preserve, he'd be using the portal at the West Station to get in and out of Tanria, which meant that they'd likely run into him. Often.

She knew she ought to give Duckers a heads-up, but she was worn to a nub after dying and resurrecting and dealing with her father and then going to a funeral. She decided that she would break the news to him on Sorrowsday morning. For now, she had every intention of going home to wallow in self-pity.

Gods, I hate funerals, she thought for the thousandth time that day and the millionth time in her life. Whenever she went to one, she was reminded yet again that she was stuck—just stuck—and she had no way to unstick herself.

Chapter Four

On Wisdomsday evening, Rosie stood on Hart Ralston's front doorstep on Walnut Street in Eternity. No one answered her knock, but she heard noises coming from inside, so she tried again. This time, the door swung inward, revealing seven-year-old Bea Ralston on the threshold. She was tall for her age, with a head full of brown curls and a pair of purple glasses perched on her nose.

"Hiya, Bea," said Rosie.

The girl gave her a perfunctory "Hi" before shouting over her shoulder, "Mo-o-m! Da-a-ad! It's Rosie-e-e!"

A moment later, all six feet and nine inches of Hart Ralston appeared in the doorway with an armful of his youngest, four-year-old Lottie, fresh from a bath and wrapped in a hooded towel. With his free hand, he cupped Bea's head affectionately. "I've got it now, Buzzy Bea. You can run along."

"Okay. Bye, Rosie!"

"Bye, Bea!"

"Hey," said Hart as Lottie leaned her head on his shoulder and sucked her bottom lip behind her top teeth. Like her sister, she had Mercy's dark curls, but the contours of her face were all Hart's. Her eyes were aster blue, the color her father's eyes might have been if he had not been a demigod. His were a striking shade of pale gray.

Normally, he would have stepped aside to let her in, but this time, he said, "Can we get a drink somewhere?"

"Sure. How does Lottie take her gin? Neat or on the rocks?"

"Let me just... Merciful?" he called over his shoulder.

Mercy stepped out of the kitchen, drying a pot, her face a question.

"I'm going to grab a drink with Rosie. Is that okay?"

"Of course." She set down the pot and came to retrieve Lottie, who was now blowing spit bubbles between her front teeth.

"Hi, Mercy. Hey, sorry about your dad."

"Thank you," said Mercy as Lottie cuddled into her full-figured frame.

Hart leaned down to kiss her cheek. "I won't be long."

"Have a nice time, Sweet-Hart."

Their eyes met for a moment, and they seemed to say all the good and right and important things to each other without having to utter a single word.

A pang of loneliness jabbed Rosie in the heart. *Why him?* some ugly inner troll asked. *Why does he get to live his life and then die and stay dead?*

She averted her gaze and berated herself for resenting a friend his happiness.

"Where to? The Salt and Key?" she asked Hart as he stepped into his boots beside the front door.

"How about Aunt Bonnie's?"

Aunt Bonnie's was a quiet neighborhood pub in the next town over. It was not a place where either of them was likely to run into many people they knew. He'd said that he wanted to talk to her, and that it wasn't anything bad, but a bud of concern began to unfurl in her gut.

"Aunt Bonnie's it is. I'll drive."

They bypassed Hart's old rust bucket in the driveway, and

it said something about Rosie's worry that she didn't tease him about it. He noticed, and she could feel him notice, but he kept the conversation light as she drove them to Mayetta in her vintage mint-green Gratton Parker series 7 coupe. Duckers liked to joke that the engine was powered by a hamster on a wheel, but it handled beautifully on land and gloriously on the sea, coasting across the waves with the aquatic grace of a seal. It was why she had bought it; she loved driving on the ocean. All that water made her feel small in a world in which she typically felt enormous. But here on the border of Tanria, they were inland and landlocked, so she steered her duck onto the highway rather than a waterway.

"Mercy's brother moved back to town," Hart said conversationally.

"I heard. Mercy must be glad to have him around again."

"She is. The whole family is. Do you know Zeddie?"

"I've never met him, but I know he and Duckers used to be a thing."

"Does Duckers know he's back for good?"

"Not yet." Rosie glanced hopefully across the front bench at Hart. "Want to tell him?"

"Duckers is my friend, and Zeddie is my brother-in-law, so I've made it a policy to stay out of their relationship."

"Coward."

"I prefer to think of it as self-preservation."

When they got to Mayetta, Rosie nabbed a parking spot two doors down from Aunt Bonnie's. She and Hart made their way along the boardwalk, passing by the trees lining Mayetta's main street. The autumn leaves shivered in the evening breeze, the colors vibrant in the light of the streetlamps.

"Evening, folks," Aunt Bonnie boomed at them when they stepped inside the pub.

"Evening," Hart said with an understated smile as he doffed his hat and hung it on a peg by the door. He was well into his forties, with grooves bracketing his thin lips and strands of gray silvering his blond hair, yet he was a softer man now than he had been during his time with the Tanrian Marshals. In those days, his mouth had been a grim slash on a face full of sharp lines and planes, even at the tender age of sixteen.

It didn't seem all that long ago.

Rosie's and Hart's paths had not crossed often in those days, but when they did, she had done her best to steer clear of him. At the time, he didn't know whether he was immortal or not, and so he was a reminder in the flesh of what she already knew (and didn't much like) about herself. Turned out he had felt the same way about her. They didn't become friends until a few years after he had left the Tanrian Marshals. By then, Hart knew he was mortal, but the fact that he had spent the first thirty-six years of his life having to wonder about it made him the only person Rosie knew who truly understood what it meant to live forever.

As expected, Aunt Bonnie's was pleasantly quiet that evening, the sort of cozy hole-in-the-wall where the polished wood and leather booths seemed to absorb sound. Hart ordered a cup of hot tea, while Rosie went for a line of prairie fire shots. Bonnie returned a moment later and set a steaming cup before Hart and five shot glasses in front of Rosie.

"You know, you could do straight whiskey and save yourself the trouble of choking on whatever goes into those," Hart commented as Bonnie left them to it.

"It's called hot sauce, and I'm not taking any sass from a man who orders tea at a bar."

"I like tea."

"Okay, but does your beverage of choice match your eyes?" She held up a shot glass full of red prairie fire next to her face and smiled like those illustrated advertisements for cleaning powder that littered the *How to Stay Home and Raise Your Kids and Clean*

Your House Without Losing Your Marbles magazines that Jocelyn used to make fun of. "Where's your sense of adventure?"

"Never had it to begin with."

"How are we friends?" She tossed back the first shot and relished the path it burned down her throat. "Also, don't give me that. You were a Tanrian Marshal. You literally took out the undead for two decades." She took another shot, which hurt even more than the first. "And let's not forget the fact that you solved the undead problem single-handedly." Another shot, and all that burning made her feel how alive she was. "And now you're sheriff of Eternity, and that town is full of weirdos, so you can't tell me you don't see wacko shit on the job." The fourth shot slid down her throat in a fiery blaze, and the hot sauce was making her eyes water. "Also, I've met your offspring, and they are walking, talking adventures, the both of them." With that she threw the last prairie fire down her gullet, and her cheeks flushed pink—not red. "How are you telling me you don't have a sense of adventure?"

Hart surveyed the empty shot glasses in consternation.

"If I drink them fast enough, I can get my buzz on for a good five minutes," Rosie explained, although she could already feel the numbness of the alcohol dwindling away.

"You died again, didn't you." It wasn't a question.

Riding her prairie fire wave, Rosie was almost cheery when she answered, "Yep."

"When?"

"Saltsday."

"Sorry."

"It is what it is." Rosie gave Hart a stoic, one-shoulder shrug.

"Did this happen on the job? Is Alma Maguire ready to have your hide again?"

"Yep."

"Want to talk about it?"

"Nope."

"Fair enough."

But Rosie did want to talk about it. Specifically, she wanted to *howl* about it. She wanted to shake her fist at the sky about it. And she wanted to know how Hart and Chief Maguire and 99 percent of the world's demigod population had gotten around this blip in the system, when she had not.

Hart studied her over the rim of his teacup. "Are you sober yet?"

"Close enough. Are we having the big talk now?"

"I told you, it's nothing bad."

"Is it something good?"

He took another sip of tea before setting the cup on the saucer. "It's something I think you should know. I've thought about telling you this for a while now, but I'm also not sure I should. I guess Roy's death got me thinking that I can't put it off forever."

Hart had never been a laugh a minute, but the seriousness with which he spoke now made Rosie squirm. The temptation to pop the tension with a joke—*Are you my long-lost brother?*—was nearly overwhelming, but she bit her tongue.

"Remember when we rid Tanria of the drudges?" he asked her.

"I'm pretty sure *you* took care of the undead problem on your own. Credit where credit is due."

Rosie was hazy on the details, but so was everyone. In the intervening years, there had been much speculation in the border towns as to how Hart had managed to pull it off. Rosie knew it had something to do with his ability to see souls, but since he was her friend now, and since he had always been reluctant to talk about what had happened, she had never pried. Now she held her breath, waiting for him to continue.

"I died back then," he told her.

Any booze that remained in Rosie's system evaporated. She sat up straight.

"You died?"

"Yep."

"Died."

"Yep."

"As in you were dead. Legit dead."

"That's right."

Experiencing roughly fifty million different emotions at one time—shock, comfort, sadness—she slapped the table with both hands. "And this is the first time you're telling me?"

Hart looked into his teacup. "Mercy had to . . . take care of me. It's not a memory we like to relive at my house."

An unwelcome image of Hart's lifeless body on his wife's prep table at Mercy's Undertakings filled Rosie's mind. How nightmarish it must have been for Mercy to take care of a body that had once contained the soul of the man she loved.

And then Rosie's brain circled around to the terrible possibility that, like her, Hart might not be able to die.

"I thought you were mortal."

"I am."

"But you said you died, and now you're . . . not dead."

"I'm glad you noticed."

Thank gods, Rosie needed that wry Hart Ralston humor right about now.

"So how did you . . . ?"

Hart fidgeted with his teacup. "I can see the souls of the dead. That's my demigod gift."

"I know."

"That's not all. When I was working in Tanria, there was a house in the middle of Sector 28, a house that only I could see."

Rosie gave a low, impressed whistle. When Tanria first opened to mortals thirty-seven years ago, it was mapped out and divided into a six-by-nine grid of sectors around which the Tanrian

Marshals organized their patrols. Each sector was given a station designation (N for sectors assigned to the North Station, E for those patrolled by the East Station, and so forth) as well as a number. But Sector 28 was never assigned to a station, because it had been Drudge Central back in the day. The undead were so thick on the ground in that section of Tanria that the marshals had stopped patrolling it a few years after the portals opened. To this day, most marshals gave Sector 28 a wide berth.

"Do you know what the house was doing there? Or who built it?"

"It looked like my home, the house I grew up in, but it was actually my death. I could see my own end, waiting there for me, although I didn't realize it at the time. You remember Bill Clark, my first partner? I told him about it, and he and I went into Sector 28 to see what would happen if I opened the door. We hoped the drudges might go inside and leave Tanria. But..." Hart swallowed, his face pained. "That ended badly."

"I remember when Bill died. I'm sorry."

Hart's first partner had been killed by drudges in Sector 28. Hart himself had been badly injured but had survived, which, at the time, had seemed like an indication that he might be immortal.

"Years later, when Duckers was my apprentice, we came under attack by a drudge cluster," Hart continued. "That kid saved my life."

"He's not a kid anymore."

"Tell me about it."

A look passed between them, a shared bittersweetness at the passing of time.

"I almost died that day, but worse, *he* almost died. And I thought, if I could get to that door and open it, if I had any chance of getting the drudges out of Tanria, I had to do it. For him. And in a way, I had to do it for myself. I didn't know if I was mortal or immortal. If I succeeded, I'd be doing something good and right with my life, and if I died trying, well, at least I'd know."

"Mother of Sorrows, you went to Sector 28? By yourself? And you managed to get past all those drudges to open the door?"

"I did."

"And?"

"And I was right. The lost souls that had been reanimating bodies in Tanria flew right in. They all went home to the House of the Unknown God. But so did I."

"Meaning, you died."

He nodded.

Rosie had the distinct sense that she and Hart were the only two people in the world at that moment, as if the universe had been distilled to this one booth with worn leather seats at Aunt Bonnie's pub in Mayetta, Bushong. "What was it like?" she asked him in a hushed, reverent tone.

"I guess you could say that I went home. But it was all the places I had ever thought of as home. My mom was there. And my grandpa. And Bill. And my dog, Gracie. Everyone I had known and loved who had gone before me. And that's when I met my father."

Rosie began to jiggle her knees under the table, anticipating the big reveal.

"Aren't you going to ask?" said Hart.

"I don't think I have to. I think you're about to tell me."

"My dad is the Warden."

Even though she suspected it was one of the death gods, to hear it announced as fact made Rosie's ears ring with shock. "You say *my dad* like you're talking about a guy who wears black socks with sandals."

"You're not wrong."

"Get right on out of town."

"He's very dad-like. I could see him in black socks and sandals."

"Wow, curveball." Rosie let this sink in before she delved deeper. "So you saw your own death, and then you died, and then you saw the afterlife—holy Three Mothers, I can't even with that. So how are you here?"

"I got a death from each of my parents, which means I get to die twice. One down, one to go."

"So basically, you get two lives."

Hart gave her a closed-lip smile, the crow's feet at his eyes crinkling more deeply than they used to. "Same difference."

"You lucky asshole."

"Can't argue with that."

Rosie put her forearms on the table and leaned in. "Is the house still there?"

"I don't know. I haven't been back."

"Can any demigod see it, or just you?"

"Just me, I think, but..." He seemed to war with himself before he went on. "Like I said, I don't know if I should be telling you all this, but I think that if I were in your shoes, I'd want to know about that door."

His pale gray eyes held her red ones, letting her know that he had an inkling of what it felt like to be Rosie Fox, with the long years stretching out before her. It was cold comfort, but she would take comfort in any temperature when she had to look her own immortality in the face.

"Thank you for telling me," she said.

He rumpled his hair with his long hands. "Mercy will have my hide if she finds out I told you."

"Mercy will also never know what it means to live forever."

"I know, and I don't think the odds are good that you'll be able to see that house, much less open the door, but..."

He looked positively wretched.

"Hey, it's not like I want out right this minute. But..." Rosie felt jittery all of a sudden, so she started building a pyramid with her shot glasses. "I'm one hundred and fifty-seven years old, and yet I'm only just now coming to grips with the fact that I'm locked in this world—in this *life*—for the long haul. Maybe that door won't work for me, but knowing that I might have an escape hatch somewhere, sometime, somehow...It helps."

Hart reached out and stilled her hands, knocking over a shot glass in the process. "I'm glad to hear that, but I want to be clear. I'm not opening the door for you."

It wasn't that she had been expecting him to make that particular offer, but now that she knew it was off the table, some cornered feral animal inside her howled in protest.

"But what if—"

"I won't do it. There's a difference between me opening that door for you and you opening it for yourself."

A long, hard pause galloped between them. Rosie's red eyes gleamed with the ferocity of her conviction, and Hart's gray eyes were stricken with his own. It wasn't until Rosie put herself in his place that she realized what she would be asking him to do.

"I understand."

"Thank you." He squeezed her hand before letting go.

The moment was too heavy, and Rosie couldn't bear the weight of it. She gave Hart her goofiest smile. "You can't do it because I'm your friend, and you luvs me."

"I do, you absolute asshole." He picked up his teacup and took a delicate sip.

"Again: you're drinking tea at a bar. Who's the asshole here?"

He raised his eyes to the altar of the sky, but since it was Hart, the gesture was restrained. The man was a giant, and yet he seemed to take up less space than most people, whereas Rosie's physical presence and outsized personality seemed to fill every nook and cranny around her.

"Don't you want to know who my divine parent is?" she asked.

"Only if you want to tell me."

She almost did. The words teetered on the tip of her tongue. But then she thought of her father, and all the feelings and baggage that came with him—and she found that she didn't have it in her to reciprocate her friend's forthrightness, not tonight.

She grimaced. "I'm not there yet."

"No worries. I get it."

He did get it, and she was so grateful to him for getting it the way no one else ever had or could. That was why she was already dreading the day that Hart Ralston would sail the Salt Sea—for good this time—along with everyone else Rosie had ever known and loved.

Chapter Five

Daaaaaaaaang," Duckers breathed as he and Rosie climbed out of her Gratton Parker in the West Station's parking lot Sorrowsday morning. Rosie followed her partner's glazed line of sight to the most luxurious and expensive autoduck she'd ever beheld, driving up the dirt road toward the West Station. The shocks were so good that the tires seemed to silence the gravel beneath them as the duck rolled majestically into the parking lot. If the engine of Duckers's beloved cherry-red muscle duck revved like a lion's roar, the black vehicle parking beside it was as sleek and stealthy as a panther. Even the Bushong dust failed to cling to the pristine paint job.

"I am in love," said Duckers, his eyes glassy.

"I want to touch it, and yet I don't want to sully it with my lowly, plebeian peasant fingers," Rosie agreed. She wouldn't trade her coupe for anything in the world, but the black duck parked next to it made her mouth water.

The driver's-side door opened, and one perfectly polished brown brogue emerged from the interior, followed by its equally meticulous mate, a crisply pressed navy-blue pant cuff hovering over each. And then Dr. Adam Lee, in the flesh, rose from the plummy depths of his magnificent autoduck, his black hair with its silver streak firmly in place, his side part as straight as a ruler. He may have been small in stature, but his dauntingly crisp bearing gave the impression of a person who towered over everything and everyone.

Dr. Lee stiffened when he noticed them, but his flat stare showed no sign of recognition, as if he encountered towering red-eyed demigods on an hourly basis. Rosie wasn't accustomed to such anonymity, not when most people gawked at her, and she wasn't sure if it was depressing or oddly comforting.

Depressing, she decided. He had made a strong impression on her the last time he was here, and she found herself disappointed that apparently, she hadn't made an impression on him at all.

"Hi," said Duckers, smacking his hand against the cab of Rosie's duck as he waved in greeting. He shook out his fingers but kept the bright smile plastered on his face.

"I am looking for Chief Alma Maguire," Dr. Lee informed them sans greeting, as businesslike in speech as he was in attire, the minuscule hint of an accent flavoring his words.

"Right this way," Rosie answered coolly, even as she snaked her hand into her front pocket and felt the silky handkerchief therein.

Chief Maguire must have spotted Adam Lee's luxury autoduck pull into the parking lot from her office window, because she was waiting to greet him in the West Station's lobby.

"Dr. Lee. Thank you for coming on such short notice."

He answered with a curt nod, impossibly out-brusque-ing Alma Maguire.

"Fox, Duckers, glad to see you made it. Let's take this into my office. Dr. Lee, can I offer you a cup of coffee or..."

Maguire let the question linger and waited for the guest to answer. Rosie was sorely tempted to see if she could crack Adam Lee's stony exterior by filling in the blank for him. *An oil change? Some fresh fruit crepes? A jazzy song and dance number? A howler monkey?*

"No, thank you."

"Then let's get to it." The chief escorted Dr. Lee down the hall-way that branched off from the lobby, with Rosie and Duckers following behind. The journey to Maguire's office was brief, but silence was not Rosie's strong suit, and the lack of basic polite con-versation was killing her. Maguire gestured at the three chairs arranged in front of her dinged-up metal desk, behind which she seated herself.

In one fluid motion, Dr. Lee unbuttoned his suit jacket and gracefully lowered himself into the chair on the far right. Duck-ers claimed the one on the left, leaving Rosie to sit in the middle, next to Adam Lee. She felt inordinately huge as she took the seat beside him, like a water buffalo hunkering down beside a fawn. She wasn't as self-conscious about her height now as she had been when she was younger, but she wasn't *not* self-conscious about it. Plus, he was so well groomed, he made her feel shabby by compar-ison, even though she was wearing an exceptional bra-and-panties combo under her monstrous uniform this morning. Not that he would ever have the opportunity to appreciate the matching con-fections in buttery-soft teal satin with a profundity of lace.

"Thank you for coming all this way, Dr. Lee, and apologies for the inconvenience," said Maguire. "Let me introduce you to Marshals Rosie Fox and Penrose Duckers. They're here to report to you regarding how the portal was damaged. Marshals?"

Ostensibly, the chief had addressed both of them, but her icy blue-green orbs landed on Rosie, prompting her to fill in Dr. Lee on the details—the details that involved Rosie's impulsive actions, which had led to this man's having to travel all the way from Quindaro on the island of Vinland to the dusty sticks of Bushong.

Despite the discrepancy in their respective sizes, Rosie sud-denly felt small. She covered her fluster with her just-the-facts law enforcement veneer, and she looked at Maguire—not Dr. Lee—when she spoke.

"Marshal Duckers and I were returning from a tour in Sector W-31 when I noticed that Louis Allen, the engineer on duty, was in the process of repairing the portal. I spotted something unusual inside the portal's inner workings, and I was pointing out the issue to Mr. Allen when I inadvertently touched a live wire, which led to some further damage to the mechanism."

Duckers gave her a surreptitious thumbs-up, gods love him.

Dr. Lee turned to Rosie, studying her face with inscrutable brown eyes. After more than a century and a half on this earth, Rosie was adept at reading other people, but Dr. Lee was a steel trap. She had no idea what he was thinking or feeling, or if he was thinking or feeling anything at all.

"I am surprised the current didn't kill you," he said.

"Well, actually—" began Rosie, but Maguire cut her off.

"Not now, Fox."

"You said you saw something unusual inside the frame. What was it?" His accent was barely perceptible, but definitely there, his voice deeper and more gravelly than one would expect from someone so slight.

"I don't know."

The answer made her sound feckless, even to her own ears.

"Can you describe its appearance?"

"Kind of shadow...y?"

Rosie experienced a sense of being outside her body. *Have you thought about using words?* suggested her snarky inner self. Gods, what was wrong with her? Why was she shrinking under Dr. Lee's relentless stare?

"Perhaps it is better if I see it for myself." Without so much as a by-your-leave, he rose and exited Chief Maguire's office, taking his oppressive lack of personality with him.

"Oka-a-a-ay," said Duckers as Dr. Lee's expensive shoes tapped out a graceful rhythm on the linoleum in the hallway beyond.

"Meeting's over, I guess," said Maguire. "Let's go."

They followed Adam Lee out the back door, arriving at the portal in time to see him whip off his beautifully tailored suit jacket and hand it to Louis, who held it as reverently as if he had been given care of Grandfather Bones's skull. He unclipped his cuff links and dropped them into his pocket, then rolled up his shirtsleeves to the elbows, unveiling the pale, graceful forearms beneath.

Rosie had zero romantic interest in the man, but those forearms could inspire sonnets. And Bride of Fortune, she was not sad to witness the way Adam Lee's impeccably tailored shirt and pants and waistcoat hugged his slender frame as he examined the scorched portal.

Three cheers for bespoke menswear, she thought.

"Marshal Fox," he called to her in the mechanical tone of a man who had never known an emotion he couldn't quash. "You put your hand in here? You touched these wires?"

Rosie felt like a student who hadn't been paying attention when the teacher called on her.

"Yeah."

"I imagine that was not pleasant."

"I wouldn't recommend it."

"The steam engine is shut off, so there's no longer power running through the wiring. Can you show me where you saw... What did you call it?"

"I believe her exact words at the time were 'shadowy blotch thing,'" Duckers volunteered.

Rosie glared at him.

"That's what you said!" he cried in his defense.

"Will you show me where you saw this shadow?"

"Sure."

She came to stand beside Dr. Lee, close enough to get a good whiff of the understated spicy, woodsy, herbal scent wafting off him. She had never smelled anyone so magnificently expensive. He was like a human bath bomb.

"It was at the back," she said. "But I don't see it anymore, maybe because everything in here is burned?"

"Could you estimate its size? Or describe its shape or color?"

"It was twisty looking, if that makes sense?"

"That makes zero sense," Duckers commented good-naturedly.

"Can it, Marshal," Maguire told him.

"It was long and narrow, maybe two centimeters wide," Rosie continued, looking abashedly at the charred remains of the portal's inner workings. "And as for color, I think it was gray? Or maybe dark brown. Does that sound like something that's supposed to be in there?"

"No." He turned to Louis. "You, there. What is your name?"

"Louis Allen, sir."

Dr. Lee indicated the open tool kit on the ground. "May I, Mr. Allen?"

Cradling the suit jacket in awed silence, Louis nodded.

Dr. Lee went to work with a screwdriver, removing a metal plate from inside the frame. He took a flashlight from the kit, wound the key, and sent its beam upward through the interior, illuminating the portal's innards.

He went still.

"What's wrong?" Rosie asked.

He didn't answer her. He set down the flashlight and went about removing another hatch door on the exterior, but Rosie could swear that his hands were trembling. The second he had the hatch open, Rosie caught a glimpse of another twisted shadow inside.

"There! You see it, right?"

Again, Adam Lee did not answer her. He didn't even tilt his head in her direction. She got the sense that he was adamantly *not* looking at her. He stepped away but kept his eyes fixed on the portal's innards. "Chief Maguire, can you see what Marshal Fox sees?"

Maguire stepped closer to the portal. "I don't see anything odd, but I have to be honest; I have no idea what this thing is supposed to look like on the inside."

Without tearing his gaze from the open hatch, Dr. Lee asked, "Marshal Duckers?"

"I got nothing."

"Mr. Allen?"

"No, sir."

Adam Lee finally turned to Rosie, his face unreadable, and yet some inner spark flickered across his features. "But you? You see something?"

"Yeah."

"What I don't understand is how something only Fox can see could cause damage to anything," said Maguire. "I'm assuming you've never seen whatever this stuff is anywhere else, Fox?"

"Not that I know of, Chief. And I think I'd remember."

"Any ideas, Dr. Lee?"

The inventor addressed Rosie rather than Maguire. "Will you describe its appearance, Marshal Fox?"

"It's like a dark, narrow smudge curling around the piston."

"Are you able to touch it?"

"Is it safe to touch it?" Rosie might not be able to stay dead, but she didn't enjoy dying or experiencing pain.

He hesitated before frowning—an actual facial expression! "Perhaps you had better not."

Neither his frown nor his answer filled her with confidence. But since she could not die and stay dead, she decided that she ought to do whatever she could to ameliorate the situation.

"Fuck it. I'll do it for science," she declared, and she reached out to touch the grayish-brownish spot.

"Stop!" snapped Dr. Lee, but he was too late.

Except, as it turned out, Rosie could not, in fact, touch the shadowy spot thing. Her fingertips passed right through it—whatever *it* was—and made contact with the cool piston beneath it.

"What's it feel like, Fox?" asked Maguire.

"Nothing."

"Meaning?"

"I can't feel anything. It's like touching a literal shadow. I can see it, but there's nothing to touch."

Rosie looked to Dr. Lee, who studied her as if she were an insect under a magnifying glass.

"I asked you to wait," he said.

"No, you asked me if I could touch it."

"And then I thought better of it, and I asked you to wait." There was an edge to his voice. Rosie couldn't say if it was anger or irritation or if he was being patronizing, but a tone was definitely present.

Rosie did not appreciate the tone.

"In fact, you did not ask, and also, you are not the boss of me."

He regarded her impassively, but Rosie got the sense that this was a man who was not accustomed to sass. She knew that her snappy comeback was unhelpful, but one of the perks of living forever was the ability to outlive even the most ill-advised retorts.

Duckers covered a laugh by pretending to cough.

"Fox," Maguire warned her, while giving Duckers the stink eye.

"I'm stating facts here. He's not the boss of me. You are."

"Well, I—your boss—am ordering you to do as Dr. Lee says."

Adam Lee adjusted his glasses, which did not appear to need straightening. "I apologize, Marshal Fox. I should not have asked if you could touch the shadow in the first place. Please understand that I have only your safety in mind."

The apology rattled Rosie. He did not strike her as the apologizing type, and she found herself wrong-footed, which was both rare and discombobulating. She suspected that most people did not care to be discombobulated, but since almost nothing cowed Rosie, she found the experience refreshing.

"Thank you."

Dr. Lee nodded before turning to the engineer. "Mr. Allen, I require your assistance. We're going to take off the entire front panel."

Louis entrusted the suit coat to Rosie's care. Flustered in the wake of Dr. Lee's apology and her own discomposure, she skulked off to Duckers's side with the inventor's jacket draped over her forearm.

"Who are you, and what have you done with Rosie Fox?" he asked her.

"Shut up."

"I think maybe that guy really is the boss of you. And it is glorious to behold."

"Fuck right off, Penny-D."

"I'm trying to figure out how someone that boring can be so intimidating. I bet I've got five inches on him, but he makes me feel tiny for some reason."

"It's the Greatness Vibe rolling off him. He's got class in spades."

Rosie surreptitiously breathed in the ghost of Dr. Lee's cologne, which haunted the woolen fibers of the jacket. The man might lack joie de vivre, but Salt Sea, he smelled divine.

Duckers, who missed nothing, asked, "And how does the Greatness Vibe smell?"

Rosie did not dignify this with a response.

The chief stood to the side and watched as Dr. Lee and Louis took out bolt after bolt around the exterior of the panel. Growing bored, Rosie nipped inside the station to nab a deck of cards from the commissary. Since there weren't enough players for a game of Gods and Heroes, she and Duckers sat on the edge of the parking lot and played a few rounds of Gods in the Corner instead, while Rosie continued to inhale the subtle aroma wafting off the coat nestled in her lap.

Duckers thought he was winning handily as he placed the Grandmother Wisdom card on top of the God of Pestilence card, the New Gods suit following the Old Gods suit. But two tricks later, Rosie wiped the endearing smugness from his face when she slapped the Briar Thief hero card on top of his War Dragon weapons card.

"Last one," Louis called from his perch on a ladder off to the left-hand side of the frame, bringing their game to a halt.

Dr. Lee backed away from the portal. "All clear. Let it fall."

Louis removed the bolt and used a crowbar to loosen the front panel. The whole thing came careening downward, hitting the earth with a ground-shaking crash and sending up a cloud of not-red Bushong dust. Rosie fussed over the beautiful suit coat, which was now speckled with a fine layer of grit, so it took a minute before she looked up to see what was inside the portal's frame.

There were pipes and pistons and cogs and tubes and wires...

And shadows wrapped around everything.

"What in Old Hell?" she cussed as she got to her feet.

"What's up, Foxy?" asked Maguire.

"This thing is chock-full of those shadowy blotch things. You can't see them?"

"No. Duckers?"

Duckers shook his head. "This is messed up."

"What do you think, Professor?" asked Maguire, sounding unsettled.

He stood with his back to them, a portrait of good posture as he studied the portal with intense focus. The seconds ticked by until, at last, he said simply, "I don't know."

"Can you fix it?"

"I don't know."

"How much time is it going to take for you to know?"

"If you are in a hurry, you could always buy a pirated portal from the Galatian crime syndicate."

"Mmm!" Duckers hummed in a quiet falsetto, expressing a sentiment similar to the laughing *Oh, shit!* of Rosie's interior monologue. No one gave lip to Alma Maguire, even in a monotone.

Maguire folded her arms, a sign that she was quickly losing patience with Absurdly Curt Genius Man. "And what happens when you die, Dr. Lee?"

The professor blinked at Maguire. "Excuse me?"

"I hate to be the bearer of bad tidings, but death is an end we all face."

Rosie gave her a sad two-fingered salute and muttered, "Thanks, Chief," but Maguire ignored her.

"A day will come when you will no longer be present on this earth, sir. What will become of the portals then? Or Tanria for that matter? There are people whose livelihood depends on the ability to work inside the Mist. Whole communities have been built up around Tanria and the business it generates. What happens to these people if they can no longer get inside?"

"I did not build those communities. I did not force anyone to move to this place."

"And yet you are responsible for all of this. If you fail, we all fail. You're not young, Dr. Lee. How many more malfunctions can you repair in your lifetime? How many more portals will you be able to build in the years you have left on this earth?"

"You have made your point."

The inventor held her gaze. Maguire nodded, but tension hung thick in the air.

"I would like to examine the portal from inside the Mist," said Dr. Lee.

"Of course. Fox and Duckers are assigned to assist you for the duration of your stay on Bushong. They can get you wherever you need to go." Maguire turned to her marshals. "You two, drive Dr. Lee to the North Station and—"

"I prefer to enter Tanria via the portal at the South Station," Dr. Lee interrupted.

Maguire raised her eyebrows at the man's temerity.

"Dang," Duckers said under his breath.

"I think you'll find the journey from the North Station much more comfortable," the chief explained with threadbare patience. "Coaches run between the Tanrian Dragon Preserve and both the North and West Stations several times a day on good roads."

"There is no transport between the preserve and the West Station at this time, clearly. And I am more than capable of riding an equimaris."

"Then you can ride an equimaris on good roads from the North Station through the dragon preserve. It'll be much faster and much easier than coming in from the south. I insist, Dr. Lee."

He answered Maguire with an abrupt nod, took his coat from Rosie, and shrugged it on before stalking toward the parking lot. He paused to gaze down at the upturned card of the Briar Thief, who was staring back at him in agony from Rosie and Duckers's abandoned game of Gods in the Corner. Then he continued on his way at a slower pace, his gait stiff.

"We need to keep that guy on a leash," said Duckers as they watched the retreat of Adam Lee's woolen backside.

Maguire pinched the bridge of her nose. "We don't have any government ducks left in the lot. You'll have to take one of your own vehicles this time."

That cheered Duckers up real fast. "I vote we hitch a ride in Dr. Lee's sexy stealth duck."

"No, sir, you are not riding in a civilian's autoduck," said Maguire.

"Aw, but, Chief—"

"Both of your vehicles are registered for mileage with the Tanrian Marshals Service. His is not. Which one of you drove?"

"Me!" cried Rosie, thrilled by this turn of events as her hand shot in the air.

Duckers was less than thrilled. "You want us to drive the good professor around in the pistachio on wheels?"

An evil grin spread across Alma Maguire's face. "As a matter of fact, I do."

Chapter Six

Adam Lee was unexpectedly amenable to riding in Rosie's auto-duck, which was a little disappointing; she had looked forward to annoying him. But as he stood beside the Gratton Parker in his neatly pressed suit and polished brogues, she couldn't help but think that he and the duck belonged together, both of them cut along vintage, classic lines.

"You're going to make me ride in the back seat, aren't you?" Duckers asked her.

In answer, Rosie unlocked the passenger-side door and pushed the front seat forward so that he could climb in. He made a moue of distaste but didn't put up a fight as he folded himself onto the back bench with its nonexistent leg room.

"I worked the northern sectors for a year before transferring to the West Station. They love me there," Rosie informed Dr. Lee as she sank into the bucket seat behind the wheel, its brittle leather cracking.

Duckers snorted behind her, but she chose to ignore him. She turned the key in the ignition, and the cheery buzz of the old-school engine filled the cab.

"Is this a series 9?" asked Dr. Lee as he examined the duck's interior with what appeared to be interest.

Rosie was gobsmacked that Reticence Personified had willingly started a conversation. "It's a series 7."

"It appears to be in remarkably good condition."

"Oh, man." Duckers laughed as Rosie's charity toward Dr. Lee unfurled like a hibiscus bloom.

She patted the endearingly hideous mustard-brown dashboard. "This baby is sixty-four years old, but in her heart, she's not a day over forty."

"All the Gratton Parkers from that era are works of art. But a series 7? This is quite special."

"And with that, he won her undying love forever," Duckers narrated from the back.

"He's not wrong. We might have to get married now."

Duckers leaned forward to better participate in the conversation as Rosie steered them onto the main road that encircled Tanria. "There are two things Fox loves most in this world: this ridiculous tin can and her underwear."

"I prefer *lingerie* or *delicates* or *intimates*. Get it right, Tighty-Whities."

Rosie glanced at Dr. Lee long enough to notice that his cheeks had gone pink, presumably at the mention of her undergarments. It was nice to know that there was blood pumping underneath that cold exterior. Maybe he was like the demigod character in one of her favorite books, *Enemies and Lovers*. The love interest was kind of a dick in that one, but it turned out he was simply shy. Maybe Dr. Lee was a secretly shy dickhead. Rosie decided to see if she could draw him out and put him at ease.

"So, where are you from, Dr. Lee?"

"Eshil Craia."

Rosie's ruddy eyebrows arched skyward. Eshil Craia was a small country on the coast of the Pritean continent. The Federated Islands of Cadmus were fairly international in scope, sitting between three different continents—the result of the world breaking apart during the War of the Gods—but it wasn't often that someone from as far away as Eshil Craia made their way to inland Bushong.

"You're a long way from home," said Duckers, perking up with interest.

Dr. Lee gave a small hum in reply, but Rosie wasn't sure what it was supposed to communicate.

"How did you wind up in the Federated Islands?" she asked.

"I walked."

Both Rosie and Duckers laughed, a response as unexpected as the humor that had inspired it.

"You think I jest," he said. Gods, the man was dry.

"No, I think you hoofed it hundreds of miles across the ocean floor," joked Rosie.

"Thousands," he corrected her.

Delighted that the professor was showing signs of life, Rosie flashed him a bright smile. She had barely returned her attention to the road when she heard a sharp intake of breath beside her.

"Dr. Lee?" she said, trying to look at him while also navigating the two-lane country road.

Duckers leaned as far forward as he could in the confines of the itty-bitty cab. "Hey, man, are you all right?"

"I'm fine," said Dr. Lee, but his hand gripped the door handle, and his teeth were clenched.

"You don't seem fine," said Rosie.

"You don't look fine either," added Duckers.

"Should I pull over?"

Dr. Lee gentled his grip on the door handle and relaxed his jaw muscles. "I have a health condition. It's nothing serious."

"It looked pretty serious for a second there."

"It isn't. I can assure you that I will not die on your watch." He stared straight ahead, his tone so dry it could cause a drought.

"I'm going to hold you to that. You are not allowed to croak on us."

A burst of air escaped his lips. If Rosie didn't know better, she would swear that Adam Lee had laughed.

"We should select some mounts first. You said you know how to ride, Dr. Lee?" asked Duckers, indicating the North Station's equimaris stable.

"Yes, although it has been some time." He glanced down at his suit pants and now slightly dirty brogues. He didn't frown or express any particular emotion, but he was likely regretting his wardrobe choices.

"It's an easy ride, but we'll take it slow," Duckers assured him.

"No need. I can keep up."

Rosie had her doubts about that. The water horses were docile enough on the coasts, but they tended to be recalcitrant this far inland and, therefore, tricky to control, especially for someone who wasn't used to riding. Even the most mild-mannered equimaris would bolt for the nearest body of water if the opportunity presented itself.

In the stables, she picked a gelding and got him saddled up in double time so that she could help Dr. Lee if he needed assistance. But true to his word, he appeared to know what he was doing, strapping on a saddlebag full of tools before he climbed into the saddle with ease. Rosie had never seen a man in a suit atop an equimaris, and the contrast was jarring. Once again, she felt shabby and underdressed in her unflattering Tanrian Marshals Service uniform.

Take strength from your intimates, she told herself.

The trio headed for the portal, where the North Station's chief marshal, who must have gotten wind of their arrival, was waiting for them.

"Chief Mitchell," Adam Lee said to the short, stocky blond woman in her chief marshal uniform, which was starched within an inch of its life. It wasn't much of a greeting, and Rosie wondered if she might be able to coach him on basic civility, such as how to say hello to people.

"Hi, Chief," she modeled for him, greeting her former boss with exaggerated cordiality.

Mitchell bypassed the greeting and went straight for a stern warning. "Don't you dare lay one finger on this portal, Fox."

Rosie had worked out of the North Station for less than a year, but apparently the old boss held a grudge. She could sense Duckers's amusement, even though he didn't make a peep.

"Come on, Chief, we had our good moments."

"You mean like the time you stuck a wool smuggler to a heart-nut tree with sap and left him there to dangle for an hour before bringing him in."

"He was mouthing off."

"He was fourteen."

"And I taught him a valuable life lesson."

"And let's not forget the time I had to come bail you and five other marshals out of jail because you thought it would be hilarious to put a Westie's autoduck on the roof of Eternity's city hall."

"Okay, but did you ever *meet* Marshal Herd?"

"Oh, *that* guy!" interjected Duckers.

"Right?"

"I had to partner up with him for a few weeks—well, before he died. You were the one who put his duck on the roof of city hall?"

"Yep."

"Classic! How'd you pull it off?"

"Oh my gods, it was so great! We—"

"I also remember the time you broke the portal," Chief Mitchell interrupted with increasing agitation. "This portal. Right here. Which I do not want you to touch."

"I didn't *break* it. I *fixed* it."

"Do. Not. Touch. It. Understood?"

"You bet," said Rosie.

Mitchell glared up at her, unconvinced.

"Have you had problems with the portal?" Dr. Lee asked the chief.

"Some flickering. Nothing the engineers can't handle."

He nodded, but he seemed distracted.

"Go ahead and let them through," Mitchell ordered the engineer on duty. But as soon as he pulled the switch, the Mist inside the archway began to flicker from opaque to sheer to opaque again in rapid succession. A person could try to go through, but it would be inadvisable. Not that inadvisability had ever stopped Rosie a day in her long life, but she did have her partner and the World Blandness Champion to consider.

"Are you kidding me right now?" said Duckers as Dr. Lee dismounted to take a look and consult with the chief and the engineer. Rosie could envision how this would play out, with Professor Meticulous dotting every *i* and crossing every *t* to get to the bottom of the issue at the North Station while everyone who needed to use the West Station's portal would continue to get rerouted, and the whole day would be wasted while a bored Duckers and an even more bored Rosie played cards until their fingers bled.

She slid off her equimaris, strode toward the portal, and pounded the frame with her fist.

"Salt Sea, Fox!" said a very miffed Chief Mitchell.

Duckers sighed dramatically, but with a certain amount of affection, especially since the Smack It Method worked this time. The portal belched steam, and the cogs and pistons began to work their magic, thinning the Mist within the archway to a transparent curtain that revealed the outline of the Tanrian landscape beyond.

Rosie cheekily cocked her ugly flat hat at her partner. "Fifty percent of the time, my friend."

"I gather that is not the first instance in which you have assaulted one of my portals?" inquired Dr. Lee, deadpan.

"I've fixed the portals a few times over the years."

"You and I may differ in our definition of the word *fix*."

"Worked, didn't it?"

"I... You can't... How?" sputtered the North Station's chief marshal.

"Go on through before she murders you," Duckers murmured to Rosie while Chief Mitchell was too pissed off to form a coherent tirade. "We'll be right behind you. I'll bring your mount."

Rosie decided not to quibble over the chief's ability to murder her and chose instead to hustle through the archway before she got into any more hot water.

Like most people who crossed the Tanria-Bushong border on a regular basis, Rosie hated the high-pressure squeezing sensation that came with passing through the Mist. The absolute silence of those seconds reminded her of how it felt to die without really dying. And then she came out the other side, where the bizarre otherworld of Tanria greeted her.

The foothills of the Dragon's Teeth mountain range rolled before her in a series of perfectly round hillocks, like enormous bubbles covered in grass the color of cotton candy. Beyond them, to her south and west, the peaks rose in bizarrely regular magenta triangles. To the southeast, she could make out the rainbow blur of the friendtree forest that covered a third of Tanria, taking up enormous swaths of the north and east sectors. It had been a while since she'd seen this view, but it was comfortingly familiar all the same. People often found the sights and sounds and colors of Tanria overwhelming, but to Rosie, it was the closest thing she'd found to home since Jocelyn died.

From outside, the Mist was a dense fog, but from inside Tanria, it was clear as glass, so that the Old Gods could look on the world they had tried to destroy and see what they were missing. Which meant that Rosie could see the response of everyone on the opposite side of the portal when a grating sound erupted from inside the frame, followed by a loud *pop* and the sad trombones of the portal winding down to its demise. She reached out to touch the space inside the archway, but sure enough, it was solid.

"Well, shit snacks," said Rosie. She could see—but not hear—the commotion on the other side of the border between Tanria and the rest of Bushong. Chief Mitchell nodded gravely as the engineer spoke to her. Duckers faced the Mist with a worried expression on his face. And Adam Lee stood motionless, his arms folded, his suit coat increasingly rumpled. His eyes darted from point to point on the portal's frame. There was something beyond cold calculation going on behind those eyes—frustration and... was that maybe a hint of concern?

Rosie rang the portal bell. Under normal circumstances, the bell notified the engineer on duty that someone needed to be let out. Now Rosie rang it to let everyone know she had made it through in one piece. Duckers sagged with relief, which made painfully squeezy things happen inside her rib cage.

"Once more, for the Penrose Duckerses in the back: I can't die," she said, even though he couldn't hear her.

Dr. Lee took off his suit coat, and this time, he didn't bother to hand it off to a groveling engineer. The woolen masterpiece hit the Bushong dust as he approached the portal opposite Rosie to remove a hatch. His body language was taut, like a rubber band stretched to its most uncomfortable limits.

It was...

Well, frankly, it was kind of sexy.

The bespoke clothing, the debonair removal of his jacket, the big brains, the intense focus, the giving of zero fucks... There was a certain allure.

And now that Rosie was taking a good look, she had to admit that the man had a handsome face, a pleasing combination of hard and soft—the jawline and cheekbones chiseled, but the lips full, the brown eyes round and liquid. And while she had only his forearms and his hands and his face as evidence, he certainly appeared to be fit under that rigorously tailored menswear.

Not appropriate, Rosie, she told herself, but she allowed one more thirsty glance in his direction before opening the portal's fail-safe hatch. Technically, marshals were only supposed to use the fail-safe mechanism as a last resort, but Rosie decided it would be better to beg forgiveness than ask permission on this one. She was about to pull out the crank when she noticed shadows within the North Station's portal.

They were more distinct now, not formless blobs but an interconnected network with shape and substance. And they weren't simply taking up residence inside the portal. Rosie detected a faint line snaking away from the archway, running parallel to the ground like a troubling crack in a house's foundation. It was difficult to make out against the sunny Bushong landscape beyond, but now that she'd noticed it, she couldn't un-notice it. Upon closer examination, she found multiple cracks branching off from the portal's frame in all directions.

"That's not alarming or anything," she said as she peered inside the open fail-safe hatch and wondered if it would be unwise to stick her hand inside.

Are you able to touch it? Adam Lee asked her in her memory, followed by *Perhaps you had better not.*

She was sure that there were times in her life—before she knew she couldn't die—when she might have felt the need for caution, but she could no longer remember what that need felt like. Which was why she put her hand into the hatch to see if she could feel the shadows this time.

She could not. Her fingers passed right through, straight to the fail-safe mechanism. Unsure as to whether she should be relieved or disappointed, she pulled out the crank and unfolded the handle. Before she could give the lever a good wind, though, she heard someone call, "Mail delivery."

Rosie turned to find Tanria's nimkilim—a tiny, bipedal deer named Gobbo—approaching her. The nimkilim were once the messengers of the Old Gods. Now they were the backbone of the Federated Islands of Cadmus's postal service. Most of them were pissy about being demoted after the War of the Gods, but Gobbo was the poster child for the chill life. Unlike his predecessors, he seemed to enjoy delivering mail inside the Mist, probably because he could get away with wearing ripped dungarees out here in the boonies.

He propped his sunglasses onto his horns and grinned, his eyes glassy. "Hey, it's Rock On or Fuck Off! What's up, RoFo?"

"Nothing much. The portal's not working, so I'm kind of screwed at the moment."

"Sucks. But cheer up, my friend. You've got mail."

He handed her a small, irregular package, badly wrapped in brown paper and twine with a kitschy postcard from the country of Stenland attached to it. She guessed who it was from before she even read the message.

Tallyho, kiddo! I'm vacationing in Stenland. Have you ever been? Very posh. Lots of castles. Anyhoo, I saw this cat in a gift shop, and since it looks like Stinky Buttcheek, I thought you'd like to have it for your collection.

Love, Dad

Rosie sneered at the message. Even on paper, her father turned her into a sulking teenager in seconds. She opened the parcel and found a small figurine inside, a calico that in no way resembled the gray-and-black-striped asshole who used her for her tuna and whose name the Trickster could not trouble himself to remember. And two of its legs had broken off, thanks to the inadequate packaging.

"Aw, that's cute," said Gobbo. He looked inside the mail satchel slung over his shoulder. "I might have some glue in here."

Probably for sniffing, thought Rosie. Aloud, she said, "Don't worry about it."

"Are you sure?"

"Yes. Because this?" She held up the cat figurine for his inspection, causing one of the broken legs to slide off the paper and land in the spiky pink grass at her feet. "This is a fucking metaphor."

Gobbo held up his front hooves in a gesture of peace, love, and understanding. "Cool cool. I can totally get behind a good metaphor."

Rosie picked up the fallen leg and shoved her father's pathetic peace offering into her pocket. She tipped the nimkilim before turning her attention to the portal, which showed no signs of life, even as Dr. Lee and the engineer worked on it on the other side.

"All right, I'm taking matters into my own hands," she declared as she grasped the fail-safe handle. "Here goes nothing."

"Sweet."

Rosie managed to crank the handle only a quarter turn before she ran into resistance.

"What do you think?" she asked the world's highest nimkilim.

"Fuck it. It's not going to let you out if you don't do anything."

"You've got a point." Rosie adjusted her grip on the handle and put some muscle into it. The entire lever came off in her hand with a sickening *crack*, and she wound up staggering sideways before she caught herself.

"Shit," said Gobbo. "I take it back. Don't do that."

"Great advice."

"Here to help."

Rosie was not ready to panic yet, but the blood drained from her face as she stared at the broken handle in her hand. "Oh dear."

"Technically, I'm a dik-dik, but I prefer to go with *deer*. Because, like, the dick jokes, man."

Rosie stared at Gobbo.

"Do I have something on my face?" He brought a hoof to his cheek. If deer could be said to have cheeks. Dik-dik cheeks?

Rosie dropped the crank and took him by his sloping dik-dik shoulders. "My dude, I am legit stuck here."

"Oh." He frowned at the fail-safe handle, which had landed in a patch of scraggy pink grass. "That blows."

The absurdity of the situation made Rosie cackle, and Gobbo laughed cluelessly along with her. On some level, she knew she was bordering on hysteria, and yet she relished the feeling of dread gurgling in her stomach. It was such a rarity for her.

"I wish I could get you out of here, but nimkilim can't carry living matter," Gobbo said in apology once the laughter had petered out.

"And there's no one more alive than I am."

Rosie thought of the carelessness with which she had whacked the North Station's portal moments ago. Now she wanted to kick Past Rosie in the teeth.

"If I make it through any portal in the next twenty-four hours, I'm going to wrap the whole thing in velvet and give it a kiss," she told Gobbo.

He nodded sagely. "Keeping it classy."

She was formulating a plan to hoof it to the East Station when the northern portal juddered to life beside her.

"Woooooooo!" cheered Gobbo as he helpfully charged Rosie and butted her toward the frame with his diminutive horns. She lost her footing and grabbed hold of the first thing she could find before she fell on her ass, the first thing in this case being the fringed shirtfront of a mail-delivering dik-dik. They both tumbled through the silent curtain between prison and freedom.

Gobbo whooped. "What the what! I've never used a portal before! That high-pressure squeeze thing? A+. No notes. Wooooooo!"

Duckers crushed Rosie in a bear hug. "Are you all right?"

"When am I ever not all right?"

"The second you went through, the whole thing sputtered out. We thought you'd been caught inside the Mist. You've got to stop doing this to me."

"This time was not my fault!"

"I know." Duckers smacked a loud kiss on her cheek before letting go of her.

Dr. Lee continued to work on the portal. Shadowy tendrils spilled out of the open hatch, and while the inventor didn't actually touch them, he appeared to be working around them as the Mist inside the portal's frame flickered in and out in rapid succession.

"Don't suppose you can see that," Rosie said to Duckers.

"See what?"

"That's what I thought." She stepped forward to get a better look when Dr. Lee threw down his pliers in defeat and let loose an Eshilese curse word, an explosive *kh* plus a vowel—possibly *ai* or *ah* or *eh*—followed by a harsh, wet *shhhhhh*. It was the same syllable she'd heard him utter five years ago when he had cut his hand while repairing the West Station's portal.

He turned away from the defunct husk of his invention, his face animated by anger (not at Rosie!) and frustration. Rosie reeled, because *that* was a face she could stare at for a long, long time without getting tired of it. He was striking in the best possible way when he chose to wear his feelings.

When his eyes met Rosie's, he blew out a long breath. "Are you all right?" he asked her, his voice extra gravelly with fatigue and— dare she think it?—concern on her behalf, which also looked delectable on him.

Rosie fanned herself. "I ought to worry you on a regular basis. You are fine, sir!"

He blinked at her for a few seconds before he puffed an incredulous laugh. Rosie's delight in wringing genuine amusement from him was short-lived, however, because Adam Lee's laughter turned into a bone-rattling cough. Alarmed by his sudden turn, Rosie put a steadying hand on his shoulder as he clutched his chest.

"Can we get some water over here?" Duckers called to the North Station staff milling around the portal. Someone held out a canteen to Dr. Lee, but he waved it away.

"Close the portals," he choked out between coughs.

"What?" asked Chief Mitchell. "What did he say?"

"I said, close the portals. We need to evacuate Tanria immediately."

The growing crowd of marshals and Tanrian employees waiting to go through the Mist went deadly quiet in the wake of Adam Lee's pronouncement.

"Whooooooooa," said Gobbo as his sunglasses slid down the long bridge of his nose.

"Isn't that a bit...hasty?" asked Chief Mitchell.

Dr. Lee's fit had ebbed, but he continued to cling to Rosie's arm to steady himself. "Two of the four portals are malfunctioning. They were all installed at the same time. If two are experiencing mechanical issues, it is likely they are all experiencing mechanical issues. We cannot run the risk of trapping people inside the Mist. If we are unable to fix the portals quickly, those people will run out of food and supplies. They can drink water and ambrosia, but nothing else in Tanria is potable or edible."

"We can deliver supplies via nimkilim post. They don't use the portals."

"And if, for any reason, the nimkilim are unable to enter Tanria?" Mitchell chewed her lip.

"It would be a death sentence, and you know it."

The chief's face drained of color. She turned abruptly to address her marshals. "Listen up: we're calling for the complete evacuation of Tanria. Now. All tourists, all personnel, every living, breathing human being currently inside the Mist needs to exit through the nearest functioning portal."

"Holy Three Mothers," breathed Duckers.

Rosie couldn't convince herself that an evacuation was actually happening. The experience was like reading a novel, requiring her willing suspension of disbelief when she had yet to lose herself in the story.

Dr. Lee released his hold on her as Chief Mitchell barked orders. He stood ramrod straight, returning to his standard Imperious Mode as he eyed the crowd, making sure they understood the gravity of the situation. Rosie suspected that they were all thinking the same thing she was. The Tanrian Marshals performed an evacuation drill annually, but those drills were a disaster every single year. And that was with all four portals in operation.

It had to be done, but Salt Sea, this was going to be a nightmare.

Duckers probably spoke for everyone present when he said, "Well, fuck."

Chapter Seven

"Cracks?" repeated Dr. Lee as the Gratton Parker sped along the two-lane highway with Rosie behind the wheel.

"Ish? I don't know how else to describe them."

"And you have never seen them before this morning?"

"No, but that doesn't mean they weren't there."

Rosie took the ramp leading to the South Station. It was the most likely exit point for tourists and staff vacating the Tanrian Dragon Preserve, since the north and west portals were out of commission, which meant that it would be the busiest of the two functioning portals. The East Station was closer as the crow flew, but the terrain between there and the preserve was difficult, especially if they were getting people out via equimaris-drawn coaches.

"Surely you would have noticed the 'cracks,' as you call them, before today."

"Not necessarily. When I step through a portal, it's not like I turn around to study the Mist. I get to work. And then, when I get off duty, I'm thinking about what I'm going to eat when I get home and taking a bath and feeding Blammo Tinky Fartface."

"You—I'm sorry, what?"

"I didn't see a problem, because I wasn't looking for a problem. It would be like having a janky pitcher in the cupboard. The only way you're going to find out it's cracked is when you make margs and all the liquid gold comes leaking out. I noticed the cracks today because I was forced to stare at the problem."

"Remarkably, I think I understand your point."

"Pro tip," offered Duckers. "Never accept a cocktail from the hands of Rosie Fox. People who can't get drunk are bad at measuring."

He was trying to lighten the mood, but even a Duckers joke couldn't lift the pall of an evacuation order. And Adam Lee had regressed to his standard automaton mode, so he was unlikely to laugh in any event.

This guy should play Gods and Heroes on the professional circuit, thought Rosie as she pressed down on the gas pedal, making the proverbial hamsters in the engine clamber to keep up.

Dr. Lee inclined his head, listening to the furious buzz of the motor as the Gratton Parker picked up speed. "This duck is magnificent," he said, his tone flat, but his appreciation clear.

Rosie gave him an emphatic "Thank you" as she shot Duckers a meaningful glance in the rearview mirror, one that said, *At least someone here appreciates the finer things in life.*

The South Station was a zoo by the time Rosie, Duckers, and Dr. Lee pulled into the parking lot. Or perhaps it was more accurate to say that it was a ranch. Almost everyone exiting Tanria arrived by equimaris, either riding astride one or catching an equimaris-drawn coach. The stable was full to bursting, even though only a fraction of Tanria had been cleared so far. Emergency water troughs had popped up willy-nilly to keep the overflow livestock from bolting, and the air rang with a cacophony of people shouting and the distressed gargling of the water horses.

The stench wasn't so great either.

They found Alma Maguire conferring with the South Station's chief marshal, Dane Longmeier, near the bustling portal. This time, Dr. Lee shook her hand in greeting and Chief Longmeier's as well.

"Aw, look at him being human," Rosie whispered to Duckers, like a proud parent at her child's halting piano recital performance. "Our baby's growing up."

Duckers puffed his lips in disagreement.

"I'm glad you're here, Professor," said Maguire. "I'd like to have you on hand in case anything goes wrong with the portal."

"Should we be on the lookout for any problems here?" asked Chief Longmeier, his drawn face taking on a deeper cast of concern.

"Not that I'm aware of. May I take a look?" Dr. Lee gestured at the portal.

"Of course."

Someone rang the portal bell from the Tanrian side of the Mist, and the inventor watched as the engineer pulled down on the main lever. The portal's steam engine chugged to life, and the Mist within the archway thinned to let out another group of evacuees. Dr. Lee nodded in approval, but he lingered beside his invention like a dragon hovering anxiously over a clutch of eggs.

Duckers nudged Rosie and jerked his head toward Lu and Annie Ellis, who stood at the center of a growing mob, each clutching a clipboard. Lu was putting on a brave face, but the extra unruliness of his corkscrew curls betrayed his frazzled state, while Annie looked like she wished she could flay someone with her eyeballs.

Rosie plowed her way through the bodies with a series of unapologetic "make ways" and "coming throughs."

"What's up?" she asked the Ellis siblings.

"Gah!" answered Annie.

"Okay then." Rosie turned to Lu for a more articulate response.

"Dad and Twyla are staying in Tanria until everyone at the dragon preserve is out. Annie and I are in charge of roll call. I'm checking off tourists. She's checking off staff."

"Want help?"

"Please!" they said in unison.

"We got you!" Duckers yelled from the back of the crowd, since he was too polite to shoulder his way through.

For the next hour, Rosie and Duckers flashed their shiny Tanrian Marshals badges and handled crowd control while Lu and Annie checked evacuees off their rosters. The stream of humanity fleeing Tanria grew sparser as the afternoon wore on, allowing Lu and Annie to sneak off to the ad hoc buffet that had sprung up inside the station, generously cobbled together by the locals who lived in the southern border towns.

When it was Rosie and Duckers's turn for a break, they tracked down Adam Lee by the portal to take him to the smorgasbord. Somewhere along the way, he had elbowed aside the engineers and had personally taken over responding to the portal bell. His hair remained impeccably coiffed, and he carried himself with his usual cool bearing, but he had loosened his tie and unbuttoned his collar, framing a slender throat with its prominent larynx.

Who knew a larynx could be attractive? thought Rosie.

She gave herself a good shake.

"Have you eaten yet?" she asked him.

"No."

The bell rang, and he pulled the switch, letting through another round of evacuees.

"The engineers are more than capable of pulling the switch. You need to get something in your stomach."

The two chief marshals on duty approached them in time to

catch the gist of their conversation. "They're right, Dr. Lee. Go eat," said Maguire.

"I'm fine."

"You won't be if you don't eat."

He huffed. It might have been laughter. Who could say?

"Don't worry. If the portal acts up, I'll give it a good whack," said Rosie.

"Touch this portal and you die, Fox," Maguire warned her.

Rosie raised one ruddy eyebrow.

"Don't give me that look. You know what I mean."

The bell rang again, and Dr. Lee flipped the switch. Rosie could swear she heard a strange sound accompanying the pumping of pistons and clicking of gears, a sort of friction that shouldn't be there.

Perhaps Adam Lee sensed it as well, because his lips thinned as he studied his invention. "The portals were not designed to turn off and on in rapid succession. We risk wearing out the main switch. It would be better to keep this one running continuously until everyone is out."

"Makes sense," said Chief Longmeier.

"I can bypass the main switch from the fail-safe."

It took a moment for his words to sink in.

"No. Bad idea," said Maguire. "You are not going inside."

"Are there any engineers inside Tanria right now?"

"I don't think so," said Longmeier.

"There are repairs that can be made only from the interior. At least one person who understands how the portals work should be inside the Mist in case repairs need to be made from within."

"Okay, but not you," said Maguire.

"Yes. Me. The failure of the portals is my responsibility. I should be the last one out of Tanria. I insist."

Longmeier pulled a sinewy hand down his haggard face. "He's not wrong."

"I don't like this," said Maguire.

"Neither do I, but needs must."

Maguire mulled this over, but it was clear she was caving. "I don't want any unnecessary heroics. If it gets dicey in there, you get out immediately."

"Understood."

Without another word, Dr. Lee picked up the engineer's tool kit, pulled the switch, and passed through the archway against the tide of fleeing humanity.

"Shit." Maguire pounced on Rosie and Duckers. "You two, make sure he gets out of there in one piece. That's an order."

Rosie and Duckers gave each other startled looks before scrambling after Dr. Lee, with Maguire's "Mother of Sorrows, have mercy" trailing in their wake.

Aside from the inevitable bottleneck and a slightly strained atmosphere, their arrival on the Tanrian side of the Mist was anticlimactic. As far as Rosie could tell, the evacuation was going smoothly. Maybe people were more cooperative when they realized that this was not a drill.

It was late afternoon, but the blue flares soaring into the sky in a coordinated pattern were easy to both spot and hear as they popped over the mesas to their west and the distant swamps and giant fungi groves to their north and east. The only way a person could miss the evacuation order was if they were hiding so deep in a mineshaft that they were probably dead.

Unsurprisingly, they found Adam beside the portal. His impassive face revealed nothing, but Rosie couldn't shake the suspicion that something was amiss as he popped open the fail-safe hatch.

"How can we help?" she asked him.

He startled. "What are you doing here?"

"We're your assigned escort, remember?"

"I don't need an escort."

"Yet here we are."

"Yep," said Duckers unenthusiastically.

"You should return to the station for your safety."

"We're supposed to ensure *your* safety," Duckers reminded him.

"So you're stuck with us," said Rosie. "I'll ask again: Need help?"

Dr. Lee glanced at her and winced. He put a hand on the portal to steady himself. "I'm perfectly well," he answered preemptively before returning his attention to his work.

It had been a long time since Rosie had crossed through the Mist at the southern checkpoint. The terrain in the immediate vicinity of the portal was flatter and drier than it was farther north. The grass was short and spiky here, the blades a dusty rose rather than the bubblegum pink found in the northwestern sectors. A flock of Tanrian turkeys yodeled nearby. They weren't really turkeys, but they were as birdlike as a feathery creature with two heads was going to get, and what else were you going to call a two-headed birdlike animal that yodeled?

Already bored, Rosie's gaze wandered back to where Adam Lee was working on the right side of the portal's frame, which was when she noticed the series of faint lines worming around the metal archway.

"Fuckity-fuck-fuck."

"What's wrong?" asked Duckers.

"More cracks."

By now, she had the inventor's attention as well as her partner's. She pointed to where one of the fissures started to the right of the frame and followed it with her finger for several feet before she came to a stop, even though the uneven line continued.

"You don't see this?" she asked her partner.

Duckers shook his head.

Rosie aimed a finger at Adam Lee. "Do you?"

He regarded her for a long moment. "I don't see anything here that I have not seen before."

"Hey!" called someone in the line to get out. "Why aren't they cranking this thing up?"

Dr. Lee stepped forward to address the crowd. "I'm making an adjustment to the switch that will allow us to keep the portal running continuously. This will allow everyone to exit Tanria without having to ring the bell and wait for an engineer to let you through.

A few cheers greeted this announcement, but a more cynical marshal said, "If you're making a repair, doesn't that mean the portal's broken?"

"It's not a repair. It's an adjustment. If you will give me a moment, please."

The *please* came with a heaping spoonful of withering disdain, and the marshal in question zipped his lips.

"Dang," said Duckers. "That guy should be busting mobsters or teaching middle school."

Rosie might have appreciated watching a petit man shutting down someone much larger than himself, except her brain kept chewing on his answer to her question a moment earlier. She dragged Duckers to the side as the inventor got to work, and treated him to her first attempt at an Adam Lee impression.

" 'I don't see anything here that I have not seen before.' "

"You've got the hauteur right, but you're missing that rusty, gruff thing he's got going on with his voice."

"No, listen to the words, Penny-D. That answer was cagey as shit."

"I'm sure he meant that everything looks normal. At least, I hope that's what he meant."

Oblivious to their side conversation, Dr. Lee retrieved a small lamp from the tool kit, which he lit with matches made in the ancient style, since New Gods technology like flashlights didn't work inside the Mist. He brought the lamp close to the portal to examine the patch of interior through the open hatch.

"Marshal Fox, do you see anything amiss here?"

Why did this feel like a trick question?

"Do you?" she hedged.

"No."

She approached the portal to peer inside the frame and was relieved to see no strange shadows therein.

"Looks fine to me."

He nodded before he reached inside and pulled out the failsafe mechanism. It gave a satisfyingly heavy *chunk* as it fell into place.

On the other side of the gateway, Longmeier poured himself a steaming cup of coffee from a thermos while Maguire smoked a cigarette. People didn't smoke much these days, and the sight of that glowing orange ember reminded Rosie of Jocelyn for one aching moment.

"I didn't know the chief smoked," said Duckers.

"She doesn't. Hasn't in ages. She gave it up before she and Hart were partners. It's been decades since I've seen her bust out a pack of smokes. That's not unnerving or anything."

"Dang," muttered Duckers.

The line of evacuees grew troublingly long as Dr. Lee tinkered inside the frame. After twenty minutes passed, the crowd grew restless and, in some cases, pissy.

"It's on the fritz, isn't it? Tell us the truth," insisted the same marshal who had busted Dr. Lee's chops earlier. Rosie recognized him, a guy who had started with the marshals before Tanria had attained national park status. He wore the green polo of the Education Division.

"Your name's Blumker, right?" Rosie asked him.

"Yeah."

"Blumker, that's Adam Lee, as in Adam fucking Lee—you know, the guy who invented this thing. Do you think he'd voluntarily come inside Tanria if he thought the portal was actually busted?"

"Um, no?"

"Exactly. Chill thyself."

"Should we think about heading to the East Station, though?" asked a nervous woman in an Alvarez Ambrosia Bottling Company uniform. She had come all the way from Sector W-7, so it was no wonder she was feeling anxious.

"Dr. Lee has the situation under control, I promise," said Rosie. "It'll be a few more minutes."

She went to stand beside Duckers as the crowd continued to fret, her smile frozen in place. "I'm starving," she told him without moving her lips.

His smile was also fixed in place. "You can't die. I'm the one who's starving."

"There is a whole-ass buffet on the other side of the Mist."

His stomach growled. "Don't remind me."

At last, the professor unfolded the fail-safe crank and gave it several hard winds, putting his back into it. Perspiration slicked his forehead. He had abandoned his waistcoat, and sweat now glued his wrinkled dress shirt to his torso, a sight at which Rosie respectfully refused to gawk (even though she wanted to). The entire archway hummed and vibrated. On the other side of the Mist, Longmeier perked up, and Maguire crushed the cigarette beneath her boot.

"Have you got it working again, Dr. Lee?" the latter called through the portal's opening.

"Yes. We're sending people through now."

He looked expectantly to Rosie and Duckers.

Duckers visibly wilted. "I just want a sandwich, man."

"It's the 'Crowd Control Reprise'!" cheered Rosie. "Let's take it from the top!" She twirled in a circle and flashed him a pair of jazzy sparkle fingers.

"You're lucky I love you, RoFo," he told her, but he helped her organize the line.

Chapter Eight

By the time the sun sank below the horizon, the South Station had set up floodlights, which blared illumination into Tanria.

Duckers remained sans sandwich. So did Rosie. So did Dr. Lee for that matter, although he hadn't complained of hunger.

Alma Maguire slipped into Tanria during a lull in outgoing traffic shortly before nine o'clock. She dispensed with the niceties and launched into an update.

"We've been coordinating rosters with the East Station. Tanria is almost clear. It's the transport to and from the dragon preserve that's taking the most time. There are only so many bodies you can squeeze onto a coach, and we're having to change out equimares to keep the teams fresh."

"I see," said Dr. Lee, whose once well-groomed hair was now falling into his face.

"You must be exhausted, Dr. Lee. Why don't you—"

"If you wish to convince me to return to Bushong, I must tell you that I intend to be the last person out of Tanria."

The chief considered him for a moment, as if she were taking his measure and finding that he was up to snuff after all. She nodded her newfound respect for him.

"You should return to the station immediately for your own safety," he told her before looking to Rosie and Duckers. "You should all return."

He had been urging his escorts to leave for hours, but for reasons Rosie could not begin to fathom, she knew there was no earthly way she was leaving this complicated man behind.

"Dream on. I'm staying until you're *not* staying."

Duckers nodded. "And I'm not going anywhere without Rosie, so you're stuck with both of us to the bitter end, Doc."

Their boss seemed like she might put the kibosh on this plan, so Rosie spoke up. "No worries, Chief. It's been smooth sailing all day. And you did order us to make sure Dr. Lee gets out safely, so . . ."

Maguire sighed heavily through her nose, but in the end, she didn't object. "Make sure you know when the last coach arrives, and once you have those folks out, you cross through the Mist, no matter what."

"You got it, Chief," said Duckers.

Maguire, who was not a person one would refer to as touchy-feely, patted him on the shoulder and gave Rosie's arm a collegial clap. "You two be careful, you hear?"

"Sure thing," said Rosie, touched by her boss's unexpected show of affection.

Alma Maguire crossed through the Mist, and Rosie shook off the paranoid premonition that she might not see her boss again anytime soon.

A half hour later, they were still waiting for the last transport from the preserve. Duckers went in search of a private place to pee, a daunting task given the open field stretching out before them. Rosie was not a fan of squatting behind a bush, much less taking care of business out in the open, so she and her bladder were hanging on for dear life.

Dr. Lee leaned against the portal, facing Tanria, his arms

crossed, his glasses lenses reflecting moonlight. Left alone with his reticence, Rosie leaned against the opposite side of the frame and attempted to start up a conversation with him to keep her mind off her bladder.

"Any theories as to what's going on here with the portals and the shadows?"

"I honestly don't know why this is happening. I wish I did."

Backlit by the floodlights, he looked weary and, if not old exactly, not terribly young either. Seeing him like this—tired and a little lost—she recalled again that chance encounter beside the West Station's portal five years earlier.

Duckers had been on vacation visiting his mom and siblings on the island of Paxico, and sans partner for the week, Rosie had had to pull a solo tour. Except she couldn't report for duty, because the portal at the West Station went down, and the engineers couldn't figure out what was wrong with it. Maguire had rerouted her and everyone else through the North Station's portal, and when Rosie had returned to the West Station at the end of her tour a week later, there was Adam Lee, crouching beside the portal, untangling a cluster of wires inside the frame with delicate fingers. His suit jacket hung from a protuberance on the portal's exterior, undulating forlornly in the breeze like a limp banner on a defeated turret in Ye Dayes of Olde. He worked by himself, with nary a federally employed engineer in sight, and for some reason, Rosie was struck by the loneliness of the scene. People were coming and going, in and out of the station a few yards away, but Dr. Lee seemed to stand apart from the hustle and bustle, adjacent to but outside the lives of his fellow human beings. It was a silly notion, of course. Rosie was certain the man had never entertained such morose, poetic sentiments. Given the blandness of his expression, she wasn't certain he entertained any emotions at all.

She had no reason to linger that day. He certainly paid no

attention to her as he reached his right arm into the frame's interior, burying it to the shoulder. And yet Rosie was mesmerized as she watched him work. As someone whose attention careened from one interest to another with little rhyme or reason, she was fascinated by his ability to focus so completely on the problem at hand. Nothing distracted him, not even a gawking, oversized demigod with red eyes.

She was about to be on her merry way when he uttered a sharp syllable in a language Rosie didn't know. He pulled his arm free and glared at the bloody gash on his hand, a line of bubbling red on the palm under the first three fingers. He spat the curse again before gingerly picking through his abandoned suit jacket with his unbloodied hand for his pocket square.

It was the curse that got her. She didn't speak whatever language he had uttered, but she knew a salty word when she heard one, and Rosie was inclined to like people who cussed. In her experience, the foulmouthed tended to be honest and authentic. Maybe that was why she stepped forward and offered, "Need help?"

"No," he said without deigning to look at her as he feebly attempted to fold his pocket square into a bandage with his uninjured hand.

"Because it kind of looks like you do. Need help."

He finally looked up at her as she held out her hand for the pocket square, but he didn't fork over the silk right away. He regarded her coldly, if a statue could be said to regard anything. He appeared to be a carving of a man, from his high, sharp cheekbones to the curve of his brown eyes behind a pair of metal-rimmed glasses. Even his hair seemed to be made of stone, obsidian strands slicked back from his forehead, with a streak of silver running through it like an icy river in a winter landscape. And since, like a statue, he did not move, Rosie made the decision for him, plucking the fabric from his grasp.

The second it touched her fingertips, she knew there was no way she was going to use it to bind the cut. As a connoisseur of high-end lingerie, she recognized quality silk when she felt it.

"My dude, this hankie is way too good for triage. Here, use mine." Without thinking, she folded the square and slid it into her pocket so that she could fish her own linen from her rucksack to use instead.

"There is no need for that," he told her in a baritone she did not expect from someone so small. At six feet and five inches, Rosie was accustomed to towering over people, but Adam Lee was uncommonly bantam.

"It's clean. I swear." She waved her handkerchief in the air like a flag of surrender before she folded it neatly and took his hand in hers to press the linen to the cut. It wasn't until she had committed herself to this endeavor that she realized how bizarrely intimate it was, to be standing inches away from another human being and holding his hand.

And what a hand it was.

Rosie had never given much thought to hands in general. What was there to notice? Most people had them, after all. But Adam Lee's hand was a lovely thing to behold—fine-boned yet strong, elegant yet calloused, a masterpiece of contradictions. And here she was, touching this hand, caring for it, feeling the warmth of it against her skin. It was like cradling a fallen bird in her palm, realizing, too late, that she ought not to touch something so precious and fragile and wild.

Well, you're in it now, Rosie, she thought, so she went on pressing the cloth against the cut for several more seconds before lifting it to get a better look at the injury. Blood immediately welled out of the gash, and she covered it with the linen once more.

"Heads and hands. They always bleed like crazy," she blathered as she tied the fabric in place. The task complete, she looked up.

And in the time it had taken her to manhandle his appendage

without permission, his face had transformed. He was not made of stone. He was flesh and blood and feelings, and the emotion painting his face in that moment was complete and utter devastation, as if his hand really were a bird, and she had crushed it in her grasp.

"Dr. Lee? Are you all right?"

"You are very kind," he answered, his voice rusty, as if he wasn't accustomed to using it.

"It's no big deal." Rosie couldn't seem to let go of his hand as he stared at her like she was the Mother of Sorrows, come to bring him mercy. All she could think to say was "You should have this looked at in the infirmary. It could get infected."

He shifted his focus to their joined hands, and when he looked up again, all hint of emotion was so thoroughly wiped from his face that Rosie had to question whether she'd seen into his soul in the first place.

"I am not concerned." He took his hand from hers without thanking her, and Rosie, dizzy with the whiplash of his changing demeanor, went to the parking lot, got in her autoduck, and promptly forgot the whole business. But from time to time, the memory resurfaced, as it had when she had spied the strange spot inside the portal's frame last Saltsday, and as it did here and now.

Rosie reached into her pocket and pulled out his handkerchief. "I almost forgot. This is yours. I accidentally stole it the last time you were here."

He stared at it but made no move to take it.

"You tried to besmirch this gorgeous silk with your blood, so I had to rescue it. You're welcome."

"You can—" He stopped abruptly. Surely, the next words were supposed to be *keep it*, but they never exited his mouth.

An expression Rosie had never seen on him before took over his usually unreadable face, betraying an unwelcome invasion of emotions. Maybe the handkerchief was special to him for some reason. Maybe someone he loved had given it to him. Or maybe it carried bad memories. As Rosie watched him war with something inside himself, she wished that she had kept her mouth shut and her pocket closed.

"Thank you," he said at last, the words clipped. He took the handkerchief, his fingertips brushing hers.

Without warning, he gasped in pain, clutching the silk as he pressed himself against the frame behind him, a substitute spine to hold him upright. Rosie watched him uselessly until his breath evened and his shoulders sagged.

"I want to ask if you're all right, but I also don't want to annoy you by asking you if you're all right," she told him.

He held up his hand, a gesture that lied, that said *I'm fine*, when it really meant *Don't look at me* and *Don't see me* and *Don't try to know me*. But then he froze, and his gaze snapped sharply to hers.

"I cut myself," he said.

Rosie's nerves twanged with alarm. "Where?"

"No, five years ago, when I was repairing the portal at the West Station. I cut myself inside the frame."

He said this as if it were a momentous realization, as if his cutting himself half a decade earlier contained the cure for cancer or the meaning of life.

"I know," Rosie said slowly. She watched, baffled, as he looked at his hand and then turned to study the portal and the Mist surrounding it. Clearly, important calculations were happening in his genius brain, but Rosie, for the life of her, could not figure out what she was missing.

The tense moment was punctured in spectacular fashion by the return of Duckers, who shouted "Dad's back! You kids can stop making out now!" as soon as he stepped into the floodlights' radius.

Rosie was about to fire off a snappy rejoinder when they heard the telltale rumble of the coach's wheels rolling toward them.

"Thank you, Bride of Fortune," said Duckers, in time for the constant, ever-present hum of the portal to wind down to an ominously silent halt.

"Fucking fuck me up the ass with Grandfather Bones's tibia," said Rosie.

On the other side of the Mist, Chief Longmeier's mouth moved, bellowing orders they couldn't hear, and the engineers swarmed the portal.

Adam Lee peered into the fail-safe hatch and spat that *kh-sh* curse word. Rosie had no idea what he was seeing when he looked inside the frame, but she sure as shit knew what she saw.

"Mother of Sorrows!" she said.

"Shadows?" guessed the inventor.

"A ton of them. I swear it didn't look like this earlier." She watched as lines of grave concern carved his face. "Can you fix it?" she asked him.

"I don't know," he answered brusquely as he dug a pair of pliers out of his commandeered tool kit.

A crash followed by several shouts drew Rosie's attention away from the portal.

"Fuck, fuck, fuck," spat Duckers.

Rosie squinted into the Tanrian landscape, or at least the part of it she could see in the station's floodlights. "What now?"

"Over there. The coach lost a wheel."

Sure enough, fifty yards away in the outermost reaches of the floodlights' radius, the dragon preserve coach hunched awkwardly on three wheels, the fourth nothing more than a thin black shadow lying flat on the ground.

"It's amazing it lasted this long. That thing's not exactly an all-terrain vehicle."

Duckers cupped his hands around his mouth and shouted, "Everyone all right?"

A general confirmation of well-being drifted their way as the passengers clambered out of their busted transport.

"How are we doing?" Rosie asked Dr. Lee.

"Almost there."

Duckers clapped his hands in rapid succession like the coach of a kids' sea polo team. "Let's go, go, go!" he hollered.

The evacuees seemed to comprehend the urgency of the situation, because they took off running toward the portal, while the equimares hitched to the coach stamped their feet and gargled their glottal anxiety.

Two passengers remained with the coach, trying to unhitch the panicking water horses as a series of clanking sounds rattled the portal.

"Gods, it's Ellis and Banneker," said Rosie.

"Twyla! Frank! There's no time for that!" yelled Duckers.

"I need help," Dr. Lee said behind them as Duckers sprinted toward the coach.

Rosie turned to find Adam Lee with a pair of pliers in each hand, both clamped on the portal's innards.

"Take these," he ordered her.

Rosie took over the pliers without batting an eye at his imperiousness. He could be as imperious as he wanted, as long as he got them out of Tanria tonight.

He bent at the waist to ferret inside the tool kit, his rear pushing against Rosie's thighs. She was too full of adrenaline to pay much attention to the physical contact, but her mind was storing this moment in her memory for later observation.

He straightened and touched Rosie's right forearm with his fingertips. "Don't move."

You are going to find all of this incredibly sexy when you have a moment, her pervy inner monologue informed her.

Dr. Lee fixed a C-clamp in place, flinching as another round of sparks shot out of the hatch, accompanied by a series of troubling screeches. Most of the sparks hit Rosie's left arm, which was bare from the elbow down, thanks to the ugly-ass Tanrian Marshals uniform. She gritted her teeth against the pain and kept her hold on the pliers in her left hand, even as Adam Lee tapped her right arm again and said, "You can let go on this side."

"Are you all right?" she asked him as he crouched beside the tool kit.

"Yes. Are you?"

"Yeah. Thanks."

He handed her the lamp and positioned her arm as if she were a gooseneck task light rather than a living, breathing person, revealing the portal's inner workings and a series of shadows dangling among the wires and tubes. His manner was stiff and efficient, but his fingers were warm against her skin.

"You're burned," he observed as he stood between her arms, parts of his backside bumping against her front as he worked.

"No worries. I'm fine. Oh, that's your line. I forgot."

He made a sound—a sigh or a laugh or a grunt of pain; it was hard to tell.

And then the shadows on the inside of the frame *moved*.

Rosie startled so hard she nearly let go of the pliers in her left hand. "Holy Three Mothers!"

"Hold on," Adam Lee told her as he spliced wires together.

The portal started up again with a painful grating noise.

"Go! Now!" he shouted at the last evacuees, who raced through the portal in twos and threes.

Twyla Banneker and Frank Ellis brought up the rear, escorted by Duckers. They were about to race through like the others when Banneker came to a sudden halt and looked behind her.

"Wait—" she began.

"No time, Banneker!" Rosie pushed her through the archway.

"Sorry, Frank!" said Duckers as he gave Ellis a good shove.

Rosie watched them both stagger safely into the Bushong side of the border. Banneker was speaking to Ellis and Lu and Annie—a frantic stream of words made tinny and inarticulate by the thickening curtain of Mist between them.

Rosie was about to hurtle Dr. Lee through the portal after them when someone called, "Wait for me!"

A tall man carrying an object the size of a kickball was walking toward them with mincing steps, his head bent as he stared down at the object in his hands.

The portal keened with a jarring screech of metal on metal, and Rosie, Duckers, and Adam exploded into a chorus of shouts.

"Come on!"

"Hurry!"

"Move!"

The man picked up the pace, but not by much, behaving as if he were holding the Bride of Fortune's birth key on a velvet pillow in his hands.

"Let's go!" yelled Duckers.

The portal made a sickening screech, and the floodlights flickered until the portal's steam engine gave out in a ground-shaking *boom* that could be heard on both sides of the Mist. The portal died, taking out the floodlights with it.

Rosie's heart throttled her from within as darkness settled over them, the kind of rush she usually enjoyed chasing. Today? Not so much.

"Everyone all right?" she asked.

"Fuuuuuuuuck," answered Duckers, which she took as *I am unharmed.*

"I'm fine," said Dr. Lee. "Are you all right?"

"Sure. Great. Never been better."

The slowpoke from the last transport finally arrived at the

portal, scarcely out of breath since he hadn't exactly exerted himself. In his hands was a white dish, glowing faintly in the darkness and containing something that on any other occasion would have smelled scrumptious.

"Is the portal . . . okay?" he asked.

"I'm going to go with no," said Duckers.

"Gods' tits! Are you kidding me?"

A light flickered to life on the Bushong side of the Mist. It was Lu Ellis, holding up a cigarette lighter next to a piece of notebook paper on which someone had scribbled one word: *ZEDDIE!!!*

Rosie turned to look at the man who had refused to run to safety, and then she took in her partner's face as he registered who was standing beside the now-defunct portal. With a lead weight in her gut, Rosie remembered the thing she had meant to tell Duckers first thing this morning.

"Hey, Zeddie Birdsall was just hired as the head chef at the fancy restaurant they're opening next to the dragon preserve."

Duckers closed his eyes as if he were in physical pain and let loose one more "Fuuuuuuuuuuck."

In the flickering light cast by Lu Ellis's lighter, the soufflé deflated into the dish with applaudable dramatic timing.

Chapter Nine

The good news was that they had four equimares at their disposal, thanks to the abandoned coach. The bad news was that one of them was Saltlicker.

Saltlicker had long been a divisive entity in the Tanrian Marshals Service. Roughly a quarter of the force found the stallion "spirited." The other 75 percent hated his ass. Rosie fell into the latter camp.

By the flickering light of the coach's lamps, the oft-reviled equimaris looked pissy as ever with his kelp-like mane sticking wetly to his long neck. His scaly violet hide was beginning to pale with age, but the water horse had some good years left in him. If by *good years* one meant *this stallion is the worst, the woooooooooorst.*

"Man, the punches keep coming, huh?" she commented to the surly water horse as she unhitched his neighbor, a mare who was much nicer than he was.

Saltlicker gave her a watery growl in reply.

"Don't hate on Saltlicker," said Duckers as he absently dodged the equimaris's teeth. "I love this guy."

"He's all yours."

"The equimares aren't saddled," said Dr. Lee, subtly eyeing Zeddie Birdsall, who gazed forlornly into the middle distance. "It will be difficult to ride bareback to the East Station."

"We're going to walk the mounts to the nearest barracks,"

explained Rosie, although she wasn't sure Zeddie was listening to a word she said. "Hopefully we'll find tack in the stable there. We can get some rest and head out first thing in the morning."

"Rest is a luxury we don't have. We need to keep going."

"These equimares have already crossed Tanria at least once today. They are not going to make it to the East Station exit unless we get them fed and watered."

"*I'm* not going to make it to the East Station exit unless I'm fed and watered," muttered Duckers as he went about unhitching Saltlicker.

"Is it ideal? No," continued Rosie. "But nothing is ideal right now. This is the best we can do."

Duckers managed to get onto Saltlicker's back from the coach, and he rode ahead to the barracks, ostensibly to start a fire in the stove and make up four beds for the night, but it didn't take a genius like Adam Lee to figure out he was avoiding his ex for as long as possible.

Meanwhile, Rosie was stuck with a brooding inventor and Zeddie Birdsall, whose white stoneware contrasted sharply with his black chef's attire as he clutched it to his chest in abject misery. They walked the three miles to the barracks in weary silence, the way lit by a coach lamp that Rosie had liberated from the wreckage.

It was nearing midnight when they arrived at the barracks. Duckers met Rosie at the stables so that the two marshals could put the equimares in their water troughs, while the civilians got their bearings inside the rustic accommodations.

"This is Old Hell, right? We're in Old Hell," said Duckers as he helped Rosie top off the troughs with well water. Generally speaking, he was a glass-half-full kind of guy. Tonight, however, his attitude was more glass-is-empty-and-broken-into-tiny-shards. Saltlicker, who was already situated in his own trough, gargled in peevish agreement.

"It's not the House of the Unknown God, that's for sure," said Rosie.

Duckers waved a hand in the direction of the barracks. "Do you believe that guy? We say *run*, and he fucking saunters."

"Pen," Rosie said in warning, but her partner cut her off.

"Nope, I get to be pissed off right now. And *you*. How could you not tell me that my ex was going to be popping into my life left and right?"

"With everything going on, it slipped my mind."

He dismissed that weak excuse with a derisive puff of his lips. "When did you find out?"

"At the funeral," Rosie admitted.

"And you said nothing?"

"What difference would it have made?"

"I could have been mentally and emotionally prepared. But you were too busy being up your own ass because you died and you were feeling sorry for yourself, and you were all *me, me, fucking me*."

Rosie opened her mouth to protest, but then it occurred to her that Duckers was correct. "I'm sorry. But also, rude!"

On that happy note, they made their way to the barracks to find Dr. Lee setting the table and Zeddie futzing around the stove.

"What are you doing?" asked Duckers.

His hands protected by a thick tea towel, Zeddie pulled the dish out of the oven. "I heated this up, unless you want to eat a cold soufflé. More like a cold omelet now." He sounded as crabby as his ex-boyfriend.

"To be clear, we're stuck inside Tanria because you didn't want your fluffy eggs to be not fluffy?"

"It's a little more complicated than that."

"So that's a yes. We are stuck inside the Mist because of a fancy omelet. This is up there with that time I had to listen to the villain speech of a hedgehog."

Zeddie set the soufflé on a trivet with a force that would have made it deflate had it not already sunken in on itself. "Feel free to not eat it if you're so miffed."

He glared at Duckers before stalking across the room to fling himself onto one of the cots in the darkened half of the barracks.

"Aren't you having any?" Rosie asked him.

"No."

A pall settled over the soufflé as the three people who remained standing stared at it in mute resignation. Duckers finally spooned some onto a plate and took himself outside, presumably to eat his late dinner in one of the deck chairs out front.

"Should we go after him?" asked the professor.

"He needs some space. He'll come in when he's ready," said Rosie, and since she was ravenous, she heaped a serving of the soufflé on Adam Lee's plate before helping herself. Then she sat down and raised her cup of water to the one person who wasn't acting like a kindergartner. "Cheers?"

Dr. Lee sat and raised his own cup. "Cheers," he said in resignation.

They ate in exhausted silence until Rosie realized that the flavors enveloping her tongue were, in fact, the opposite of Old Hell. She'd had sex that wasn't half as good as the masterpiece she was currently devouring, and she groaned with the sheer, unexpected pleasure of it, her eyes shut in ecstasy. When she opened them again, she found Adam Lee staring at her, his soft lips hanging slightly ajar, a forkful of eggy goodness held halfway between his plate and his mouth.

"What? It's delicious," she said defensively.

The bite fell from his fork and splatted on the table. He looked to his plate as if he were surprised to find food there. "Yes. Phenomenal."

"Thank you" came Zeddie's muffled reply from the other side of the room.

"Come eat with us," said Rosie. "You should reap the rewards of your labor."

"You're not mad at me?" he asked as he joined them at the table and helped himself to his soufflé.

"I wouldn't say that, although your food is doing a great job of buttering me up. Why don't you explain what happened."

"I started this job three days ago, so I didn't know what the flares were for. I thought there was some kind of celebration going on. It wasn't until Twyla and Frank tracked me down that I found out the truth." He took a bite of his own cooking, pondered its flavor, and made a face. "Not my best."

"Feed us your best, and we will definitely forgive you. Right?"

Rosie turned to Dr. Lee. His eyes had gone dreamy with culinary appreciation, which made him look fairly delicious himself. "I wasn't angry to begin with," he said.

"All I'm saying is, feel free to make us your best whenever you want to."

"Well, that's just it," said Zeddie, who ate his food in the continental way, like Adam Lee—knife in the right hand and fork in the left. It made Rosie feel like an uncouth gorilla whenever she switched between knife and fork with her right hand. "I'm supposed to be making five-star meals at the Dragon's Lair, but I'm having to figure out how to cook old-school style since New Gods technology doesn't work inside the Mist. I'm used to gas ovens and burners. Wood-burning stoves and open flames? Not so much. I've got a month to put a menu together, so I've been figuring out what I can and can't do with what I've got. Trial and error—mostly error. This was my fifth attempt at a soufflé today, but the first one that didn't collapse when I took it out of the oven—and by oven, I mean a big-ass wood-fired brick oven."

"Sounds like a challenge."

"Gods' tits, it is. But that's what I wanted. A challenge to up my game. Plus…" Zeddie pushed a soft, delicate mushroom around his plate. "My father sailed the Salt Sea recently."

"I know. I'm sorry."

"My condolences," added Dr. Lee, and he sounded like he meant it.

"I should have been around more for my family. For Pop. That's why I came home, to spend more time with the family I have left."

Rosie put her hand over his, the one that was poking at a mushroom the way Rosie was poking at poor Zeddie's wounds.

"Still mad?" he asked her ruefully.

"Nah. We'll get out tomorrow. The East Station's portal is working fine. And even if that one breaks down, the northern exit has some juice left. Plus, we have the guy who invented the portals on our team. We're in a good position here, right, Dr. Lee?"

The professor cleared his throat. "Right."

"See? And if worse comes to worst, someone can slap a pirated portal onto the Mist, and out we'll go. I've busted enough poachers to know there have to be a few in the FICBI's evidence lockers. I'm not worried at all."

She was, in fact, slightly worried, but in her experience, 99 percent of the things people fretted over came to a whole lot of nothing in the end. It was the unexpected twists that bit you in the ass.

"Okay, that makes me feel better. Thanks, Marshal," said Zeddie.

"Oh my gods, call me Rosie."

"Thanks, Rosie." Cheering up, he got into the spirit of enjoying the meal. "I've heard a lot about you over the years. I know you're friends with Mercy and Hart. I'm glad I finally got to meet you."

"Back atcha."

Rosie and Zeddie kept up a stream of light conversation over the rest of dinner, occasionally drawing in Dr. Lee, who was more inclined to watch and listen than to participate. But as Zeddie filled his belly, the food seemed to weigh down his eyelids so that he was half asleep by the time they finished eating.

"I'll take care of the dishes," he volunteered, but Rosie took his plate.

"The cook shouldn't have to clean up, and you look dead on your feet. Go to bed. I can handle this."

"I'll help," added the professor.

Zeddie seemed like he might protest, but then he sagged with fatigue. "Thanks," he said before shuffling to the other side of the barracks to collapse on his cot.

Rosie glanced toward the barracks' front door, wondering if she ought to check on Duckers.

"I can wash the dishes if you would like to speak with your partner," Adam Lee told her, relieving her of the plate she had taken from Zeddie seconds ago.

"I'm not going to make you clean up on your own. Duckers will live. Let's roll up our sleeves and get 'er done. Except your sleeves are already rolled up, and the sleeves of this hideous uniform are short."

The skin on Rosie's arms was pale and smooth, the burns from the sparks that had shot out of the portal earlier in the evening having already healed. She wondered whether Adam Lee had noticed. In either case, she had no intention of pointing it out to him.

Duckers had fetched plenty of water from the well before their arrival, so Rosie took up the cake of soap at the old-fashioned basin sink and got to work.

"There are dish towels in that cupboard over there," she told Dr. Lee, indicating with her head since her hands were elbow deep in dishwater. He retrieved a towel and came to stand beside her, and suddenly, Rosie was extremely aware of his physical proximity. Although she was head and shoulders taller than he was, she felt the enormity of his presence keenly.

"You dislike the uniform?" he asked her as she handed him a wet plate, and she was grateful that he had stepped so dramatically out of character as to start up small talk.

"*Hate* is a more accurate term. *Loathe* would also work. *Despise* and *abominate*? Also good options." She handed him another plate.

"So you are a thesaurus in addition to being a Tanrian Marshal."

The comment was delivered in so deadpan a manner, it took Rosie a moment to realize that he was joking. She stopped mid-scrub and gaped at him.

"Was that sass? Are you sassing me?"

"It appears that I am." He knitted his brow in confusion, as if his own sense of humor had surprised him.

"Good. Someone ought to keep me in line," she said as she handed him the forks.

"Noted."

Salt Sea, this man was dry in the best possible way. Rosie could listen to him say the word *noted* in that gruff baritone many times over and not get tired of hearing it.

As she handed him the dripping soufflé dish, she couldn't help but notice his forearms once more. *How romance-novel cliché of me*, she thought as she forced herself to stop ogling the guy's appendages and look elsewhere. But *elsewhere* was the formerly sleek hair that had fallen across his forehead, the casually unbuttoned vest that hung from the straight line of his shoulders, the open collar of his increasingly wrinkled shirt, which revealed the long column of his graceful neck. Honestly, who could blame her for staring? Anyone who bothered to look at Adam Lee long enough would begin to notice that the Three Mothers had crafted him with exquisite artistry. He was as finely cut as his elegant attire, and his smooth skin had a translucent quality, allowing her to see the verdant veins snaking beneath the surface.

Rosie could feel her own pale skin flush. Great. Now she was redder than usual, even if it was a pink kind of red.

He cleared his throat. "I believe I'm missing some context. Do Marshal Duckers and this Zeddie person have a history?"

"Zeddie Birdsall, and yep."

"A romantic entanglement gone awry?"

"You got it."

He considered this information as he dried the knives. "I'm afraid that matters of the heart are not my forte."

"Because you like to think you're dead inside?"

Rosie had never had a whole lot of impulse control, but even she could hear how bad that sounded.

"Wow, that came right out of my big mouth, didn't it?" she said, turning even pinker. "I'm sorry. It's been a long day, and the filter is gone."

"There was a filter?"

Rosie did a double take. "You are on fire tonight, Dr. Sassafras."

He rewarded her with another one of those startled bursts of laughter. She suspected that he was not accustomed to laughing, and the fact that she could elicit an amused response from him made her lightheaded.

"But for real, I'm sorry," she said as she scrubbed a dish to cover her fluster.

"For what? You did not accuse me of being dead inside. You said that I like to *think* that I am dead inside." He paused, staring off into the middle distance as he held a half-dry tin cup in one hand and a damp dishcloth in the other. "Which is not inaccurate."

"For what it's worth, I don't think you're dead inside."

"Is that right?"

Rosie handed him the scoured spoons and pointed at her eyes with wet fingers. "It's the freaky red eyeballs. I can see right through your chest cavity to your warm little heart."

For the span of one breath, he seemed to marvel at her, and Rosie's own warm little heart got a whole lot warmer in response.

"Those eyes see a lot," he said warily.

She shrugged away the bewildering blossom of emotion in her chest and rinsed off a plate. "Maybe it's my demigod gift."

"What does 'freaky' mean?"

"You know, *weird, unnatural, kind of scary*. Hey, look at me, your friendly neighborhood thesaurus, hard at work yet again!"

He met the freaky red eyeballs in question as he took the dripping plate from her hand. "Your eyes are not something to be ashamed of."

It was not often that anyone looked at Rosie Fox and got any further than *Golly, her eyes are disturbing*, but she could swear that a flattering adjective was buried somewhere in that sentence. She leaned against the basin and cocked her head at him.

"You know, when you first showed up this morning, I thought you didn't remember me. But now I think I was wrong about that."

His forehead furrowed again, making two minuscule dents appear between his eyebrows.

"You are difficult to forget."

"Well, you could've fooled me."

"One does not forget a stunning woman with eyes like garnets."

His own eyes widened, as if the words had astonished him as much as they had astonished Rosie. Neither of them spoke or moved for several seconds, long enough for Rosie to notice that she wasn't breathing.

In unspoken agreement, they both returned their attention to the washing of dishes in mildly agonizing silence until Duckers finally came inside.

"Hey," he said meekly.

Rosie put her finger to her lips and nodded toward Zeddie's sleeping form.

He nodded in understanding and whispered, "Sorry about tonight. I know I'm being a baby about this. I just"—he glanced again at Zeddie—"did not see that coming."

"It's my bad. I totally forgot to tell you."

"Don't worry about it."

"I am turning in," announced Dr. Lee as he hung up the dish towel with surgical precision.

"Good night," Rosie replied, because that was what you said to people who announced that they were turning in. Yet he seemed surprised, as if no one had wished him a good night in a very long time, which, for all she knew, might be the case.

It was a shame that her demigod eyes did not allow her to see what was going on behind the exterior he presented to the world. But he turned away from her and went to lie down on the cot next to Zeddie's, so she would have to crack open his mysterious carapace on a different day. For now, she tapped the plate in her partner's hand and said, "Admit it. This was the best thing you've eaten in years."

"Ugh. It was fucking delicious."

She put her hand on his shoulder and gave him a squeeze. "Go easy on Zeddie. He didn't know what the flares were for. Plus, he's got a lot going on right now, and he just lost his dad."

"I know."

She took his dishes from him to reward him for his future good behavior. "I'll wash these."

"Best partner ever," he said, his whole body drooping with relief and exhaustion.

"I'm telling Hart you said that."

"Best partner ever, tied with Hart."

"Too late. No take-backs. You said what you said." Rosie bumped him in the direction of the cots with her hip. "Go to bed, Penny-D. I got this."

He started in that direction, but he paused. "We're getting out of here tomorrow, right?"

"Absolutely. We'll leave first thing in the morning and saunter through that portal before Maguire's had a chance to pick up doughnuts. We'll be stuffing our faces at the Salt and Key by lunchtime. Piece of cake."

Bolstered, he nodded and went to bed. As Rosie washed his plate and fork, she prayed to the Bride of Fortune that she was right.

When she finally turned in for the night, she didn't fall asleep right away despite her bone-deep fatigue. An analysis of Adam Lee's use of the word *stunning* kept her awake. Her mind pulled on rubber gloves, busted out a scalpel, and got busy doing some exploratory linguistic surgery.

Stunning as in *gigantic*?

Stunning as in *overwhelming*?

Stunning as in *creepy*?

I really am a thesaurus, she thought.

She turned onto her side and put her pillow over her head, as if that could make her brain go quiet. But no matter how hard she tried to tamp down her poorly timed attraction to a man about whom she knew next to nothing, she couldn't help but think that when Adam Lee had uttered the word *stunning*, he might have meant something other than *tall* or *loud* or *ox-like*.

He might have meant *pretty*.

Chapter Ten

The journey to the East Station was not a piece of cake, as it turned out.

The marshlands of the southern sectors proved impossible to avoid. Fresh ambrosia from Tanria's many brooks was tasty, but those streams emptied into the bogs, where the ambrosia turned thick and syrupy. Towering fungal forests full of long tubular mushrooms in lurid colors that swayed in the breeze protruded from the stagnant marshes, composing some of the most bizarre scenery Tanria had to offer. This was the area with which Rosie and Duckers were least familiar, and they had to consult their map often.

Once again, Adam Lee stayed true to his word, sitting his mount as if he'd been born there. He faced forward, but Rosie could see most of his profile. As she studied his features, she found herself wondering how old he was. The debonair silver streak in his glossy jet hair spoke of his having at least half a century under his belt, but his face showed only a hint of lines around his eyes and across his broad forehead. Even if he had been staggeringly young when he had invented the portals, he would have to be at least approaching sixty by now, wouldn't he? Rosie was tempted to ask him about his age, but she knew mortals were sensitive about that kind of thing. No one wanted to admit that they were growing old, which was hilarious; she would kill to get wrinkles and arthritis, to sense an ending on the horizon.

She held Zeddie's reins as well as her own since he wasn't accustomed to riding, and it was challenging to handle both equimares at once. With the ambrosia underfoot, the water horses wanted to wander deeper into the bogs, and it was all Rosie could do to keep them from rolling in the sticky muck. But while the equimares delighted in squelching their way across the southeastern wetlands, their riders had to deal with the gelatinous liquid that flooded their footwear and stuck to their clothes and filled their nostrils with a sickly-sweet scent akin to rotted fruit.

It was slow going, and they were at least an hour behind schedule when shit got weird, even by Tanrian standards.

A colony of graps hopped about in the middle of the trail several feet in front of them. This, in and of itself, was not unusual. The furry, frog-like creatures were common throughout Tanria. What was remarkable in this instance was the fact that they had taken up residence on a clump of shadows that sprawled across the path from between two giant fungal tubes. To Rosie's companions, it must have looked as though the graps were floating in midair.

"What the fuuuuuuuuck?" said Duckers.

Zeddie puled. "I want off the weird train."

"Hate to be the bearer of bad tidings, but Tanria *is* the weird train," said Rosie. She slid out of the saddle with a *splat*, handed her reins and Zeddie's to Duckers, and cautiously approached the spectacle.

"They're not floating, y'all. They're hopping around on those shadow thingies."

"Uh...how?" asked Duckers.

Zeddie rubbed his eyes with the heels of his hands. "Seriously, stick a fork in me. I am done."

As Rosie drew near, she could see the shadows more clearly, dark smudges and irregular lines crisscrossing each other without order or sense. Although words like *shadows* or *lines* or *cracks* no longer seemed apt. They looked . . . alive.

"I think they might be plants."

"Plants? What kind of plants?" said Duckers.

"I don't know. They're viny, I guess?"

A grap jumped from one opaque "branch" to another. It looked at Rosie and said *Graaaaaap*, as if to express complete nonchalance, like, *Oh, you know, just another day hopping around on a whole lot of insubstantial shit.*

Bemused, Rosie crouched low and sliced her hand through the shadow-filled air beneath the graps. Dr. Lee hissed in protest as Duckers snapped, "RoFo, don't do that!"

"Why not? There's nothing to touch." She waved her hand dramatically through the shadowy plant.

"What in Old Hell?" whimpered Zeddie.

"I can see shadows no one else can see," Rosie explained to him. "Should have brought you up to speed on that sooner. Sorry."

"Oka-a-ay."

Rosie looked to Dr. Lee. He had been excruciatingly hard to read all morning, which was disappointing after the whole *eyes like garnets* thing the night before. But now the unflappable professor was showing signs of flappability, and Rosie wanted to keep him that way.

"You. You're a scientist. Any theories?"

"No." He unhooked his gold-rimmed glasses from behind his ears and wiped the lenses on his shirtsleeve. The action was unremarkable, but his demeanor had changed in some way, as if his body had suddenly hummed to life. There was tension under the skin.

"How far is it to the portal from here?" he asked as he put on his glasses.

"Another hour's ride, if we're lucky," answered Duckers.

"Then let's move along. We can give...this"—he nodded toward the graps—"a wide berth."

Without waiting for the marshals' say-so, he spurred his mount forward, circumnavigating the grapping graps and leaving his companions to follow in his wake.

Rosie's heart sank when they finally arrived at the East Station's portal.

"FYI, this looks bad," she told the others.

"Do I even want to ask?" said Duckers.

"Those vines or whatever are now visible on the outside of the portal. I don't even want to think about what it looks like on the inside."

Zeddie raised a finger like a lawyer getting ready to shout, *Objection!* "He didn't actually ask."

"I don't know what to tell you, my dude. I'm speaking the truth here."

Zeddie opened his mouth to say more, but movement on the Bushong side of the Mist caught his attention. An assembly of marshals and engineers and all four chiefs of the Tanrian Marshals, including Alma Maguire—who was once again smoking like a chimney—were gathered around the portal. But it was the group of people behind the Tanrian Marshals Service staff that stunned Rosie—people like Hart Ralston and Mercy Birdsall, sitting in lawn chairs while their kids ran around the dusty Bushong landscape, tossing around a sea polo ball; people like Lu and Annie Ellis, playing cards on a picnic blanket while their dad and Twyla Banneker watched the Mist intently. Bassareus, the foulmouthed rabbit who used to deliver mail in Tanria, shared a flask with Horatio, an owl who, like his nimkilim colleague, now worked for Mercy's Undertakings. There were dozens of familiar faces from the border towns, especially Eternity.

"Are they here for us?" asked Zeddie. "Are we the only ones left inside Tanria?"

Rosie scanned the faces in the crowd, connecting each of them, one by one, to herself and to Duckers and to Zeddie. Their family and friends had come to welcome them home. Except none of these people were waiting for Adam Lee, were they? Unless Rosie counted Alma Maguire, which was a stretch. Granted, he was far from Quindaro and even farther from Eshil Craia, but it twisted Rosie up on the inside to think that no one waited for him on the other side of the Mist to welcome him home, to tell him that they were glad he was alive and well.

Where was home for Adam Lee? Were there people who loved him and were anxiously waiting for his return? Because she had the sneaking suspicion that the answer to that question was no, that there was a reason, after all, why he walked through this world making sure nothing and no one could touch him.

Well, Rosie Fox did have people waiting for her and a home whose bathtub was calling her name, so she turned to Dr. Lee, jerked her head at the portal, and said, "This thing looks bad. Think we should risk it?"

"The evidence suggests that the situation is unlikely to improve."

"That was a yes, right?"

"That was a yes."

"Once more, with feeling!" cried Duckers as he approached the portal, adding sparkle fingers to add levity as Zeddie trailed behind him.

"Five, six, seven, eight!" Rosie snapped gamely, because she, too, adhered to the school of Laugh So That You Don't Have to Cry. She even threw in a few dance moves before she rang the portal bell to alert the station's engineer that they had arrived.

They couldn't hear the response on the other side, but they could see it. Anyone who had been sitting was now on their feet, and there was obviously a lot of celebrating going on. Rosie didn't want to miss out on the excitement, so she dubbed in the cheering for the enjoyment of her three companions on the Tanrian side of the Mist. "Woo-hoo! Yay! They're alive!"

Maguire wasn't the chief marshal of the East Station, but she was the one who nodded to the engineer on duty and counted down on her fingers for the benefit of the four people who could not hear her.

Three.

Two.

One.

The engineer pulled the lever.

And nothing happened.

No clicking of gears. No pumping of pistons. The engine puffed steam into the Bushong sky, but the portal remained as silent as the four people in Tanria who stared at it in varying degrees of disbelief and horror.

"Fuck," said Zeddie.

Rosie put a hand on his shoulder to steady him. "Nobody panic. Lots of options remain on the table."

Maguire gave an order, and someone handed her a notebook and pen. She scribbled a message and held up the page as the steam engine whined piteously.

Try the bell again.

Rosie rang the bell. It must have worked, because Maguire gave a thumbs-up. She flipped the page of her notebook, jotted down another message, and held it up.

Fox, Duckers, Lee, Birdsall: Are all four of you together and safe? Use Marks Code to respond.

Marks Code was a way of communicating using short or long pulses of either sound or light, named after the guy who had invented it. Each letter of the alphabet had its own code, so you had to spell out any message you wanted to send. It was cumbersome, but it was all they had to work with at the moment.

Y-E-S, Rosie replied via the bell.

Maguire's next message read *Can you access the fail-safe?*

Rosie spelled *Y-E-S* as the portal's inventor pried open the fail-safe panel, but a single glance at the open hatch told her that the whole thing was choked with vines.

Dr. Lee looked at Duckers and gestured to the crank. "Care to do the honors, Marshal?"

"Are there shadows in there?" he asked Rosie.

"Do you want me to say, 'It looks peachy keen,' or do you want the truth?"

He shook his head as he approached the fail-safe. "If I end up with hives and shit from touching an invisible plant, you all owe me a beer."

"If you secure our release out of Tanria, I will buy you the entire pub," said Dr. Lee.

"Now that's the kind of halftime locker room speech I signed up for, Coach Lee. Watch the magic, folks."

He wound the fail-safe past the uncomfortable protests of the portal's inner workings, and the machine juddered to life.

"Whoa, whoa, whoa!" cried Rosie when flames shot out of the frame on the Bushong side, sending the onlookers running. Duckers dropped the crank as if he had accidentally taken hold of a rattlesnake and needed to get rid of it posthaste.

They watched in numb denial as marshals scrambled to put out the fire.

"Gods' tits and testicles!" Zeddie dug his fingers into his mop of golden curls and began to pace.

"That's not helpful, Z," snapped Duckers.

"Fuck you, Pen. And you don't get to call me Z. My name is Zeddie."

"Fine, *Zeddie*. Losing your shit is not optimal right now, *Zeddidiah*."

"I can lose my shit if I want to, *Penrose*. We're trapped inside the Mist, in case you haven't noticed."

"Let's stay calm." Adam Lee intervened. "As Marshal Fox said, we have multiple options for vacating Tanria. I'm sure that I or the engineers can repair one of the portals." He looked to the marshals on the other side who had started a fire brigade and were now throwing buckets of water on the flames that were shooting out of the archway. "Perhaps not this one," he added, unnecessarily.

"This is not happening." Zeddie chewed on his thumbnail as he continued his frenetic pacing.

"Dr. Lee is right," said Rosie. "Even if it takes a few days to repair one of the portals, we're getting out of here, one way or another. And I bet someone could get their hands on a pirated portal if push comes to shove."

She looked at the faces beyond the Mist, at all the friends who watched in dismay as reality settled in on the other side of the portal.

"We should signal that we're okay, assuming the bell works," said Rosie. It felt good to make a suggestion, to have the first step of a plan, to take action.

Duckers perked up slightly. "Good idea. Let's do that."

Rosie began to signal *We're okay*, but she only got as far as *we* when the portal lurched and the frame cracked open. Cogs and wheels and scraps of metal shot out like bolts from a pistol crossbow. Something slammed into Rosie's chest, searing her with pain as it tore through an organ or two that were fairly important to most people's survival.

"Shit! Rosie!"

Duckers caught her as the entire portal fell onto the Bushong side of the Mist, sending the fire brigade scattering for cover. His face loomed over hers once he had laid her carefully on the ground. She wanted to tell him how sweet it was that he freaked out every time this happened, even though he knew she'd be up and running in a matter of hours. But the pain was excruciating, and her lungs weren't working right, and she was making horrible gurgling noises, and she couldn't stop shaking, and fuck, it hurt so much.

The next thing she knew, Adam Lee was crouching next to her, getting her blood all over the knees of his beautifully tailored wool trousers. If she hadn't been in so much pain, she would have considered this a travesty. He looked at her the way he had five years ago with a face full of devastation, which made her chest hurt even more. His lips moved, but Rosie couldn't understand what he was saying, so she let the rough cadence of his words wash over her.

I could listen to that voice for at least three lifetimes, she thought as he took a clean linen handkerchief from his pants pocket with a shaking hand and pressed it over Rosie's wound.

The last thing she thought before she died was *That's my handkerchief.*

Chapter Eleven

Rosie's heart came pumping to life sometime later, but it took a while for her lungs to start working again. Her sense of touch returned next. She was no longer on the ground, of that she was certain, and she didn't think she was outside either. Beneath her, she felt the light discomfort of a too-small government-issued cot. She must be inside a marshals' barracks, although she couldn't imagine how she'd gotten here.

"She's breathing," said a sandpapery voice, so her hearing had returned, too. She could sense Adam's physical presence, standing beside her prone, unmoving body.

Duckers sat on the edge of the cot. "Twice in one week, Foxy? Could you be a bigger asshole?"

"Week and a half," Rosie managed feebly.

"A week and one day does not a week and a half make." He held her hand, the size and shape and texture of his own achingly familiar to her. How many times had he sat beside her, waiting for her heart to start beating again? Gods knew she didn't deserve him.

She opened her eyes, and there he was, wearing a bittersweet smile as he stared down at her.

"How was this my fault?" she asked him, her throat painfully dry.

Zeddie swooped in with a cup of water and handed it to Duckers, who propped Rosie up to help her drink.

"All I'm saying is that you have got to stop dying on me all the time."

"How many times have we been over this? I. Can't. Die."

"Yes. You. Can."

"You know what I mean."

"Well, you definitely weren't living thirty seconds ago, so stuff that in your pipe and smoke it."

Despite Duckers's thin stabs at humor, a pall hung in the air. Adam stood off to the side and watched Rosie charily, while Zeddie stalked away to busy himself by the stove.

"I'm so traumatized right now," the latter muttered as he made a lot of noise involving kitchenware. "I'm going to need years of therapy when this is over."

It was nice to know that Zeddie was thinking positively, assuming *when this is over* meant *after we escape Tanria*.

"Where are we?" Rosie asked Duckers.

"The barracks in Sector E-30."

"How did you get me here?"

"Dr. Big Brains made a gurney out of friendtree limbs and my rain poncho so that Saltlicker could drag your dead ass here."

Rosie looked to Adam. He had swapped his bloodstained wool slacks for a pair of Tanrian Marshals Service uniform pants that someone must have left behind in the barracks. They were too large for him, so the olive cotton ballooned from the belt cinching them at his waist. All that was left of his bespoke apparel was the increasingly dirty white dress shirt. And the belt, she supposed. He looked horribly uncomfortable, and not simply because he wore clothes that didn't fit. His arms were crossed tightly over his chest as if he were holding himself together, and his face had gone alarmingly pale.

"Oh hey, I'm immortal. Surprise!" she said, but the words came out limp and half dead and not particularly funny.

"I noticed."

Rosie suspected that he had been grasping for his usual arid humor, but what came out of his mouth sounded more like an accusation. He crossed his arms more tightly and looked anywhere but at her.

It hurt, to be honest.

No one responded well to the fact of her immortality. It made some people deeply uncomfortable, while others went all in, asking questions that felt bizarrely personal to her. ("How many times have you not died?" "What happens if someone cuts off your arm?") Navigating these responses was the main reason why she kept her immortality close to the chest whenever she could. But for some reason, she had expected better of Adam. He could barely manage a facial expression in the most dire of circumstances, but now, all of a sudden, he looked as though he might be sick.

"Thank you for making a gurney, because it's way nicer to wake up in a bed than in the dirt," she told him, trying to lighten the mood, but he remained grim as he stood off to the side of the bed.

He nodded briefly and said "Excuse me" before stepping outside the barracks.

Sensing Rosie's ridiculous hurt feelings, Duckers said, "Don't read into it. He's probably taking a piss."

"Or running away from the unsettling immortal in our midst. How about you, Zeddie? How are you handling this?"

"If I never see that much blood again, it will be too soon," he called from the stove. Compared to Adam, he was taking it rather well.

Rosie tried to sit up on her own, but Duckers had to prop her up with pillows. She was wearing a clean shirt and a pair of boxer shorts, but traces of blood stained what she could see of her skin.

And she wasn't wearing a brassiere. She wondered if Adam and Zeddie had gotten an eyeful of her naked bits while poor Duckers cleaned her up. She had an inkling that most people would find this scenario embarrassing, but Rosie was a good century past blushing over nudity. She was more upset about the loss of her pretty teal brassiere—a masterpiece that had given her bust magnificent height and shape—and it was easier to focus on the loss of her lingerie than to stew over Adam's reaction to her immortal affliction.

"What's the game plan?" she asked now that she was semi-upright and resigned to the loss of her satin and lace.

"The game plan is to let you rest and be more alive, after which we'll figure out the real game plan," answered Duckers.

"But—"

"But nothing. We'll sort shit out tomorrow. Burning question for you, though: What is that, and why was it in your pocket?"

Duckers gestured to the bedside table next to Rosie's cot, where the two-legged cat figurine lay on its side, its broken appendages scattered forlornly in front of it.

Rosie sighed. "It's a metaphor."

A clatter that sounded more like self-expression than accident erupted from the kitchen.

"Is Zeddie cooking?" Rosie asked hopefully, welcoming the diversion.

"I'd hardly call this cooking," said Zeddie. "I have nothing to work with here. Nothing. Would it be too much to ask for some bacon? Thank gods for salt at least."

After several minutes of clanging and muttering, the blessed aroma of a decent meal in the making filled the barracks. Rosie caught Duckers watching Zeddie as he whipped up a miracle.

"He's cute when he's grumpy," she said.

Duckers sucked his teeth at her.

"Don't suck your teeth at me. I almost died today."

"You did die today, asshole."

She put her hand on his arm. "I love you, too."

"He-e-ey, mail delivery," called Gobbo, and a moment later, he stepped inside the barracks, trailed by the expressionless version of Adam Lee that was carved out of marble. "Feels like a downer in here."

"I can't imagine why," said Rosie.

Clueless, Gobbo held up a letter. "It's addressed to you two marshals. Who wants it?"

"She's half dead. I'll take it," said Duckers. He opened the letter and read aloud.

To Marshals Fox and Duckers,

The engineers are assessing all intact portals for repair, but the North Station looks like our best bet. I advise you to head in that direction. If Dr. Lee has any special instructions regarding repairs, please send them with Gobbo. We are also working on an alternative method of getting you out. More on that soon.

I have sent along clean clothing for everyone as well as food stores to get you through the next few days. Please update us as to your location and well-being as soon as possible.

We're all pulling for you and doing everything in our power to bring you home.

Best,
A. Maguire

" 'Best'? She closed with an honest-to-gods salutation?" Rosie asked in disbelief.

"Doesn't bode well," Duckers agreed as Adam immediately set about writing down the requested advice for the engineers.

"But at least one portal can be repaired, right?" Zeddie said as he set a trivet on the table followed by a cast-iron pan of scrambled eggs.

"With time," said Adam. "Although I can't account for the—for whatever Marshal Fox is seeing."

"Speaking of which, we should send a report with Gobbo to update the chief on our adventures today." Rosie hauled herself out of bed, retrieved the requisite writing materials, and sat down at the table.

"Don't forget the floating graps," said Duckers as Zeddie returned with another platter.

Gobbo's long face lit up. "Dude! Biscuits! Can I have one?"

"They're called scones," Zeddie informed him. "I found strawberry preserves in one of the cupboards, and I did my best to make a clotted cream substitute."

"Sweet." Gobbo was blithely oblivious to the glares he was getting from the human and demigod population in the room as he piled food onto a plate.

Duckers shook his head and joined everyone else at the table. "Maguire said they're banking on the northern portal. That's going to be a sucky ride from here."

Zeddie made a strangled cry of despair as he set a bowl of fruit salad on the table.

"Hey, Gobbo," said Rosie. "Where's the stuff Maguire sent?"

The nimkilim blinked his bloodshot eyes at her before catching up. "Oh yeah." He dug a couple of boxes out of his mailbag—neither of which looked like they could have fit inside—and set them on one of the cots. Rosie armed herself with the kitchen shears and headed for the one not labeled *perishable*.

"What is this?" she cried as she stared into a cardboard box full of khaki and dull olive. "We need clean clothes, and they send us Tanrian Marshals Service uniforms? If I have to be stuck in Tanria, I at least deserve a flattering cut."

"You have never been more Rosie Fox than you are right now," Duckers commented affectionately, but Rosie's mood was growing fouler by the second. Because underneath three packs of men's boxers in various sizes were several pairs of flesh-colored cotton granny panties, the kind with stalwart, no-nonsense waistbands that came up to a woman's eyebrows. And the brassieres were even worse, constructed out of some horrific white fabric with bands so wide they required four sets of hooks and eyes to close them and shoulder straps thick enough to support a pair of fully ripened watermelons. Outraged, she held a pair of enormous panties in one hand and a farcical excuse for a brassiere in the other and waved them furiously through the air like war banners.

"Are you kidding me? I refuse to wear this... this... *insult* to intimate apparel! I refuse!"

"RoFo, you're giving Dr. Lee a heart attack," Duckers informed her.

Rosie's emotions careened from outrage to alarm as she hustled to where Adam sat at the table with a half-eaten scone before him.

"What's wrong? Are you having another one of your attacks?"

"I'm fine," he answered shortly, his shoulders hunching, at which point Rosie realized that she was touching one of the aforementioned shoulders.

She snatched her hand away as Duckers and Zeddie both tried to stifle their snickering.

"What?" she demanded.

They shared a look and proceeded to laugh openly.

"Well, aren't you two chummy all of a sudden?"

"Keep waving your panties around, Foxy, so we can play a few more rounds of Let's Torture the Straight Guy," suggested Duckers.

"They're not my panties." Rosie turned to Adam. "I would never wear intimates this not-sexy on purpose. I only allow high-quality materials to touch my skin."

"I really don't need to know this," said Adam as he folded his letter to Maguire with a concentration usually reserved for complex surgery, the color on his cheekbones high. Rosie wondered if it was the intimate apparel that made him blush or her, personally.

Zeddie wiped away a tear of hilarity. "This almost makes getting trapped inside a prison meant for gods worth it."

"Almost," said Duckers with the first genuine smile he'd given his ex since this debacle began.

Rosie was about to tease them when the view over Zeddie's shoulder made her brain go *sproing*. Hanging neatly on the drying rack, freshly laundered and permanently bloodstained, was the handkerchief Rosie had used to tie up the cut on Adam's hand five years ago, the one he'd pressed against her wound this very day. She had completely forgotten about it.

And now she was fairly certain that her cheeks had gone pinker than Adam's.

"So, like, what are you guys going to do about the plant?" asked Gobbo as he helped himself to another scone.

The dik-dik's casual question caused another *sproing* to go off in Rosie's head. "The what?" she asked.

"Dude. The plant." The nimkilim gestured broadly with one hoof, his tone mystical.

"You can see it?"

"Yeah?" he answered, as if this were a trick question.

"And it is, in fact, a plant?"

"Ye-e-eah?"

"How long have you been able to see it?"

He screwed up his long face in concentration. "I first noticed it about five years ago, I guess?"

"Years?" exclaimed Duckers.

"Yeah."

"Did you tell anyone about it?"

"Um . . . no?"

"Why not?" Rosie and Duckers demanded in unison.

Gobbo screwed up his face again.

"You know what? Never mind," said Rosie. "Can you tell us what it looks like to you?"

"Kind of brown. Kind of gray. Big-ass thorns. Looks familiar actually, like I've seen it before. Maybe that's why it didn't freak me out when it first showed up around Tanria."

"Can you touch it?"

"I would but . . . big-ass thorns." He shrugged in apology. "Like, at first it was no big deal, but lately it's been getting out of hand. This plant is everywhere all of a sudden."

Zeddie made a sound that was somewhere between a laugh and a sob. "Great. Wonderful," he said before shoving half a scone into his mouth. Rosie doubted he was even tasting it, not that she could blame him; she was experiencing an uncommon amount of dismay herself.

Adam spoke not a word through this exchange, and his face was the steeliest of steel traps. Rosie fought the urge to clap in his face and say, "What's going on in that giant brain of yours?" Instead, she turned her focus to the more pressing task of cobbling together a report for the chief.

Gobbo lingered over the meal while Rosie scribbled away and everyone else jotted quick notes to family and friends—everyone except Adam, whose sole missive was addressed to Alma Maguire.

"Is this everything?" asked the nimkilim as he gathered up the outgoing mail.

Rosie was about to answer in the affirmative when her eyes

landed on the broken cat figurine, a reminder of the Trickster's half-assed gifts over the years, of his pathetic attempts to play at being a decent father, of his excruciating failure to be a meaningful part of the life she had shared with Jocelyn. As she sat in the shabby barracks, stuck in Tanria for the foreseeable future—a place intended for Old Gods like the Trickster, not for the daughter he had abandoned a hundred times over—she found that she wanted to tell her father where he could stuff his cat figurine, and she had enough paper and ink to get the job done.

"Hold on, Gobbo, I have one more letter I want to write, if you don't mind?"

The dik-dik helped himself to another plateful of magnificent Zeddie Cuisine as Rosie pulled a clean sheet of paper to herself.

Dear Old Dad began the scathing screed that poured out of her pen. Her cold fury bubbled up like the water from the bottom of a fountain, frothing to the surface.

You didn't give a shit about my mother, she wrote, pressing the nib so hard to the paper that she etched the words into the tabletop beneath it.

You were never there for us.

I don't need you.

Stay out of my life.

Rosie had always thought it would take hours to rake her pathetic excuse for a father over the coals, but in the end, she knocked it out in ten minutes. Though she felt lighter for having poured two lifetimes' worth of resentment onto a single sheet of paper, her hand shook as she gave the letter to the nimkilim along with the last copper lingering at the bottom of her pack.

As Gobbo bid them adieu and let himself out, only Adam seemed to notice Rosie's discomposure. He studied her with his trademark enigmatic consideration before she caught him staring and he looked away.

Adam?

When had Rosie started thinking of him as *Adam*, rather than by his full name or Dr. Lee or Professor Stick Up His Ass?

The bloodstained handkerchief dangling from the drying rack answered the question for her.

Chapter Twelve

Rosie woke at first light, and not wanting to rouse the others, she snuck out the front door as quietly as she could to get a head start on saddling the equimares. Outside, the Painter was brushing the eastern sky in shades of violet and pink and orange, while the heads of gray tuft flowers in the barracks' yard bobbed in the breeze in time to the grapping of graps and the first chirps of Tanrian birds.

It all brought Rosie to a shockingly tearful standstill.

When was the last time she had bothered to watch the sunrise? When was the last time the world had made her pause and think, *That's amazing*? When was the last time she had been adequately grateful to be alive?

Yesterday, she had survived an injury that would have killed anyone else; today, she was glad to be basking in the soft light of dawn, here and now, even if "here" was Tanria and "now" was a shit show.

She lingered, waiting until the sun peeked an eyelash of blazing light over the horizon before she continued on her way to the stable. But as she rounded the corner of the barracks, the sight of another astounding natural wonder brought her to a stuttering halt.

Adam stood beside the well, naked from the waist up, his back to Rosie as he sponged off with a dingy washcloth.

The Three Mothers knew what they were doing when they crafted this man. Each line of his body was elegant, each lean muscle delicately drawn. Even the Painter seemed to approve as the god's morning light lovingly caressed Adam's smooth, damp skin.

The entire scene would have made Rosie unbearably thirsty were it not for the three long scars running diagonally across his back from his right shoulder to the waistband of his pants and beyond. The gashes had healed, but recently; they were the same angry red as Rosie's irises.

"Holy shit, what happened to you?"

He spun to face her, clutching the dripping washcloth to his chest as if the small square of cotton could cover his unclothed torso. His body was spare, but there was grace and athleticism in his slender frame, and the defined ridges of his abdominal muscles were clearly visible below the washcloth's hem. Rosie wrenched her eyes away from his naked stomach, but not before internally moaning, *Good gods.*

"My apologies. I should have done this in the bathhouse," he said, assiduously avoiding eye contact. His face was drawn in a way that made him look like a schoolboy who had been caught mid-wrongdoing.

"You didn't answer my question," said Rosie, annoyed that there were now two things gumming up the friendly progress she had made with Adam Lee: her immortality and his scars.

"It's nothing." He took up the shirt that was neatly folded on the rim of the well and put it on.

" 'Nothing'? Like your 'medical condition'?"

He busied himself with the buttoning of his shirt. "There is no cause for concern. My wounds healed a long time ago."

"A long time ago, my ass."

Thoroughly buttoned up now, he stood grim-faced before

Rosie in the uniform that Maguire had sent yesterday. While it fit him well enough, and while the colors suited his warm complexion, the prêt-à-porter khaki diminished him in some way, making Rosie think of a snail exposed to the world without its shell for protection. And here she was, figuratively poking a literal wound.

"I'm sorry. It's none of my business," she said, even though she wanted to make it her business.

He nodded, but his acceptance of her apology did nothing to lessen the strain between them.

"'Morning," called Duckers as he stepped outside, carrying two rucksacks containing the supplies Maguire had sent the night before.

Rosie welcomed her partner's cheery early-bird interruption the way a small child reached for a security blanket. "'Morning," she answered.

Adam, unsurprisingly, said nothing.

"Did you saddle up?"

"Not yet. I was on my way."

"Is there anything I can do to assist you?" Adam asked them, or, more accurately, he asked Duckers.

"You can help Zeddie pack up breakfast and lunch. We're eating on the road today," Duckers told him with a nod toward the barracks.

It seemed that Adam would depart without so much as a second glance at Rosie, but he stopped and turned back.

"Forgive me, I have yet to ask you: How are you feeling today, Marshal Fox?"

He didn't look her in the face, but given recent events, the fact that he was asking the question at all melted the tension in Rosie's shoulders.

"I'm fine. I always am."

"Good. That's good," he said before walking to the barracks, his posture ramrod straight, his gait stiff. Rosie wondered if his mysterious scars caused him pain or if the stiffness was a result of his mortification at having been caught half-naked by a freak who couldn't die.

"It's so weird to see Dr. Lee in a marshal's uniform," Duckers said as he and Rosie made their way to the stable. "The poor guy's slumming it now."

"I doubt he realized he'd be traipsing about the Tanrian countryside when he packed for this trip. Cut him some slack."

"I was joking."

"Well, joke nicely. He's stuck in here as much as we are."

"Okay, dang."

As they saddled the equimares in brooding silence, it was not their increasingly dire circumstances that Rosie had front of mind; it was Adam Lee and the wounds on his back. What could have caused them? What kind of life had he been leading that would result in an injury that must have bordered on fatal? She had been picturing him in a stale, sterile lab puttering away on stale, sterile projects, not taming lions. What had he been up to? And now that she was thinking about it, why had the wounds healed as if he hadn't received decent medical attention? None of it added up.

She nearly mentioned the scars and her musings to Duckers, but she thought better of it. She suspected that Adam would not want her to share such personal details with anyone else.

"You know, he was really upset yesterday when you d—when you looked like you were dead. FYI," said Duckers, finally puncturing the silence.

"Who? Zeddie?"

"You know who I mean."

Rosie did know who he meant. She remembered in detail

Adam's unguarded devastation as he pressed the handkerchief—*her* handkerchief—to her wound, but she shrugged it off, the picture of nonchalance when she felt anything but.

"He straight-up panicked, started shouting all sorts of shit," said Duckers. Rosie knew a verbal trap when she heard one, but she took the bait anyway, because how could she not?

"What did he say?"

"I don't know. It was all in Eshilese, I think. The point is, your dead-but-not-dead ass freaked him out, which is probably why he's acting funky around you now."

"I don't care how he acts around me. Why would I?"

Rosie finished tightening the saddle strap on Zeddie's equimaris when she realized that her partner was scrutinizing her with narrowed eyes.

"What's that look for?"

"Sweet Mother of Sorrows, I knew it. You like Dr. Lee."

Rosie readjusted the strap, which did not need adjusting. "I guess. He's nice-ish."

"No, RoFo." Duckers took her by the arms and spoke to her like she was five years old. "You. Like. Him."

"What, like, *like*-like?"

"Mm-hmm."

This morning's vision of Adam Lee, shirtless and damp and scarred and vulnerable in the soft light of dawn, filled her head like a mural. She squirmed out of Duckers's grasp and wished she could squirm away from his perspicacity as easily. Because, crap, she did like Adam, in a world's worst timing kind of way.

"Are we in the fourth grade right now?"

Duckers folded his arms and treated her to his best shit-eating grin. "I will have you know that I had this exact conversation with Hart Ralston re: Mercy Birdsall, and I was right. And I called Twyla Banneker and Frank Ellis getting together."

"You're wrong about this, though," said Rosie, as much to convince herself as her partner.

"Am I wrong, or are you in denial?"

"You're wrong."

I'm in denial. Leave me here, she thought.

"Nope. I have decided: you're in love with Dr. Monotone. L-O-V-E. You want to have cute little demigod babies with the uptight pocket man from the University of Quindaro." By the time he got to *University of Quindaro*, Duckers was singing his words in a soulful falsetto.

Rosie was not having this, and it was easier to fall into her usual banter with Duckers than to contemplate their dire circumstances.

"First of all, pocket men deserve love as much as tall guys, so stop being small-phobic."

"Touché."

"Secondly, all I did was say that the man might be nice-adjacent. Maybe he has hidden depths, you dickweed."

"Oh? Did he show you his hidden depths?" Duckers waggled his eyebrows suggestively.

"I'm trying to be charitable."

"Because you lo-o-ove him!" belted Duckers.

"I am not in love with Adam Lee!"

"We are ready if you are."

This last statement came from directly behind Rosie, spoken in the raspy baritone with a slight accent that had become familiar to her, no matter how rarely its owner put it to use.

She turned to look at Adam with chagrin, a feeling with which she, a thoroughly shameless person, was unfamiliar. For a few seconds, Rosie tried to convince herself that there was a minuscule possibility Adam had not overheard any part of her conversation with her partner, but Zeddie's attempts to tamp down his laughter forced her to abandon that hope.

Opting to behave as if nothing had happened, she slung a rucksack full of ugly underwear over her shoulder and said "Let's hit it" with applaudable insouciance. Once everyone was mounted, she led the train toward their planned route to the North Station.

Duckers sidled up to her. "Wow, that was so embarrassing, it had to hurt."

"Fuck you very much," Rosie told him before riding ahead.

The eastern sectors were heavily forested with Tanrian friendtrees, *trees* being loose with the language. Like most living things created by the imprisoned Old Gods, friendtrees did not have a healthy respect for the New Gods' laws of nature. They wove their rainbow-colored branches together from root to treetop like the fingers of two hands intertwining in a manner that must have appeared friendly to the person who had named them decades ago.

Rosie knew this area of Tanria as solidly as she knew the lyrics to every Brigitte Porcel ballad. She had worked out of the East Station for a quarter century before getting transferred, and the forest trails burned bright in her mental map of the area. Sadly, that map did not include translucent vines that rambled over the trails on a regular basis, causing her to get the whole group turned around on more than one occasion. For the most part, she could ride around these obstacles, but halfway to their destination, they came to a truly gnarly thicket in the road.

Adam halted beside her when she reined in her filly, but Duckers and Zeddie and their mounts sauntered straight through the plant as if it weren't there. Once they were on the other side, they were slightly obscured from sight, as if Rosie were looking at them through Jocelyn's yellowed lace curtains.

"That's disturbing," she said.

Noticing that Rosie and Adam weren't with them, Duckers stopped and turned in the saddle. "What's up?"

"You two waltzed through a big-ass plant thing in the road."

Duckers shivered. "Fuck me, Grandfather Bones."

"Is that going to cause horrible side effects?" asked Zeddie. "Are we going to break out into hives and pustules?"

"I think you are safe," said Dr. Lee.

"You *think*?"

"There's nothing we can do about it now. We should focus on getting to the northern portal," said Adam.

"Hold on." Rosie slid out of the saddle and foisted her reins on Adam, ignoring the impatience wafting off him.

"Be careful," he said as she stepped close to the bramble.

"Being careful is not my strong suit." She reached out, but once again, her fingers met nothing but air. When she looked back to Adam Lee, she was surprised to see him breathing a sigh of apparent relief.

"How is it that graps can hop around on this plant, but people and equimares can pass right through it?" she asked the group.

"I wonder if the dragons can see it," said Duckers.

Adam stiffened. "We should move along. Marshal Fox?"

He gestured toward the path, indicating that Rosie should lead them on their merry way, but the uncanny plant life made everything look unfamiliar. She mounted up and stood in the stirrups to get a better look ahead.

"I hate to say it, but this might not be the best trail to take to the North Station."

"Ugh," moaned Zeddie, who was surely saddle sore.

"Keep it together, Z," said Duckers, aggressively mopping sweat off his face with his yellow kerchief. Rosie threw him a speaking look. He rolled his eyes but added, "—eddie."

"The situation sucks, *Penrose*. Am I not allowed to express the fucking truth?"

Duckers's eyebrows took a nosedive. He opened his mouth, but Rosie cut him off with "Don't" as yesterday's glimmer of hope that a truce had settled in between the exes flickered out.

Saltlicker cantered sideways, his huge nostrils flaring, probably catching the scent of a nearby stream. Suddenly, Duckers had his hands full keeping the stallion in line, and he dropped Zeddie's reins.

"Knock it off," he warned the equimaris as the scaly beast snorted in protest and shook out his seaweed mane.

Saltlicker's bad behavior was infectious, egging on the other equimares. Both Rosie and Adam got their mounts under control quickly, but Zeddie's gargled churlishly as she sniffed the air. When it became clear that Zeddie was about to lose control of his equimaris, Duckers and Rosie began to shout advice at him.

"Show confidence! She needs to know you're in charge!"

"Pat her neck! Talk softly!"

"What?" he asked, his eyes going wide.

"Don't panic!" Rosie and Duckers and even Adam shouted at the same time.

The equimaris reared, and for one awful moment, Rosie thought the mare was going to toss Zeddie to the forest floor. But Zeddie held on for dear life, even as he went deathly pale.

"I'm panicking!" he yelled, and as soon as his mount's webbed front feet hit earth again, she bolted. In stunned silence, the remaining trio watched as the equimaris galloped off, weaving in and out of friendtree stands and plowing through thickets neither equimaris nor rider could see. Zeddie's cry lingered, a long, shifting vowel of terror—"Aaaaiiiiiiieeeeeaaaargh!"—that grew fainter and fainter as his equimaris ran farther and farther away.

Rosie turned to her partner and said, "Not it."

"Grapshit! We're flipping a coin."

"Don't have one, and I already called not-it. Now go before he breaks his neck."

"I wish he *would* break his neck," Duckers muttered darkly, but he kicked his mount into action and took off after Zeddie and the errant mare.

And with that, Rosie found herself alone with Adam. He remained erect in the saddle, staring fixedly at the path Duckers had followed after Zeddie and very fixedly *not* looking at her. How could the inroads she had made with him over the past two days be so utterly eradicated by her immortality?

"Well, let's air it out," she said.

He looked at her in confusion.

She made a winding motion with her hand, that circular gesture that said, *Move it along.*

"What do you want to 'air out'?" he asked cagily.

"I died, and now I'm not dead, and you clearly have some beef with it. And then I saw your scars, and you're not thrilled about that either."

"To have beef? Is that your way of saying I take issue with your dying?"

"And with me getting an eyeful of the wounds on your back."

"I don't care that you saw my back."

Lies, thought Rosie, but she didn't want to interrupt Adam.

"And of course I take issue with your dying. When someone you—" He cut himself off and started again, more quietly. "It is unpleasant to watch someone die, especially when that death is painful."

"But I'm fine now. So what's the problem?"

"I'm...I was..." His voice trailed off as he, true to form, hesitated.

"Horrified?" suggested Rosie.

"No."

"Grossed out?"

"No." That *no* had been half laughed, so maybe there were a few inroads left unscathed.

"Then what?"

"I was worried. About you."

Warmth spread through Rosie's body, as if she had gulped down three rounds of prairie fire in quick succession. The Salt Sea take Penrose Duckers for making her see the truth. She did like Adam Lee—Adam Lee, who was not even remotely dead inside. She liked him in that fizzy way she had pined for Ralph Windermere in the seventh grade, even though Ralph had been at least a foot shorter than she'd been in middle school. She had thought her ability to experience a giddy crush was long behind her, but here she was, stuck in Tanria with the dreamiest pocket man she had ever met.

What was truly staggering was the fact that this brilliant, mysterious man with a sense of humor so dry it could only be described as *desiccated* seemed to maybe possibly find her attractive in return.

As a general rule, men did not like Rosie, romantically speaking. She was too tall, too loud, too red. Too much. And the ones who did like her wanted her for all the wrong reasons—reasons that had more to do with getting it on with an exotic-looking demigod than with falling for the woman behind the creepy eyeballs.

Not that any of this had stopped her from enjoying the finer things in life. If she wanted sex, she had sex, and the word *regret* rarely entered into it.

But relationships were another matter. She had thought herself in love twice, once in the previous century and once in this one. But after a few years, those relationships had fizzled out. It was hard to stay in love with someone once she'd heard him slop and slurp his way through a bowl of breakfast cereal or mansplain her own job to her. And it was hard to watch the subtle way a lover changed and aged over the course of years, while she herself remained as she ever was. Maybe it was easier to believe that love could last forever when you were confident that your own life could not.

Whatever the case, Rosie had come to accept that tying her heart to a person who would inevitably die was a bad idea. Now, out of nowhere, she found herself falling hard and fast. Ill-equipped to handle the bewildering surge of emotions, she decided to duck behind her usual breezy indifference.

"You don't have to worry about a gal who can't die."

"Do you think you don't merit concern because you cannot die?"

Considering the fact that he tended to hide who he was behind his glasses and a three-piece suit, this willingness to look at her—to truly look—flustered her all the more.

"Yes. No? I don't know, to be honest."

"I imagine that it is not easy to come back from death the way that you do."

Most people would be fidgeting by now. Hart Ralston and Mercy Birdsall aside, few people spoke of death and dying and not dying with this much ease. But Adam sat unwavering in his saddle, his bearing an ode to good posture, as he regarded her with a placidity she was beginning to recognize as sympathy. And now she couldn't bring herself to play off her inability to die as a joke, not when he seemed to see right through her.

"It isn't," she admitted.

"How many times has it happened?"

"I have no idea. Over a hundred?"

He raised his eyebrows in surprise, and Rosie congratulated herself on inspiring those black slashes to budge.

"I used to work in a traveling circus. Coming back to life was my act."

"How old are you?"

"One hundred and fifty-seven."

He gave another huffy laugh, probably because he was stunned to discover her age. When the Old Gods were around, there were more immortal demigods like her, but most of them joined their divine parents on the altar of the sky hundreds of years ago. That was before Rosie was born, and no one had given her that option. So now she was one of the few non-divine immortals walking the earth, a distinction she didn't want.

"One-hundred-plus non-deaths in one hundred and fifty-seven years is an absurd average," she conceded.

"Not necessarily. An immortal naturally takes risks that a mortal person would not attempt. But in your case, every time you come back to life, it's a reminder that you cannot die."

With that last sentence, he cut through her carapace of carefree cheerfulness and got himself a good look at the tender heart she was usually much better at protecting. She hadn't realized that she had been wearing armor until he had so deftly removed it, and now here she was in the middle of nowhere, laid bare to a man she hardly knew at all. She wondered if this was how he'd felt this morning with his literal scars on full display.

"And so I was worried, because that sort of thing can weigh heavily on a soul," he continued, like the human emotional wrecking ball he apparently was. "But I thought it would be presumptuous of me to say that to you, so I..."

"So you avoided me like the plague," Rosie filled in for him, scrabbling for the remnants of her armor.

"I would not phrase it that way."

He gave her a ghost of a smile, as if the memory of how to experience joy haunted his face, before he put his teeth away behind his soft lips. But she had caught a glimpse of their imperfection. They didn't line up neatly in a row. Not that he was snaggle-toothed, but his parents definitely hadn't taken him to the orthodontist when he was a kid. Maybe they didn't have orthodontists in Eshil Craia at the time, but that would make him much older than he looked.

Something about this scratched at the back of Rosie's mind, like an itchy tag on a new shirt, but she couldn't pinpoint exactly what was bothering her. She cocked her head to the side and studied Adam the way Duckers always seemed to scrutinize her when she least wanted it.

"I told you how old I am. Your turn. How old are you? And don't tell me that you're older than I think. I want numbers."

Adam seemed to turn to stone, the hesitation of all hesitations.

Rosie was tired of his masks and his demurring and his evasions. "This is not a hard question, Adam. What the fuck?"

"It's harder than you think. The answer is that I don't know." He held her gaze, but he had retreated behind his facade. His eyes gave away nothing now.

"What do you mean, you don't know?"

"I don't know how old I am."

"Are you an orphan or something?"

"Yes, that's right," he said slowly, as if he needed to mull over his answer. "I am an orphan."

The truth of it seeped into Rosie's bones. "Wow, I am such an asshole."

"No, you're not."

"Yes, I am. Total asshole, right here."

"It's all right, Marshal Fox. It was a long time ago."

"I think we can dispense with the formalities at this point. Call me Rosie."

"And you may call me Adam."

Rosie pressed a hand to her heart. "Oh, Adam, I already gave myself permission."

"Yes, I noticed."

What a magnificent desert he was.

"Friends?" asked Rosie as she stuck out her hand.

For one terrible moment, Adam stared at it, his cool exterior buttoned firmly in place. But then he relented and took her hand in his, and it was precisely how Rosie remembered it from the day she had bandaged it—an elegant mix of masculine lines and delicate bones. His grip was unexpectedly strong and comfortingly warm, and Rosie had the bizarre urge to keep holding on to him. Stranger still was the fact that Adam didn't let go. They went on sitting atop their equimares, staring at the place where their hands came together. Adam's thumb moved, brushing over the back of her hand, so slowly that Rosie almost thought she was imagining it.

The friendtrees all around them rustled and shivered, as if a breeze was blowing through them, but the air was calm. At the same moment, Adam gasped and gripped Rosie's hand so hard she squawked in pain. He immediately held up his free hand in that *I'm fine* gesture.

Rosie let go of him in exasperation. "Don't give me that! You are not fine!"

He shook his head and muttered a handful of sharp and bitter syllables in a different language as he rubbed his chest. Rosie had seen Adam's caginess, his caution, his kindness, and even his humor. But his bitterness was something new, and she wasn't sure how to dance around it.

"What did you say?"

"Nothing that matters."

A flare went up to their north, a bright pink, sizzling flame against a blue sky. Rosie had an entire suitcase of questions to unpack with Adam, but with Duckers's flare going off—at least she assumed it was Duckers who had fired it—she had more pressing matters to worry about.

"Is there trouble?" asked Adam.

"A flare is usually not a good sign. Are you okay to ride?"

He nodded, and they took off in the direction of the pink flame as it sank beyond a stand of friendtrees. Zeddie and Duckers couldn't have gone far in such a short span of time, but since Rosie found the vines increasingly disorienting—and she could swear they were multiplying by the second—she and Adam took a circuitous route around them. Once the flare was out of sight, they followed Rosie's compass as they picked their way through the clearest path she could find, arriving on the scene forty-five minutes later.

"Took you long enough," said Duckers when they emerged into a large and unexpectedly vine-free clearing in the middle of the woods.

Zeddie sat hunched and miserable on a fallen log beside his picketed equimaris, while Duckers stood ten feet away from him, holding his mount's reins, ready to go as soon as their companions showed up.

Rosie surveyed the clearing. "I don't recognize this place at all. Where in the Salt Sea are we?"

"I don't think this clearing existed until recently. Hence, my flare. Which you took forever to answer."

Taking a closer look at their surroundings, Rosie saw what he was getting at. An entire stand of friendtrees had come down in a giant clump, their shallow roots flailing from the ground to ten feet in the air like a landed squid. She had seen stands come down before, usually when the God of Wrath's storm blew through, but not on this scale.

Rosie picketed her equimaris and climbed up the roots to get a better look. When her head crested the top, she found that a tangle of thick, shadowy vines had brought down the entire stand.

"The plant?" asked Duckers.

"The plant," Rosie affirmed as she climbed down, jumping the last few feet.

"So the magical briar that only twenty-five percent of present company can see and zero percent can touch pulled down a bunch of trees?" asked Zeddie.

"That about sums it up."

"Great. That's not terrifying or anything."

Duckers glared at his ex, but Rosie thought he was being uncharitable. Zeddie's tone had been more resigned than pettish. She made a mental note to punch Duckers in the arm and tell him to lighten up later.

For the time being, the falling of a huge grove of friendtrees had resulted in a blessedly clear pathway heading toward the North Station, and time was a-wasting.

"I vote for calling this a win," said Rosie. "Who's ready to ride?"

Chapter Thirteen

The North Station was a bustling hive of activity, but only Tanrian Marshals Service personnel were present this time—all four chiefs, a handful of marshals milling about, and more engineers than Rosie had seen in one place at any given time. Half of them were gathered around a folding table, going over what she had to assume were technical drawings of the portal, while the other half were actively investigating various aspects of the machinery. Like the West Station's portal, the entire front panel had been removed and set off to the side.

Gone were the festive environment and the supportive family and friends, which didn't bode well. If the Tanrian castaways were going to escape today, surely more people would be here.

The fact that the vines seemed to be growing around the portal at an alarming rate wasn't a great sign either.

Maguire and the other chiefs looked rumpled and sleep-deprived as they conferred with one another. There was a buffet table behind them with a canopy set up overhead and a grill to the side. Rosie spotted Maguire's wife, Diane, filling a plate under the canopy. A moment later, she interrupted the chief's discussion to hand the giant fortifying meal to her spouse. Rosie couldn't hear them, but she could easily narrate their conversation.

You need to eat.

I'm fine. I'll eat later.

You're no good to anyone if you wear yourself out. Now eat.

Despite being a sweet, diminutive woman, Diane Belinder was the only person who could strong-arm Alma Maguire into doing anything. The chief caved and took a bite of her hamburger, and her wife dabbed away the mustard from the corner of her mouth. The entire scene was charmingly domestic.

Duckers shuddered. "It's so disturbing when you have to see your boss as a real person with a real life."

"Great couple, though."

"Yeah, Diane's the nicest," agreed Zeddie. "Are we ringing the bell?"

"I'll do it," said Rosie, but she paused when she noticed a vine snaking close to the lever she needed to pull. It was translucent, but it was no longer blurry. She was definitely looking at a plant, one she could see with increasing detail.

"Is it me, or are the thorns getting longer and sharper?"

"It's definitely you," said Duckers.

"You can't even see it."

"Exactly."

She couldn't argue with that, so she rang the bell to alert Maguire et al. of their arrival.

The chief hurriedly handed her plate to Diane and took a notebook and pen from a marshal in the hubbub that followed. She jotted down a few words on the paper and held it up for the inadvertent prisoners to read.

Is everyone all right?

Y-E-S, Rosie answered in Marks Code.

Duckers gave her a strong side-eye.

"You want me to tell her in Marks Code that I died again? Do you know how long it would take to spell that out?"

Maguire flipped the page and scribbled another note.

Portal is functional but flickering. Working on it. Hang tight.

"For how long?" asked Zeddie.

Duckers clenched his teeth in irritation, but Rosie thought it was a good question.

H-O-W L-O-N-G, she signaled.

The question was simple enough, but answering it involved Maguire conferring with the engineers and the other chiefs for an unsettling amount of time. The answer, when it came, was equally unsettling:

Unknown.

Zeddie burst into a fit of laughter. Rosie looked at him with concern.

"Come on," he said. "You have to admit, it's fucking hilarious."

His laugh was infectious, and the next thing Rosie knew, she was giggling along with him.

"We're still here!" she wheezed.

"Right? Let's ride for hours and hours through an overgrown forest only to be met with a big pile of not-going-anywhere!"

By now, Adam was peering into the opened fail-safe hatch with the crank dangling out of it, the one Rosie had broken on Sorrowsday. It felt like a lifetime ago, which seemed deeply comical at the moment and made her laugh even harder, which made Zeddie laugh even harder. And then Duckers lost it, too, and the three of them had to hold each other up because they were laughing so hard.

Meanwhile, an unamused Adam Lee examined the portal and behaved as the only functioning adult left.

"How's it looking, Doc?" Zeddie asked between gasps for air.

"Grim," Adam answered succinctly, inspiring fresh peals of laughter from the other three.

"Hey, RoFo, where are the thorns?" said Duckers.

Rosie indicated a thicket to the left of the portal. Duckers posed against them and made a face full of comical mock agony.

"What are you doing?" she asked.

"I'm the Briar Thief!"

Rosie, Zeddie, and Duckers howled with pure mirth, while Adam took off his glasses and rubbed his eyes. Rosie wasn't sure if he was tired of his companions or just plain tired, but she sobered up and nudged Duckers to do the same.

Taking the hint, Zeddie dug a parcel from his saddlebag and asked, "Who's up for some lunch?"

For the next several hours, the mood remained high as Rosie, Duckers, and Zeddie played cards, sang, and argued about the lore of the *Old Gods* comics series. Adam spent the time futzing with the portal and, more often than not, jotting down notes to send to the engineers on the off chance they wound up stuck in Tanria for one more night.

That chance looked more and more likely as the sun wheeled westward.

"I hate to say it, but I suspect we're in for another fun night in Barracks Town," said Duckers, trying to maintain a cheery demeanor.

"No. Nope," said Zeddie.

"Come on, Z—I mean, Zeddie, we—"

"The Dragon's Lair is maybe ten miles from here. And that's a good road, right?"

"So?"

"So, do you know what's at the Dragon's Lair? Fresh vegetables, the best cuts of meat, butter, cheese, wine, all going to waste while we eat hot dogs at the barracks? I don't think so. Who wants real food tonight?"

Rosie's hand shot into the air, and when Duckers and Adam continued to stare at Zeddie like he had a third arm growing out of his head, she thrust her other hand in the air.

"What's wrong with you eggheads? Of course we want real food! And I say that as the only person present who does not actually require food to keep living. Put your hands in the air!"

"What in Old Hell am I doing? Count me in." Duckers raised his hand.

Everyone looked to Adam. He stared them down, his face a cool mask while the gods knew what churned behind his poised exterior. He simply said, "No."

"It's not that far," reasoned Duckers.

"And there's wine," said Zeddie.

"We should stay close to the portal in case I or the engineers are able to repair it."

Maguire held up her notebook for the first time in hours.

Progress made, but everyone's exhausted. Sending people home. But we will get you out.

Any humor that lingered in the air evaporated.

"I vote we call it a day and have a decent meal," said Zeddie.

Ignoring Maguire's note, Adam tinkered inside the frame. "I don't think it's a good idea."

"What part of *the professional chef is cooking* don't you understand, though?" asked Duckers, genuinely confused rather than snarky.

"Plus, dragons," Rosie added.

Adam hissed a curse, baring his teeth, his whole body suddenly alive with fury. "I said no!" he shouted before chucking his pliers and storming off along the main road toward the nearest barracks, leaving his companions stunned in his wake.

"What just happened?" asked Zeddie.

"I think we broke him," said Duckers.

Rosie trotted down the path, quickly catching up to the runaway inventor. He stared straight ahead as he continued to march forward, not deigning to look in her direction as she fell into step beside him.

"Adam."

He didn't acknowledge her. He kept walking.

"What's wrong?"

"I can't."

"You can't what?"

He stopped but said nothing. Rosie could tell he was chewing on something big and difficult, so she kept her lips sealed as she waited him out. At last, he spoke, his entire demeanor as thorny as the mysterious briar that seemed to be taking over Tanria.

"They call it the Dragon's Lair—a restaurant. Isn't that cute? Isn't that clever? Dragons slaughtered entire villages during the War of the Gods, but now it's a joke to you people."

Rosie's hackles rose, but she forced herself to consider his words and the manner in which they were uttered. Because in this moment, Adam Lee was not being cagey for a change. Whether he knew it or not, he had, for the moment, ceased to hide behind his usual facade.

"I don't think anyone is trying to diminish what happened in the war," she answered carefully. "The Tanrian dragons aren't the same as the Old Gods' battle dragons."

"Intriguing theory, one which I have no interest in testing."

"You're afraid," Rosie realized aloud.

Adam glared at her, but he trembled, a good indication that she was right. Rosie couldn't do much about their current predicament, but she could at least assuage his fears.

"Do you know what Duckers calls the Tanrian dragons? 'The purse dogs of the gods.' They are the toy poodles of the dragon world. I'm telling you, these things are safe as kittens in a basket. And they're cute. Straight-up adorable."

"Then go without me."

"Adam—"

"You have no idea. You don't understand."

"Then help me understand."

"Why do you care?"

"Because I do. I care. Ta-da!"

He opened his mouth and promptly shut it again before he cried out and bent double, grasping his loose pant legs in tight fists. He panted for half a minute until the agony subsided and he caught his breath once more.

"That's it!" burst Rosie. "What is going on? What is this fucking 'health condition'? Does it have anything to do with those scars on your back?"

"I am perfectly well," he lied, as if she couldn't see his drawn face with her own two red eyes.

"Grapshit! Tell me one thing that's true about you! One thing, Adam. I'm begging you."

He looked so breakable it made Rosie's chest hurt.

"One thing?" he asked.

"Preferably more, but sure. Let's start with one."

"I fucking hate dragons," he told her, his voice rougher than usual.

A tenderness in Rosie's chest pulsed, growing larger by the second. She wanted to sit across a table from this short, slender, nearsighted man with less-than-pristine teeth and a hard outer coating. She wanted to look at his face in the candlelight as Zeddie Birdsall set down a five-star meal before them. She wanted to share a quiet corner with him and take the time to appreciate the amalgamation of supposed imperfections that somehow added up to a man who was achingly beautiful to behold.

"Come to dinner," she urged him. "The restaurant overlooks the lake where the dragons hang out, but they're homebodies. They stay close to the preserve, and they've never hurt anyone."

This was not entirely true. One of them had smacked around a few mobsters while rescuing Frank Ellis a few years ago, but Rosie decided to keep that tidbit to herself.

"Think of the deflated soufflé Zeddie made. Imagine what he could do with an entire kitchen at his disposal. Come on. Have dinner with us."

Adam had yet to don the tattered remains of his cold-blooded exterior, so Rosie could see the instant he began to cave. Without thinking, she pounced, taking his hand in hers, and all their previous hand-touching came flooding in on contact. Rosie could still feel Adam's thumb brush the back of her hand. She could recall in perfect detail the feel of his hand in hers as she bandaged the cut on his palm with the handkerchief he had then kept.

He nodded, a gesture that seemed more like defeat than acquiescence.

"Thank you," she told him, giving that elegant hand a squeeze before relinquishing it. She was unnerved by how much she did not want to let go.

You like him, Duckers teased her in her memory.

And that is very inconvenient right now, she informed him in her brain.

They walked back to where they'd left Duckers and Zeddie, neither of them speaking. Rosie couldn't shake the feeling of his hand in hers, the way his touch sparked a sensibility that she hadn't felt in such a long time. Years. Decades. She wanted to ask him about the handkerchief, where it was now, and why he had held on to it to begin with. But the concession from Adam to go to the Dragon's Lair was fragile at best, so she decided not to push her luck.

Since when does Rosie Fox not push her luck? she wondered.

Chapter Fourteen

The salmon is iffy, but everything else here is in play," Zeddie happily declared as he surveyed the state of his kitchen at the Dragon's Lair. Now that he was in his element, he seemed far more confident and at ease than Rosie had ever seen him. Of course, the only time Rosie had encountered Zeddie Birdsall before they trudged all over Tanria together was at his father's funeral. She remembered her mental note to punch Duckers in the arm and made a mental note to remember her mental note as soon as she was able to get a word alone with her partner.

Zeddie rubbed his hands together as he giddily contemplated the menu. "I'm thinking we should go with the rib eye, maybe with a spicy mustard on the side? Let's knock out this asparagus before it goes limp on us and maybe throw in some carrots for color. Are we feeling polenta or potatoes for our starch?"

"I think we're feeling ravenous about any of this," answered Rosie, increasingly gladdened by their choice to decamp to the Dragon's Lair for the evening, even if a certain attractively competent inventor was crabby about it.

"You," Zeddie said to Adam. "You strike me as the only person here who can be trusted with a knife, and I could use a sous-chef."

"Hey," protested Duckers.

"No offense, Pen, but I've seen you chop onions."

"Ten years ago."

Zeddie raised a single eyebrow at him. Duckers thinned his lips, but he let the nickname and the criticism pass without comment.

"Duckers and I are going to make this place sleepable while you two do your thing," said Rosie. "This joint is nicer than all the barracks of Tanria combined."

"We're staying here tonight?" asked Adam, his body gone rigid. It was subtle, but Rosie knew him well enough now that she saw it. He startled when she put a hand at his back and ushered him toward the door leading to the dining room. His warm flesh beneath the ugly uniform shirt was slight but solid, and only then did it occur to her that maybe she shouldn't assume she could touch him like this.

Too late now.

"Zeddie, can we borrow your sous-chef for a minute?" Rosie didn't wait for an answer. Remembering the scars on Adam's back—and wishing she could figure out a reasonably sensitive way to ask him about them—she took him by the shoulders instead and gently but firmly guided him into the restaurant proper, with Duckers coming along for the ride since she had, after all, said *we*.

"Where are we going?" he asked.

"It's about time for sunset, right?"

"I think so." A bright smile spread across his face as he understood what Rosie was getting at. "Let's go have a look."

"A look at what?" asked Adam.

"You'll see."

Rosie guided him across the restaurant floor. As they approached the terrace door, however, Adam balked the way he had when Zeddie first floated the idea of coming to the Dragon's Lair. But Rosie had moved him then, and she had every intention of moving him now.

"Once you see them, you won't be afraid anymore."

Duckers, catching on to the issue, joined in the fray. "Aw man, the dragons are great! They're like toy poodles in sweaters, except they're vegetarian. And they don't wear sweaters. And they don't fit on your lap. You can't come to Tanria and *not* see the dragons."

Unlike his partner, Duckers had no compunction about grabbing Adam by the arm and escorting him—or possibly dragging him—out the terrace door. Rosie scrabbled to catch up, and the three of them burst onto the wide veranda that overlooked Lake Vanderlinden, where the dragons spent most of their daylight hours before flying off to their nests at sundown.

Adam pulled himself free of Duckers's grip and plastered himself against the far wall, while Rosie and her partner stepped up to the railing for a better view. The Dragon's Lair perched on a ridge to the east of the lake, affording an excellent view of the sunset. Tonight's show was spectacular, with the Painter coloring the long fingers of wispy clouds over the horizon in pinks and purples and oranges. A handful of dragons swanned on the water below, floating gracefully on the surface, a few bobbing their heads in the lake for plants to eat. The pale light shimmered on their iridescent pink scales.

"I never get sick of this," said Rosie.

Duckers hummed in agreement. "It's been months since Maguire assigned us to preserve duty. We should get on her about that. Assuming we still have a job when all this is over."

"Hope for the best." Rosie decided to skip the part about expecting the worst. She turned and extended her hand to Adam, who had become one with the wall. It was like holding out her hand to a stray dog without knowing if she was about to make a new friend or get her hand bitten off.

Apparently, the dog wasn't biting today, because Adam took a step away from the wall, then another and another, the set of his angular jaw determined as he took her hand and came to stand between her and Duckers.

The scene before them was serene. The strange night calls of exotic Tanrian birds filled the air, along with the rhythmic grapping of graps in the cattails bordering the water. Hatching season was long over, but there was a mother dragon with a sweet, overgrown fledgling swimming in her wake and a mated pair near the shore, grooming each other.

"See?" said Rosie, acutely aware of Adam's hand in hers. "They're nothing like the ones we read about in storybooks growing up, are they?"

"No, they're not," he murmured.

The mother dragon chirped to her baby—the *meep meep* call that always struck Rosie as comically incongruous, given the size of the creatures. The little one climbed onto its mother's back, and the adult shook out her fuzzy antlers before sprinting across the reflective surface and taking to the sky.

Adam recoiled, but Rosie held tight to him as the other two dragons followed suit. They were many yards away from the three human beings on the terrace as they wheeled through the air on huge pink wings and careened toward their nests deep in the Dragon's Teeth mountain range. Several moments passed with Rosie, Duckers, and Adam staring after them in awed silence.

When the dragons disappeared from view, Rosie turned to Adam. He looked wan and shaken as he took his hand from hers, and she wondered if she had made a horrible mistake, bringing him out here to face his fear.

"Better?" she asked, more plea than question.

He nodded, the barest movement of his head. "I had better help Zeddie" was all he said before walking slowly across the veranda to the restaurant door.

"Don't let him bully you," Duckers called after him. "He's a monster when it comes to mincing garlic."

"Noted," said Adam before he exited through the veranda door.

"Did my eyes deceive me, or did Dr. Lee experience a facial expression?" asked Duckers once Adam was out of earshot.

"Quit being mean."

"I'm not being mean. That was a legit question. What was up with the tragic face? Everyone knows the Tanrian dragons are nice."

"They are big, though. Hey, before I forget."

Rosie punched Duckers in the arm.

"Ow! What the fuck, RoFo?"

"That was for glaring at Zeddie earlier."

"What are you talking about? I've been playing so nice!"

"Play nicer."

"Salt Sea." Duckers rubbed his arm. "Come on, Little Miss Teacher's Pet. If we're supposed to make the Dragon's Lair sleepable, we should get to it."

"You think Dr. Lee is into me?" Rosie asked casually, the way she might say, *Oh, this dress? I've had it for years.*

"Paging Clueless, party of one."

With that parting shot, Duckers broke away from her and scooted down the hall before Rosie could punch him in the arm again.

Perfectly roasted asparagus and balsamic-glazed carrots on a bed of creamy, buttery polenta. Rib eye so tender it melted in Rosie's mouth. Bold red wine that sang on her tongue without leaving behind a nasty tannin residue. Crème brûlée served with coffee brewed to perfection. And then more wine. All of it served in the wood-paneled main room of the Dragon's Lair with its gorgeous polished oak tables and hand-carved chairs with red silk seat cushions and an extravagant chandelier with sparkling crystal tears refracting light into tiny rainbows. The only luxury they lacked was the presence of professional musicians softly playing the pre-modern instruments left behind on a small dais off to the side.

"This might be the greatest meal of my life," Rosie declared as she hovered on the verge of a food-induced coma.

"It ranks high for me as well," marveled Adam, evidently surprised to be eating a meal this good, in Tanria or otherwise.

Rosie had wanted to sit across from him at a candlelit table, but now that she had her wish, she wasn't sure it was such a great idea after all. She couldn't look at him, because if she looked at him, she would moon over the way the candlelight warmed his skin and flattered the poetic lines of his face. And if she mooned over Adam Lee, her partner and dear friend was sure to take note. And if Duckers noticed how utterly besotted she was, he'd be like a dog with a bone, urging her to make her move. And if she made a move and Adam was not receptive to that move, she would have to live with the humiliating rejection while being trapped inside a literal prison with him for an "unknown" amount of time. So Rosie, keeping her usual lack of impulse control in check, forced herself to stop ogling the enticingly mercurial man sitting across from her.

It was torture, but a nice, boozy torture. Thanks to the unending wine coming her way grâce à Zeddie Birdsall, she had maintained slight inebriation for a solid ninety minutes.

Realizing that Duckers had yet to thank Zeddie for the meal, Rosie kicked him under the table. He glared at her, but he raised his glass in a vague toast that seemed to be directed at the opposite wall as opposed to the person who had created this edible miracle in the midst of a full-blown crisis.

"Compliments to the chef," said Rosie on her partner's behalf.

"Cheers," said Adam, a toast as small and contained as he was himself.

Zeddie flushed with pleasure and shrugged in humility. "I do my best."

"He-e-ey, mail delivery," called Gobbo before he entered the main room of the restaurant, his shirt fringe swinging, his mail-bag slung across his chest. He surveyed the restaurant, nodding his approval. "So this is where you all ended up? Dudes, I love this place. This place is swanky."

"How are things on the outside?" asked Duckers, pulling out a chair for the dik-dik.

Gobbo plopped himself down as if his weary bones had given out on him. "Stressful, man. The vibe is killing me. And, like, the plant is messing with my ability to get in and out of Tanria."

With that depressing news, he pulled up the flap on his satchel and began distributing letters like a dealer at a card table.

"Does anyone have tip money?" Rosie glanced around at her companions, lingering last and longest on Adam. Their attention snagged on each other for longer than was socially acceptable before Adam swallowed, the lump in his throat bobbing as he shook his head. And now that Rosie had noticed how prominent that lump was, she had the inconvenient urge to lick it, kiss it, nip it playfully with her teeth.

She averted her eyes and said "So, tip?" to the whole group, her pitch too high and her volume too loud.

"Would you take some ludicrously expensive wine in place of cash, Gobbo?" suggested Zeddie, picking up an as yet unopened bottle of red from the table.

Gobbo took it, nodding in appreciation. "Sweet. Oh, one more thing." He unearthed a large cardboard box from his bag and set it down in front of Rosie.

"Oh, oh, oh! Is this...?" She untied the twine and peered inside the box. "It is!"

"What is it?" asked Duckers, drunkenly amused.

"I sent a letter to Hart and Mercy last night asking them to check on my apartment and to pack up some real clothes for me." Rosie held a soft cambric shirt with its sweet mother-of-pearl buttons to her chin, hugging it to her along with the memory of being able to wear whatever she wanted to work. She draped it fastidiously over a nearby chair and took out her beloved brown leather pinch-front hat, which she placed on her head. "Fare thee well, shitty Tanrian Marshals Service flat-top hat," she said, sighing in contentment.

She read the enclosed letter before digging into the box's remaining contents.

Dear Rosie,

Hart and I and the girls checked on your apartment yesterday and picked up your mail. Everything looks fine. Bea and Lottie loved your place so much that we about had to scrape them off your belongings with a spatula. We refilled the dish on your altar and touched salt water to your mother's key. We'll keep looking in until you're able to come home (soon!).

Per your instructions, I've packed up some of your clothes for you. I'm sure I went overboard on the underwear, but if I were in your shoes, I'd want as much clean underwear in my arsenal as possible. Speaking of shoes, I packed your ostrich leather boots, too. (Have I ever told you how much I love these boots? Don't tell Hart, but I'm tempted to marry them.)

I do all of this in the faith that you won't need much, if any, of it—I know we'll get you out of Tanria any minute now. We can't wait to see you and hug you.

Love,
Mercy, Hart, Bea, and Lottie

P.S.—Do you have a cat? There was a gray-and-black cat yowling and scratching at your kitchen window. I wasn't too sure what to do with him, so I fed him a can of tuna I found in the cupboards. I hope that's okay!

Rosie could imagine Mercy and Hart and the kids letting themselves in the front door with the spare key, the way the girls would squeal at the sight of so much feminine decor—beads hanging from mantels, big fluffy pillows with embroidery in vivid colors, candles and vases and artwork and dried flowers. She wondered if Bea and Lottie had invaded her closet to dress up in her scarves and hats and high-heeled shoes the way Rosie had tried on all of Jocelyn's pretty things when she was a kid.

An insidious voice in the back of her mind whispered that she might never see Bea and Lottie again, or Hart and Mercy. She tamped down the sudden dread as best she could and returned her attention to the box. She pulled out two more neatly folded shirts, three pairs of high-waisted denim trousers cut lean enough to tuck into her beloved ostrich-hide boots. And there, wrapped in tissue, was a collection of Rosie's pride and joy—seven matching sets of clean, luxurious brassieres and panties in a rainbow of silks and satins and lace.

She clutched as many as she could hold in her long hands and held them to her heart. "Bride of Fortune, thank you, Mercy Birdsall!"

Adam stood so quickly that his chair toppled over. "I'll wash the dishes," he announced, picking up his plate and utensils and the platter closest to him before speed-walking to the kitchen.

Rosie watched the door swing shut behind him. "That was sudden."

"Clueless," Duckers coughed into his fist.

"There's a message from Maguire here," said Gobbo. "I was going to give it to the stone-cold sexy little guy who doesn't get mail, but like, he left."

Rosie surveyed the paper loot that the nimkilim had dropped off. She had her package as well as letters from the Ellises, and both Duckers and Zeddie had a thick stack of mail from concerned loved ones. But Adam had nothing, which was probably why he had secreted himself in the kitchen. It had to feel shitty to watch other people receive love and support when you evidently had none to speak of. Surely someone had at least notified the University of Quindaro of the situation. How could he have no mail?

"I'll take it," Rosie told the nimkilim, the ache in her chest labeled *Adam* growing achier. She read the note aloud.

To Marshals Fox and Duckers, Dr. Lee, and Mr. Birdsall,
I've received your report re: the possible plant that you're seeing in Tanria. Given the fact that you began to see whatever this is when the portals started to break down, Marshal Fox, I think it best to gather as much information as you can. I want a detailed description of what you're seeing. Try to make a decent drawing of it, if you can. I want to know where you're finding it and how fast it appears to be growing, especially in the vicinity of the portals. And if you can figure out a way to get it out of the portals, so much the better.

As you know, we are coordinating our efforts at the North Station's portal, which appears to be the best candidate for repair. While it is not yet fully operational, the engineers inform me that they are making good progress. (Thank you for your helpful notes, Dr. Lee.)

In the meantime, the Joint Chiefs of the Tanrian Marshals are investigating an alternative method of getting you out of Tanria. Specifically, we are in the process of acquiring a handful of pirated portals, but this will take time, as we have to work in cooperation with the Federated Islands of Cadmus's Bureau of Investigation and, sadly, the Galatian mob. But this is all to say that we are far from giving up, and we hope that you are keeping the faith that we will get you out of there.

We will continue to send supplies and anything else you might need or want. We ask that the four of you stay together for easier communication. Please report your whereabouts, well-being, and any other matters through Gobbo. We'll see you soon.

Sincerely,
Alma Maguire

" 'Sincerely' and her first name. Salt Sea, that's bleak," said Duckers.

"I love that they're breaking the law for us. Getting a portal from the Galatian mob? Life goals," Rosie joked, but that insidious voice of doom inside her was getting louder.

"Does this mean that we're stuck here? Like, indefinitely?" asked Zeddie, visibly deflating.

"Yes, Zeddie, that's what it means," said Duckers in a long-suffering voice. "Do you need one of us to fetch the smelling salts?"

"That was uncalled for," Rosie snapped at him.

"Yeah, ouch, man," added Gobbo.

"Give me a break! He's the reason we're stuck here, in case you have forgotten, so can we please stop coddling the baby?"

Zeddie set his wine goblet on the table with hefty deliberation. "Right. I'm a baby. I am aware of that, because my whole life, that's how everyone has treated me: like a fucking baby. *Zeddie's so young. Zeddie's so feckless. Zeddie doesn't know what he wants or what he's doing, because he's the baby.* Well, news flash, Penrose: I'm thirty-two years old now. I have a bank account and a budget and a retirement plan and a career, and I'm about to have a mortgage, if I ever get the fuck out of here. I worked hard to get where I am, and I did it all by myself like a big boy. I'm sorry that we're trapped here. I'm sorry that I fucked us over with my fucking soufflé. You have no idea how sorry I am. But I made that mistake because I'm a human being, not because I'm a child. Now, if you'll excuse me, I'm going to go clean up the kitchen with Adam like the responsible fucking adult I am."

He stood and dabbed his lips with his napkin before taking himself off to the kitchen, leaving a thick silence behind him.

"Du-u-ude," said Gobbo. "That was rough. I'm out. See you guys tomorrow, if I can get through the thorns."

Rosie folded her arms and glared at Duckers as Gobbo left through the front door. When her partner continued to push a carrot around his plate without meeting her eye, she said, "That was unacceptable. You need to go talk to Zeddie and set things right."

"It's not my job to make him feel better. He *is* a baby. He will always be a baby."

"You're acting like he done you dirty. *You* dumped *him*, Penny-D, not the other way around."

"I am allowed to be pissed off right now. We're trapped here because of him."

"No, we're trapped here because the portals broke down, probably due to an invasive, semi-invisible plant that is taking over Tanria. It's not like you to take out your stress on someone else, so quit being pissy with Zeddie."

Duckers leaned against the chairback with a sigh. "I think I'm more pissy with myself than with him, to be honest. I dumped the guy, and I know it was the right thing to do at the time, but I never had to face the consequences, you know? He left, and I moved on. Being around him now dredges up the past, and I feel guilty, because I know I shattered his heart into a million pieces ten years ago. And then that crap with the soufflé happened, and now we're stuck here and, ugh, it's fucking awkward."

"Okay, but you feeling guilty isn't his fault. Heartbreak is an inevitable part of life, and even if you did shatter his heart into a million pieces, look what a good job he did putting himself back together."

"I guess." Duckers rubbed at a spot on his wineglass that wasn't there, and Rosie experienced the rare thrill of getting to be the one to see right through her friend rather than vice versa.

"Ooooooh. I get it," she said smugly.

"What?"

"You're not mad at him about the soufflé. You're mad because he got over you. You thought sweet little Zeddie Birdsall was pining away on Medora, when in reality, he was killing it in his career and moving on without you. And by the looks of it, he's been working out, too, because he is jacked. Did he always look like that?"

"No, the whole jacked thing is new, but if I don't get to short-shame your boyfriend, you don't get to objectify my ex."

"Step off. Adam is not my boyfriend."

"Oh yeah? Do you always hold hands with not-your-boyfriends?"

"He needed moral support!"

Duckers flapped his hand at Rosie. "Here, hold my hand, RoFo. Spread some of that moral support around."

She smacked his hand away. "We're not talking about me. We're talking about you, and how it's a blow to your ego that your ex got over you, even though you still find him attractive."

"Everyone finds him attractive. He's universally attractive. That doesn't make being trapped in Tanria with my ex suck less, especially since he can barely ride an equimaris without falling off."

"Again, not his fault."

"Yeah, yeah, yeah." Duckers toyed with his wineglass, rolling the stem in his fingertips. "Sounds like Maguire wants you to take a good look around Tanria for this plant, and I don't think you should go it alone."

"Don't you worry. I am making you come with me."

"We'll have to cover a lot of miles in shitty terrain. If we keep this up, Saltlicker is going to go rogue."

Rosie walked to the windows that overlooked Lake Vanderlinden and stared out, even though it was too dark to see anything.

"If only we had a faster, more efficient way to get around Tanria," she said, her eyes glinting with evil glee. She turned to Duckers, who looked at her in confusion before he mirrored her sinister smile.

"Fuck yeah," he breathed.

"But first, get your ass into that kitchen and apologize to Zeddie."

"Ugh," he said as he got to his feet. "I hate it when you're right."

Duckers went into the kitchen as soon as Adam came out of it.

"Hey," Rosie heard him say to Zeddie, and she caught Zeddie's answering "Hey" before the kitchen door swung shut. She scurried over to press her ear to the wood.

"What are you doing?" Adam asked her.

"Eavesdropping, clearly."

"Why?"

Rosie waved at him to turn down the volume. "I want to make sure Duckers apologizes and doesn't weasel out of it."

"Why does he need to apologize?"

Exasperated, Rosie turned to him with a finger to her lips. She was about to press her ear to the door again when Duckers pushed it open, smacking her in the face.

"Ow!" She rubbed her sore cheekbone and scowled at her friend.

"Serves you right. I can handle this solo. Shoo."

"Is something wrong?" Adam asked Rosie as the door swung shut again.

"They got into a tiff after you left the room."

"Ah. Young love." He sounded wistful.

"Have you ever been in love?"

He hesitated before answering, "Perhaps."

"I'm not going to get any more from you than that, am I?"

"No, you will not."

"That's all right. I need to tell you about our brilliant idea, anyway." She highlighted the words *brilliant idea* with sparkle fingers before diving into her sales pitch.

"No, absolutely not," Adam said before she was twenty seconds in. It was amazing how daunting he could be when he chose to be imperious.

"They're literally made for riding."

"No, they're literally made for killing people."

"What's literally made for killing people?" asked a far more relaxed Duckers as he and an equally relaxed Zeddie emerged from the kitchen. Apparently the apology went well.

"He thinks the dragons are going to kill us," explained Rosie.

"Are you kidding? They're like big pink plushies."

By now, Adam had reverted to his cold, blank exterior. But Rosie knew that a roiling mass of emotions hid beneath the surface, especially when it came to dragons. Some people feared spiders. Adam Lee feared giant flying lizards that spat glitter. She couldn't fault him for it.

"What are we talking about?" asked Zeddie.

"Rosie's supposed to gather intel on the plants, so we want to try getting around Tanria on dragons," explained Duckers.

"That makes sense, I guess."

Adam stared at Zeddie with mild incredulity. "Flying makes sense to you?"

"I've heard the dragons are nice—nicer than equimares, right? It's worth a shot."

"Excellent point, Mr. Birdsall," said Rosie.

"No, not excellent." The more upset Adam got, the colder he became, like iron left outside in winter.

"I'm going to test-drive a dragon first to make sure it's safe before Duckers takes one out for a spin. What's the worst that could happen?"

"You could fall. You could—" He stopped himself, but Rosie finished the thought for him.

"Break my neck and die?"

"I'm aware that you cannot die, but you can get hurt, as we have seen. And I don't think any of us want to witness that again. So perhaps we should not encourage Marshal Fox to fly on a pink behemoth." He addressed the last bit to Duckers and Zeddie, like a stuffy school principal trying to shame a couple of ne'er-do-wells.

"Speak for yourself, Doc. *I'm* flying on a pink behemoth," said Duckers.

"How do you steer, though?" asked Zeddie. "Are there bridles and reins for these things?"

"Nah, their antlers are empathic. You hold on to their horns, think about where you want to go, and that's where they go."

"Can I try it?"

"No," said Adam. "None of you should try it."

Rosie spoke to him with as much patience as she could muster. "I get that you're not thrilled about this, but the vines are making it hard for me to see where I'm going on the ground, and if Maguire wants a full report, I need to be able to get around. And, gods forbid, if we have to head to one of the other portals for some reason, it's going to take time we may not have to ride on equimarisback the whole way. This is not about good ideas or bad ideas or who's right and who's wrong. This is a logical solution to a difficult problem."

"You don't care about logic. You just want to fly."

"That, too."

"This is a terrible idea."

"And yet we are going to do it. And so will you, if the necessity arises."

Adam went so stony that Rosie's words seemed to smack into him and stagger away half-conscious and bleeding. He turned and stalked off toward one of the sleeping areas Rosie and Duckers had set up in the restaurant's four corners, where they had tacked tablecloths to the low ceiling, creating small "rooms" for privacy.

"He'll come around," said Rosie.

Both Duckers and Zeddie scoffed.

Chapter Fifteen

I call dibs on Mary Georgina. She's my girl," said Duckers as he and Rosie hiked to the Tanrian Dragon Preserve, leaving Zeddie behind with the disapproving genius.

"I don't care which one I get, because I'm going to be mother-fucking flying. But I'm serious about test-driving one first. I promised Adam."

"Oh yes. *Adam.*"

"Don't start with me."

"Start what? I think it's sweet that you're on a first-name basis with the good professor."

Rosie grumbled under her breath, which amused Duckers even more.

"Dang, you have it bad for this guy. It's never been this easy to tease you."

"Feel free to not tease me, then."

"RoFo, how many times have you croaked on me over the years? How many times have you croaked on me *in the past ten days*? You owe me my fun."

It was a beautiful morning with a cloudless blue sky overhead. The hike was an easy one, since the roads around the preserve were well used and kept in good order, thanks to a robust tour-ist trade. For Rosie's part, the fact that she was wearing her own clothing—a soft cambric shirt in a flattering muted shade of turquoise, specially ordered high-waisted denim tucked into the butter-soft leather of her teal ostrich-hide boots, all worn over the magnificent intimates hidden beneath—made her feel a million times more optimistic about their prospects for getting out of here sooner rather than later.

She had also dabbed her wrists and neck with the lavender scent that Mercy had included in the box of material joy. If she couldn't be at home, she could at least smell like home. And perhaps a teeny-tiny part of her had had Adam's cologne on the brain when she had unstoppered the bottle this morning.

Her hat, however, she left at the Dragon's Lair; she had no reason to wear it when she was about to fly.

They arrived at the north end of Lake Vanderlinden after a twenty-minute walk. Normally, the only way to access the north lakeshore was via the dracological research center, but there was an access road used by the Tanrian Marshals assigned to preserve duty. Of course, Rosie and Duckers were not currently assigned to preserve duty and, therefore, did not have the key to the gate of said access road. What they did have was a bolt cutter from Adam's tool kit, which Duckers used to cut through the old-style padlock with a satisfying *ka-chunk*.

"It's not considered breaking and entering if we're law enforcement officers, right?"

"Act first, think never," said Rosie. "Let's go."

They trekked along the access road and made it to the shore in time for the dragons to come flying in from their nests for their daily routine of gliding on the water and sunning themselves on the shore. The dragon population of Tanria was small, but there were a good two dozen out and about this morning, chirping their cute dragon chirps, their pink scales iridescent in the morning sunlight.

One of the dragons farther out on the water lifted her head, whiffed the air, and perked up. Her tail lifted and began to wag, and her antlers quivered with excitement.

Duckers cupped his hands around his mouth and hollered, "Mary Georgina-a-a!"

Meep! Meep! Chirr-chirrup! cheeped the dragon in a high-pitched tweet that did not match her enormous size before she sailed across the lake toward them, posthaste. Duckers jumped up and down at the water's edge, pumping his fist in the air and cheering as the dragon came tearing at him. She knocked him over like a mind-bogglingly large and enthusiastic golden retriever and snuffled his neck affectionately.

"I missed you, too, darlin'," he told her in a passable imitation of Frank Ellis, who had raised this particular dragon from a hatchling. It was difficult to comprehend that this six-ton pink lizard had been small enough to attach herself to Ellis's torso ten years ago, but since Duckers had been partnered up with Frank Ellis and Twyla Banneker at the time, Rosie had no choice but to believe it.

Another dragon swam in, larger and statelier than Mary Georgina, curiously sniffing the newcomers from a distance that respected personal boundaries.

Duckers crawled out from underneath Mary Georgina's affection and got to his feet. He nodded toward the other dragon. "I think that's Eloise. She's the one Twyla rode to the rescue that time Frank got kidnapped by the Galatian mob and an evil hedgehog."

"Good times," said Rosie as she stepped forward.

Eloise approached her, tilting her large fox-shaped head as she studied Rosie. If Rosie's intestines could have spoken at that moment, they would have said, *Shit snacks, that thing is a lot bigger than I realized. Shouldn't I be running away?*

She could almost hear her mother's tinkling laugh in her ear.

You're made of sterner stuff than that, my darling rose, Jocelyn had told her on more than one occasion, usually when the other kids teased her at school for her red eyes and her height, but it applied here, too.

Eloise lowered her head and nudged Rosie's hand with her warm snout. Her heart pumping hard with adrenaline, Rosie stroked the top of the dragon's scaly head and beamed when Eloise made a trilling sound like a cat's purr—a much nicer cat than Blammo Tinky Fartface.

Gods, she missed that little asshole.

Pushing the feline-induced heartache to the side, she brushed the dragon's plush salmon-colored antlers, remembering what Duckers had said about their horns being empathic. She could sense the dragon's contentment pulsing through her own veins, at once disconcerting and intoxicating.

"What do you say, Eloise? Are you game?" she asked, trying to convey her intent as she continued to run her fingers along the silky fuzz of the antlers.

The dragon blared a trumpeting call that Rosie hoped was the reptile's version of *Fuck yeah!* and not *How dare you?*

Eloise lowered herself to the ground, her front leg creating a convenient step, as if her body had been designed for it.

"Ha!" whooped Duckers in triumph. "Get on, RoFo!"

She tamped down the mild hysteria bubbling up inside her as she pulled herself onto the step created by the joint in the dragon's leg and hauled herself onto Eloise's back. The depression where head met shoulders seemed tailor-made for a rider. Rosie settled in, letting herself grow accustomed to being so high off the ground.

Because she was about to go a whole lot higher.

With an excited chirp, Eloise flattened her antlers, putting them within easy reach for her rider. Rosie's hands trembled with excitement as she took hold of the silky horns. A sense of calm settled over her then, and she realized that it didn't come from within but from without—from the dragon. Eloise seemed to be telling her, *No worries, sister. I've got you.* And with that, the dragon raised herself to her full height. But rather than taking a running start across the shore, she turned toward the lake. With a single flap of her long wings, she lifted herself so that her webbed feet hit the water's surface, and she took off running, splashing Rosie in the process. The dragon pumped her wings once, twice, and on the third pump, they took to the air. Rosie's stomach lingered several feet below them as they climbed up and up.

"Wooooo!" Duckers cheered from the lakeshore.

A euphoria like nothing Rosie had experienced before filled her veins. She crowed in jubilation as her hair whipped behind her and the air rushed past her ears in a deafening *whoosh*. The steady *whump-whump-whump* of the dragon's wingbeats matched the rhythm of her heart.

Eloise channeled her own excitement through her antlers, as thrilled to have a rider as Rosie was to be the rider. The dragon trumpeted at the same time Rosie whooped, a pair of outlaws out for a rollicking good time. They circled the lake, wheeling thirty, forty, fifty feet in the sky. Below, Duckers clapped his exuberant approval as they passed by him.

Where to? Eloise asked, not in words so much as in pure vibes. Rosie was so stoked to be flying that she didn't care where they went. The dragon chirped and flew farther afield, taking her passenger over the southernmost range of the Dragon's Teeth. How many times had Rosie served tours in the mountains? How different they looked from this perspective—small and insignificant, as if they hadn't burned her lungs a hundred times over when she had climbed their peaks.

Eloise dipped lower, gliding gracefully through mountain valleys to give Rosie a better view.

"Show-off!" Rosie shouted, and she could swear she felt the dragon's laughter through the antlers gripped tightly in her hands.

Something flickered in her peripheral vision as Eloise soared upward once more. Rosie turned her head. The wind whipped her loosened hair into her face, but she could see Duckers plain as day, flying Mary Georgina, and hear his "Woohoo!" over the wind howling past her ears.

Annoyed, she squeezed Eloise's antlers, mentally asking the dragon to find a place to land. This time, Rosie left her stomach above rather than below as Eloise dove, coming in for a sudden (and mildly terrifying) landing in the foothills.

"What are you doing?" Rosie demanded when Duckers and Mary Georgina alighted beside her and Eloise.

"What does it look like I'm doing? I'm flying! Like an eagle! On the back of! A fucking dragon!" He pumped both fists in the air, forcefully reminding Rosie of wee baby Duckers, the kid he had been when they had first partnered up.

Mary Georgina chirred happily, joining in her passenger's excitement.

"But I promised Adam I would test-drive first to make sure it was safe."

"Well, I made no such promises. And let's be real, Dr. Cold Fish cares a lot more about you breaking your neck than me breaking my neck. Which sucks, by the way, because I'm the one who could actually die in that scenario. Come on, RoFo, we're partners. We should be doing this together, right?"

He gave her his best sweet puppy eyes, knowing that Rosie was powerless in the face of such pure Duckersness.

"It's the dream," she reluctantly agreed.

"It's the dream!"

Rosie took Eloise's antlers in hand again. "Hey, Duckers."

"What?"

"Race you!"

Meep-meep chirrup! twittered Eloise as she took off down the hill, leaving Duckers and Mary Georgina in her dust. Rosie heard Duckers shout "Punk!" before her dragon flapped her wings and took to the air once more.

Eloise let Mary Georgina catch up to her, and for the next ten minutes, the two dragons raced each other in the sky across Tanria while their human riders pretended that they were the ones racing, the partners shrieking insults at one another and laughing their fool heads off. But as they flew near the West Station, a stunning proliferation of shadowy vines caught Rosie's eye. Eloise wheeled back and landed so that Rosie could take a better look.

Getting on the dragon was a lot easier than getting off, as it turned out, especially since Rosie's legs had turned to jelly with all the adrenaline coursing through her veins. In the end, she wound up sliding down the dragon's neck as if it were a piece of playground equipment, and she could swear that Eloise laughed at her clumsy landing.

"Hush, you," she told the dragon, who meeped in what sounded like amusement at her expense.

Rosie walked toward the Mist on unsteady feet. The vines now grew so thickly around the West Station's portal that they obscured her view into Bushong. From there, the plant branched out in all directions, threading the Mist in some places with branches as thick around as her arm.

Mary Georgina came in for a landing beside Eloise. Duckers slid down her neck with the same comical gracelessness as Rosie.

"What's up?" he asked her when he joined her by the portal. To him, it must have looked like Rosie was staring at a whole lot of nothing on the other side of the Mist—the West Station, the parking lot, and the dusty Bushong landscape dotted with the occasional acacia. But to Rosie, it looked like a cataclysm.

"I'm officially calling it. This plant is the problem," she said after she explained the situation to her partner.

"Pretty sure we already figured that one out."

"Is it me, or are the vines looking a lot healthier all of a sudden?"

Duckers leaned against the frame, facing Rosie. "It's you, because I can't see them. We've been over this."

"They're growing way faster than any normal plant should."

"Growing in a nice, friendly way or in a they're-coming-to-get-us way?"

"Well, shit, I never considered the possibility that these things could be malevolent. Thanks for planting that terror in my brain, Penny-D."

"If I have to low-key panic on the inside, so do you."

"I'm trying to have a positive outlook here." Rosie stared at the plant as her mind tried to fit together the puzzle pieces of this bizarre situation. "I don't get it. Before, they were scraggly and thorny—and they still are—but now they seem...I don't know...better hydrated? And greener, like they're beginning to bud leaves. Is that a good thing or a bad thing, do you think?"

"I think anything that's good for this plant is bad for us."

"But what changed? These vines show up out of nowhere, and now they're straight-up invasive. What plant food are they eating?"

"No clue. I'm still on 'Where the fuck did these things come from?'"

"And 'How can we send them to Old Hell?'"

"For real."

Rosie raised her hand, which Duckers gamely slapped. "We should probably head back before Adam has a conniption. But if we're stuck here tomorrow, I'm going to do a tour of the Mist. Maybe I can track this thing, figure out where it started and where it's going. For what it's worth."

"If there are benevolent gods, we will not be here tomorrow. But if we are, I'll come with you."

"You don't have to."

"Hello? I'm your partner."

"And flying is fun."

"Fuck yeah, it is." Duckers pushed himself off the frame and gave a start when he glanced at the Bushong side of the Mist. "What's going on over there?"

Rosie found a break in the vines through which she could get a good view of the West Station.

A middle-aged man in a blue dress shirt and khaki slacks stood outside the low, blocky building before a crowd of reporters, his silver hair swept off his high forehead, his pale skin in extraordinarily good condition for someone his age. He looked stoic yet tragic as he spoke, the journalists hanging on his every word. Rosie had never seen him before, but she knew who he was, and though she couldn't hear a thing he was saying, she didn't have to. He was, as ever, full of shit.

She had told him to stay out of her life, yet there he was, a father basking in the glow of his daughter's personal tragedy. It shouldn't have surprised her, much less hurt her, but it managed to do both with searing precision.

"This is so typical," she fumed.

"Do you know who that is?"

"He's..." She couldn't bring herself to say *my father*, so she said "a god" instead.

"Which god is he?"

Rosie didn't say a word, but she could sense the spark plugs of Duckers's brain firing.

"Wait. Is that your dad?"

"You mean the guy who knocked up my mom and then popped in and out of our lives whenever he felt like it to serve his own narcissistic ends while never actually doing a single thing to help either of us? Yeah, that's him."

"Holy shit, I've never seen a bona fide god before."

"God. Bag of dicks. Tomato. To-mah-to."

Rosie glared at the silver fox filling a bunch of journalists' ears with what was sure to be the most self-aggrandizing tale of the century.

Duckers put his hand on her back. "I've said it before and I'll say it again. You don't have to tell me anything."

"He's clearly outing me as his offspring right now to all the world, and I'd rather you heard it from me than the front page of the *Eternity Gazette*. He's the Trickster."

"Your dad is the *Trickster*?"

"Yep."

He gave a long, low whistle and stood quietly by her side, watching the silent scene play out for several moments before he spoke again.

"Thank you for telling me," he said, his friendship as warm and comforting as Rosie's favorite sweater on a crisp autumn day. "Hoo boy, this is a lot to take in. That's an *Old* God out there. Isn't he the last one left?"

"Yeah. He sided with the New Gods in the big war—supposedly—so he didn't wind up in Tanria with the rest of them, and he didn't go to the altar of the night sky when the Old Gods finally caved after being imprisoned for a couple of millennia. Salt Sea, this is just like him. He always has to sweep in and try to rewrite the story so that he's the big hero."

"But isn't he usually the villain in most stories?"

"Do not get him started. The world done him wrong. He is much aggrieved." Rosie watched her father dab a crocodile tear from his eye as he spoke to his rapt audience. "And now he's plastering the details of my life all over the front page of every newspaper from here to Eshil Craia so the whole world can say, *Poor guy! His daughter is stuck inside the Mist, and he is clearly distraught because he loves her so very much!*"

Her emotions got the better of her, and the last few words came out of her mouth a garbled, tearstained mess. She thought of that stupid cat figurine he had sent her, the one with two broken legs that didn't look anything like Blammo Tinky Fartface, and an even stupider sob bubbled up from her lungs.

"Need a hug?" offered Duckers.

"Yes," Rosie cried in a pathetic staccato.

Duckers wrapped his strong arms around her narrow waist, and she nestled her cheek against his tight curls.

"I don't know why I'm being like this," she said, trying not to get snot in his hair. "It's not like him hogging the spotlight is a big shock or anything. I just...I wish he was something other than what he is. I wish he were a real dad instead of some asshole cardboard cutout of a dad. If I had to have an immortal parent, why'd it have to be that jackass? Why couldn't it have been Jocelyn?"

"I'm sorry. I know you miss your mom."

"And I know you miss your dad." Rosie gave him a good squeeze before letting go. "Thank you."

"You good?"

"Good enough. Listen, can we not tell Zeddie and Adam about...him?" Rosie waved a hand toward the Mist without looking at the Trickster again. "I know they'll find out eventually, but..."

"Sure, no problem. I mean, I don't want to talk to one of them, and the other one doesn't want to talk at all, so this'll be easy."

Rosie pointed at his face. "Be nice."

"I'm speaking true facts here," said Duckers, nudging her toward the dragons. "Come on. We should get back to the lake before Dr. Lee turns into a statue of repressed rage."

"Penny-D!"

"I'll be nice, I promise."

The return trip to the lake took only twenty minutes, proving Rosie's theory that dragons were a much more efficient way to get around Tanria, especially if they needed to cover some serious distance.

Zeddie was waiting for them on the lakeshore, jumping and pumping his fist and acting remarkably like Duckers. Maybe there was hope for them yet.

Duckers landed, but as Rosie approached the water, an image filled her mind without thought or intent, the memory of a cold man in need of a three-piece suit and a warm hug, scowling at her as she asked him, *What's the worst that could happen?*

Instead of landing beside her companions, Eloise veered east, straight for the restaurant. Evidently, Rosie's heart was doing the driving rather than her brain.

Adam stood on the veranda, a speck coming into sharp focus as they barreled toward him. He staggered backward when Eloise hovered in the air beside the railing with the powerful beating of her great wings. Rosie leaned over to find Adam pinned to the wall by an anguish that made her insides ache for him. Her own Trickster-inspired hurt seemed paltry by contrast. She wanted to lift that burden from his shoulders, whatever it was that had crushed him and continued to weigh him down, a terrible load that seemed to be represented by the dragon before him.

"Come on. Come closer. She won't hurt you," Rosie said in the soothing tone she had used two years ago to coax Blammo Tinky Fartface to come to his first can of tuna.

Adam shook his head, tears streaming down his cheeks, his mask decimated in the face of the awesome creature hovering before him. The flapping of Eloise's vast wings blew his silver-streaked black hair out of his tragic face in pulse after pulse.

"Adam." Rosie extended her hand to him, even though there was no way for him to reach her.

She didn't think he would move. She didn't think he would come anywhere close to the dragon or to the hand that had been offered to him. And so when he took his first hesitant step and then the next and the next, he might as well have cracked Rosie's chest open and taken her tender heart in his careful grasp. He came all the way to the rail and reached his trembling hand up and up, and Eloise bent her neck to nuzzle that hand and sniff his face and his forehead. Adam closed his eyes as she knocked his glasses loose, letting her catch his scent.

The dragon's antlers communicated sentiments rather than words, so Rosie wasn't certain what Eloise wanted to tell her. The emotion she sent through her rider's bloodstream now was thick and sorrowful. If Rosie had to name it, she would have called it pity.

The effort of hovering in place was beginning to wear out the dragon. Her lungs became a bellows, and sparks of gold glitter plumed from her nostrils. Rosie knew she couldn't ask her to stay here forever. So although she was loath to leave Adam in his precarious emotional state, she communicated to Eloise that they could return to the lake.

She looked over her shoulder as the dragon soared away. Adam stood at the rail, unmoving, growing smaller as the distance grew between them.

And yet she felt closer to him now than she had ever been before.

Chapter Sixteen

Adam wasn't at the Dragon's Lair when they returned, but there was no need to go looking for him, because he'd left a note on the table that the four of them had co-opted as officially theirs.

Went to work on the North Station's portal. I will be back before dinner.

—A. L.

Rosie didn't have to be fluent in Subtext to understand that what the note really said was *I need space. Leave me the fuck alone.*

"So...what should we do now?" asked Zeddie.

Rosie toyed with the end of one of her ruddy braids. "There's nothing much to do but wait."

They stood around the table, silent for a long moment. In the wake of riding dragons—or in Zeddie's case, watching Rosie and Duckers ride dragons—they had come back down to earth, as it were, to the reminder that they remained stuck in a formidable prison, and whether or not they escaped was out of their hands.

"I guess I'll take a nap," said Zeddie.

Duckers slanted a look toward his ex-boyfriend's "bedroom."

"It's stuffy in here. I'm going to go for a walk," he announced as he rolled up his sleeves, revealing the tattoo that contained his soul. Zeddie's gaze lingered on it before Duckers made for the door.

Rosie wondered if either of them knew what their eyeballs were up to.

She picked up Adam's note—the act of holding his neat, compact handwriting thrillingly intimate—and decided that she had no intention of leaving him the fuck alone. She suspected that he had been left the fuck alone in this world for far too long.

"I'll go check on Adam."

Duckers paused at the restaurant's main entrance. "I don't think he wants to be checked on."

"Oh well. Sucks to be him."

"You know, I've never seen you in love before. It's nice," he said, leaning against the doorjamb, a wistful smile on his face.

"Are you and Dr. Lee a thing?" Zeddie asked Rosie. "Did I miss that?"

"No, we are not a thing. There is no thing."

"She's practically making out with the guy's note," Duckers told Zeddie. At least the two of them were getting along now.

"Fine," said Rosie. "A smidgen of attraction might be involved, but there is an ocean between *like* and *love*."

"Mm-hmm. You keep telling yourself that. Bye! Have fun with your pocket man!"

"Stop short-shaming!" Rosie shouted after Duckers as he scooted out the door.

"It's not shaming if you really do want to put him in your pocket!" he shouted in reply as the door swung shut behind him.

Rosie growled in irritation before she noticed Zeddie regarding her with a gleam in his eyes. "Don't you start with me."

"I didn't say a word."

Zeddie's gaze drifted toward the main door, and his face fell.

"Want to talk about that?" Rosie offered.

Caught staring after his ex, Zeddie stood up straight. "No, ma'am."

"Got it. I respect that."

Rosie was walking toward the door when Zeddie stopped her. "Just kidding. How's he been? For the past ten years?"

She raised her eyebrows at him.

"Hart and Mercy were always skimpy on the details," he admitted. "And I was always skimpy on the questions."

"He's had good days and bad days like anyone else, but on the whole, he's been doing well."

"Good." Zeddie nodded and scrubbed a hand through his hair, making his golden curls stand up. "We were kids when we were together, especially me. I had a lot more growing up to do back then."

"Mission accomplished," said Rosie. Unlike her partner, she had only known Zeddie as he was now, and as far as she could tell, he was a grown-ass adult.

"Thanks."

"He broke your heart, huh?"

It was presumptuous of Rosie to ask him a question like that, but she'd had this story from Duckers and was curious to know Zeddie's point of view.

He mulled over the question. "*Losing him* broke my heart."

"What's the difference?"

"The difference is that he didn't do anything wrong. He was right to break things off. And honestly, that's what got me to pull on my big boy pants and grow up. I'm a different person now—a better one, I hope. And Pen has changed, too. It's just that . . . You never stop being who you were, do you? You may be on page 120 of the novel that is your life, but that doesn't mean page 37 no longer exists. Pen and I had a lot of pages together in the early chapters, so it's weird being here with him all of a sudden in the middle of the book."

"That makes sense."

Zeddie gave Rosie the same wistful grin Duckers had worn

moments earlier. "Gotta say, being stuck in Tanria is a nightmare, but I'm glad that I've gotten to know you over the past few days."

"Hard same, Z. Can I call you Z?"

"Sure, RoFo."

Rosie beamed at him before continuing on her way to the front door.

"Hey, Rosie, a word of advice?"

She turned.

"If there is a smidgen of like or love there, you may as well go for it. Those smidgens can be hard to come by."

She wondered if he was talking about her or if he was referring to something Duckers-shaped. And if he was talking about her, she wondered if she was this transparent to Adam. She hoped not.

"Thank you," she said, smoothing a wisp of coppery hair that had come loose from her braids, as if that action could put her dignity back in place. "And this conversation never happened."

"Understood."

"Enjoy your nap."

"Enjoy your pocket man."

"I can't believe you went with Saltlicker," Rosie told Adam, her way of announcing her arrival at the portal, although surely he must have heard the slap of her equimaris's feet as she approached.

Holding a wrench in his right hand, with the innards of the portal splayed at his feet along with several tendrils of thorny vine, he gave her a questioning look.

"The equimaris," she clarified. "You chose the orneriest, most recalcitrant dickhead in the Tanrian Marshals' stable as your mount today."

"I like him. He's intelligent and responds well to authority."

"That asshole?"

Saltlicker stood peacefully at his picket, the first time Rosie had ever seen the equimaris in a decent mood. He seemed to give her the equine version of a shrug. Rosie shook her head, picketed her filly beside the stallion, and came to stand beside Adam at the portal.

"How's it looking?"

"Terrible."

"No need to sugarcoat things. I can handle the truth."

He huffed his laugh-adjacent amusement as he dropped the wrench into his toolbag and rubbed his forehead. Rosie wondered if he knew that his cold exterior was flaking away more and more with each passing day. She certainly had no intention of pointing it out to him.

"How was your survey of Tanria?" he asked her.

"Also terrible. The vines are getting worse."

She filled him in on her findings at the West Station. He took in her news, nodding somberly.

"Listen, Adam—" she began, wanting to apologize for flying a dragon straight at his face, but he cut her off.

"I don't want to talk about it." He picked up a screwdriver and studied the portal again.

"Okay."

"Okay?"

"Yep. Okay."

He eyed her with suspicion.

"What?" she said. "You saw a dragon today. You don't want to talk about it. I saw my dad today. I don't want to talk about that either. We're even."

"You saw your father in Tanria?"

"No, he was on the Bushong side of the Mist. *And* I don't want to talk about it."

For once, Adam was the one who seemed like he wanted to ask a million questions, but in the end, he respected Rosie's wishes.

"I could use your assistance, if you are willing," he said, indicating the portal with his screwdriver.

"Willing and able. What do you need?"

For the next couple of hours, Rosie handed him tools like a surgeon's assistant and held tubes and wires and various mysterious bits out of the way so that Adam could get at other mysterious bits. Her hand continued to pass through the plant, but there was friction involved now, as if she were sticking her fingers into a gelatin mold.

"Have you ever tried smacking it?" she asked him as he dropped a socket wrench into his bag with a fatalistic air.

"I admit that hitting my invention with blunt force has never occurred to me."

"Works at least half the time."

He gestured at the portal. "Be my guest."

"Really?"

"It could not possibly make things worse."

She cracked her knuckles, made a show of adjusting her stance, and slammed the side of her fist against the frame. The whole thing rattled like a tin can, and an important-looking tubular object dropped out of one of the open hatches. Predictably, the portal remained dead as a drudge with a skewered appendix.

She stepped away from the frame and faced Adam. "It didn't work."

"I see that."

"Felt good, though."

"I imagine that it did."

"You should try it. Might be cathartic."

She did not for one minute think that he would take her up on this suggestion, so she was delighted when he stepped up to the portal, his bearing distinctly martial, and thwacked the frame with an athleticism that was the sexiest thing Rosie Fox had seen in her century and a half of living. She felt the reverberations of that *thwack* in her gorgeous pink silk panties.

"Gods," she moaned before she could think better of it.

He turned to face her and said, completely straight-faced, "It didn't work."

"I see that." Rosie swallowed the lump of pure lust that sprang up from her sexy bits, and decided that a change in topic was in order. "Any thoughts on where this plant came from or how to get rid of it?"

"If I knew how to get rid of it, we wouldn't be trapped here."

He gave the portal another solid pound with his fist, this time with an animosity that Rosie would have found both surprising and appealing if he hadn't hissed in pain.

"Are you all right?"

"Yes," he said, but a trickle of blood dripped from the side of his hand, a striking mirror of the moment he'd cut himself on the West Station's portal five years ago. As he reached into the back pocket of his government-issued uniform pants, Rosie pounced on the opportunity to bring up a sticky subject.

"I've been meaning to ask, where's that handkerchief?"

He held up his recently returned pocket square in answer to her question before pressing the silk to the cut on his hand.

"You are determined to ruin this thing, aren't you?" Rosie liberated the pocket square from Adam and tied it firmly around his hand.

"Thank you."

"You're welcome, but you know this is not the handkerchief I'm talking about. Where's the other one—mine?"

Rosie's pulse ratcheted skyward as she watched him realize he had been caught. She had taken many risks in her life, but she couldn't shake the sensation that this one came with real consequences that could actually hurt her. When he hesitated, she crossed her arms, her body rather than her mouth telling him, *Do not try to weasel out of this.*

Accepting defeat with grace, he produced her linen handkerchief, not from his pants pocket but from the left breast pocket of his khaki Tanrian Marshals shirt, and he held it out to her. "I apologize for the stains."

She stared at it, noting the faded brown splotches marring the fabric, wondering which had belonged to her and which had belonged to him. "I don't care about the stains. I want to know... why do you have that?"

"You gave it to me."

"No, I mean, why do you *still* have it? Like, now, on your person?"

Since Rosie had made no move to take the handkerchief, Adam retracted his arm and stared down at the linen in his hand. "Sometimes, a small kindness can be quite... large... to the recipient."

Rosie recalled that day beside the West Station's portal, how easy it had been for her to tie a hankie around his hand and walk away, how quickly she had forgotten a man who did everything he could to be overlooked. How lonely must he have been— how lonely must he be now—to care about an act so simple and insignificant as one person showing basic human decency to another?

He stroked the linen with his thumb before holding it out to her again. "Take it. It's yours."

"No, you keep it," she told him in a rush, bending over to fold his fingers more tightly around the stained cloth. When she looked up, she found herself nose to nose with Adam.

Adam, whose face had gone soft.

Adam, whose focus dropped from her eyes to her mouth.

A pang in Rosie's chest bloomed, fanning out like a rose, petal by petal, as her lips went plump with expectation.

He winced and stepped away from her, taking his hand and the handkerchief and the possible intent to kiss her with him.

"Your medical condition?" she guessed.

"Please don't ask me if I'm all right." He looked wan in the aftermath of his pain, so he probably wasn't going to be in the mood to kiss her anymore. Maybe he hadn't wanted to kiss her in the first place. Maybe that had been wishful thinking on her part. Maybe Adam's mysterious health condition had saved her from humiliating herself.

It was bitterly disappointing.

Adam avoided the inevitable awkwardness by foraging through his toolbag. "Since we appear to be returning items to one another, I have something for you."

He retrieved a plain envelope and handed it to her. Inside, folded in a blank piece of paper, was the offending cat figurine, plus its two disembodied legs.

"You forgot to pack it before we left the barracks in Sector E-30. I thought you might want it, so I put it in my bag. I apologize that I forgot to give it to you until now."

Rosie snorted. Because of course. Of course.

"You don't want it?" asked Adam, regarding her with open curiosity, while she, yet again, was the one who didn't want to answer questions.

"Who wouldn't want the metaphoriest of metaphors?" she deflected as she tucked the envelope—broken cat and all—into her pocket. She was about to ask him if he was ready to head to the Dragon's Lair when she noticed a dramatic change to the vines around the portal.

"What under the altar of the sky?"

"What do you see?" Adam asked her.

"It's got leaves. Not buds. Honest-to-gods *leaves*. They were not here five seconds ago, I swear. What in Old Hell is happening?"

As soon as she turned to him, he flinched and shut his eyes tight as if he couldn't bear to look at her. "I'm sorry. I'm so sorry. I will get you out of here. All three of you. I swear that I will."

"I believe you," said Rosie, and she meant it, but it didn't seem to assuage the storm that was brewing inside him.

As they made their way back to their makeshift home base, she mulled over Adam's odd apology. He had behaved as if he were solely to blame for getting them trapped inside Tanria. It seemed to Rosie that he had added an important piece to the jigsaw puzzle that was their predicament.

She wished that she knew where it fit.

"He-e-ey, mail delivery," called Gobbo as they were finishing up a dinner of chicken spiedini. He entered the dining room from the kitchen this time, pushing open the doors so they swung wide as he stepped into the main room. "That was fun! I'm totally coming in through those doors from now on."

While Gobbo seemed as chill as ever, there were several gashes in his clothing, and the right sleeve of his fringed shirt dangled off his dik-dik shoulder.

"What happened to you?" asked Rosie.

"No big. Had a tough time getting through the spectral plane. I've got a letter for all of you. Who wants it?"

Duckers put out his hand. "Is this all there is?" he asked.

"No, but that's the most important thing, so I put it on top."

Duckers opened the letter and read aloud.

To Marshals Fox and Duckers, Dr. Lee, and Mr. Birdsall,
We anticipate the arrival of a new (albeit pirated) portal in
excellent working condition tomorrow afternoon. Our plan is
to try to get you out via the North Station's portal first. If that

modus operandi goes awry, we will use the alternative method.
One way or another, we are getting you out of there tomorrow. If
you can arrive at the North Station by 1600 hours, we can move
forward on this plan. Please send confirmation with Gobbo.
Once you are at the North Station's exit, notify us via portal bell
(assuming that it is functional) and we'll get things moving.

Looking forward to seeing you in person tomorrow afternoon!

All my best,
Alma Maguire

Rosie turned to Adam. "I thought you said the northern portal looked terrible."

"It does. I suspect they would prefer to rescue us via the official portal but are relying on the pirated version."

"We're getting out of here tomorrow?" asked Zeddie, his entire being laced with excitement.

Duckers held up the letter, a smile lighting up his face. "She used an exclamation point and everything."

"You're getting out of here, my dudes!" Gobbo thrust his hooves in the air in triumph.

Duckers and Zeddie both leaped to their feet, knocking over their chairs in the process as Rosie stood to take the letter and read it for herself. Sure enough, there it was, plain as day. By this time tomorrow, they'd be on the Bushong side of the Mist.

And she felt...

She wasn't sure what to call what she was feeling, but it wasn't entirely joy.

"May I?" Adam asked her, hardly audible over their companions' shouts of exultation. He held out his hand, and Rosie couldn't help but notice that he didn't seem overjoyed either. She gave him the letter, her fingers brushing his in a way that was not at all accidental.

"We're getting out of here!" Duckers sang as he swept in and jostled Rosie in a side hug before letting go to perform his signature celebratory dance moves. She tried to join in the fun, but for reasons she could not begin to articulate, her heart wasn't in it.

"Gods' tits and testicles, yes!" cheered Zeddie. He danced along with Duckers, and somehow in the midst of all that jubilation, they wound up hugging. They both seemed to realize it at the same time and relinquished each other in a mutual display of *We'll just pretend that didn't happen.*

"But wait! There's more!" said Gobbo. He handed letters to everyone but Adam and then hefted a good-sized box out of his satchel. The nimkilim set it on the table in front of Zeddie, who dug in with gusto.

"What is it?" asked Duckers.

"I was inspired by Rosie and asked Lil to send me some of my things." He pulled out a short-sleeved button-down shirt with a bright yellow paisley pattern printed all over it and held it up to his broad chest.

"I see your sense of style hasn't changed," said Duckers.

"I'm going to consider that a compliment."

Gobbo set his bag on the floor, pulled a suitcase out of it, and rolled it toward Adam. "Package for you, friend."

"I asked Maguire to see if the hotel would send it along," Rosie told him. "I thought you might like to have your own things. Guess it's a moot point now, but it's the thought that counts, right?"

She made the mistake of making eye contact with Duckers.

You just want to see him in suits again and swim in his cologne, his eyeballs accused her.

I will cut you, her eyeballs fired back.

"Thank you," murmured Adam without tearing his eyes away from the suitcase.

Gobbo next placed a cardboard box redolent of cinnamon into Duckers's hands.

"Are those your mom's snickerdoodles?" asked Zeddie as Duckers tore into the package.

Duckers held the box under Zeddie's nose. "Have one."

"Bless you." He closed his eyes as he took a bite in evident reverence.

"Do you and the cookie need some alone time?" asked Rosie.

"You don't understand. These are the greatest cookies of all time. I've been trying to re-create this recipe for years, and I've never gotten it right."

"It's a family recipe. Mom won't share it," explained Duckers.

"How is your mom? How's the whole fam?" asked Zeddie, and Duckers launched into a good-natured report on his mother and his three younger sisters.

"What about your brother?"

"He's a punk."

"Still?"

Rosie intervened in defense of her partner's much-maligned youngest sibling. "He's about to finish his degree in finance. He's already landed a fancy job in Diamond Springs after graduation. He's an upstanding member of society."

"And a punk," finished Duckers with a fond grin.

Zeddie topped everyone's wineglasses and raised his own. "To our imminent escape!"

"To our imminent escape!" Duckers repeated with alacrity. Rosie joined in with a lack of enthusiasm that she covered with false good cheer. She couldn't for the life of her figure out why she'd be anything other than overjoyed to be leaving Tanria at four o'clock tomorrow afternoon.

Adam simply raised his glass, so he wasn't even trying. She added this to the ever-growing list of things to unpack once they'd made it safely to the other side of the Mist. He wheeled his suitcase to his makeshift bedroom, and the other three dug into their mail.

Rosie was glad to find letters from Hart, Annie, and an old friend from her circus days—a tightrope walker who had retired a decade ago. But her stomach sank when she discovered a letter from the Trickster in the mix.

She remained livid with him over his antics outside the West Station, but a worm of regret uncoiled in her conscience as she recalled in detail the venomous letter she had sent him two days ago. Sadly, her "act first, think never" rule did not apply when it came to her father—he would remember that letter fifty years from now. He would remember it fifty *million* years from now. He would file it away with his many grievances and trot it out for centuries to come whenever he popped up unannounced in Rosie's life, even though she'd told him to stay away from her.

Hilarious how he couldn't get away from Jocelyn fast enough, yet he always managed to show up in Rosie's life when she least wanted him.

Against her better judgment, she read the letter.

Hey, kiddo.

I got your note. Gosh. Not gonna lie, that was a punch to the proverbial solar plexus. Fortunately for you, it's going to take more than a little youthful rebellion to turn away your old man. (Or I guess I should say, your Old God. Bah dum tsss!)

All joking aside, I need to set you straight on a few things, my Rosa-loo, but I'd rather do that in person. We'll set up a father-daughter date as soon as you come home. Dinner's on me!

In the meantime, I want to let you know that I am worried sick about you. I can't eat or sleep (not that I need to, but you get the picture). It is so dang hard for me to know that my own daughter is trapped in Tanria when I'm the only Old God who managed to evade that fate. Doesn't seem fair, does it?

I hope you know that I'm here for you every step of the way, and I'm thinking of you constantly.

Love, Dad

Rosie had poured over a century's worth of hurt and anger into the message she had sent her father, and the Trickster replied with a fucking rim shot? After which he blathered on about how hard her situation was on *him*? She would go to Old Hell before she let him "set her straight" on anything.

Inwardly steaming, she took the envelope containing the cat figurine and both of its broken legs from her pocket and crumpled the Trickster's letter around it.

This is garbage, she thought as she regarded the wad in her hand, *and the first thing I'm going to do when I get out of here is throw it away in the nearest trash can I can find. How's that for a metaphor?*

She set it aside in disgust before opening Hart's letter to cheer herself up.

Dear Rosie,

Rumor has it that Alma is busting the four of you out of there soon, but I wanted to write to you all the same. While I'm certain that you're holding up like a champ, it can't be easy.

I thought I should let you know that my children have adopted your cat for the time being. He is currently residing in our home, which he has taken over like a king. We're calling him Tinky since Mercy put her foot down on calling him Fartface. Apologies.

Anyway, I'm sure you have better things to do right now than to read a long-winded message from an old grump, but I wanted to let you know that Mercy and I and Bea and Lottie are thinking of you, and Mercy, being a far better person than I will ever be, has been making offerings to the Bride of Fortune every day.

Your friend,
Hart

Gods love Hart Ralston; he did make her feel a million times better after the pile of grapshit her narcissistic man-child of a father had sent her way.

Rosie was opening her letter from Annie when Gobbo piped up.

"Is it cool if I head out? I want to leave before those vines make the spectral plane any more jacked up."

"That's alarming," said Duckers.

"But we're getting out tomorrow," said Zeddie. "What does it matter?"

"It'll matter if everything goes tits up."

"Which it won't," said Rosie, handing the nimkilim a bottle of wine as his tip. "Go ahead, Gobbo, and be careful."

"Aw, that's sweet." He gave them a cheesy bow before pushing through the kitchen doors.

Chapter Seventeen

The following afternoon, the four of them stood in a line outside the restaurant, shoulder to shoulder, staring at the kitchen door, none of them inclined to move yet.

"Is it weird that I'm going to miss this place?" asked Zeddie.

"Either it's not weird or we're all a bunch of weirdos," said Duckers. He gazed at the door one last time before nudging his shoulder against Zeddie's. "Come on. Time's a-wasting."

They chatted affably as they mounted their equimares, and Rosie was glad to see they'd cleared the air, even if she hadn't been able to eavesdrop on the good stuff. She was about to climb onto her filly when she realized that Adam hadn't budged. He continued to gaze at the restaurant, his expression difficult to make out.

"I suppose this is goodbye," he said at last before he climbed into the saddle.

The four of them took off down the road with Duckers and Zeddie in front and Rosie and Adam following behind.

"You look like the gallows await you. We're supposed to be happy like those two yahoos," Rosie said with a nod to Duckers and Zeddie.

"It has been a long time—a long, *long* time—since I did anything that resembled living. But here...I was alive for a few days. And I find that I don't particularly want to return to the life—no, the *non*life—that is waiting for me in Quindaro."

Ahead of them, Duckers said something that made Zeddie laugh, a tinkling sound incongruous with the fragility of Adam's unexpected opening up at the eleventh hour. When he spoke again, it was in a voice so bone-weary that he sounded as ancient as the gods themselves.

"I get up. I go to work. I come home. I sleep."

"Presumably, you eat on occasion."

"Sometimes." He gave Rosie a rueful close-lipped smile.

"What exactly is your job?"

"I'm a professor of design."

"Meaning you invent shit all day?"

"Yes, in fact, the university pays me to 'invent shit' that makes people's lives better. I have my own laboratory."

"That sounds fun," said Rosie, wondering again how he'd managed to get those scars on his back. The life he described did not sound particularly dangerous.

"It can be rewarding."

"But you don't like it?"

He considered this question before he answered. "I don't dislike it. I don't love it. I don't hate it. I don't feel anything about it."

"There's more to life than work."

"Not for me."

"Then don't go back to that life. Start living a new one."

"Yes, I probably will," he mused, as if starting a new life was a task he had done a hundred times before.

Rosie had sensed the loneliness he kept at bay beneath the surface, but now she had a taste of it, and it was as vast and salt rimmed as the sea itself. Maybe, in some regard, he was as stuck in his life as she was in hers.

"I know you said you're an orphan, but isn't there anyone important to you? A family member? A friend? A...more than friend?"

"No, there isn't any—" he began, and for the first time during the course of this weighty conversation, he faced Rosie. The second their eyes met, his darted toward the road in front of them. "I'm better off on my own. Trust me."

Rosie thought about the dearth of letters addressed to him in Gobbo's mailbag and the fact that no one appeared to know or care that he was trapped in Tanria. She did not think he was better off alone.

"I hate to break this to you, but you're stuck with me, literally and figuratively. I hereby declare myself a Person Who Is Important to Adam Lee, no matter where we end up. And I'm going to live forever, so you can't shake me."

He dropped his head and cast his laugh-adjacent laugh at the pommel of his saddle. "I honestly don't know what to do about that."

"Eh, we'll figure it out."

He didn't look in her direction again, but one corner of his mouth twitched skyward.

By the time the northern portal came into view, Duckers and Zeddie were both fizzing with excitement, but for Rosie, the moment was bittersweet. While she wanted to go home to her apartment with her mementos and her pretty things and her bathtub and her Brigitte Porcel records, the idea of not being able to return to Tanria anytime soon, if ever, gnawed at her. Sure, she'd been in a rut lately, but what would her life be without this place? What purpose would she have? Suddenly, the prospect of finding her way again in the mortal world made her immortal life yawn before her like the gaping black maw of some mythological beast. It scared her in a way it never had before.

And what about Adam? She had promised him that he would

be stuck with her for the foreseeable future, but did she have any control over that? Where would he go if he didn't return to the University of Quindaro? The world was enormous, and he had already traveled so far in his life. He could go anywhere, do anything. He might not want to be stuck with her outside the Mist.

She felt as old as Grandfather Bones as she approached the North Station's portal with two young men who shone as brightly as a pair of new copper coins. But Adam, however old he was, seemed ponderously ancient beside her, which was oddly comforting.

"Would you look at that," said Zeddie as they got closer to the Mist.

Between gaps in the vines Rosie saw a large gathering near the portal. At the forefront stood the Joint Chiefs, somber and serious and talking among themselves. Behind them, a majority of the Tanrian Marshals in the service and, by the looks of it, a good many retirees, too, had gathered near the station. Opposite them were the family and friends of those who were trapped inside Tanria—the Birdsall family, the Ellises, Twyla Banneker, and Duckers's mom and sisters and brothers-in-law and nieces and nephews, and even his brother.

"Look at that punk," joked Duckers.

A much larger crowd fanned out in all directions behind a line of barriers and a significant FICBI presence. There were reporters with notebooks and cameras, but there was also an entire ocean of average, everyday people gathered together to watch four castaways come home at last. While the throng behind the barriers held up encouraging signs, the relatives and friends of those who were trapped—well, of at least three of the four people who were trapped—watched on with anxious faces.

Alma Maguire stood closest to the Mist, puffing away on a cigarette.

"When we get out of here, I'm going to have words with the chief about the bad habit," said Duckers.

"I'd love to be present for that," Rosie told him.

"What's the worst she could do to me? Fire me?"

So apparently Duckers understood that their career prospects were in the toilet. At least toilets were one thing to look forward to in Bushong.

Someone came out of the North Station's back door, a handsome man in his middle years, looking dapper and self-important in a sports coat and dress pants. He strode along the path that led to the portal with an officiousness that made Rosie's blood boil, and stood in front of the Birdsalls and the Ellises and the Duckers family. He even stepped ahead of the Joint Chiefs of the Tanrian Marshals and behaved as if he were calling the shots. Maguire took a long drag on her cigarette, as if it would stop her from saying something she might regret to the Old God.

This was the Trickster at his core, the father who sailed in and out of Rosie's life however it suited him and expected her undying love and adoration for doing nothing more than siring her, the god who bumbled through the history of the world without thought or care, ruining people's lives and wondering why no one built him a shrine. And now here he was, using his daughter in order to play the hero, when he'd let her mother die in poverty because she was no longer the young, beautiful dancer who had caught his eye decades earlier.

"Who is that?" asked Zeddie. "He looks important."

"He isn't," said Rosie. She turned away from the spectacle that the Trickster was making of himself and looked instead to her companions, the most important people in her life, now and for years to come.

"What say we ring that bell?" she suggested.

Duckers squinted at the sky, a habit all marshals developed to estimate the time of day. "It's not sixteen hundred hours yet."

Zeddie jerked his thumb toward the gathering at the North Station and beyond. "I don't think they'll mind."

Rosie looked to Adam. He nodded, his face grim, as if going back to the regular world was a boning knife and he was the fish.

"We're not crossing the threshold into the House of the Unknown God here. Cheer the fuck up," she told him, even though she herself had complicated feelings about returning to everyday life.

Adam gaped at her before blessing her with one of those puffs of laughter that seemed to rise out of him without his full consent or agreement. "Care to do the honors, Marshal Fox?" he asked, gesturing to the portal bell.

"Ro-sie! Ro-sie!" Zeddie chanted.

"I'm on it." Rosie cracked her knuckles and pulled the bell lever. She knew immediately that it worked, because everyone on the Bushong side of the Tanrian border startled. She gave the bell another good ring, and the gathered crowd burst into cheers. Not that she or her compatriots could hear the celebration, but they could certainly see it: people jumping up and down, clapping, fist-pumping, shedding tears.

"Gods' tits, I did not expect to deal with a bunch of emotions today," said Zeddie, laughing at himself as he dabbed a tear from his eye.

Maguire stomped out her cigarette and fumbled for her notepad. Rosie decided to mess with her by spelling *N-O S-M-O-K-I-N-G* using Marks Code. The other chiefs and a good many of the marshals laughed. Hart Ralston wore the biggest grin Rosie had ever seen on the man. Even Maguire had to laugh at herself. Pettily, Rosie was glad to see the Trickster look around, completely clueless and trying to figure out what the joke was.

The chief held up the first page in the notebook. It read, simply, *Ready?*

Duckers and Zeddie clapped and whooped as Rosie used the bell to answer *Y-E-S*.

The chief flipped to the next page and held it up.

The engineer is about to pull the lever. Hold for five seconds on my mark before crossing through the Mist so that we can ascertain that it is safe. Do you understand?

Rosie looked to her companions. "Everyone got that?" she asked them, breathy with nerves, when Rosie almost never felt nervous about anything.

Duckers blew out a breath and said, "Yeah."

"Wait for Chief Maguire to count down from five. Got it," said Zeddie.

Adam nodded, cool as a cucumber.

Rosie faced the portal and rang the bell again: *Y-E-S.*

On the other side of the Mist, Maguire nodded to an engineer. It was Louis Allen, of all people. Louis, who had been on duty the day Rosie had electrocuted herself. Louis, who had helped Adam detach the front of the portal's frame. *How very full circle of you, Bride of Fortune*, Rosie thought as she waited for the big moment.

Louis wiped beads of sweat from his forehead, and then he grasped the main switch and pulled down on it.

The portal hummed to life, the cogs and pistons chugging along as they ought, a sound so familiar to Rosie that it may as well have been a favorite song.

"Fuck yeah," said Duckers, tension coating the words.

Maguire held up her hand and counted down with her fingers: *five, four, three*—

"Gods, please," Zeddie prayed.

Two—

A buzzing noise erupted from the frame, and the entire structure lurched.

"No," someone said, but Rosie couldn't say who it was. She was too distracted by the lightning-like bolt that shot across the archway, where they should be passing through right now.

On the other side, Maguire's mouth moved, and Louis shut down the portal again.

Zeddie clasped his hands on top of his head, his elbows jutting out to the sides.

Duckers put his arm around his waist. "It's all right. Remember what Dr. Lee said? They knew the regular portal was a long shot. But they've got a shiny new pirated portal that they're sticking on the Mist. The vines haven't had a chance to mess with it yet. We're getting out of here. Right now."

He was telling Zeddie that everything would be all right, but he did not look or sound like he meant it. The pair of them had been so cheery en route to the portal, but now Rosie saw that cheeriness for what it was—a cover for terror.

Gods, this is it, she thought. *If this doesn't work, we're fucked.*

They *were fucked*.

How had she so blithely ignored her misgivings for the past four days? How had she been so oblivious to what Duckers and Zeddie and Adam were facing? If she got stuck in Tanria for weeks or years or decades, what would it matter? She'd live. But how long could three mortals last inside the Mist with nothing to eat, especially if Gobbo could no longer get in and out with supplies?

Duckers and Zeddie stared into the desperate faces of the people they loved most. Duckers's mother clung to his sister, her lips pinched between her teeth as tears streamed down her cheeks. The rest of the Duckers clan linked elbows. Hart crossed his arms tightly over his chest as if he needed to contain his own heart, and Mercy wrapped her arms around him. Zeddie's sister, Lil, and her husband, Danny, clasped hands, both of them pale as the dead. The Ellis family and Twyla Banneker huddled together, all of them watching the Mist with tense foreboding. Rosie had always known she'd lose each and every one of them someday, but to lose all of them at once? How in Old Hell could she face that alone? Because that was what she'd be, one way or another: utterly and completely alone.

Maguire turned the page and held up the notebook again, telling them what they already knew.

We are going to try the alternative method now. Move ten feet to your left.

Four people inside the Mist and many, many more outside of it watched on in various shades of dread as two more engineers attached the pirated portal ten feet to the left of the North Station's dysfunctional one.

"Shit!" cursed Rosie, but of course, the engineers couldn't hear her, nor could they see the vines crowding that exact section of the Mist with thorns and leaves.

Zeddie's head snapped in her direction. "What?"

There wasn't time to explain. The engineers flicked on the pirated portal, and Rosie watched in horror as the vines twisted into its cogs. Adam lunged for the portal bell and signaled *S-T-O-P*. Maguire's mouth moved, and the engineers immediately shut off the portal. It all happened in less than five seconds.

"Is it broken?" asked Duckers, his lips barely moving.

"I don't know," answered Rosie. "Some vines got caught in it."

Zeddie shook his head emphatically. "That doesn't make sense. How can this plant that only one person can see and no one can touch mess up machinery?"

"Because the machinery sucks in the Mist to manipulate it, and the vines are thriving in the Mist. That's my theory, at any rate," Adam explained before signaling a new message to the other side.

S-E-N-D L-E-E P-O-R-T-A-L.

Maguire wrote down each letter until Adam had finished the

message, then showed the page to the other chief marshals. They spoke briefly among themselves before Maguire faced the Mist again and gave them a thumbs-up. The engineers were pulling the illegal portal off the Mist when Alma Maguire addressed everyone gathered at the North Station to tell them the bad news: Rosie Fox, Penrose Duckers, Zeddie Birdsall, and Adam Lee would not be coming home today.

Rosie turned away, shaking like the crisp autumn leaves shivering on the trees outside Aunt Bonnie's the night Hart had told her about his house in Sector 28. She could not bear to look at him or anyone else now. She couldn't face the bleak reality setting in on the other side of the Mist.

"So . . . they'll fix another portal, right?" said Zeddie.

No one replied. Rosie didn't feel up to lifting his spirits when her own were spiraling down the vortex to Old Hell.

"I mean, it's not like we're permanently trapped here."

Again, he was met with an ominous silence.

"Oh gods, we're trapped."

"No," said Duckers. "No. No!"

He flew at the Mist and pounded his fist against it, which had to have hurt.

"No!" he howled.

Zeddie got to him first, pulling him away from the invisible boundary. Duckers struggled and yelled "Let me go!" but Zeddie wrapped him up, pinning down his arms.

"Get me the fuck out of here!"

Zeddie was crying, but he kept his hold on Duckers, who continued to struggle but was quickly losing steam. And then he hung limply in Zeddie's arms and looked at his mom and his family and started bawling.

"I want to go home!"

"I know," Zeddie told him. "I know."

Duckers turned and buried his face in the crook of his ex-boyfriend's neck and screamed a sob into his flesh. Zeddie cupped his head and whispered again, "I know."

Duckers might as well have reached into Rosie's chest cavity, ripped out her heart, and thrown it against the Mist. If she could die, she would gladly sacrifice her own life for Penrose Duckers—for any of them—yet here she stood, watching him suffer and powerless to do a thing about it.

On the other side of the Mist, the Trickster strode forward in the guise of a middle-aged politician. He grew in height until he towered several feet over the crowd, most of whom shrank from him in fear. His eyes went solid white, veined with lightning, and his fingers turned to black-tipped talons as he reached for the barrier that separated him from his daughter. Again and again, he tore at the Mist, splintering his claws, bloodying his hands, but to no avail. Rosie had to assume that a wall created by the New Gods to keep the Old Gods in could easily keep one out.

It was the first time in her life that he had seemed godlike to her, but more importantly, it was the first time he'd struck her as *father*like. She didn't realize that she was crying until Adam brushed her elbow with his fingertips and offered her her own handkerchief.

She wiped her face with her sleeve. "I don't want that one. I want yours."

"This one is better for..." He faltered. In his defense, it was probably awkward telling a bawling demigod that linen was way better for snot than silk.

"I don't care," said Rosie, sounding like a baby. A six-foot-five baby.

He tucked her stained linen hankie into his breast pocket and produced his silk handkerchief from his pants pocket. "I washed it last night."

"Thank you."

She dabbed at her nose with the insufficient scrap of silk. It smelled like him, and she had no intention of ever giving it back.

Adam regarded the Trickster, who stood panting on the other side of the Mist.

"Is that your father?"

"Yes."

He waited for her to say more, but this was not a conversation Rosie wanted to have in the face of nihilistic anguish, so she blew her nose instead.

Getting a grip on himself, Duckers pulled away from Zeddie and looked at the toes of his boots. "Sorry."

"Hey, I freaked out on day one," Zeddie told him. "You've held your shit together for five whole days."

Duckers gave him a watery laugh. "Yeah, I'm totally winning on that."

"Totally."

On the Bushong side of the Tanrian border, the Trickster stared daggers at the Mist, which would not give way to him.

Maguire held up her notebook.

Sending portal to you as soon as Gobbo can get through. Stay positive. This isn't over yet.

Rosie and Duckers and Zeddie and Adam gathered in a circle as the weight of pure hopelessness pressed against them. Maguire could tell them it wasn't over yet all she wanted. It didn't matter.

Because it felt over.

Chapter Eighteen

Rosie took over the kitchen since Zeddie was morally crushed, which meant they were eating hot dogs with a side of carrot sticks and some canned pears. Not that she couldn't make a nicer meal, but she was in no mood to put in a whole lot of effort.

There were so many hard truths and horrifying possibilities staring them down, but her mind kept circling the Trickster. She had never seen him wear a genuine emotion, and yet there beside the Mist, with his eyes gone white and his hands turned to talons, he had seemed to her more alive and real and . . . human than she had ever seen him. For the first time in her life, he appeared to care about her, and she didn't know what to do with the emotion that came with this revelation, and she resented having that emotion foisted upon her. So she plated the pathetic dinner she had created and made her way to the dining room, where someone—possibly Adam—had assembled a respectable array of the restaurant's beer selection.

"This sad excuse for a meal does not deserve the Dragon's Lair's stash of craft brews," she announced as she set a platter of wieners on the table.

"I find that processed meat and craft beer pair well with existential despair," said Zeddie.

"Is that your expert opinion, Chef?"

"Absolutely."

Rosie opened a bottle of pale ale with a satisfying *hiss* and clinked her bottleneck to his. "Cheers."

Dinner was a somber affair, eaten in silence, save for the occasional mumbled request for someone to pass the ketchup or mustard. Empty beer bottles began to populate the dining table at an alarming rate, mostly around Adam. Either he wasn't drinking as much as Rosie thought he was drinking, or he had a remarkable tolerance for alcohol. All she knew was that she'd had one bottle so far, while Duckers and Zeddie had polished off another six bottles between them, but there were thirteen empty bottles on the table. The only person she saw consistently drinking was the statue with a pulse sitting to her left.

She watched him open another bottle of stout.

"Are you okay?" she asked him.

"Are any of us?"

"I mean, are you . . . ?"

He looked at her blankly.

"Drunk off your ass?"

"No."

He didn't look drunk. His eyes were clear. His face showed no sign of a boozy flush. He moved with his usual assured grace. Yet those bottles on the table told a different story.

"Touch your nose," she said.

Without batting an eye, he obeyed.

Rosie couldn't believe she'd actually gotten him to do it.

"Other hand," she tried.

Sure enough, he touched his nose with the pointer finger of his left hand.

"Sing a sea shanty while dancing a jig."

He gave her a withering look.

"Can't blame a girl for trying."

"The man holds his drink like you do, RoFo," observed Duckers a half second before Gobbo staggered through the kitchen door, cut and bleeding, scaring the ever-loving crap out of everyone present.

"Mail delivery," he moaned.

"Mother of Sorrows, Gobbo! Are you okay?" asked Rosie.

"That entry was kind of rough."

"Here, sit down."

Rosie took him by the dik-dik elbow and guided him, limping, to a chair, while Zeddie opened the craftiest bottle of craft brews and pushed it across the table toward him. The nimkilim inexplicably dumped it over his head like a fizzy lava flow, shivered, and handed the empty bottle to Zeddie. "Thanks, man."

"Um, sure thing?"

"Want us to bandage you up?" asked Duckers.

"Nah. I'm immortal, you know? It's no big. The good news is that I got in, right?"

"Yay," said Zeddie, trying to muster some enthusiasm.

"The bad news is that I might not be able to come back. Assuming I manage to get out of here at all."

"Oh," said Zeddie, mustering some very real consternation.

Gobbo clapped his hooves and smiled brightly, as if he hadn't dropped a metaphorical bomb in the room. "Okay, the Number-One-Super-Priority delivery of the day goes to Dr. Adam Lee!"

He reached into his mailbag and pulled out the enormous archway. Duckers got to his feet to help Adam lean it against one of the dining room's walls.

"And this is for all four of you." Here, Gobbo lifted a huge crate labeled *perishable* from the depths of his satchel and set it on the table, shaking plates and rattling silverware in the process. Already, he had stopped bleeding and was looking healthier by the second. "And this." He heaved another heavy box onto the table's surface. "And this, and this, and this."

He stacked three more boxes in a tower next to the table, like a child playing with building blocks. Everything was labeled *perishable*, hammering home the bleak fact that they were irrevocably trapped in Tanria.

"And here's the nonedible mail for the whole gang," said Gobbo, bringing forth a huge crate full of letters to set on Zeddie's lap.

"Oof! What is all this?"

"Messages of moral support. You're front-page news right now, dudes. Like, you're a big deal."

Duckers selected a letter at random and read it aloud.

Dear Sinners,

The Unknown God is punishing you for putting your faith in the unworthy New Gods. You have defiled the memory of the Old (Rightful!) Gods by desecrating their sacred land. Repent and return to the way of righteousness before you are trapped in Tanria forever! And may those who follow the path of the New Gods rot and burn in Old Hell until the end of time!

Signed,
Mary Remis

Duckers, Rosie, and Zeddie looked to Gobbo questioningly, while Adam popped open another beer.

The dik-dik grimaced. "Well, most of them are messages of moral support, but, you know, kooks are everywhere."

Duckers set the letter on the table. "How do you get in and out of here, Gobbo?"

"Through the spectral plane."

"What does that mean?"

"You know the story about how the Old Gods finally surrendered, and the Warden cut a door into Tanria so that they could get out and become stars on the altar of the sky?"

"Yeah."

"That's how."

"There's a door?" asked Zeddie.

"Yeah."

"Can we use it?"

"No."

"Why not?"

"Because it's not a *door*-door, if you get me?" Gobbo nodded as if he and Zeddie were in complete understanding.

"Not even a little," said Zeddie.

"You can't go through a door in the spectral plane. And if you did, you wouldn't come out again."

"You mean, like, we'd...die?"

"Yeah." The dik-dik smiled and gave Zeddie an encouraging pat on the shoulder, congratulating him on getting the answer right.

Rosie thought of Hart's house in Sector 28. What would happened if she could open that door? Did it connect to Gobbo's woo-woo spectral plane? The question felt far less theoretical than it had a week ago.

A sickening realization dawned on her then, one that made her short-lived charity toward her father drain out of her like pus from a septic wound.

"Wait a minute. Can a god go through that door?" she asked Gobbo, preparing herself for a good old-fashioned rage fest.

She was almost disappointed when the nimkilim answered, "No way, at least, not right now."

"Why not?"

"It's a size thing, spiritually speaking. Like, I'm a dinky dik-dik soul, and it's a tight squeeze for me with a bunch of big-ass thorns in the way. So a god trying to get in here? Ain't gonna happen. Exempli gratia, I bumped into the Trickster on my way in, and it was no dice for him."

Adam snapped out of his lethargy. "The Trickster was trying to get into Tanria?"

Again, Rosie recalled the sight of her father, panting and desperate on the other side of the Mist. She swallowed her indignation of a moment ago with a bitter pill of regret.

"Yeah."

"Why?"

"No clue. But that reminds me, Big T wrote a quick note for you, RoFo, and shoved it in my pocket when I was on the way in."

Gobbo reached for the folded paper, which was how he discovered that his pocket had been ripped to shreds. His hoof popped out the gaping hole.

"Shit, it must have fallen out."

"No worries," said Rosie, disconcerted by how badly she wished she could read her father's message when she hadn't been glad to receive a letter from him since she was a kid.

Zeddie rubbed his temples. "I am so confused right now. Why would a god be sending Rosie a letter?"

Duckers nudged him and shook his head. Zeddie gave him a questioning look, but he dropped the subject.

Rosie glanced at Adam to gauge his reaction to Zeddie's question, but he turned away from her before she had a chance to read him. He took another swig of beer, but there was a tension under the surface that hadn't been there a moment ago, his bearing like a rubber band stretched to its limits.

"Okay, I'm out," announced Gobbo.

"You're leaving so soon?" Zeddie asked with the barely masked desperation they were surely all experiencing. Rosie certainly didn't relish losing their connection to the outside world.

"I need to get out of here before those vines get any worse. If I don't see you again, hugs?"

He threw out his arms in invitation, followed by the most

awkward group hug in the history of group hugs, minus Adam, who remained seated at the table.

"Are you going to be all right?" Rosie asked the nimkilim, resisting the urge to cling to his sleeve and never let go.

"Sure. Totally can't die. Catch you later! I hope!"

With that, Gobbo made his dramatic exit through the swinging door of the kitchen, leaving the four prisoners to resume their depressing dinner.

Rosie stared at her plate, lost in thought, perplexed by the Trickster's actions. She probably ought to tell Zeddie and Adam that the god was her father, although it wouldn't take a genius to figure it out after today. And Adam actually was a genius.

She looked his way, and sure enough, he was eyeing her askance, a bottle held to his lips. A small white circular scar on the side of his hand seemed to stare back at her.

On impulse, she snatched the beer from Adam's grasp, took his hand in hers, and turned it to look for the wound he'd self-inflicted when he whacked the portal, the one she'd bound up with his pocket square only yesterday. But he had given her that same handkerchief—freshly washed—this afternoon, and there was no bandage covering his injury now.

He pulled his hand free, his bland mask fixed firmly in place. "I heal quickly."

She thought of his behavior throughout the past several days— the way his body had stilled when he had first looked inside the West Station's portal, the way he'd worked around the shadows spilling out of the North Station's portal before it went down, the way he'd known to stop when a briar tumbled across their path, the way he'd signaled for the engineers to halt when they had placed the pirated portal in a section of the Mist infested with vines.

I don't see anything here that I have not seen before. That was what he had told Rosie at the South Station's portal. Because he *had* seen it before. And he could see it now. He had seen it all along.

Her eyes narrowed to blazing red slits. "You fucker."

"Hey, now, things are bad enough. Let's not argue," said Zeddie, but Duckers leaped onto Team Rosie without hesitation.

"What'd he do, RoFo?"

"He can see the plant."

Rosie's glare never left Adam's face. He said nothing, but he didn't have to. The jig was up, and he knew it.

"Are you messing with us?" Duckers asked her.

"I wish I were."

"What is going on?" asked Zeddie.

"What's going on is that Dr. Grapshit here has been holding out on us from day one."

Adam's lips parted as if he might deny it.

"Stop. Just stop. I know you can see it, so can we quit pretending that you don't?"

Still he said nothing.

"Are we having a staring contest? Because I have all the time in the world."

"Wait," said Duckers. "Is he a demigod?"

"No," Adam answered, breaking his silence. There was a whole mood in that *no*.

"Look at his eyes. Do they look like a weird shade of brown to you?" Duckers asked Rosie and Zeddie.

"My eyes are perfectly unexceptional, and I wear glasses."

"That doesn't mean anything."

"I have never met a demigod who required vision correction. And demigods are generally tall, whereas I am five foot five."

Duckers raised one doubtful eyebrow at him.

"In shoes," Adam amended.

"Five three," Duckers coughed into his fist.

"The point is that I am not a demigod."

"Then who are you?" asked Rosie.

"You know who I am."

"Do I? Do any of us? Does anyone actually know you?"

"You're being ridiculous," Adam insisted.

"You can see the plant. You heal the way I heal. You've put away a metric ton of beer tonight, but you're steady as a rock. And why haven't you received a single letter since we got stuck in here? Doesn't anyone in your life know you're missing?"

"It's complicated."

Rosie folded her hands and rested her chin on them. "Well, as it turns out, we have nothing but time on our hands."

"I'm all ears," said Duckers, keenly interested.

"Yeah, I'm intrigued," said Zeddie.

"You don't know what you are asking."

"I am asking for your life story," said Rosie. She turned to Duckers and Zeddie. "Are you guys cool with that?"

Zeddie nodded, while Duckers said, "Sounds good to me. Dr. Lee?"

Cornered, Adam turned into an icy statue before them, his lips frozen shut.

"No, sir," said Rosie. "Incorrect. You don't get to do that thing where you retract into your mechanical Adam-shell like a clockwork turtle and pretend that nothing can touch you."

He inhaled sharply, his nostrils flaring as he transformed in front of them, the ice sculpture of a man melting into a real person of flesh and blood, seething with an anger Rosie never would have guessed he contained within him if she weren't bearing the brunt of it now.

"You think you know me so well. You think that you have me all figured out, that your eyes see more than anyone else's eyes because a god calls you Daughter. Well, let me ask you this, Marshal Fox: What secrets are *you* keeping?"

"Don't *Marshal Fox* me."

"Then answer the question."

"I'm not the one keeping secrets here."

"Is that right? In that case, who was that man with the chief marshals at the portal today? And why is the Trickster sending you letters?"

"Step off, man," Duckers warned him.

"Gladly."

Adam pushed away from the table and made it halfway to his makeshift bedroom before he cried out and fell to his hands and knees. His spine arched as a paroxysm racked his body.

The other three raced over to him. Rosie dropped to her knees and wrapped her arm around his shoulders, much good it did him. He keened in pain as he pressed a hand over his chest and writhed.

"It's okay. It's okay," she said like a prayer, as if repeating the words could make them true, even as blood pooled between Adam's fingers and began to drip onto the floor.

"I'll get the first aid kit," said Zeddie, dashing toward the bar, as Duckers got down on the floor with Rosie and Adam.

In the seconds it took Zeddie to return with the kit, Adam's attack had subsided. He sucked in ragged breaths, his blood-coated hand clutched tightly to the left side of his chest. He sat back on his haunches, pale and shaking, and looked at each of his companions with tormented eyes.

"I need to tell you something," he said before he pulled his trembling hand away from his chest. At first, all Rosie could take in was the blood staining his clothes. But then she saw it, clearly visible through a tear in the cotton fabric of his shirt and a hole in his undershirt.

A delicate tendril of vine peeking out of his skin.

"The Tale of the Briar Thief"
from *A Child's Book of Heroes* by Susan Lacy,
illustrated by Emily Schroen

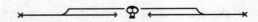

Parents tell their children that stealing is wrong. But there once was a hero who tried to steal something precious, yet he was a good man. No one remembers his name anymore. That is why we simply call him who and what he was: the Briar Thief.

They say that he was born a prince. There used to be princes and kings and queens in the time before the War of the Gods, and in those days, the oldest son of a king would become the next king. The Briar Thief was not the eldest, but he did not mind. He preferred books and learning. He liked to tinker and to create, to make things that helped people.

He lived so long ago that he was alive when the Old Gods went to war with the New Gods. And what a difficult time it was to be a mortal on earth when the gods raged! But what truly upset the Briar Thief was a dragon.

One of the battle dragons of the Old Gods had taken up residence in the forests around his kingdom. And when that hideous dragon wasn't flying its god into the fray against the New Gods, it was terrorizing the countryside and all who dwelled there.

Unable to bear his people's suffering any longer, the Briar Thief begged his father to let him slay the dragon. But the king would not allow him to risk his life, for surely the dragon would kill him. This did not deter the Briar Thief. He went to speak to the crown prince instead.

"Royal Brother, we must kill the dragon," he said.

The crown prince wrung his hands. "But we are mortals. How can we possibly defeat a battle dragon when even the gods cannot?"

"Leave it to me," said the brave younger brother.

When all the preparations were ready, both princes went into the forest with their bravest guardsmen to hunt and kill the monster. They walked for a day and a night before they found the dragon's lair.

The beast was curled up in a vast cave, but even in sleep, it was terrible to behold. Its rough hide was covered with sharp-edged silver scales, and its enormous fangs jutted over its hideous purple lips like a pair of deadly swords. An array of jagged horns crowned its head and ran down the length of its long spine.

On silent feet, the men arrayed themselves around the mouth of the lair, armed with bows and special arrows crafted by the Briar Thief's own hands. Tied to each one was a tube full of saltpeter and sulfur and ashes, which would explode when they struck the dragon's fiery-hot hide.

"Now!" commanded the Briar Thief.

The men let loose their arrows, which burst against the dragon's scales—*Boom! Boom! Boom!*—making it roar in pain and fury. White sparks plumed from its nostrils as it sprang like a copperhead and went on the attack. The men continued to shoot their fire arrows, and between the gunpowder and the scorching breath of the dragon, the air grew heavy with smoke.

In all the confusion, the Briar Thief became lost. He felt terribly alone and afraid when the dragon appeared out of the smoke, and before he could think or run or do a single thing, it grasped him in its talon-tipped fingers and would not let go. As the dragon brought him toward the gaping maw of its mouth to eat him, the Briar Thief sent an arrow flying down the dragon's throat.

The beast staggered and guttered until it crashed to the earth, dead. The Briar Thief was alive, but the dragon had left three long claw marks down his back.

As the smoke cleared, he hobbled about the forest in search of the crown prince and the guardsmen who had come with them. Time and again, he found the body of a fallen comrade, until at last, he discovered his brother. Grandfather Bones had already called to the crown prince's soul and sent him sailing over the Salt Sea.

Wounded and bleeding, the Briar Thief took the crown prince's body onto his shoulders and carried him home. Upon seeing his oldest child dead, the king raged against his second son and cast him into a dungeon.

Over time, the Briar Thief's wounds scabbed and healed, but his heart and soul remained sick. He neither ate nor slept. The food they brought to him in his dungeon cell he offered to any god who would listen. "Stop this war. Have mercy on your poor, fragile people."

Many days passed like this until a god came to him at last: the Trickster.

"Why do you cry?" he asked the Briar Thief.

"My brother is dead, and my people suffer because the gods fight one another and let dragons roam the land."

"What would you say if I told you that you could level the playing field between mortals and immortals?"

"How?" asked the Briar Thief.

"Do you know the story of the Salt Sea and his lover, and how the soul came into being?"

"Of course."

"What if you could steal the flower that gave a thousand thousand years to a mortal man? What if all the mortals created by the New Gods could live as long as the gods themselves? What would you say to that?"

The Briar Thief remembered his reason for wanting to slay the dragon in the first place. He had wanted to save his people. If he could do that—once and for all this time—then perhaps his brother's death would not have been for nothing. And yet he was a clever man, and not easily swayed by the Trickster's deceptions.

"If it is so simple a task, why have you not already stolen this gift of a thousand thousand years for humanity?"

"I have sided with the New Gods in this awful war. If I enter the garden, the Old Gods will know, and they will snuff out my life, and I will be nothing more than a star on the altar of the sky. But you, little human, are just the person for the job. You are brave and clever. If anyone can steal immortality from the gods, it is surely you."

"What must I do?" the Briar Thief asked the Trickster.

"You must sail the Salt Sea, but you will not go to the House of the Unknown God. You must direct your boat to the island where the Old Gods live, and take a cutting of the briar in the garden to bring home with you."

"But the only way for a human to sail the Salt Sea is to die."

"Nonsense! I am the Trickster, am I not? I am older than the gods of death and more powerful. I will stop your heart to trick the Salt Sea and Grandfather Bones, and in that moment, you will find yourself on the shores of the Salt Sea. A boat will be waiting for you. In the boat, you will find a pot and a knife. You must fill the pot with the soil in the garden and plant your cutting in it. The flower will not grow in the mortal world without it. Now if you are ready, lie down," instructed the god.

The Briar Thief wondered if he would ever return from this perilous journey, but he had made his choice, so he did as he was told.

Slowly, painfully, the Trickster eased his divine hands into the living man's chest, past bone and muscle and sinew. He took hold of the prince's heart and squeezed it in his tight grip until it stopped beating.

The Briar Thief found himself standing on the shore of the Salt Sea. It was nighttime, and the stars shone brightly above and sparkled in the water below. Not a creature stirred, and the soft shushing of the ocean was the only sound.

There was a long dock before him, and at the end of that dock was a boat, just as the Trickster had said there would be.

Perhaps this is not one of the god's jokes, he dared to think. *The Trickster did side with the New Gods, after all. Maybe he wants me to succeed.* With that encouraging thought, the Briar Thief walked down the gangway.

A figure appeared, holding a lantern aloft. It was an old man, so ancient that his sunken eyes appeared to be nothing more than dark shadows in his head, and the hollows of his cheeks were black, yet the Briar Thief did not fear him, for he seemed to be a welcoming old fellow.

This must be Grandfather Bones, thought the thief.

"You are welcome here," said the god as he stepped aside so that the mortal could embark on his journey.

The Briar Thief found a knife and a large terra-cotta pot inside the boat, as the Trickster had promised. He had no sooner settled himself when a sail unfurled from the mast. Grandfather Bones blew a gusty breath into it, and away the boat went, skimming over the Salt Sea, which also seemed to whisper, *Welcome. You are welcome here.*

The Briar Thief saw an island in the distance, and on that

island was a house, the sort of place he would wish to inhabit had he not been a prince in a palace. How nice it would be to come home to a cozy cottage such as this, the windows lit with warm firelight.

But no, he thought. *I must find the island where the Old Gods live. I must go to their garden and take a cutting of the briar.*

He looked around him, and there on his right was the shadowy outline of another island—a dark, craggy place that did not call to him in welcome. It seemed to say, *Stay away.*

Setting his jaw with determination, he adjusted the sail so that Grandfather Bones's breath hurtled him in the new direction.

As soon as he came ashore, he moved quickly and quietly, carrying the pot and the knife with him. The homes of the Old Gods loomed over him, unlit and irregular in shape, some sprawling across the land like an octopus, some towering higher than a dragon could fly, and all of them silent as graves in a shipyard.

Eventually, the thief came to the garden at the heart of the island. There was only one plant in that cramped, ugly space—a chaotic riot of thorns that cascaded over every surface. Here and there, a flower dotted the vines, as darkly crimson as blood, with a scent so sweetly heavy it seemed to weigh down the air.

Without wasting a moment, he crouched and began to dig into the earth with his hands, scooping the strange, shimmering soil of the garden into the pot for what felt like hours. He wasn't sure if he had collected enough, but it would have to do. It was time to steal a thousand thousand years.

The briar was as large and monstrous as a dragon. Close to the ground, the stems were as thick around as the thief's waist. He would have to climb the plant to cut fresh new tendrils from the top.

At first, the thorns were so enormous that he could use them like the rungs of a ladder. But as he climbed higher, the barbs grew smaller and snapped off under his feet, so that he feared he would fall. The higher he climbed, the more the briar snagged his clothes and scratched his skin. He rose so far above the garden that he could scarcely see the pot below him. The thorns were now the size of teeth, and they cut as sharply. His hands bled and ached, and yet he continued to climb, all the way to the top of the briar, where, at last, the vines grew slim enough to cut.

He took the Trickster's knife and cut three long tendrils, which he tucked into his belt. He was about to descend when he noticed the House of the Unknown God in the distance. The soft firelight that gleamed from the windows seemed to say, *Welcome. You are welcome here.*

My brother is in that house, he thought.

Perhaps it should have been a comfort to the Briar Thief, to know that his brother was somewhere safe and warm. But in that moment, he was filled with longing and remorse. He would return to the land of the living while his brother remained here, and it broke his heart.

He was thus lost in his thoughts when a giant claw grabbed him around the middle and picked him off the vine the way you might snatch a squash bug from a pumpkin patch. It was the God of Wrath, and how wrathful she was to find a mere human taking something that belonged to the Old Gods.

"Do you think you can be equal to a god? How dare you!" she raged as the Briar Thief struggled to release himself from her grasp. "If a briar is what you want, a briar is what you shall have."

With that, the God of Wrath carried the thief to the longest, sharpest thorn in the garden—the Thorn of Eternal Life—and she hung him there as easily as a child might drape a cloak on a coat hook. The barb pierced his heart, and as his life ebbed away from him, he could feel the moment that the Trickster let go of his heart in the mortal world, and he could hear the wily god laugh at him.

"What a fool you are!" cried the Trickster, and perhaps he was right. Like the bloom that hides the thorn, unending life comes with more pain than joy. But we celebrate the Briar Thief anyway, the good man who tried to make the world a better place, not for himself, but for everyone.

Chapter Nineteen

Adam refused to lie down, so they cushioned his seat with folded tablecloths and made him put his feet up on an extra chair. Thankfully, the hole in his chest had stopped bleeding.

Rosie and Duckers slumped in their own chairs, staring at him, while Zeddie paced behind them, muttering "How is this my life?" under his breath. As she stared at the slender green cirrus coiling out of Adam's open collar, Rosie performed a series of mental calisthenics, trying to make sense of what Adam had told them.

"But you can't be the Briar Thief," she said at last.

"Why can't I be the Briar Thief?"

"Because he died! He's dead! He got a giant thorn through the heart!"

"The Thorn of *Eternal Life*," Adam said slowly and evenly, helping her connect the dots.

"So there's a *plant* growing inside you? That's your medical condition?" asked Duckers.

"Yes."

Duckers cupped his face in his hands. "Fuuuuuuuuuck."

"And it's the same plant that gave the Salt Sea's lover a thousand thousand years," said Rosie.

"That's right." Adam removed his glasses and ran a hand down his face.

"How old were you when this happened?"

"Thirty-three."

"So your body is thirty-three years old? Forever?"

"Correct."

"But what about the hair?" She indicated the silver streak.

"If I want to stay in one place for a few decades, I must make it appear that I'm aging. It's simply a lock of hair that I bleach and dye. You would think it would take more than that to fool people, but I interact with others so rarely that they see what they expect to see. I have a means by which I can add wrinkles, too, if I must."

"Is that why you wear glasses, to make yourself look older?" asked Zeddie as Adam hooked the arms behind his ears once more.

"No, I wear glasses because I'm nearsighted."

"But you're immortal."

"Yes, I'm trapped in my thirty-three-year-old body, with my thirty-three-year-old eyes, which were and continue to be nearsighted."

"So you got saddled with immortality, but it didn't fix your eyeballs?"

"Or my scars or my teeth."

Rosie sat up. "Oh my gods, Adam, your scars! You got them when you fought the dragon. And that's why you hate dragons so much."

"Yes," he said quietly.

"What scars?" asked Duckers.

Adam turned in his seat and raised the hem of his shirt, offering a peek at one angry red gash.

Zeddie stopped long enough to get a look. "This is real. Right. Totally makes sense," he said before he restarted his pacing.

"You got a raw deal, that's for sure," said Duckers.

"Nearsightedness and a few scars are not the worst things to carry with you for millennia."

A thick silence followed as Adam's companions contemplated what might be the worst thing to carry with you for millennia.

"I should have told you long before now," said Adam, "but I didn't know how to broach the subject or if you would believe me if I did."

"I get it," said Duckers. "I mean, how do you tell someone, 'Hey, I'm a legend'? It's not like that comes up in casual conversation unless a fucking invisible vine pops out of your chest."

"Perhaps, but my behavior tonight was unacceptable."

"All in favor of forgiving the guy who tried to save humanity during the War of the Gods?" asked Rosie.

The question was met with unanimous *ayes*.

"That's settled, then. So, Adam, has the briar ever...you know...grown on the *outside* of your body like this?"

"No."

"Should we be concerned about that?"

"I don't know."

"Because I am feeling very concerned about that."

"That makes two of us."

Zeddie waved a hand to get everyone's attention. "Excuse me. Do you all realize this man is two thousand years old? What the fuck?"

"The war was two thousand and twenty-five years ago, so technically, I am roughly two thousand and fifty-eight years old. But I never calculated the shift from a lunar calendar to a solar calendar into my age, and to be honest, I've lost track of my time on Earth." Adam looked to Rosie. "When I told you that I didn't know exactly how old I am, that was true."

Rosie sat with that. A half hour ago, she had thought of herself as older than the hills. Now she realized that she was a spring chicken compared to Adam.

"Let's get some things straight. Gobbo said that he first noticed the briar in the Mist five years ago, so our current dilemma started when you cut your hand in the West Station's portal, correct?" asked Rosie.

"Yes, that does seem to have caused…this." Adam gestured toward the veranda and the increasingly vine-covered landscape beyond it.

Duckers raised his hand. "What are you two talking about?"

Rosie filled in the backstory, leaving out the emotional bits and sticking to the facts.

"I don't understand why the briar took root then," said Adam. "I tried cutting it out many times before, and it didn't work."

"Gonna need you to elaborate on that," said Rosie.

"Do we need that?" asked Zeddie. "Because I'm not sure I can deal with any more blood tonight."

"It's why I invented the portals, but perhaps I should put this in context," said Adam, ignoring Zeddie's squeamishness. "Before I became immortal, I was always tinkering, making everyday objects more efficient, creating things that made life easier. When I found myself facing down a thousand thousand years, I focused on working rather than on living, on inventing things that would help people. Sanitation, mostly. Running water, which eventually led to toilets, that kind of thing."

Duckers cackled. "You invented *toilets?*"

"Yes."

"You absolute king. What else?"

"Printmaking, the printing press, ballpoint pens—much later, though—"

"What?" exclaimed Zeddie.

"—gas technology, including lighting, ovens, autoducks—"

"Autoducks?" Rosie thought of her beloved Gratton Parker series 7 coupe and fell a little harder for Adam.

"I also invented the gramophone and, more recently, transistors."

By now, Rosie was so giddy she was beginning to feel light-headed. "Holy shit snacks."

"In fact, I have watched you use one of my inventions," Adam told her.

"Not the toilet."

"No, thank gods. Marks Code."

"But that was named after the guy who invented it."

"Yes, I am aware of that."

Rosie stared at him, both confused and delighted by the reappearance of Dry Adam.

"That was when I was using the name Joseph Marks," he explained. "New life. New name. I have had many lives and many names."

"So your name's not Adam Lee?" asked Duckers.

"It is now. I've cycled through Adam Lee a few times over the years."

Rosie's mind was spinning, trying to take it all in. "Let's come back to that. What do all of these inventions have to do with the briar?"

"Those particular inventions had nothing to do with the briar, other than doing something worthwhile with my time on Earth, if not for my own benefit, then for the benefit of humanity in general. But the portals? Those I created for myself."

"How so?"

"Early on, I tried to bleed this eternal life out of my veins, but it didn't work. The plant grew inside me and would not take root elsewhere. I needed soil from the land of the gods and the dead, but I was never able to go back, so I turned my attention to Tanria. It's a place for the Old Gods, so perhaps my briar could take root here. After a century of trial and error, I made a portal that worked. I bled in this land every way I knew how, but the plant never left my body. Eventually, I gave up and shared the technology with the rest of the world. There was no reason why humanity shouldn't reap the rewards of my failure."

"So why did the plant begin to grow here when you cut your hand in the portal?" asked Rosie. "What made that time different from your other attempts?"

Both Duckers and Adam gazed intently at Rosie.

She squirmed under the weight of their probing attention. "Me?"

"You," said Duckers, and Adam nodded.

"What did I have to do with anything?"

"Who was the god standing with the Joint Chiefs at the portal this afternoon?" asked Adam, the same question he'd hurled at her before, delivered far more gently this time.

Click click click went the puzzle pieces, and Rosie buried her face in her hands.

Zeddie plopped onto an empty chair, joining the group. "I have no clue what you people are talking about right now."

"My father is the Trickster," Rosie told him, the admission muffled by her hands.

"Okay then." Zeddie sprang to his feet and began pacing anew.

Rosie pulled her hands away from her face, and the tendril poking out of Adam's shirt was a surprise all over again. "You must hate his ass," she said.

"I admit that I am not fond of him," Adam answered carefully.

"Understandable. I'm not fond of him either."

"I can't believe you were a prince," said Zeddie.

"Prince, nothing. The guy's a *hero*," added Duckers.

"I am no hero."

"You are a literal hero in the literal books about literal heroes."

"I am the literal reason you are trapped in Tanria. I repeat, I am no hero."

"Incorrect," said Rosie. "The Trickster is the literal reason we're stuck here and the literal reason for your 'medical condition.' Blame where blame is due. And for the record, I don't call him Father or Dad. I tend to use terms like *Entitled God-Baby* or *Ugh, Him Again*."

"Noted."

Their eyes met, and Adam didn't attempt to hide behind a mask of cool indifference. His warmth and sadness and humor were all on display, and for the span of three rapid heartbeats, Rosie forgot about Duckers and Zeddie and Tanria and the world outside the Mist as her alarming affection for this man took off like a bottle rocket.

Then Adam winced, and Rosie watched in real time as his vine pushed farther from his chest. She squinted at it until it stopped moving. "Mother of Sorrows."

"What is it?" asked Duckers.

"Adam's vine grew a titch."

Zeddie whimper-laughed. "We are so screwed."

"No, this is good. We know what the problem is now, which means we can fix it."

Duckers gestured to Adam. "He's been trying to fix it for two thousand years."

"But now he has me."

Adam grunted in pain.

"Not to be a dick, Foxy, but I think you're making it worse."

"Am I making it worse?" Rosie asked Adam.

"How could you make anything worse?" he replied, and Rosie could swear the subtext was *You make everything better.* She filed the swoony sentiment away for later obsession before she stood and clapped her hands.

"All right. It's time to stop moping and start problem-solving. We've got one more chance to get out of Tanria, using the portal the chief sent with Gobbo, and we are going to own it. I suggest a three-pronged approach here. Adam will repair the portal while I scout out vine-free places in the Mist to make our escape, and Zeddie can keep us fed."

"Sure thing. I can inventory the food they sent and make a meal plan," said Zeddie.

"What about me? Want me to fly with you?" offered Duckers, even as his eyes drifted in Zeddie's direction. Rosie would have liked to have had company, but she decided to do her partner a solid instead.

"What are you going to do? Guess where vines are and are not growing? Feed me bonbons while I bust my ass? You're better off staying here and holding down the fort. I'm sure Adam and Zeddie could use an extra pair of hands anyway."

"I'm cool with that, but I have to wonder..." Duckers trailed off as he chewed on an unpleasant thought.

"Spit it out, Penny-D."

"You're the conduit for this vine, right? Doesn't that mean you'll make things worse the more you travel around Tanria?"

"I don't think that's how it works," said Adam.

"Why?"

"Call it...instinct? What's the word?"

"A hunch?" suggested Rosie.

"Yes, call it a hunch."

Duckers gave him a dubious look.

"Surely you operate on such hunches in your line of work, Marshal Duckers?"

"I do, but oh my gods, you do not have to call me Marshal, Adam."

"What should I call you?"

"Duckers," he said at the same moment Zeddie said "Pen" and Rosie said "Penny-D, obviously."

"Maybe I'm missing the boat here, but shouldn't we try to

figure out how to *kill* the plant?" asked Zeddie. "Wouldn't that solve all of our problems?"

"I don't see how we can get rid of the plant when only fifty percent of us can see it, and zero percent of us can touch it," Duckers pointed out.

"I can," said Adam. "I can touch it."

He fanned his fingertips over the tendril poking out of his shirt, clearly moving it, to Rosie's eyes at least. She knelt beside him to get a better look. When his hand fell away, she gave it a shot, but her fingers passed through the vine as they always did, albeit with the same friction she had noticed before. She leaned in for a closer look at the plant and gawked as the vine produced a tiny green leaf.

"Did that hurt?" Rosie looked up from the plant to find him staring down at her, his eyes unfocused, his full lips soft and slightly open while her face hovered inches away from his chest. This close to the skin laid bare by his open collar, she caught a whiff of his delectable cologne. He must have put some on since his suitcase's arrival at the Dragon's Lair.

"You sprouted a leaf," she told him, mesmerized by his unguarded face and the intoxicating scent of him.

"Did I?" He looked at the leaf in question, and his brow furrowed, creating those two delicious dents between his eyebrows. "It didn't hurt."

"Rosie, get your hands off Adam before I'm forced to report you to Maguire for harassment," said Duckers.

Rosie realized that her left hand perched on Adam's shoulder and her right hand rested on his thigh. She snatched them off his body and fisted them over her heart. "Shit! Sorry!"

"It's nothing." Adam stood and walked to the veranda windows. The other three watched him warily, but for a man who'd recently bled all over the dining room floor, he moved with his usual grace.

"I don't think we should try to kill the plant," said Duckers, the unspoken words screaming through the minds of everyone present: *We don't know what killing the plant would do to Adam.*

"Then we're agreed," said Rosie. "Adam will work on the portal, Zeddie will handle the food situation, and I will fly through Tanria like a badass god."

The statement inspired Adam to turn around, his expression admonishing. "Feel free to exercise a modicum of caution."

"I will, but again, I can't stay dead, so."

"Be cautious anyway."

"This is what I've been saying for years," Duckers chimed in. "I don't like it when you die. He doesn't like it when you die. Zeddie, how do you feel about Rosie dying?"

"I'm not a fan."

"See? No one likes it when you die."

"So be careful," said Adam, completing Duckers's argument. "Please."

That *please* and the hint of concern that went with it made Rosie blush from the roots of her flaming hair to the tips of her ostrich leather–encased toes.

Chapter Twenty

At first light, Rosie walked alongside Adam and Duckers as they gingerly carried the portal out of the restaurant and down to the stable, where Adam would have more room to maneuver as he made repairs.

"Sure you don't want help with that?" she offered. The pirated portal was large enough to let a human being pass through and little else, so it didn't require more than two people to carry it, but Rosie was worried about Adam after seeing him bleeding on the floor last night.

"I am perfectly well. How many times must I tell you, I will not perish on your watch?"

"As many times as you have to tell me to be careful?" she replied.

"No one could ever tell you that enough," said Duckers.

Adam laughed, a sound that went beyond his usual contained burst of amusement. Everything about him was looser this morning—his shoulders, his facial expression, the way he moved. Rosie wondered how long it had been since he told anyone the truth about who he was. Was that a question you could ask a legendary hero? Rosie had never been much good at navigating the rules of polite society—especially since she tended to outlive social mores as they came and went—but she was in seriously uncharted waters here.

By now, they had arrived at the restaurant's stable, where their four equimares looked forlorn in the cavernous space. It was unusually large and grand in order to accommodate the coaches and equimares bringing customers to the Dragon's Lair for lunch and dinner every day but Allgodsday. Not that it had gotten much use. The restaurant hadn't opened to the public yet, and now it seemed unlikely that it ever would.

"The investors are going to take a bath on this place," said Rosie.

"Lots of investors are going to take a bath on lots of things in Tanria," Duckers observed as he helped Adam prop the portal against a wall.

"And on that happy note, I'm going to go wrangle me a dragon."

"Be careful," Duckers and Adam said in unison.

"When am I ever not careful?" asked Rosie, blowing them a kiss and scampering off before Duckers could cough up a snappy comeback and Adam could do anything else that would make her any more smitten than she already was. A half hour later, she was winging along the Mist on Eloise's back.

At first, she thought it was overcast, but the sky beyond the Mist was blue and cloudless. Upon closer examination, Rosie discovered that the plant had grown so high into the dome covering Tanria that it was beginning to filter the sunlight.

That can't be good, she thought, and felt a commiserative pulse through Eloise's antlers. Leaving Tanria might solve the problem for Rosie and Duckers and Adam and Zeddie, but it didn't solve the real problem at all. The dragons would still be here, and the graps and the Tanrian turkeys and all the weird flora and fauna that would never be able to escape. What in the Salt Sea would happen to them?

Eloise sent another pulse, one that conveyed worry and fear, held at bay but simmering constantly under her gleaming magenta scales. Rosie wanted to stroke her neck to comfort her, but she couldn't let go of the antlers while they were airborne.

Circumnavigating Tanria on dragonback took only a couple of hours; finding a spot relatively free of the briar that was also low enough to the ground on both sides of the Tanrian border to allow four people to escape without sliding down the Mist and breaking their legs on the other side took considerably longer.

At first, Rosie was glad of her extended solo flight. It gave her the room she needed to breathe and think. But the more she considered their predicament, the less she wanted to think at all.

Five days ago, the situation hadn't been great, but it hadn't been dire either. But that was before Rosie had understood what the shadows were, before the plant had grown completely out of control, before she and Duckers and Zeddie had found out about Adam's true identity.

Now the more Rosie considered the peril that the briar posed to her friends, the more her panic on their behalf grew. She and Adam could survive what was coming if they failed to get out. Duckers and Zeddie almost certainly would not, and all Rosie could do about it was fly around on a dragon in search of a spot in the Mist where they might be able to punch a hole out of Tanria.

With this emotional morass poking her heart like a thorny thicket of her own, Rosie kept an eye out for possible escape routes. Whenever she spied a promising lead from the air, she had Eloise land so that she could get a better look. In most cases, the vines still presented a problem, and by midafternoon, she had found only a handful of possible exit points, mostly in the Dragon's Teeth mountains. The most promising location, however, was in southeastern Tanria, hemmed in by the ambrosial swamps. She meticulously marked its location on her map.

Worn out, she allowed herself a fifteen-minute break on the

ground to cry and eat the sandwich Zeddie had packed for her that morning. Eloise meeped in sympathy.

"Right? What a shit show," Rosie said to the dragon as she dabbed a tear from her eye. "But this sandwich is fucking amazing. What did Zeddie put in this thing? Sex?"

Meep-chirr-chirrup, said Eloise, by which Rosie assumed she meant *You wish*.

"Don't start with me. I need to keep my focus on finding a way out of here. No offense."

Meep?

"Listen, I'm still processing the whole Adam-is-immortal thing. My whole life, I've been stuck in a doom loop of caring about people only to lose them, over and over. Now suddenly, here is this person who's like me, who's not going anywhere, and it feels big and important and overwhelming. But what if our connection here is dictated by the circumstances? What if we cross through the Mist and find out that nothing about the past six days is real or lasting? What if he's all, 'Nah, I don't like you, so please stay the fuck away from me' in the normal world?"

Chirr-chirr-chirrup.

"You're right. First things first. I'll worry about my big feelings after we get out of here."

Rosie climbed onto Eloise's back once more, and off they went. But no matter how far they flew and how hard Rosie looked, that spot in S-54 appeared to be the last hope of escape. With both of them wilting, Rosie signaled that it was time to call it a day. Once they'd landed by the lake, she slid off and nuzzled the dragon's snout.

"Sorry, Eloise. Seven hours in the air, and all we have to show for it is one lousy spot on the other side of Tanria, which doesn't help you at all."

The dragon snorted wearily. Rosie was about to bid her farewell for the day when she noticed that a vine dangled from one of Eloise's wings. A thorn had punctured the leathery membrane, and glittery dragon blood dripped from the wound. Instinctively, Rosie reached for the briar to pull it out, but her hand passed through it as always.

For the second time that day, tears streamed down Rosie's face, but unlike her earlier crying jag, these were tears of anger—anger at herself for getting Eloise hurt, anger at the vine for shutting down the portals, and most of all, anger at her father for causing this nightmare in the first place. The Trickster was the one who had brought this monstrous plant into being. He was the one who had ruined Adam's life. He was the god who'd thoughtlessly used a mortal woman named Jocelyn Fox without ever considering the consequences of that seduction. And now here was Rosie, the product of that ill-fated union, trapped by a problem of her father's creation along with three other precious human beings who did not deserve this fate.

Eloise trumpeted to a dragon swanning nearby on the lake, who came ashore to grasp the vine in her toothless mouth and tug it free. The dragon in question had a baby on her back, which hopped down and skipped toward Rosie like an excitable puppy.

"Aw," cooed Rosie, grateful for the adorable distraction as she petted the hatchling between the two antler nubbins on her fox-like head. The baby sneezed, which would have been cute, except it spewed a staggering amount of sparkling gold snot all over Rosie's front. She could swear Eloise laughed at her.

"I guess you're fine, then," said Rosie. The dragon meeped at her before taking off again, this time heading for her nest. It was odd, since the dragons didn't usually leave the lake until the sun began to set. The other dragons followed, the entire flock taking to the sky to turn in for the evening. It did not take long to figure out why.

As Rosie made her way to the Dragon's Lair on foot, Tanria's one and only storm came along and opened up a deluge directly above her. The God of Wrath may have surrendered alongside all the other Old Gods centuries ago to become a star on the altar of the sky, but the ominous gray cloud she had created while imprisoned in Tanria ping-ponged around inside the Mist, dumping her unending vengeance upon the unlucky. Today, the unlucky was Rosie.

The storm followed her, drenching her clothes without washing away the glittery dragon goo splattering her shirt and pants.

"Fuck my life," she muttered a half second before a bolt of lightning struck her and she died for the third time in a week and a half.

The sun had fully set by the time Rosie dragged her ass through the kitchen door of the Dragon's Lair to find her three companions in the dining room, all of them sopping wet from head to toe. Zeddie was peeling off his dripping shirt, revealing an impressive physique, when he caught sight of Rosie and froze.

"Guess I'm not the only one who got caught out in the rain, huh?" she said.

"What happened to you?" asked Duckers.

"Lots of flying, dragon snot, pissing rain."

Zeddie wrinkled his nose, his shirt half-off, half-on. "What's that burning smell?"

"Please tell me you weren't struck by lightning again," Duckers begged Rosie.

"I would, but lying is wrong, Penny-D."

Rosie looked to Adam to gauge his response to her most recent resurrection and was immediately distracted by the way his white shirt, made sheer by the rainwater, clung to his wiry frame.

Perhaps she should stand under the frigid, torrential rain for a bit longer.

"I want to ask if you're all right, but I also don't want to annoy you by asking you if you're all right," he said, his humor dry, his body deliciously wet.

"I see what you did there, Dr. Sassafras."

"So, situation normal: all fucked up?" asked Zeddie.

"Yep."

"Then I am putting on dry clothes."

He finished pulling off his shirt, at which point Duckers finally clocked the half-naked ex-boyfriend to his right and turned away abruptly, while Adam—who was wearing an uncharacteristic scowl—stalked off to his curtained-off bedroom to change.

"Not to objectify you, Zeddie, but you're kind of hot," Rosie informed him.

Adam coughed from his corner nook. Or, at least, it sounded like a cough. A judgmental cough.

"Oh, uh, sorry," said Zeddie, holding the sopping shirt over his chiseled chest. "I shouldn't be stripping down right in front of you. I wasn't thinking."

"Feel free to not think in my presence any old time."

"Salt Sea, RoFo," Duckers muttered before he fled for his own corner.

"She claims to have a filter, but I have seen no evidence" came Adam's disembodied voice from behind the tablecloth-curtains. Did he honestly not know that his deadpan humor delivered in that sexy rasp did more for her than five strapping young Zeddie Birdsalls? She opted to keep this tidbit to herself since she did, in fact, have a filter. A flimsy one, but it was there.

Rosie stepped into her own curtained-off area to change clothes and inspect her beloved intimates. Both brassiere and panties were soaked, but her clothes had saved them from the perils of baby dragons and lightning. Since the storm continued to pour down the God of Wrath's displeasure upon the roof, she hung her lingerie from the fireplace mantel to dry, the buttery yellow satin and lace downright cheery in the firelight once she had a blaze going.

Meanwhile, Duckers had set four white porcelain mugs on the group's adopted table and was now filling them with bliss in a cup, a hot drink that involved strong black tea, honey, whiskey, and occasionally, lemon juice.

Zeddie caught a whiff of it in the air. "Are you making Hart's 'medicine'?"

Duckers looked up and met his ex's gaze for a lingering moment. "With fresh lemons and everything. I helped myself in the kitchen. I hope that's okay?"

"I can't imagine a better use for a lemon."

The brief exchange between the two men was oddly tender. Rosie hated to pop the romantic bubble, but she'd had a fucking day, and she deserved some medicine.

"The Three Mothers bless you," she told her partner as she plopped into a chair in front of a steaming cup. Duckers and Zeddie sat on either side of her, so Adam took the seat across from her, facing the fireplace. His damp hair looked extra glossy, and the warm light of the fire flattered the sharp planes and soft lines of his face as his eyes went dreamy and distant. Even the sprig of briar curling out of his shirt looked lovely and poetic against his skin.

Zeddie raised his mug. "Cheers."

"Cheers," echoed Rosie and Duckers.

Adam startled, snapping out of his reverie. He fumbled for his mug and took a fortifying drink, which brought color to his cheeks.

"How'd y'all wind up caught out in the rain?"

"Adam needed help taking the front panel off the portal," said

Zeddie, so apparently everyone was calling him Adam now. Rosie wondered if she would ever have the opportunity to ask him what his real name was.

"I could have done it myself, but since time is of the essence, I thought it best to ask for assistance," said Adam, even as his gaze slid away from the conversation. He was oddly distracted this evening.

Duckers cupped his hands around his mug. "I saw the storm blowing in when we were done, but I thought we could make it here before it caught up to us."

"I didn't know that much water could come out of one cloud," said Zeddie.

"They didn't call her the God of Wrath for nix," said Rosie, still smarting from having been struck by lightning. Again.

It wasn't until after the words had popped out of her mouth that Rosie woke up to her own insensitivity. She grimaced apologetically at the man whom the God of Wrath had impaled on the Thorn of Eternal Life two millennia ago, but Adam didn't acknowledge her gaffe. His focus remained fixed on a point over Rosie's shoulder.

She gave him a befuddled look before asking Zeddie, "How's the food situation?"

"Pretty good, enough to last us two weeks, more if we're strategic. And from what Adam says, it sounds like the portal will be ready way before that."

Adam once again dragged his attention back to the conversation. "Yes, that's correct."

"What about you, Rosie? How'd you fare today?" asked Duckers.

"Not awesome. First of all, for those of you wondering whether or not the dragons can see or touch the briar, the answer is yes."

"That's not good," said Zeddie.

Duckers swirled his mug ruminatively. "I have a theory about who can see and/or interact with the plant. The Mist, graps, dragons…they're all part of Tanria. Me and Zeddie, equimares, the stuff we bring in from outside? None of that belongs here."

"What about me?" asked Rosie. "Why can I see it? I'm not from here."

"You're the daughter of the god who made it."

"But I can't touch it."

Duckers gave her sparkle fingers. "Magic."

"Moving on to more pressing issues," said Rosie as she smacked one of his hands en route to retrieve her pack. She moved her cup and Duckers's to the side to make room and accidentally flashed the entire table as she bent over to spread out her map of Tanria. Fortunately, Duckers didn't care about boobs in general, Zeddie didn't seem to care about her boobs in particular, and who knew what in the Salt Sea Adam thought about boobs, hers or otherwise? When she snuck a glance his way to see if he'd noticed her inadvertent display, he downed the contents of his mug, reminding Rosie of herself, lining up shots in a feeble attempt to get drunk.

"The best place I've found so far is in Sector S-54," she explained, tapping the location on the map. "The Mist is clear in a couple other locations, but this is the only spot that's level with the landscape on the Bushong side. We should be able to walk straight out."

Zeddie nodded as he stared at the map, but Duckers bit his lips between his teeth and flashed Rosie a worried look, one that said, *That's going to be the shittiest of shitty rides.*

Problems for Future Us, she mentally replied before refolding the map.

"That all sounds terrifyingly hopeful," said Zeddie as he rose from his seat. "In the meantime, I'll get started on dinner."

"I'll help," said Adam, casting one last look over Rosie's shoulder before following him to the kitchen.

As Rosie set the table, she glanced up from Adam's place setting and realized what had been distracting him: a brassiere and matching panties in buttery soft yellow satin and copious amounts of lace, dangling from the fireplace mantel.

Adam Lee, you horndog, she thought smugly.

Chapter Twenty-One

You know what would kick ass right about now? A gramophone. Or a transistor," said Duckers as they sipped their post-dinner aperitifs later that evening.

"Music would be nice," Zeddie agreed.

"And dancing," said Rosie, remembering her mother and the way they used to dance together in their apartment to the music of the buskers drifting in through the windows.

Adam rose from his seat and walked over to the Old Gods–era instruments on the dais. "Which one of these do you want?"

Rosie, Duckers, and Zeddie shared a confused look.

"Seriously?" asked Zeddie.

"I've had a great deal of time to fill in my life. I can play many instruments."

"Can you play the guitar thing?" asked Duckers.

"It's a lute." Adam picked it up with the confidence of a sea polo captain saddling his equimaris. It looked enormous in his grasp—at least half his size—and yet he seemed perfectly at ease handling the huge instrument.

Once he seemed satisfied with tuning it, Adam got himself settled and proceeded to play an extremely complex piece of music, the fingers of his left hand pressing the fretboard with precision as he plucked the strings of the body so quickly that it boggled the mind. Music filled the dining room, alive and lovely, making

Rosie's insides lurch with affection for this marvel of a man who never stopped surprising her.

"What the fuck!" laughed Duckers as soon as the song was over.

The audience of three leaped to their feet in a standing ovation. Rosie stuck two fingers in her mouth and whistled, while Zeddie said, "For real, that was amazing." Adam bowed his head, but Rosie caught a faint smile on his lips, as if he were genuinely pleased with himself.

Adorable, she thought, but she kept that sentiment to herself. Adam didn't strike her as a person who had ever thought of himself as cute, and surely none of them were feeling terribly adorable at this juncture anyway.

"I wonder...," he said, his fingers experimenting with a few chords, his eyes gone distant as he listened to the mysterious progression he was stringing together. And then, out of nowhere, he played the unmistakable intro to "Having My Sugar" by Brandey Chandler, one of those cheesy pop songs with inane lyrics and a catchy melody that turned it into an ear worm of the highest order. It was at least twenty years old and had descended into cult classic territory, the sort of song grandmas knew as well as ten-year-olds on the playground.

If someone had put a pistol crossbow to Rosie's head and asked her, *What's the last song Dr. Adam Lee of the University of Quindaro would know, much less play on any instrument ever?* she would have answered *"Having My Sugar" by Brandey Chandler* without batting an eye.

"Holy shit!" Duckers cackled, while Zeddie dug his fingers into his curly hair, his eyes goggling in delighted amazement. But no one was more amazed or delighted to see and hear Adam play a fizzy pop song—on a lute no less—than Rosalie Emmaline Fox.

Oh, shit snacks, she thought, *this is love, and that's all there is to it.*

She and Duckers and Zeddie belted out the lyrics. Duckers took Rosie by the waist and danced with her between the tables, and then Zeddie cut in to dance with her, and then Duckers and Zeddie wound up dancing with each other, and all three of them sang their fool heads off until the song came to an end.

"What else you got?" Duckers asked Adam as he caught his breath. His face had that shining quality one gets when they're truly happy, and Zeddie looked much the same. What a miracle Adam had wrought, to make them forget the darkness, if only for a little while. He seemed to know it. He even seemed to be glad of it. Small miracles.

"Do you know any Brigitte Porcel songs?" asked Rosie.

"Ah, Brigitte Porcel," Adam said wistfully. He placed his slender fingers on the fretboard and began to pick out the opening melody of "He Thinks You're on My Mind." And Rosie, who had not sung professionally in years and years, began to sing along.

When she was a child, Rosie used to sing with Jocelyn all the time.

"What a voice you have, my darling rose!" her mother would exclaim, and she had trained her daughter from a young age how to use it. It never occurred to either one of them that a red-eyed demigod would never have a career onstage, not then at least. That was a lesson Rosie had had to learn the hard way, through rejection after rejection. Jocelyn went on singing and dancing in show after show, never getting her big break, until her knees gave out on her at last, and her cancer caught up to her. And the only gig in entertainment Rosie could find was in the traveling circus, dying and reviving rather than singing.

But now she sang, remembering how good it felt to draw air into her lungs and support the music, holding each note exactly where it was supposed to be, how right it was to weave the tender emotion of the lyrics into every word. The world had not let Rosie Fox be a singer, but she was no longer in that world. She was in this one, and in this world, her audience of three listened and cared. They had no interest in telling her who she was not allowed to be; they were fine with her as she was.

In her mind, she imagined herself singing with Jocelyn again, even though Jocelyn had died long before Brigitte Porcel's day— long before gramophones for that matter. She sang with her mother in the cramped apartment in Morton City, even as she watched Adam play the lute and Zeddie pull Duckers into a slow sway of a dance, and for the first time in a long while, she was at peace with herself and the way things were.

When the song came to an end, Duckers and Zeddie stopped dancing and started clapping, but Rosie only had eyes for Adam. She knew she ought to do a better job hiding her feelings, but he had given her—given all of them—this gift of an evening, and she couldn't bring herself to wipe away the lovesick look on her face. He regarded her with an expression of soft wonder, but whether it indicated admiration for her musical talent or a welcome mat for her affection, she couldn't say.

She liked it either way.

Rosie and Duckers got cleanup duty since Zeddie and Adam had made dinner. As Rosie got started on the plates, Duckers leaned against the counter, his arms folded in that *I'm going to say something you don't want to hear* pose.

"Out with it," she told him.

"That spot you scouted is about as far from here as you can get in Tanria."

"It's not right next door, that's for sure."

"On equimarisback, we'd either have to cross through the bogs or circumvent them, and I think we're agreed that time is of the essence, right? Every second we're stuck in Tanria makes it that much harder to get out."

That helpless panic she had felt as she flew around the Mist clawed its way into her gut once more. "I know."

"Which means that the second Adam has the portal repaired—and I mean that second—we need to move."

"I know."

"Which means your boyfriend is going to need to buck up and get his ass on a dragon."

"He's not my boyfriend, and I can't help but notice that you are not helping me wash these dishes."

"I'm trying to have a serious conversation here."

"So am I, but look at me! Talking *and* washing!"

Zeddie chose this opportune moment to step into the kitchen and say, "Hey."

"What's up?" she asked him, glad for the interruption.

"Adam turned in early, and I wanted to talk to you two alone. Listen, I know he has a messed-up history with dragons, but with the vine growing all over the place, I think it makes more sense to fly wherever we need to go rather than take the equimares."

"My point exactly," said Duckers.

At least Zeddie wasn't teasing her about her "boyfriend," but an image of Adam, scared and angry and recalcitrant, filled her memory, the desperation in his voice when he had told her, *You have no idea. You don't understand.* She had informed him that getting on a dragon might be a necessity, whether he liked it or not, but now that she knew his story, she couldn't stomach the idea.

"How are we going to get the portal to the exit point?" she countered, grasping at straws.

Duckers put a finger to his chin. "If only we had a genius with us who could figure that out."

Well, he had her there.

"All in favor of flying to the exit, say aye," said Duckers.

Zeddie put up his hand as he and Duckers said, "Aye." Duckers turned a stern look on Rosie. Denial wasn't a viable option anymore. She reluctantly raised her hand.

"Good. All in favor of Rosie being the one to convince Adam that he has to get on a dragon, say aye."

Zeddie put both hands in the air. "Aye. All the ayes. So many ayes."

"And the ayes have it."

Rosie scowled at them.

"You know we're right," said Duckers.

"And Adam does seem to like you best," added Zeddie, moderately apologetic.

Duckers turned to him. "Does he *like* her or does he l—"

"Zip it!" Rosie glared at them. "Fine, I'll do it. But you two jerks can do the dishes."

Since there was no reason to put it off, she dried her hands on Duckers's dish towel and marched to the dining room door like a soldier facing the battlefield.

"Or does he lo-o-ove her?" Duckers sang quietly under his breath behind her. She spun around to find him smirking at her in ornery glee, while Zeddie clamped his lips in an attempt to contain his laughter. Rosie gave them both the stink eye before pushing open the door and making her trek across the dining room.

Lamplight glowed behind the curtains of Adam's sleeping area, so, assuming he was awake, she knocked on the wood panel outside.

"Come in," he said gruffly from behind the wall-cum-tablecloth.

Rosie had not anticipated being invited inside what was

essentially Adam's bedroom at the Dragon's Lair. It felt presumptuous, letting herself into his private space, but she was a demigod on a mission, and needs must.

She stepped beyond the tablecloths and found Adam sitting cross-legged on his bedding, leaning against the wall. He set the book he had been reading face down on his thigh, using his leg as a bookmark. He was wearing a pair of pale blue pajama pants and a white cotton T-shirt with the vine forming a long, irregular bump beneath the fabric, a sight so intimate that Rosie wanted to fan herself. She decided that she had better cough up a joke before she spontaneously combusted.

"Shouldn't you find out who's knocking before you invite them in? I could have been a serial killer."

"Serial killers in Tanria are not my greatest concern at the moment."

Rosie caught a hint of his cologne wafting in the air. Either he was perplexingly dedicated to smelling good even in the most dire of circumstances or he had put it on with someone in mind, a thought that made her heart beat so hard that her pulse pounded in her eardrums.

He traced the spine of his book with one tapered fingertip and said, "To answer your question, yes, I will do it."

"How do you know what I'm going to ask?"

"Call it an educated guess."

She thought of Adam pressing his entire body against the back wall of the terrace in terror, of the way he'd squeezed his eyes shut as Eloise nuzzled him, of his ferocity when he told Rosie, *I don't want to talk about it.*

"You'll fly? You'll really do it?"

"Yes."

"On the back of a dragon?"

"I doubt I could ride on its front."

She regarded him carefully, expecting to sense his trepidation, but he radiated resignation instead.

"Thank you," she said.

"I understand that it's necessary."

"You don't have to ride solo. You can ride with me. Or Duckers," she hastened to add. Adam might not relish sitting between her legs, after all.

Gods, now she was thinking about Adam between her legs. Mother of Sorrows have mercy.

"I may take you up on that offer," he said, and there was the trepidation at last, bleeding through his attempts to keep his shit together. She wanted to tell him how brave he was, how much strength of character it took to face his fear like this. But what right did she have to be proud of him? What did he care what she thought?

Unless the dab of cologne at his neck meant he cared more than he let on.

"I'll let you get back to your book," Rosie told him, the unexpected intimacy of being here with him in his pajamas suddenly overwhelming. His clean, spicy scent lingered in the air between them like a cloud of unarticulated emotions. "Where did you find a book, by the way? Are there more hanging out around here somewhere?"

"I packed two in my luggage. Would you like the other?"

"As long as it's not in Eshilese."

He reached toward his open suitcase. Rosie spotted the book in question sitting beside his neatly folded ivory-and-blue-striped silk boxer shorts before his hand made contact. Her eyes locked on his underwear, and the realization that his exquisite taste in menswear extended to his undergarments gave her heart palpitations. She had to tear her gaze away from his intimate apparel so that she could focus on the novel he was kindly loaning her.

Then she realized which book he held in his hand, and smiled so wide she nearly cracked her face in two.

"You know it?" he surmised as she took the book from him and held it tenderly.

"I love this one. Everyone goes gaga over *Enemies and Lovers*, but *Blandishment* is my favorite C. Redfern book."

"And why is that?"

"It's bittersweet. All that sadness under the surface makes it more powerful when Katherine Morgan and Captain Danforth finally get to be together after so many years apart. And what's not to love about a hero who spends ninety percent of the book pining away in wretched desperation?"

"You enjoy a man's yearning and suffering?"

"Fictionally speaking? Very much."

"I'm glad I brought it, then."

"Maybe it was fate."

"Maybe." His voice was little more than a rumble in his chest now.

"Well, thank you for the book. And for...everything else."

Rosie ran out of breath, and perhaps Adam couldn't breathe either, because he simply nodded in response.

"Good night, Adam."

"Good night."

With no excuse to stay, she left his curtained-off room and headed for her own. As she walked, thoroughly weak in the knees, clutching the borrowed book to her chest, it occurred to her that Adam had yet to utter her name aloud. And she wanted him to. She wanted to hear what *Rosie* sounded like in that familiar, husky voice.

Maybe, he said again in the privacy of her mind.

Maybe.

Chapter Twenty-Two

With nothing left to do but wait for Adam to finish repairing the portal, Rosie spent the following morning after breakfast cocooned in her hidey-hole, reading *Blandishment* to take her mind off all the things that could go wrong with their last shot at getting out of Tanria. The story hit differently this time around. It wasn't the agonized yearning that called to her; it was the slow evolution of the main characters, the way they changed over the years until they were even more perfect for each other than they had been when they were young.

Rosie's appearance could not be called butterfly-like when she emerged from her corner cocoon after turning the last page. Her hair was no longer singed, but the burnt-feathers scent of yesterday's demise clung to her. As she cobbled together a half-assed lunch of hard-boiled eggs and carrot sticks and apples slices, she decided to forego the effort of drawing a bath and opted for a dip in the crystalline waters of Lake Vanderlinden.

Following the sounds of laughter, she found Duckers and Zeddie on the terrace, playing a game of Gods in the Corner, both of them leaning over the café table as if they were magnets pulling on one another.

"Is Adam working in the stable?" she asked.

"Probably?" said Duckers.

"Way to pay attention. FYI, I'm taking a bath in the lake, so can you two make sure I have privacy for the next half hour or so?"

"Sure thing." Duckers directed his answer at Zeddie rather than Rosie. Zeddie gave him a brash grin from across the table.

"I feel like you're not listening to me," said Rosie.

"Hmm?" asked Zeddie as he played the Briar Thief card and won the match—a match that neither player seemed to be paying much attention to.

"I said I'm taking a bath," she repeated. "In the lake."

"Oops. Looks like I won again," Zeddie told Duckers.

"Card shark," said Duckers in a way that sounded positively lascivious.

Salt fucking Sea, this was practically foreplay.

"Hello?" said Rosie. "My naked boobies are about to be on display, so..."

"Have fun," Duckers tossed over his shoulder at her.

"And then I'm going to tango with a hippopotamus while juggling chain saws and wearing a headdress made of lit sparklers."

"Want to go for another round?" Zeddie asked Duckers suggestively.

Rosie gave up and went to fetch her bath kit from her rucksack. Before she left, she hollered, "Get a room!"

"Hey!" yelled an offended Duckers.

Rosie came to the terrace windows and flipped them both the bird. "I'm taking a bath, dickweeds."

On that cheery note, she hiked the short distance down to the lake. The shoreline nearest the Dragon's Lair was wooded with pale yellow Tanrian willows, but there was a clearing in the trees with a small beach that led downhill into the water. The ground was damp in spots from yesterday's rain, but Rosie found a reasonably dry patch to set down her towel and shuck her clothes. Wearing nothing but her birth key on a chain around her neck, she sank into the crystal clear water with a sigh of pleasure. The experience did not match the luxury of her claw-foot tub with its lavender bath salts, but given her current circumstance, the full-body dunk plus soap and a good shampoo felt like a spa day.

Mary Georgina popped by to meep hello, but for the most part, the dragons stayed near the north side of the lake so that Rosie could enjoy a little peace and quiet as she floated in a dream state of cleanliness. But then her birth key bobbed by her chin, and for the first time, it occurred to her that she didn't know what would become of Jocelyn's birth key on the altar in her apartment. She had been forced to write a will when she first joined the Tanrian Marshals—it was government policy at the time—but she hadn't taken it seriously for the obvious fact that she would never need it. No matter what life threw at her, she had always come home to touch salt water to her mother's key.

It was bizarre to think of the world going on without her in it. She had loved and lost so many people over the years; she had never considered the possibility that the people who loved her in return could lose her. If she got stuck in Tanria, wasn't that essentially...dying?

A breeze rippled the lake, and Rosie tried to imagine the cool water carrying off her troubles along with the dirt and grime that had accumulated on her skin. As the water calmed, her mind drifted to more pleasant topics.

Topic, actually. Singular.

Adam.

Adam's tapered fingers on the lute, and the way he had gazed at her when the song was over.

Adam in his pajamas, handing her his copy of *Blandishment*.

Adam and every iteration of Rosie's handkerchief, from the moment she had tied it around his hand five years ago to his pressing it against her wound to her tucking it into the palm of his hand—his marvelous hand—and folding his fingers around it.

Adam buttoned up in his suit and slowly coming unraveled

over the course of seven impossible days, while every glimpse Rosie got of what hid underneath his crisp exterior made her want to know more and more and more.

Adam, who was the Briar Thief.

Adam, who knew what it meant to be stuck.

She wished she could linger in this Adam-inspired reverie, but she did tell Duckers and Zeddie that she wouldn't be long, so she made herself vacate the lake. On the shore, she slipped into her favorite set of intimates, constructed in a silky mesh fabric in a vibrant peacock pattern. Gorgeous feathers fanned out over her pubic bone, while the brassiere boasted a teal-and-sapphire eye over each nipple. The set was so gorgeous that it almost seemed a shame to cover it, which was just as well since Adam chose this exact moment to crest the small hill that led down to the lake.

He froze, unmoving save for the stuttering of his breath. His face, completely unguarded, displayed a bald hunger that would have put *Blandishment*'s Katherine Morgan and Captain Danforth to shame. Rosie soaked it in like a flower opening to sunlight.

She was well aware that her body, permanently hovering some-where in her midtwenties, was above par—smooth, unblemished skin, flaring hip bones, a flat stomach, and small but not insignif-icant breasts that required no intimate apparel to make them look good.

But the intimate apparel she wore now made them look, quite frankly, phenomenal.

Adam finally unstuck his tongue and looked anywhere but at her.

"Apologies. I didn't know that you were...What are you doing?" he asked, his tone accusatory.

"Taking a bath."

Adam cleared this throat, then cleared his throat again. "I was...I needed some air. I decided to take a walk, and..."

His gaze caught once more on her half-naked body, and he lost his train of thought. The sight of a stunning woman with eyes like garnets in nothing but her designer intimates and a birth key had fried his big, brilliant brain, leaving nothing behind but the truth: he longed for her as much as she longed for him. He saw her and he understood her, and he wanted the woman he saw and understood.

Rosie felt soft and beautiful under that gaze.

She clocked the moment he realized that he had let her get a good, long look at his heart. He closed his eyes, his face a rictus. "Will you please put your clothes on?"

She smiled beatifically, sloppy in love with him. "I have clothes on."

"Put *more* clothes on." His gravelly voice was rubble at this point.

"No."

He opened his eyes and stared levelly at her, putting his mask on as if she hadn't already witnessed what lay behind it.

She stepped into her boots and walked toward him.

"Marshal Fox," he said, a feeble attempt at admonishment.

"Dr. Lee," she said, imitating his tone as she continued to walk uphill without missing a beat.

He swallowed hard, a tell he couldn't hide, not with that delectable bump in his throat.

"Rosie."

She halted, letting the two simple syllables wash over her. It was the first time he had uttered her name aloud, a weary supplication that savaged his voice. If he didn't want her to come any closer, he had another think coming, because his mouth had transformed the letter *o* into a mating call. She closed the distance between them, stopping inches in front of him, the incline making their faces almost level.

"Adam," she said, filling his name with knowing affection.

He had no defense left against the enormity of what was happening between them, a story that had begun five years earlier, when their fates had become irrevocably intertwined and led them inexorably to this moment.

She hooked a finger in one of his belt loops, and his entire body went taut.

"Will you say my name again?" she asked him, her breath skating across his lips.

Helpless, he sighed, "Rosie." And then he took her face in his hands and treated her to the slowest, deepest, most heart-meltingly passionate kiss of her life.

His full lips opened hers with a rapt inevitability. He didn't spear her mouth with his tongue; he let it unfurl against hers, little by little, his pace languid, as if he was savoring the feeling of her mouth against his. This was no obligatory hand wave at foreplay. The kiss was the point, and dear gods, did he make it matter.

Rosie's cheek smudged the lenses of his glasses and set the frames askew. She wanted to set all of him askew. She dug her fingers into his silky hair and mussed it. She grabbed him by the shirtfront to pull him closer and wrinkle the fabric in her balled fists.

His hands stroked downward, from her cheeks to the long line of her neck to her bare shoulders and the naked skin of her arms, and all the while, he kissed her with a tenderness she wanted to swim in for years.

Adam slowed the kiss to the softest touching of his lips to hers before breaking it off. He bowed his head and trotted out the *kh-sh* curse before telling her, "I should not have done that. I apologize."

Rosie straightened his glasses for him. "Take your apology and shove it. Every other kiss of my life is now garbage, thanks to you.

No one else can kiss me again after that. Your lips are the gold standard. Your tongue is a masterpiece. I will accept nothing less."

He gawped at her before huffing an incredulous laugh.

"Are we... What are we?" she asked him, feeling shy all of a sudden.

He put a hand to her cheek and studied her face, his eyes amber in the sunlight. "You will have to leave Tanria to find out."

It was like he'd walked into a dark room and turned the gas sconces all the way up, filling the space with blinding light.

"You fixed the portal?" she guessed, buzzing with anxious hope.

"I fixed the portal."

"Ahhh!" Rosie hugged him while jumping up and down, setting his glasses askew all over again. But then she noticed that his vine had sprouted another leaf. As a matter of fact, the vines encroaching all around them looked a whole lot greener than she had realized.

"Is it me, or—"

He pressed a kiss to her cheek. "We should tell the others."

"Yes! Let's get the fuck out of here!"

Rosie snatched his hand and made to leave, when he stopped her.

"What's wrong?"

"Your clothes."

In the excitement, she had forgotten that she was wearing nothing but her peacock-patterned brassiere and panties and her foxy ostrich leather boots. She flipped her damp hair. "I thought you might prefer me without my clothes."

"I prefer you however you are, but..."

He blew out a breath, and Rosie could not fail to notice what his beautifully tailored pants could not hide. She put her hands on her hips and let him take one last look before she got dressed.

"Do you have any dinner plans tonight?" she asked him.

He was so unaccustomed to showing his feelings that even his smile looked sad.

"My calendar is remarkably clear."

Duckers and Zeddie were still on the terrace, sitting side by side, looking out over the lake, when Rosie and Adam returned to the Dragon's Lair. The glass muffled their conversation, so Rosie could pick up only the warmth passing between them rather than the words themselves. Zeddie turned toward Duckers, and even in profile, the smile that lit his face could have melted diamonds. It drew Duckers's eyes like iron to a lodestone, and he reached out his hand to place it over Zeddie's.

"Let's give them a moment," said Adam. He went to stand behind the bar and asked Rosie, "Would you care for a drink?"

She sat on a stool across from him, but when it occurred to her that there was a whole-ass bar between her and the man who had turned her into mush, she moved to join him on the other side.

"So you're a bartender as well as a genius and a lute player? A lutist?"

"I've had two thousand years to fill with learning all manner of things."

Rosie raised one lascivious eyebrow at him, and his face darkened.

"I can't die, but if you continue to look at me like that, you might give me a heart attack."

"Tempting," she said. "How do you feel about prairie fire shots?"

With a quiet, competent efficiency that made Rosie swoon, he set up a line of shot glasses.

"I didn't think it was possible, but you just got sexier."

He paused between the whiskey and the hot sauce. "You really have no filter."

"It's flimsy, even on the best of days. Which is today! Today is the best of days!"

"Cheers," he said, ever subdued as he handed her a glass.

"Cheers."

She clinked her glass against his before they both downed their shots.

"You can't get drunk, can you?" she asked him as they each reached for another shot glass, Adam unapologetically brushing Rosie's fingers with his own.

"No, but I can *approach* drunk."

"Is that what we're doing right now?"

"We are letting our friends do whatever they need to do while I work up the courage to ride a dragon." He threw back his second shot, but his hand shook as he set the glass down on the bar. Rosie took it between her own, this hand that she had bandaged twice now.

"You're the bravest person I know."

"I don't feel brave."

His eyes glistened, a sight that torqued her heart. Rosie wondered if those unshed tears were for his brother.

Two thousand years of loss, she thought, trying to fathom the sheer scale of it.

"You don't have to *feel* brave to *be* brave."

She leaned down to kiss him—a chaste, comforting kiss—but it was enough to make Duckers shout "Called it!" when he stepped into the dining room and caught them in the act.

Rosie and Adam snapped apart to find Duckers and Zeddie watching them from the terrace door, both of them rumpled.

"Called! It! In your face, RoFo!" yelled Duckers.

Zeddie applauded. "I see Adam took my advice."

"I didn't, actually."

"What advice?" Rosie asked Adam.

"You don't want to know."

"I told him that you two needed to bang it out."

Adam pinched the bridge of his nose, while Rosie clutched her nonexistent pearls. "What do you take me for? I'm at least going to treat him to a nice dinner first."

Adam sighed.

"You say that like we're busting out of here today," said Duckers.

"We are. We were waiting for you two to finish canoodling on the terrace."

Zeddie perked up like a terrier. "Wait, really?"

"The portal is ready whenever you are," replied Adam.

An explosion of triumphant whoops met this news. Zeddie hugged Adam, while Duckers wrapped an arm around Rosie's waist and spun her around the room. Rosie celebrated along with them, but when she caught Adam's eye, she saw in him the same bittersweet reluctance she felt, now that it was finally time to go.

Chapter Twenty-Three

They hitched a coach to the four equimares they had commandeered on their first night in Tanria to transport the portal to the lakeshore, after which they set the water horses loose. Three of them were thrilled to be given free rein beside Lake Vanderlinden, but Saltlicker fretted on the shore like an unwanted dog that knew he was about to be abandoned in the countryside. Which he sort of was.

"Go on, Saltlicker. Go have the fun you've always wanted to have in Tanria," Duckers pleaded. He'd always had a soft spot for Saltlicker—the equimaris had once saved his life, after all—so he was near tears when the stallion tossed his head and slapped a webbed foot on the ground as if to say, *Fuck you. I do what I want.*

It was Adam who got him to run free in the end. He pulled the stallion to the side, stroking the beast's scaly neck and murmuring gentle words in a language no one else present could understand. But Saltlicker seemed to get the gist, because he bent his huge head to snuffle Adam's cheek and upset his glasses before running toward the lake with a surly snort of acceptance.

"Fare thee well, dickhead," Rosie said softly, slinging an arm over Duckers's shoulders as they watched the equimaris swim across the lake, dragons shying away from him left and right.

"Think he'll be okay?"

"I do. If anyone is going to come out on top, it's that asshole."

That earned her a laugh, and what could be better in this world than earning a laugh from Penrose Duckers?

With Saltlicker taken care of, they turned their attention to calling in the dragons.

Adam stood on the lakeshore next to Rosie, going rigid as soon as Eloise perked up on the water and began swimming toward them. She clapped a supportive hand on his shoulder. (It was a beautifully crafted shoulder.)

"Know what my motto is? Act first, think never, because fifty years from now, no one is going to remember this anyway."

"I will most certainly remember this fifty years from now."

"You got this."

"I don't got this," he replied faintly.

"Was that shoddy grammar coming out of your mouth? I'm so proud."

"Please don't make jokes right now."

"Who's joking?"

Rosie was absolutely joking, but in her defense, she was mildly worried that he might pass out if she didn't distract him.

"Gods' tits, they are huge," said Zeddie with a smidgen of dismay.

"But in a good way," said Duckers before calling "Mary Georgina-a-a!" at his favorite dragon.

"Gods' tits and testicles!" Zeddie none-too-subtly darted behind Duckers in case he needed to use him as a human shield.

Adam took a shuddering breath as the dragon he and Rosie would be riding drew near.

"This is our friend Eloise. You've already met," Rosie reminded him quietly, trying to keep him calm.

Adam gasped and took a step backward as the dragon drew up to the shoreline. Eloise sniffed Rosie's torso and then turned her great pink head toward Adam. He didn't balk, but Rosie could see him trembling, his chest hitching on staccato breaths. The dragon chirred at him, the same sound Rosie had once heard a mother dragon use to encourage her fledgling baby to take the first terrifying leap off a cliff and spread her wings.

Rosie reached out to touch the antler closest to her and felt the jolt of Eloise's friendliness pulse through her veins. Adam extended his own shaking hand and let his fingertips brush the plush horn closest to him. Eloise must have sensed his trepidation, because she moved out of Rosie's reach and offered both antlers to Adam. He made himself take hold of the horns, his lungs working so hard that Rosie thought he was at risk of hyperventilating. But slowly, surely, Eloise worked her magic, and his breathing evened out.

"You good?" she asked softly, barely audible over the whoops of Duckers and Zeddie, who had already mounted Mary Georgina.

"Yes," he said as if the answer surprised him.

"You can do this."

He nodded, grim-faced with determination.

True to Duckers's prediction, Adam had devised a feat of engineering to secure the portal to Mary Georgina's rump with ropes and a couple of equimaris saddles. With four sets of hands, the entire operation took under a half hour.

When it was time to take off, Rosie climbed onto the step created by the bend of Eloise's leg and heaved herself onto the dragon's back. Then she held out her hand to Adam, who would have to climb onto their mount's leg in order to reach it.

To his credit, Adam did not hesitate. With athletic grace, he pulled himself onto the dragon's ready-made step and took Rosie's hand to let her pull him up. Though Rosie gave him room to settle in, their proximity to one another was steeped in intimacy, in the sweet, unspoken negotiations of figuring out how to be around each other in the wake of their first kiss. Once they were in flight, they would have no choice but to plaster themselves to each other, which seemed inappropriately sexy, given the circumstances.

Rosie was looking forward to it.

Eloise stood, and Adam startled backward, wedging his ass between Rosie's thighs.

Yep, she was enjoying this far more than she ought to.

"Do you want to steer?" she offered.

"No."

"Fair enough."

She reached for Eloise's antlers, but the dragon pulled free of her grasp. She tried again, but all she could sense from the dragon was a sentiment that felt like *Nope* before Eloise moved out of reach again.

"Uh, Adam?"

"Yes?" he answered tightly.

Rosie leaned over and saw that he had closed his eyes, so obviously he didn't see what was going on right in front of him.

"I think she wants you to drive."

His eyes popped open. "What? No."

"I don't think Eloise is giving you a choice here, tiger."

"Did you call me 'tiger'?"

"Yep. Grab them thar antlers, tiger, and let's get this party started!"

Tiger? Them thar? Grandmother Wisdom, had she been possessed by some lingering lost soul in Tanria? What in the Salt Sea was coming out of her mouth right now? It was just so hard to think straight with Adam's tight derriere saying hello to and shaking hands with her pants feelings.

Adam's entire body started to shudder. Rosie internally smacked herself for letting her libido distract her at a time like this and was about to start up another inane pep talk when she realized that he wasn't quaking with fear.

He was shaking with laughter.

Not sort of smiling in his stony *I forgot how to use my face muscles* way. Not merely coughing up one single, amused puff of air. He was legitimately cackling, the kind of laughter that came from his lean belly and made his shoulders bounce up and down. And the sound of his beautiful, glorious laughter made Rosie wish she could bottle it up and listen to it at leisure.

She leaned over to get a look at his face. His mouth grinned wide, making adorable wrinkles fan out around his eyes and bracket a smile that she never would have guessed could be so infectious. She wanted to bottle that up, too.

"Everything all right?" she trilled, delighted by the sight of his precious levity.

"I am trapped in a prison designed for gods, sitting on a dragon while the most astounding woman I have ever met calls me a tiger," he told her through tears of mirth. "What could be wrong?"

Now she was going to have to add *astounding* to her list of What Does Adam Lee Mean When He Says These Things to Me? words.

Mary Georgina swooped down and hovered over them and meeped at Rosie and Adam and Eloise in a way that seemed to say, *Let's fly, bitches!* Eloise spat a spray of glittery gold slime at her, but it was more playful than anything.

"Are we doing this or what?" called Duckers.

Adam reached for Eloise's antlers. "Hold on, Marshal Fox," he said, his usual steady confidence spiked with a new bad-boy-in-a-black-leather-jacket vibe that Rosie found as intoxicating as his cologne.

Meep-meep-meep-chirrup! Eloise crooned as she took a running start before flapping her vast wings and soaring upward.

Adam cursed bilingually, his *kh-sh* cuss word morphing into a truly eloquent "Shhhhit!"

The force of the dragon's speed pushed Adam's entire body

against Rosie's. She wrapped her arms around his middle and held on tight, his shoulders in a straight line beneath her shoulders, his back curling into her front. Despite all evidence to the contrary, they fit together. In a world where women were supposed to be small and men were supposed to be strong, Rosie had spent too much of her life bemoaning the fact that she towered over everyone she had ever dated, when what she really needed was a guy who was as vast on the inside as she was on the outside.

As they flew over Tanria, Rosie looked down and took in the sheer magnitude of the briar's invasion of the countryside—entire forests and grasslands overrun with vines and thorns. And those vines were greening up quickly, the buds uncurling into leaves to drink up the sunlight. Clearly, their decision to fly to Sector S-54 had been a good one. Rosie wondered if they could have made it on equimarisback at all.

An hour after takeoff, they soared over the ambrosial wetlands that had made their slog from the barracks in S-52 to the East Station completely miserable last week. That seemed like a million years ago now.

Once they had cleared the bogs and giant mushrooms of the southeast, they landed on the spongy earth between the wetlands and the Mist. This time, there was nothing on the other side but dirt and tumbleweeds—no marshals, no FICBI agents, no reporters, no family or friends.

No self-absorbed god manipulating the world's attention for his own gain.

Once they were on the other side, they would have to hike to the South Station, or if worse came to worst, they could probably hoof it to a nearby ranch or hitch a ride somewhere along Highway 10.

"Let's get this done while we have light," said Duckers.

Rosie led them to the best spot she had scouted out the day

before and frowned when she noticed a few tendrils snaking their way through the Mist.

"I swear, it was totally clear before," she said for Adam's benefit since the other two couldn't see the vines.

"All the more reason to act now."

Working together under Adam's direction, they unhitched the precious portal from Mary Georgina and carried it to the Mist.

"It's going to work this time, right?" asked Zeddie once the portal was in position.

Adam nodded slowly. "Yes."

"I detected a slight pause there," said Duckers.

"It will work. Stand back, please."

Duckers obeyed, and as he did so, Adam's eyes flicked to Rosie and darted away as quickly. His face was the picture of calm, but a drop of unease seeped into her bloodstream.

The portal in place, they gave Adam space to do his work.

"Where are you staying in Eternity? With Hart and Mercy?" Duckers asked Zeddie.

"No, Lil and Danny and the kids are putting me up until I get my own place. Are you still in the same apartment?"

"Nah, I got a two-bedroom rental a few years ago over on Sycamore Street. It's got a spare bedroom if you need a place to crash."

"I'm good, but let's be clear." Zeddie took Duckers's arm and kissed the stoppered bottle inked on his skin. "If I come over to your house, I'm not staying in the guest room, you jerk."

Rosie insinuated herself between them and pulled them in for a group hug. "Aw, I'm so happy for you guys."

"It's ready," said Adam, his somber pronouncement cutting through their jocularity. Their laughter and jibing fell away, immediately replaced by a nauseating combination of hopeful excitement and hopeless terror.

"Salt Sea, someone tell a joke," said Duckers.

Adam spoke in a monotone as he worked a button loose from his expensive shirt. "A sandwich walks into a bar. The bartender says, 'I'm sorry, we don't serve sandwiches here.' The sandwich asks, 'Why not?' And the bartender says, 'Because we don't serve food after eleven.'"

With one last tug, he pulled the button free of the shirt and looked up to find his three companions gaping at him in stunned silence.

"You said to tell a joke."

"Dry as a desert wind and every bit as hot," marveled Rosie.

Adam placed the button in Zeddie's hand. "I'm about to turn on the portal. Will you toss this through the Mist on my mark? I want to ascertain that the technology is working before anyone attempts to pass through."

"Of course."

"Hey, wait," said Duckers. "If New Gods tech doesn't work inside Tanria, is that thing even going to power up?"

"It embeds itself into the Mist, so in theory, it should work."

"In theory?"

"There's only one way to find out if it works in practice." Adam faced Zeddie. "Ready?"

Zeddie blew out a nervous breath and nodded.

Duckers did his sea polo coach clap. "You got this, Z."

"On my mark," Adam repeated, and then he switched on the portal. The pirated versions were small compared to the official portals at the Tanrian Marshals' stations, which meant that they were also quieter.

And less powerful.

And prone to breaking down, catching fire, and occasionally, exploding.

But this one appeared to be in working order. Rosie dared to hope they would finally be busting out of Tanria.

"Now," said Adam, and Zeddie lobbed the button through the Mist. Rosie and Duckers rushed forward to get a better look and whooped when they saw it bounce through on the other side.

There was movement in Rosie's peripheral vision. She looked up to see the slender new vines reaching toward the portal.

"Adam—"

"I see it. Go on through."

Zeddie turned to Duckers and held out his hand. "Ready, sugar?"

"Ready as I'll ever be."

Duckers grasped him by the hand and went through the archway, dragging Zeddie behind him. Rosie could hear their jubilation when they hit the Bushong dirt, although it sounded tinny through the thinned Mist.

"Wooooo! Come on, you two!" cheered Duckers.

"Go," Adam told Rosie, gazing steadily at the switch in his hand.

Rosie beamed at him. "Let's go together."

"It's all right. Go ahead."

The drop of unease turned into a deluge of dark suspicion, flooding her veins as the young shoots of the vine threaded their way into the pirated portal's frame. She remembered how sad his smile had been when he told her that his calendar was remarkably clear this evening. He had dawdled at the Dragon's Lair on the pretense of letting Duckers and Zeddie have a moment together. He had gone to the bar like a man on a mission.

I don't feel brave, he said in her memory, but no one in the history of the world was as brave as the Briar Thief.

Or more willing to sacrifice himself.

"You go first," she told him.

"I'll be right behind you."

Rosie's suspicion solidified and sank into her stomach, a lead weight. "I don't think you will be right behind me," she said reedily as the encroaching vines began tunneling into the portal's inner workings.

His mouth said nothing, but for once, his face said everything.

"Because you can't, can you? If you take your hand off that switch, it won't work."

The vines thickened, twining around the outside of the frame. Adam winced in pain, and his hand tightened on the lever. He gritted his teeth. "Go."

"Not until you take your hand off that switch and prove me wrong."

His hand didn't move. He stared back at her, silent.

Helpless.

"You fucking fucker." She seethed at him.

"Rosie? Adam?" called Zeddie from the other side.

"Come on," yelled Duckers.

Adam's face went bloodless. "Go."

"And leave you here? Abandon you? Have you lost your fucking mind?"

A spray of sparks shot out of the portal's frame on the Bushong side of the Mist, forcing Duckers and Zeddie to scurry out of the way.

"Come on! Move it!" they shouted through the failing archway.

Adam's hair fell into his eyes. His glasses slid halfway down the bridge of his nose. Part of his shirt came untucked as he hunched in pain, and sharp thorns grew from the vine in his chest. Panting, he drew himself upright, his hand never leaving the switch. "You have to go! Now!"

"No, sir! Incorrect!"

The portal rattled violently.

Adam's eyes were alight, the lines of his body taut and alert. He was more alive in this moment than Rosie had ever seen him.

The vines came into sharp focus behind him, green leaves unfolding in the afternoon sunlight. Rosie had never beheld anything as beautiful as a living, breathing, disheveled Adam Lee, standing before a world bursting with life.

"Rosie, go," he begged her. "Please."

"Rosie!" bellowed Duckers, equally distraught. But he had Zeddie and Hart and Mercy and Twyla and Frank and Lu and Annie. He had his mom and his sisters and his punk of a brother.

Adam had only her.

"Change of plans. I'm staying here with Adam," Rosie called through the portal.

"No!" Adam said at the same moment Zeddie cried, "What?"

"The fuck you are," hollered Duckers. "Get out of there, both of you!"

"We can't leave, Penny-D."

"Yes, you can. So do it," Adam insisted.

The entire portal shuddered.

"No!" shouted Duckers.

"Come on!" pleaded Zeddie.

"I'm okay," she told them, her goodbye teary. "We're both going to be okay."

Adam's face crumpled with misery. "Go," he begged her one last time.

She took his face in her hands and gazed at him with love and outrage. "Dream on."

A sob bubbled up from within him, and he went slack in her hands. She turned toward the portal and shouted "I love you guys" before she reached over and took Adam's hand off the switch. The whole thing went dead in an instant and broke off the Mist in three vine-clogged chunks, completely, irrevocably busted.

Adam shook himself free of her grasp and glared at her as the realization of what Rosie had done settled over both of them.

Simmering with rage, he began to pace. When he could muster words, he berated her from here to the House of the Unknown God, but he was so livid that he delivered the entire vengeful tirade in a stream of virulent Eshilese. It went on and on, and the more pissed off he got, the more Rosie fell in love with him.

He finally came to a stop a few feet in front of her and shouted a single word she could understand: "Why?"

"Because I'd rather be stuck in here with you than stuck out there without you, you fucking asshole."

He sucked in a deep, wrathful breath before marching straight at her. Rosie didn't have a moment to retreat or even think before he reached up, grasped the back of her head, and pulled her down into a desperate kiss, all teeth and tongue and anguish. If she had been questioning her choice—which she had not in the slightest— this kiss would have convinced her that she had made the right decision and then some.

He broke away and pressed his forehead to hers and murmured sweetly in Eshilese.

"What does that mean?" she asked him.

"I called you a fool."

"Really? It sounded so nice."

"It literally means 'You are a soft cantaloupe.'"

Wrung out, he pulled away from her, put his back to the Mist, and slid down until his butt hit dirt.

Rosie came to sit next to him. "So, to be clear, you knew that you couldn't get out when you found me by the lake?"

"I knew by then that the only way I could make the portal work was to operate it manually." He leaned his head against the Mist like the ancient, exhausted man he was. "I should not have kissed you."

"Of course you should have kissed me."

"I didn't want you to have any remorse when you left. But I

was selfish, and I decided to let myself be happy, if only for a few hours."

"Did you honestly believe that it wouldn't gut me to leave you behind in Tanria, whether you kissed me or not?"

He looked at her warily. "Yes?"

"That makes me want to strangle you."

"I am the one who should strangle you," he said, his temper on the rise again. "I will never understand why you stayed when you could have left."

"How is this hard to understand? I'm in love with you, you soft cantaloupe."

Adam opened his mouth, then promptly closed it. The tips of his ears went pink. "You don't know me."

"Stop. Zip it. I know what I know." Rosie picked up his hand and kissed his palm. "This is the part where you tell me that you love me, too."

"I love you, too," he repeated helplessly, linking their fingers.

"Oh! That was easier than I thought it was going to be."

Adam huffed his small Adam laugh, which was growing incrementally larger in size each time Rosie inspired it.

"Do you feel up to flying back to the Dragon's Lair, or would you rather get to the nearest barracks?" she asked him.

"Let's go home."

"Ha ha. That's hilarious."

"I'm not joking. Would you believe me if I told you that a restaurant in Tanria feels more like home to me than anywhere else I have lived for the past..." He raised his eyes to a bank of clouds crossing the late afternoon sky as he made his calculations. "Four hundred years at least?"

"No, it makes sense. I've been feeling the same way, but I wasn't sure how to put it."

He lifted his head off the Mist and glowered at her.

"What's that look about?"

"It is about your foolish, nonsensical decision to stay here. You could be at home—your *real* home—in your bathtub, listening to your Brigitte Porcel records, but instead, you're here with a miserable old man."

"I have no regrets."

"Then I will regret that decision for you. I will regret it now, tomorrow, and every day for the rest of your life."

"That's a lot of regretting."

"We have a lot of time to fill."

"Regret all you want, but I can think of better ways to fill our time." She dropped his hand, straddled his legs, and kissed him before he could do any more regretting.

"I—we shouldn't—" he stammered as Rosie took off his glasses and set them neatly to the side. Barefaced, no jacket, no vest, no tie, his shirt rumpled with a vine peeking out of the alluringly visible skin of his chest—he was scrumptiously disarmed, and Rosie was in the mood to devour him.

"Why shouldn't we? What on earth is stopping us?"

A hungry look took over his face. "Nothing. Absolutely nothing."

He pulled her into a fiery kiss that made Rosie forget about things like portals and the prospect of living forever. There was only this moment in the present with Adam and his lips and his tongue and his teeth and his hands.

"Unless...," Rosie said as he left a trail of wet, burning kisses down her neck.

"Unless?" he rasped. Gods, that voice was unreal when he was turned on. He opened the third button of her shirt and ran the tip of his tongue along her collarbone.

"That's very distracting," she informed him dreamily.

"Good."

"Unless this brings on one of your attacks," she managed as he went to work on the other collarbone.

"Hmm?"

No, wait, this was, in fact, an important subject to discuss *before* they got any sexier. She put a hand on either side of his face and forced him to look up at her.

"Your attacks seem to be related to me, to us. Like when I make you crack a smile or laugh. Or when our hands touch. Or when I give you a handkerchief."

His lust-clouded gaze cleared somewhat. "I know. It seemed wiser to get you out of Tanria before you made that connection for yourself."

"Sorry that I outsmarted you and foiled your grapshit plan."

"But when I kissed you today, I felt no pain. Even now, I'm fine. I feel...happy. I don't understand it."

"You can think about that and kiss my neck at the same time, if you want to," she suggested.

He ran his hands down her sides and clamped them on her hips. "You make it impossible to think clearly."

Rosie noticed then that Duckers and Zeddie hadn't moved on. They stood outside the Mist in serious conversation, their faces tearstained. Her eyes welled up at the sight of them, and she felt very unsexy all of a sudden.

"They're still there?" Adam guessed, his hands relaxing their grip on her hip bones.

"Yeah."

"They should go home." He stroked her cheek. "And so should we."

Chapter Twenty-Four

By the time Eloise and Mary Georgina dropped them off by the Dragon's Lair, the sun was little more than an eyelash on the western horizon, and the stars that had once been gods began to blink to life on the violet altar of the sky. Rosie and Adam stood once more on the small beach by the lake where they had first kissed, and watched the dragons take off across the water. In the haunting light of the gloaming, Rosie saw that the briar had grown more in their absence, the vines weaving in and out of the drooping branches of the Tanrian willows bordering Lake Vanderlinden.

"It's growing so fast now," she said. "Is it because my father is the Trickster? Is that what's causing this?"

"I suspect that is why you can see the briar, but it's not the reason for the plant's invasion of Tanria."

Adam took Rosie's hand in his and led her toward the path to the Dragon's Lair.

"The briar has always caused me pain. Whenever I care for someone, it grows inside me. Zeddie and Pen have caused me more than a few twinges as well."

"Is that why you've done your best to stay away from people over the years? To avoid the pain?"

"Yes."

"So you kind of stopped living."

"I certainly tried."

"But this." Rosie gestured to the ever-encroaching thicket weaving through the trees along their path. "I know it began when you cut your hand in the portal, but how did it get this bad, this quickly?"

"I can't be sure, but that day..." He stopped and toyed with her hand. "You were the first person to touch me in a long time— such a long time, Rosie. I won't say that I fell in love with you then, because I didn't. How could I? I didn't know you, and you didn't know me. But I came alive in that moment. It was like an old story when the prince kisses the sleeping princess and she wakes. I couldn't go back to sleep after that. And so the briar awoke, too."

He got them walking again.

"And the plant has been slowly worming its way through the Mist ever since?"

"Apparently. And the more time I spent in your presence once I returned to Tanria, the more my affection for you grew, and so the briar grew as well. When I made the connection, I endeavored to halt those feelings. But then I watched you die..."

"And things got out of hand?" Rosie said gently.

"Yes. Very. Especially once I realized you were like me, some-one who could understand what it means to live and live and never die, who might...be with me."

"Maybe that's why the vines looked shadowy to me in the beginning. The harder I fell for you, the clearer they became." She squeezed his hand. "So I'm basically fertilizer for the Love Plant."

"I'm sure we could land on a more romantic metaphor."

"How long had you been trying to get the briar out of you in Tanria?"

"I arrived in Bushong shortly after the Old Gods surrendered and became stars."

"That was over two hundred years ago." This time, it was Rosie who brought them to a halt. "Wait a minute. When I asked you how you wound up in the Federated Islands, you said you walked. Did you literally walk here?"

"Oh, that. Yes."

"You *walked* here from Eshil Craia?"

"No, I was in Stenland at the time."

"That's not the relevant detail in this scenario."

Adam shrugged. "I wanted to see the ocean."

"Weren't you constantly drowning? Weren't you hungry?"

"I'm not like you. I don't die and revive. I go on living no matter what. But I did grow quite hungry after several months. And a shark ate me."

She shoved her fingers in her hair and squeezed her head, as if her brain might explode if she didn't contain it immediately. "What the fuck?"

"You don't want to know."

"I super do, though."

He shook his head and put a hand on her back to get her walking again.

By now, they had reached the kitchen door of the Dragon's Lair, which Zeddie had left unlocked, thank the Bride of Fortune. Adam stepped through first and pulled Rosie after him. Suddenly, his every movement seemed to contain intent and direction. He lit the nearest lamp he could find, its flame casting a flickering golden glow in the enormous kitchen, before he rapped twice on the kitchen counter and said, "Sit."

"What for?"

He took her by the hips and looked her dead in the eye. "Rosie. Sit. Please."

"I'll do it, but you're not the boss of me."

"Yes, I think you have made that abundantly clear."

As Rosie hiked her tush onto the counter, her feet dangling inches from the floor, Adam kicked a step stool toward the cabinet on which she sat. When he had it where he wanted it, he took a step up, so that they were now eye level with each other. He tilted his head, squinting as if he were making complex calculations in his head.

"Yes, this will do."

He took off his glasses and set them on the counter behind Rosie's ass before he cupped her jaw with his right hand and kissed her.

Kiss was an understatement. Rosie had been kissed before. This was something else entirely. This was a kiss two thousand years in the making.

She kicked off her boots and crossed her heels behind his back to pull him in close and press herself against him, making both of them groan.

He pulled away long enough to say between ragged breaths, "I should have asked if this was amenable to you first."

"Very amenable. You would not believe how amenable. If there was an award for Most Amenable, I would win, hands down." She popped open the button of his tailored pants and pulled down the zipper, revealing a peek at his blue silk boxers and making room for his evident arousal.

He followed her lead, opening her soft cambric shirt, button by mother-of-pearl button. "If I have to live one more second on this earth without seeing you in your—what is that word you love to use?"

"Intimates?" she suggested, her hand snaking into the tasteful silk of his drawers and making him hiss. This was far and away the most fun Rosie had ever had in a kitchen.

"Your intimates," Adam repeated, making the word sound positively filthy. "If I have to live one more second on this earth without seeing you in your precious intimates, I might perish at last. And I will perish if you keep doing that, so . . ."

Here, he took her by the wrist, pulled her hand out of his pants, and placed it firmly on the kitchen counter. Rosie made an unsexy grunt of annoyance. She had been enjoying herself.

"I would like to last longer than five seconds, and you are entirely too good at that," he told her.

"Just checking to make sure the cantaloupe isn't soft."

He cussed his signature Eshilese curse as he undid the last button of her shirt and slid it off her shoulders, running his hands down her arms until the cambric pooled around her hips on the kitchen counter. She wore nothing from the waist up now but her birth key and her mesh peacock-patterned brassiere with the feathers' eyes over her nipples.

"What do you think?" she asked him, even though his smoldering assessment made his opinion perfectly obvious.

"I think you are a thousand times more beautiful in peacock feathers than a peacock could ever hope to be."

"That's so sweet, but all I heard was *cock*."

"You are utterly, perfectly ridiculous."

"I take that as a compliment."

"It is." His fingertips traced the delicate gold chain around her neck until he was touching the birth key that dangled halfway between her throat and her heart. "Is this yours?"

"Yep. Seemed easier to wear it than to keep handing it off to people only to get it back when they die and I don't."

He ducked his head and pressed a kiss to the burnished metal, a soft, sweet gesture that made her chest ache with emotion. And then he bent lower and brushed his lips over the thin fabric covering her breast. And then he nipped her gently with his teeth. And then he latched on with mind-blowing ferocity, at which point Rosie couldn't muster a rational thought if her immortal life depended on it. Her toes curled with pleasure, and her hands fisted in the cotton-linen blend of his shirt.

"Take this off," she demanded, tugging at the shirt in question.

He came up for air long enough to tell her, "You're not the boss of me."

"Yes, I am."

"Yes, you are," he agreed, standing straight so he could undo his buttons while Rosie watched on in appreciation. He peeled off his shirt, taking care around the protruding vine, and toed out of his shoes, lost the socks, and shucked the pants, all while balancing on a narrow step stool. His thumbs were in the waistband of his silk boxers when Rosie called a halt.

"Let me enjoy these for one moment," she said as she ran her hands over the luxury fabric covering the taut curves of his backside. "I have a deep appreciation for quality undergarments."

"I noticed," he said huskily.

"I suspect that you, too, have an appreciation for quality undergarments."

"I have an appreciation for *your* quality undergarments. I'd like to see how they look hanging from a doorknob or dangling from that wall sconce."

A bud on the slender tendril snaking out of his chest slowly unrolled into a tender green leaf as he spoke. She put her hand on his chest but felt only skin and lean muscle.

"Does it hurt?" she asked him.

"No."

His breath stuttered as Rosie's hands wandered. She relished the shape of his square shoulders, the graceful strength of his wiry arms, the slimness of his waist, and the firm ridges of his stomach. Most of all, she relished the way he gazed at her, his eyes smoky and half-closed.

"What if we're in the middle of things and you have one of

your attacks?" she asked him, even as she slid her hands past the waistband of his boxers to pay her respects to the smooth skin of his hind end.

"I'm willing to take that risk."

Rosie's fingers ran over a thick ridge of scar tissue. She took him by the hips and turned him sideways to get a better view. There, scraping down his back from shoulder blades to buttocks, were the three long gashes left behind by a war dragon thousands of years ago. She ran her fingertips down the scar nearest to her and teared up, thinking about the suffering that must have come with these wounds.

"None of that. No pity for me tonight. That time is over and done with." Once again, he hooked his thumbs into the elastic waistband of his underwear. "I'm taking these off, if the boss approves?"

"Permission granted," said Rosie, glad to return her focus to the present moment. She watched with deep appreciation as he stepped out of his boxers and stood on his stool like a god on a pedestal. He was delicately built, but every line of his body was sumptuously masculine.

"I like it when you look at me like that," he told her, the picture of sultry.

"How am I looking at you?"

"Like you want to eat me alive."

"Tempting. Makes me jealous of that shark. By the way, you have yet to reveal fifty percent of my intimates."

"Yes, I am in danger of perishing."

He reached between them to undo the button of her pants and tug down the zipper. With laudable dexterity, he lifted her hips and dragged down her pants while leaving her panties in place, the peacock feathers fanning out over her mound. Staring at the silk-clad apex of her body, he uttered that gorgeous guttural curse in appreciation, which made Rosie's skin heat from head to toe.

"You need to teach me that word."

"Later," he rasped before dropping to his knees on his stool and performing the same ritual with his lips and tongue and teeth over her panties that he had carried out over the mesh cups of her brassiere moments ago.

"I'm not even naked yet. How are you this good?" she whimpered as she gripped the edge of the counter.

"Two thousand years of study and practice," he answered as he and his mouth made their way to her stomach.

"Gods, I hope I'm up to snuff. I haven't done this in a while."

"Neither have I." He reached around her and deftly unclasped her brassiere with one hand.

"I mean, my sexy times skills are pretty good, but I have to think that over the course of two millennia, you've had fun with a few people who are far hotter than myself."

He stopped her mouth with a kiss, one that was light and affectionate rather than ravenous. "If I may borrow a few phrases from a wise woman: Stop. Zip it. I know what I know."

She laughed in relief as he removed the hair ties from her braids.

"No one is better than you, because no one else *is* you." He loosened her plaits as he spoke, combing his fingers through her not-red hair. "It's true that I have fucked many people, many times, in many ways. I have fucked every kind of person imaginable— every size, every shape, every nationality, every gender, and of every persuasion under the altar of the sky. I have fucked my way through entire years of my life simply to forget the fact that I cannot die. But I promise you, my ruzhkel, I have never made love with someone before now."

Rosie melted. "Neither have I."

"So we are both somewhat inexperienced tonight."

"What was that word? Are you calling me a mushy lingonberry or something?"

"My ruzhkel. My rosebud."

She put her hand over her heart. "I want you to call me that forever."

"Of course, my ruzhkel. What else do you want? Tell me."

"I want to hear you say *fuck* some more, because your voice turns the word *fuck* into a five-star snack."

He leaned in and obediently whispered "Fuck" in her ear as he slid the straps of her peacock-patterned confection down her shoulders.

"Fuck," he said again, going husky as he took in the sight of her naked breasts, his eyelids fluttering.

For some time after that, he was too occupied to say anything at all, but eventually he relieved her of the last scrap of her intimate apparel between her legs. "Fuck," he moaned, leaning long and hard on the *f* as Rosie propped the heels of her feet on the counter.

He knelt on the stool and called her his ruzhkel once more, extending the nickname in an intoxicatingly proprietary way to the firm bud at her center before he made her soul leave her body—or, at least, that's how it felt to her when stars exploded behind her eyes.

Rosie tugged on his hair. "Get up here!" she insisted when she was capable of putting words together again.

He nearly tumbled off the stool as he got to his feet, but Rosie caught him between her legs, and they were kissing again, their hands roaming freely, their bodies twining.

"Now," she demanded. "Right now."

"Should we do this somewhere else?"

"Where? Somewhere more proper? Like a pile of tablecloths on the floor of an abandoned restaurant?"

"We're in a kitchen. There's a colander hanging over your head."

"You're the one who started this. You, with your *sit* and your step stool."

"I know. Forgive me."

"There's nothing to forgive. I don't care if we're doing this in a bed or on the roof or riding a dragon; I want you wherever we are."

"I will rot in Old Hell before I make love to you on a dragon."

"I have eternity to convince you otherwise." She took him in hand and enjoyed watching his face contort with tormented pleasure as she spoke. "Now, let's get down to brass tacks. My body won't let me get pregnant or catch some dread illness, so you can dispense with the condom."

"That's good, because I don't have one," he told her through clenched teeth. "And the same applies to me."

"You can't get pregnant?"

"No, I'm afraid that I cannot."

He pounced on her, lightning quick, pressing his mouth over hers and kissing her hard. He sucked in a breath, stealing the air from her lungs and making her dizzy with want. Then he took her by the thigh and hiked her leg over his hip. "Are you certain about this?"

"I honestly don't know how much more amenable I can get. Do I need to make a sign with markers and glitter saying, *Take me now*?"

"But most women don't find release with … with …"

"With dicking?"

Adam laughed and strung together the soft cantaloupe syllables of Eshilese.

Rosie pressed her hands over his heart and felt his pulse thrash beneath her touch. "It's not about the orgasm—although you've earned an A+ on that front already. It's about connection. It's about intimacy. I love you and I want to be with you. That's all, and that's enough."

His entire demeanor softened like candle wax in her hands, and Rosie enjoyed getting a front row seat to his endearing lovesickness.

"In that case, I'm going to do my best to make this extremely pleasant for you," he said a heartbeat before he made good on his throaty promise. His thumb pressed rhythmically to the side of her rosebud—*his* rosebud—setting the bundle of Rosie's building pleasure alight. A bilingual stream of consciousness accompanied the movement of his body—begging, praising, pleading, loving. The more he lost himself in her, the more the words tilted toward Eshilese alone. He propped his knee on the counter beside her and canted her hips upward, an angle that sent Rosie spinning toward her release.

His chest heaved and his rhythm stuttered.

"Does it hurt?" she panted, worried, but also so close to release her head spun.

"This is the opposite of pain."

He lost himself inside her with a sharp cry as her own release radiated from her core. Adam pressed his face against Rosie's shoulder in exhaustion, but he continued to gently knead her with his thumb until the aftershocks had passed.

Rosie sat up, holding his cheeks in her hands and kissing him softly all over his blissed-out face.

"What were you saying?" she asked.

"When?"

She raised an eyebrow at him.

He laughed quietly. "I can't quite remember."

"Because you were having an out-of-body experience?"

"No, I was most definitely in my body." He put his hands on the counter to either side of her hips and leaned in to brush her lips with his. "I was speaking of my love and devotion. Mostly."

"Mostly?"

"The rest was..." He buried his face in her neck.

"Absolutely filthy?" she supplied.

"Mmm, let's call it 'my specific plans for what I'd like to do with you in the future.'"

"All I know is that soft cantaloupes were not involved."

Adam sighed and shook his head.

"You love me for picking the low-hanging fruit," Rosie told him.

"I love you for many reasons, your terrible jokes included."

"This from the guy who told the sandwich joke." Rosie clasped her hands around Adam's neck. "Teach me to cuss in Eshilese. What's that word you use when you need to roll out the big guns?"

"Khäsh," he said, making it extra guttural and spitty and dramatic to humor her.

"Khhhhhhehshhhhhhh," she repeated, impersonating him.

Adam clamped his lips between his teeth, but she could see that he was laughing at her.

"What? Did I mess up?"

"*Khäsh* literally means *scrotum*, but the way you pronounced it made it sound like the word for *yogurt*." He started to giggle—honest-to-gods *giggling*.

"Say it again."

"Khäsh."

Rosie listened intently and repeated him.

"Almost," he said. "The vowel is a diphthong, like your short *i* plus your short *a*. Khäsh."

"Khäsh."

"That's right."

"Khäsh! I accidentally hit Adam over the head with a cast-iron skillet after he made fun of me!"

He narrowed his eyes and said a different word in Eshilese.

"What does that mean?"

"Smart-ass."

"Good, I want to learn that, too." Rosie perked up on her countertop perch. "How do you say your name? Your real name."

"Lidojozháis Mäkherkis Ödamika."

Rosie's jaw dropped.

"Princes had long names in those days."

"No kidding. Say it again."

She watched his mouth intently as he formed the syllables of his birth name: "Lidojozháis Mäkherkis Ödamika."

Rosie tried to repeat the name. Adam burst out laughing, the widest smile and the loudest laugh she had coaxed from him yet.

"Stop laughing at me!" she said in semi-mock offense.

"You called me a 'flying water monkey'!"

"I'm trying!"

"Try harder. Lidojozháis Mäkherkis Ödamika."

Rosie tried harder. Adam laughed harder.

"Lido," he prompted before Rosie got mad at him.

"Lido," she repeated.

"Jozháis."

"Jozháis."

"Mäkherkis."

"Mäkherkis."

"Ödamika."

"Ödamika."

He strung together all the syllables of his long name for her. "Lidojozháis Mäkherkis Ödamika."

"Lidojozháis Mäkherkis Ödamika," Rosie repeated slowly, carefully.

"That's right."

"Lidojozháis Mäkherkis Ödamika."

"Correct." He kissed the tip of her nose. "But my friends called me Ödam."

"Are you fucking with me?"

"Is that what your people call a 'trick question'?"

"You asshole! This whole time, I could have been calling you Ödam?"

"No. I have not been Ödam in a long time, and I don't want to be that man again. You can call me Ödam when you are angry with me. Tonight, I am Adam. I am your Adam."

He wrapped his arms around her, pulled her into him, and kissed her long and deep. "Come sleep with me on a bed of table-cloths, my ruzhkel."

Chapter Twenty-Five

They lay on their sides, facing one another in Adam's "bedroom." A single lamp burned on the other side of the tablecloth curtains, casting a faint golden glow over them. They had stayed up so late talking and touching and making love that they had crossed the bodily meridian past exhaustion, and now neither of them could sleep. And since they couldn't sleep, they chatted in quiet, lazy, looping conversations that never seemed to bring the sunrise any nearer.

They spoke of their mothers, of their childhoods, of the places they'd been, of the people who had been important to them over the years.

As dawn crept into the Dragon's Lair, Adam told Rosie stories of his brother—of their childhood pranks, their teenaged rebellions, their partnership in the face of their domineering father.

"You must have loved him very much."

"I did. He was more than a brother to me. He was my best friend. A prince—especially a child prince—is lonely in a palace full of servants and obsequious officials, and so he was everything to me. We were everything to each other."

He gazed at the low ceiling, his eyes going soft and distant. "I haven't spoken of him to anyone in ages. Centuries, I think."

Rosie brushed Adam's cheek with the backs of her fingers, small comfort that it was. "I'm sorry."

"Don't be. I like telling you about him. I feel lighter, as if I had been carrying a yoke around my shoulders only to have it lifted unexpectedly."

"I'm sorry anyway."

"Why are you sorry? None of this is your fault."

"No, but it is my father's fault," she said as he kissed her fingertips one by one.

"You are not your father."

"I'm glad you noticed."

Adam sighed in fond exasperation.

"It's amazing to me that the Trickster found the time to mess up your life so thoroughly, because he was superlatively not there for my mother and me."

She almost said more, but thought better of it.

"You don't want to talk about him?" guessed Adam.

"He always turns a conversation about someone else into a conversation about himself, and I don't want to do that to you."

"You're not. I want to know everything about your life, and your life includes your father."

"*Father* is a stretch."

When she clammed up again, he stroked her hair. "Go on. If you want to," he said, and so, haltingly, she did.

"He would show up at random and expect us to drop everything because he had deigned to acknowledge our existence. And when I would get my hopes up that he might be a part of our lives for good, he would up and leave all over again without so much as a goodbye."

Adam ran a comforting hand down her arm. "I wish you had had a better father."

"I wish we had both had better fathers."

"Perhaps kings and gods make better kings and gods than parents."

"Maybe." Rosie felt herself tearing up. "Sorry. I don't talk about my father much. Or ever."

"You can talk about anything you want to talk about with me."

She nodded, but she didn't think she would say more.

Until she did.

"He gave me a pink unicorn music box for my thirtieth birthday. It was a gift you'd give an eight-year-old girl, not a six-foot-five-inch woman trying to grapple with her newfound immortality. And it was three weeks late.

"He was always late, and that was when he bothered to show up at all. He'd tell me that he was coming to see my mother in whatever show she was in, but he'd barely make it to curtain call. That jackass was even late for her funeral, showed up three days after the fact with a bouquet of shitty, half-dead daisies. He wasn't there for her a day in her life. Couldn't he have had the decency to show up for her death? Especially when—" Gods, she was going to cry. "Especially when I was so lost and alone and I needed him. Where was he then? Where was he ever?"

Adam wiped her tears away with the pads of his thumbs.

"I hate that he can still do this to me after all these years. Such grapshit."

"I suspect that there is no time limit."

"He said from personal experience." She pulled away so that she could look at Adam and his beautiful, sympathetic face. "I don't want to waste another second of my precious time with you talking about *him*. I want to talk about you. The gods know I have so many things I want to ask you."

"Go ahead."

"How did you get back after you went to the garden of the Old Gods?"

"That part is difficult to remember. In the garden, the pain seemed to stretch on forever. And before you tell me that I don't have to speak of this, please understand that it's all right. There's a kind of pain that ends and a kind of pain that goes on and on. The pain I experienced as I hung there in the garden was excruciating, and it changed me, but it didn't last. It was there and then it was over. I remember feeling pain, but I can no longer remember the pain itself.

"I have no idea how much time passed while I hung there on the thorn. I only know that one day, a woman came. She said she heard my cries, and all at once, I was no longer stuck. I can't explain how she got me down from the briar. One moment, the thorn pierced my heart; the next moment, I was in a place that reminded me of my grandfather's house. My mother would bring me there to visit my grandparents from time to time, and it was more home to me than my father's palace ever was. The woman who saved me reminded me of my mother. She wore the same perfume. She braided her hair in the same way. She had the same kind eyes.

"I don't know how long I was in that house either, but when I was whole again, the woman opened the door for me. The moment I stepped through it, I was in Eshil Craia again, in the forest where my brother and I came to slay a dragon so long ago. But it didn't look the same. Time moves differently on the other side of the Salt Sea. Decades had passed while I was gone. My mother and father had long since sailed the Salt Sea by then. My brother's children were old and did not remember me. No one remembered me. I thought it would be best to start a new life. The first of many."

Rosie traced the lines of his face with her fingertip. He looked different without his glasses, vulnerable. "Gods, you lost everything."

"We're immortal. Loss is inevitable." He looked at her, his eyes dark and fathomless. "Loss upon loss."

"Loss upon loss," she agreed. She thought again of Jocelyn, but they were speaking of Adam's losses now, not hers. "That woman who helped you—do you think she was the Mother of Sorrows?"

"I have wondered that myself. She called me by my name, again and again."

"Lidojozháis Mäkherkis Ödamika."

Adam's lips turned up. "Ödam. Only Ödam, as my own mother said it. She called me by my name until I remembered who I was. She said, 'You will walk a long road, Ödam, my son, but the road always leads home eventually.'"

"Do you think she meant here? Tanria?"

"No. I think she meant here." He kissed the palm of her hand and pressed it over his heart, and Rosie imagined her own heart fanning open like a flower, petal by soft petal. As she leaned in to kiss him, her fingers brushed the vine draped across his chest.

She felt it.

She touched it, and it moved.

"Adam?"

But he was already looking, his eyes going wide as a bud neither of them had noticed until now unfurled like Rosie's heart, petal by soft petal, into a beautiful red bloom.

Chapter Twenty-Six

They stood on the terrace, mugs of expensive coffee steaming in their hands, and watched the world come into focus as the sun rose behind them. Like Adam, Tanria was in bloom, covered in red flowers, the sweet scent light but present in every breath Rosie drew.

"It's so beautiful," she said, aware that the word *beautiful* was inadequate.

"Yes."

"Does it hurt?"

"No, not at all."

"That's good, right?"

He didn't say anything, but his face seemed to be telling her something she didn't want to hear.

"Why are you looking at me like you're about to inform me that my dog died?"

"We need to kill the plant. It's the only way to free Tanria."

"How do you propose we kill all of this?" Rosie asked with a wave of her hand.

"By killing this one." Adam set down his mug on a café table and began to unbutton his shirt.

"What? No. Bad idea."

"You can touch the plant now. That means you can pull it out of me."

"Have you lost your mind?"

But already, he stood before her, his naked torso pale and lovely and delicately drawn in the morning light. "I can't pull it out myself. It's too deeply rooted. It needs torque from the outside. It has to be you."

"Excuse me, I don't think I made myself clear before: *fuck* no."

"Rosie—"

"Listen to yourself! Can you hear what you're asking me to do? Because what you are asking me to do is to pull the thing out of your body that is literally keeping you alive. If I do it—which, to be clear, I will not—you could die. Right here. Right now."

"I don't think I will," he said with maddening calm.

"You don't know that. You *can't* know that."

"In the Salt Sea's tale, the lover doesn't die immediately. He simply becomes mortal again. He has time." Adam took her hands and cupped them between his own. "I don't think removing the vine will kill me."

"But it might!"

"That is a risk worth taking."

Rosie yanked her hands from his grasp. "How is that a risk worth taking? You could *die*, Adam!"

"I know that."

He didn't need to say more. The bittersweet look on his face said everything.

I love you, but I have a chance to come to the end.

Let me end.

Rosie felt like the Mist of Tanria was closing in on her, and there wasn't a blessed thing she could do about it. "After all this time, we finally found each other. How can you expect me to go on living without you? You know what that would mean—you, of all people."

He pulled her to him, his arms around her waist, his ear

pressed to her heart. She wrapped him up tightly, memorizing the warmth of his living body against her own.

"I'm not eager to go, not now, not anymore. But you and I both know..." He released her to gaze up into her tear-ridden face. "I have lived long enough."

She couldn't hold herself up. Her shoulders hunched, and her torso caved in on itself. She cried the way a child cries, the way she'd cried when Jocelyn had died and left her utterly, completely alone.

Adam took her handkerchief from his pocket and wiped her face, which made her cry harder.

"How long before the briar chokes out the rest of the native flora here?" he asked her, taking on the mythic cadence of a parent reading a tale of the gods to his child. "How long before the birds have nowhere to nest, before the grap habitats are destroyed? How long before the dragons die out?"

She wrenched the linen from his hand and stalked to the railing, wiping her face as the dragons flew from their nests to alight on the lake. She knew he was right, and she hated herself for knowing that.

He came to stand beside her and put his hand at the small of her back.

"Do this for Tanria," he said so gently, so careful with her.

"I don't give a shit about Tanria."

He knew it wasn't true, but he didn't argue with her. He said, "Then do this for me," because he knew she couldn't say that she didn't give a shit about him. It was so unfair.

She looked him dead in the eye.

"Would you do it for me?"

He didn't insult her by insisting that he would, that it would be easy, that he'd do it willingly, or that he'd do it at all.

"I think I would," he answered at last. "I *hope* I would. I'm sorry to ask this of you."

"But you're asking me anyway."

He had the decency to hesitate before he nodded. "I'm asking you anyway."

Rosie blew her nose and tucked the hankie into her own pocket, since she couldn't very well hand Adam a linen square of her own snot.

"I expect you to launder that and return it to me," he told her.

"I expect you to live so that I *can* return it to you. When are we doing this?"

Rosie did not sound fragile, but she felt as breakable as the cat figurine the Trickster had given to her.

"Now," answered Adam, determination painting him from head to toe.

"Kiss me first."

She bent down, and he kissed her long and tenderly, his hands in her hair, brushing salty tears from her cheeks, caressing her jaw. When their lips parted, he held her face in his hands, searching for the answer he needed. Rosie thought of Hart Ralston, sitting across from her at Aunt Bonnie's, telling her, *If I were in your shoes, I'd want to know about that door.* And she got it. She understood. If their roles were reversed, she would ask Adam to do what he was asking her to do now. And she loved him enough to give him the end he deserved, the end everyone deserved.

She nodded, resolute, when she wanted to be anything but resolute. He kissed her again, a brief touch of gratitude and love, before stepping back and taking a fortifying breath.

Rosie placed her hand over the vine, which had grown long enough to begin to wind around his shoulder. The flower's petals were soft beneath her hand and released their heady scent.

"There aren't any thorns," she said.

"I know. They seem to have disappeared."

"When I first saw the briar, it was brown and gray and twisted and gnarly. It didn't have leaves. It was thorny. It looked half-dead. Did it look that way to you?"

"Yes."

She gazed out over Tanria, at Lake Vanderlinden and, beyond that, a sea of lush green peppered with bright red blooms.

"You should fall in love more often," she told Adam, because a joke always made things suck a little less.

He humored her with his going-to-the-gallows smile. "I prefer to fall in love only once."

Rosie tried to take comfort from that, but she was struggling mightily.

"Ready?" she asked him.

He gripped the railing and nodded grimly.

She twined the green tendril around her hand, and sending up a prayer to the Bride of Fortune to go fuck herself regarding this turn of events, Rosie pulled.

The first few inches slid easily from Adam's flesh, but then Rosie met resistance, and Adam grunted in pain. She stopped.

"Don't stop," he snapped, but he softened when he saw the devastation on her face. "Please. It's going to hurt no matter what, but you have to keep going."

Rosie exhaled her frustration and pointless fury. "You owe me big time for this."

"I know. I'm not worthy of licking your boots clean."

"They're fantastic boots," she said tearfully.

"Yes, they are. Please, ruzhkel, pull."

"I'm so mad at you."

"I know."

"I love you."

"I love you, too."

Giving the moment the full-throated cussing it deserved, Rosie took hold of the vine once more and continued to drag the plant out of Adam's body. His knuckles went white on the railing, but still she pulled, strangling the vine in her grasp and wishing she could squeeze the life out of it rather than make Adam go through any more agony. Hadn't he been through enough?

The vine gave several inches, sliding out of his chest millimeter by resentful millimeter until, suddenly, it refused to budge. Furious, Rosie dug in her heels and yanked. Adam clamped his jaw, but that didn't prevent a cry of pain from shoving its way up his windpipe. The vine snapped in two halfway between them, sending Rosie tumbling to the terrace floor, where she barked her knee.

She was on her feet in an instant, limping to Adam as a trail of blood oozed down her shin. By the time she reached him at the railing, her knee didn't hurt anymore, and the bleeding had stopped.

Adam's face was blanched, and his whole body seemed to flag as he clung to the rail. Blood seeped from his chest, but like Rosie, he healed quickly.

"Are you all right?" she asked him, touching his face.

He put his hand over hers and pressed his cheek into her palm. "Yes."

"Should I keep going?"

She desperately wanted him to say no, but she was shocked when he did, in fact, answer, "No."

He nodded toward the piece of vine that she had torn free of him. It was beginning to set down roots in the grout between the veranda's terra-cotta tiles.

"Even if you pull the whole thing out, it will grow and thrive here." He leaned his head against her arm. "I'm sorry. I know that was terrible for you."

"I get to keep you a while longer, so I've decided to forgive you."

Rosie rested her chin on his head, unspeakably relieved that it was over. Adam nestled closer, and they stood at the railing, their arms wrapped around each other, watching the dragons on the water.

"I wish that we could simply put it back where it came from," he said after some time had passed.

Rosie wished he hadn't said it, because all at once, she was thinking of Hart again, of that night at Aunt Bonnie's when he had told her how he'd rid Tanria of the undead.

There was a house in the middle of Sector 28, a house that only I could see.

"Adam," she said. She didn't want to say the rest, but she knew that she had to. She owed him this.

It looked like my home, the house I grew up in, Hart said in her memory, *but it was actually my death. I could see my own end, waiting there for me.*

Rosie forced the words out of her mouth: "There might be a way."

Adam gave her a quizzical look. "How? I've tried to return many times. I have never found my way back to the garden."

She could see Hart, sitting across from her, radiating his misgiving as he rumpled his blond hair.

"There's a door—a door to the afterlife—right here in Tanria."

Chapter Twenty-Seven

They took their time.

They read Zeddie's recipe book and cooked elaborate meals. Not that either of them would die if they didn't eat, but it was nice to enjoy a fancy dinner each evening. They talked about how much they missed Zeddie's finesse in the kitchen and Duckers's good humor.

They drank as much expensive coffee in the morning and as much fancy wine in the evening as they could hold.

They wondered if Gobbo would show up again, but he never did.

They swam in the lake.

They rode Eloise one afternoon, sticking close to the Dragon's Teeth range. Even that small tour of Tanria reminded them how little time they had, so they came home.

They made love. Often.

They slept the deep, unencumbered sleep of two people who had already made the tough decision and had no regrets left.

A morning came when Rosie woke to find Adam propped up on one elbow, gazing down at her wistfully.

"So it's today, then," she said.

"Yes, if you are willing."

He had dispensed with wearing a shirt to bed since the vine made it uncomfortable. Rosie smoothed her hands over his chest and shoulders, her eyes memorizing his face, her fingers memorizing the rest of him.

"It might not work," she reminded him.

"I know." He slipped his hand inside the undershirt that Rosie had taken to wearing at night, one of the ones Zeddie had left behind.

"There's a good chance it won't."

By now, he had the cotton rucked up over her breasts. "I know."

"And even if we open that door, we might die the moment we step over the threshold."

"Which is why you shouldn't come with me."

"I'm sorry, sir, but I'm under orders to accompany you for the duration of your stay in Tanria."

She pulled his head down to her and sighed with pleasure as he took the pink bud of her breast into his mouth. She wanted him to hold all of her inside him, as badly as she wanted to hold him inside her.

They took their time in this, too. Even when Rosie straddled him, her movements were slow and sweet, lingering until urgency won out. Adam strained against the makeshift pillows, his neck unbearably vulnerable, his pulse beating beneath his skin.

They took their time over breakfast. Rosie made mediocre pancakes that Adam insisted were delicious.

They took their time getting dressed, with Rosie joking, "What does one wear to the afterlife?"

"Nothing," Adam answered archly.

"Cad."

In the end, Rosie put on her softest cotton shirt—blue-and-green plaid—with her most broken-in dungarees and her ostrich leather boots. Under it all, she wore her peacock-patterned intimates (washed, of course)—her favorite, Adam's favorite. He wore navy blue wool-blend trousers and his loosest-fitting shirt, in a pale gray, the collar open to give the vine room. He polished the lenses of his glasses and did his best to shine his brogues.

They took their time as they strolled along the path that brought them to the north shore of Lake Vanderlinden, sidestepping the encroaching vines that snaked across the trail.

But time seemed to be speeding up.

They arrived too soon at the lake, where Eloise swam toward them without needing to be called. Before Rosie and Adam knew it, they were spooned together on the dragon's back, ready to fly together. They would do everything together, to the end.

It was a half hour's flight to Sector 28, but it felt shorter, and all the land passing by in a blur beneath them was covered with the briar... which was no longer particularly thorny or briar-like. The invasive flora had become soft and lush, with countless red blooms opening to the sunlight. Rosie wondered if it resembled the tree her father had first created, but it was difficult for her to imagine the Trickster creating anything so beautiful.

They circled above the broad plain, searching for a house neither of them should have been able to see. But Rosie did see it, even before Adam shouted "There" over the wind whipping past their ears.

It was in the middle of Sector 28, like Hart had said it would be, the shape of an old-fashioned two-story farmhouse, covered in a mass of green vines and red blossoms.

Adam directed Eloise to land as close to the house as she could.

The only problem was, she couldn't.

The instant her webbed feet touched down, she was entangled in the vines.

Meep-meep! she trumpeted in alarm, her vast wings beating hard to pull herself up and out, but to no avail.

"Hang in there, Eloise!" shouted Rosie. They were hovering ten feet in the air, but Rosie decided she liked those odds.

Adam, guessing what she was about to do, turned his head long enough to holler, "Bad idea!"

"Great idea!" she corrected him, before sliding off Eloise and falling into the vines below.

There were no thorns left, but there were plenty of sticks and stems to scratch up Rosie's skin. It had been so long since she had chased this kind of high that she couldn't bring herself to care.

Eloise continued to fight free of the vine, thrashing in the air with an increasingly panicky *meep-meep-meep-meep!* and jostling poor Adam in the process.

"We need to cut her free, but you'll have to jump first," Rosie called up to him.

"No, thank you."

"I'll catch you."

"That is not reassuring."

"It's not like you can die. Jump!"

Seeing sense, he screwed his eyes shut and let himself fall off the dragon.

Rosie caught him. Sort of. It would be more accurate to say that she let him land on her to soften the blow, and they both wound up buried in a thicket.

Rosie clawed her way out of the stems and leaves, tugged her foldable knife from her pocket, and began sawing at the vines holding Eloise in place. One vine was as thick around as her wrist, and if she didn't cut through it soon, the dragon would have no way to take off from here. They needed to free her while she was airborne. Cut and bleeding, Adam joined in, yanking smaller vines out of the way as Rosie hacked at the biggest one.

At last she broke through, and Eloise surged skyward, sending Rosie and Adam tumbling into the thicket again. By the time Rosie got herself out of it, the dragon was a speck in the north-western sky, her parting *meep* of good luck echoing behind her.

"There goes our ride," said Rosie, giving Adam a hand up. "If this doesn't work, it's going to suck to get out of here."

He smoothed down his ruffled hair and shrugged with elegant nonchalance. "I walked across the ocean floor."

"And got eaten by a shark."

"Yes, returning to the Dragon's Lair will be easy by comparison."

"I really want the details on the whole shark thing."

"I assure you, you do not." He frowned at the house-shaped jungle looming over them. "If your friend is correct, we shouldn't be able to see or touch the actual structure, only the briar."

Rosie stared dubiously at the vine-coated front steps and tested the bottom tread with the toe of her boot. "Think these will hold?"

"The plant nearly trapped a dragon."

"Good point."

They took the steps together, side by side, and walked across what appeared to be a front porch. It was an unnerving feeling, as if there was nothing beneath the verdant tapestry but air. The sensation reminded Rosie of walking across the trampoline that the trapeze artists and tightrope walkers used during rehearsal in her circus days.

"Do you see a door?" she asked Adam, squinting at the front of the house in the dim light beneath the living canopy that covered the porch.

"There," he said at the same moment she spotted it, the faint rectangular outline to their left and the doorknob-shaped bulb jutting outward. Adam looked at her, and she nodded. He grasped the leafy doorknob, and incredibly, it didn't crumple in his hand.

"Can you turn it?" asked Rosie.

Miraculously, he could, but when he pushed on the door, it didn't budge. Pulling on it didn't work either. "It's locked."

They both stood and stared at the door, unmoving.

"Part of me's relieved, and part of me is pissed that we're this close and can't do anything about it."

"My sentiments exactly."

A dark shadow beneath the doorknob snagged Rosie's attention. She bent to get a better look, pushing aside a leaf that had gotten in the way. "Does that look like a keyhole to you?"

"Perhaps. But we don't have the key."

Rosie reached inside her collar to pull up on the gold chain around her neck and let her birth key dangle for Adam's inspection. "Worth a try, right?"

He stepped aside to give her room. She took the chain from around her neck and inserted the key into the hole. She could feel friction, like sticking her key into the door to her apartment above Wilner's Green Grocer in Eternity.

"Holy shit," she said, because she knew—she knew before she even turned it—that the key was going to unlock this door.

And it did.

The invisible tumblers rolled into place. Rosie unfolded her knife to cut around the perimeter, and when the last vine gave way, she opened the door.

A dark, blank nothingness awaited them on the other side of the threshold.

"Does this look familiar?" Rosie asked Adam hopefully.

"No."

He grinned at her then, teeth and all, and Rosie saw reflected back at her the same giddy feeling she always got when she was about to plunge headlong into some ill-advised adventure with no idea as to how it would turn out in the end.

"It's funny," she told him. "Before all of this happened, I was starting to feel stuck. My whole life stretched out before me with no end, and I didn't know what to do about it. And then I got literally stuck in here with you, and it's the best thing that could have happened to me. It's like I needed to get stuck to get unstuck. How does that make any sense?"

"It makes perfect sense." He took her hand in his. "Are you sure about this?"

"I'm sure about *you*," she said, holding tight to his hand. "Ready?"

"Ready."

And they stepped into the unknown, together.

Chapter Twenty-Eight

They burst into the apartment on Seventh Street in Morton City. It was nighttime, and the parlor was lit by the warm, gauzy light of two lamps, the shades covered with floral scarves to diffuse the brightness. There wasn't enough room for a sofa, so the parlor hosted a worn armchair and a love seat with cushions so threadbare Rosie could see the faded linen covers peeking out between the warp and weft of the cottage rose upholstery. Whenever a gentleman caller stayed late, Rosie had slept on that love seat, listening to the sounds of her mother's tinkling laughter in the one and only bedroom. How on earth had she fit, even as a child?

She sensed that it was past midnight, but the slapping of equimaris feet and the rumbling of carriages and the music of buskers and the leering calls of drunks on the street below never stopped. They composed the white noise of Morton City, as constant and as soothing as the ocean's waves.

The bedroom door was open, and the single bed she had shared with her mother—where Jocelyn had let her stay up way past her bedtime as they giggled together under the sheets—was neatly made with a large, faded silk scarf draped artistically over a yellowed chenille bedspread. The scarf was torn in one corner and was missing some of its fringe, and Rosie knew it was placed strategically over a rusty stain on the bedspread.

It was unbearably beautiful, all of it.

This place had been the center of Rosie's world when she was a child, and though it radiated homeyness, she could see what she had not understood in her youth—how poor she and her mother had been and how hard Jocelyn had tried to make a dump look splendid.

And how much the Trickster had failed them both.

Adam touched her arm with gentle fingertips. "Where are we?"

"The apartment I grew up in—my home."

But Adam was her home now, too.

"It smells like you here," he said.

Rosie inhaled, taking in the familiar scent of her childhood, the one she had carried with her all her life. "Lavender. It was cheap, so it was the only perfume my mother could afford."

"Home," he repeated, and she understood that he meant her, that she was home to him, too, and so home smelled like lavender.

The noise on the street carried on as it always did, but a single strand of music stood out from the others, an alto singing a bawdy, funny song that had been popular in the days when Rosie's mother had been a chorus girl.

Rosie knew that voice.

Her heart reacted before her mind could catch up.

"Jocelyn!" she cried, choking on raw emotion as she flung open the apartment door and dashed through it.

"Rosie, wait!"

Adam followed hard on her heels. They should have found themselves in the narrow hallway outside the apartment with its cheap, wrinkled rug and creaking floorboards and the faint odor of cat piss. Instead, they looked out on a softly undulating sea under a starlit sky.

And the door snicked shut behind them.

Rosie turned. The apartment was gone. The entire building was gone. Morton City was gone. And Jocelyn Fox was most certainly gone. Instead, Rosie was staring at what appeared to be a door in a stone wall that stood eight feet high—a door without a knob or handle or any visible means of opening it.

The overwhelming grief filled her all over again, as if she had lost her mother five seconds ago rather than more than a century ago. She pressed her hands to the smooth wooden planks of the impenetrable door. "No! Jocelyn!"

Adam placed his left hand over her right, but he wasn't looking at her. His eyes were fixed on the unfamiliar structure before them. It was difficult to make out details in the dark, but the place wasn't what Rosie would describe as a house, more like an enclosure.

"Where are we?" she asked Adam.

"This was my grandfather's estate."

"So this is the House of the..." Rosie couldn't bring herself to say it aloud. "This is *the* house?"

Even that question sounded absurd. It was one thing to believe that a person's soul went to the House of the Unknown God when they died; it was quite another to be standing on the doorstep.

"I believe so."

"Was this how things looked when you were here before?"

"No. I saw this house from a great distance. I never came near it. I entered the way the dead are supposed to enter, on the opposite shore, and I took a boat to the island where the Old Gods lived."

Rosie gazed out at the dark waters of the ocean before them. "So this is the Salt Sea?"

"Yes."

She found herself short of breath and dizzy. "I know that this was the plan, but holy shit, we are in the land of the dead. I am low-key freaking out right now. Do you know how to open this door? Because I don't love the idea of being stuck on this side with no way to get out."

"My grandfather lived in a great estate. The door could only be

324

opened by his guardsmen from the inside, and it was kept bolted, especially at night."

"Khäsh," cursed Rosie.

"Yes, khäsh," Adam agreed.

"I swear, I hear someone out here" came a muffled voice from behind the wall, and a moment later, the door swung inward, revealing a tall man silhouetted against warm yellow light.

"There *is* someone out here," he called over his shoulder to a fresh-faced young woman with light brown hair, who stood at the counter of what appeared to be a comic book store. Rosie was certain she had never seen her before, but the shape of her face and her mannerisms and her bright blue eyes seemed familiar. She smiled at Rosie and Adam before returning her attention to the comic book splayed open on the counter.

By now, Rosie's eyes had adjusted to the light.

"Hart?" she asked in disbelief as she gawped at the man standing before her.

A warm smile spread across his face. "You know my boy?"

Rosie took a closer look. He was shorter than Hart, and he wore a very un-Hart-like outfit—a loose short-sleeved shirt with palm trees printed all over it, a pair of cargo shorts, and black socks with sandals.

"You must be the Warden," she said faintly, starstruck. Sure, her father was the Trickster, but the Warden was a death god, and not one people ran into every day, for obvious reasons.

"Yep. And you are . . . ?" He held out his hand, which she shook while valiantly not squealing, *Fuck me, Grandfather Bones—the Warden!*

"Rosie Fox."

The death god released her and consulted a clipboard that had appeared out of nowhere. His brow furrowed before he looked expectantly at Adam.

"I have had many names," Adam hedged.

Rosie leaned in and stage-whispered, "I think he probably wants Lidojozháis Mäkherkis Ödamika."

"No kidding? Huh!" The Warden goggled at Adam in wonder before he leaned his head out of the door and looked in both directions. "Where'd you come from?"

"From in there." Rosie pointed behind him, wondering why the world on the other side of this door looked nothing like her home or Adam's—unless Adam's grandfather had been a comic book fan.

"*From* here? Not *to* here?" He studied his clipboard, looked at Rosie and Adam again, and frowned at the clipboard once more. "You're definitely not supposed to be here right now."

"We entered through your son's house in Tanria," Adam explained.

"Really? Plot twist. I did not see that coming."

"Quick question," interjected Rosie. "Are we dead?"

The Warden squinted first at her and then at Adam. "No, you're not dead. Huh!" He scratched his head, mussing his blond hair as Rosie and Adam surreptitiously sagged against each other in relief.

"Honey, I'll be right back," the Warden told the woman at the counter before joining Rosie and Adam on the shore of the Salt Sea, letting the door swing shut behind him.

"You can open that again, right?" asked Rosie.

The Warden looked mildly offended.

"I guess that's basically your job."

"I guess it is," he agreed. "All right. Start talking. What are you two doing here?"

"It's a long story," Rosie began, but Adam cut in.

"We're here to take the briar out of my body and return it to the garden of the Old Gods in the hope that we might save Tanria from the invasive vine that has taken over inside the Mist."

Rosie stared at him, nonplussed.

Adam shrugged in apology. "Time is of the essence, my ruzhkel."

"Right." She turned to the Warden. "I stand corrected. Short story: we need to get to the garden of the Old Gods. Can you help us?"

"I would—because any friend of Hart is a friend of mine—but I can't leave my post. The last time I did that, we ended up with an undead problem in Tanria. I can get you transportation, but past that, you're on your own."

"That's more than fair."

"Yes, thank you," said Adam.

"You bet." The Warden gathered them in an unexpected group hug, smashing Adam's head against Rosie's right boob. "If you live through this, will you be sure to tell my boy that I said hi and I love him and Mercy and the grandkids?"

Rosie awkwardly patted the death god on the back. "Will do."

"Okay then, follow me."

He led them down a long gangway to a dock that Rosie could have sworn was not there moments ago. Tied to a cleat was a single weathered rowboat, bobbing like a toy in a bathtub. It looked impossibly small against the vastness of the Salt Sea. Rosie looked at it dubiously.

"I don't get out much," the Warden explained with an embarrassed cringe before giving them directions. "If you head straight, you'll wind up at the shore between life and death. You don't want to go there. What you want to do is row toward that dark mass to our left. You see that?"

Rosie gazed at the horizon in question until she spotted an oily smudge slightly darker than the starry night around it. "Yeah, I see it."

"That's where the Old Gods used to live. No clue how it's held up over all these years, but whatever is left of the garden should be there."

"Great. Thank you."

Rosie nudged Adam, but he was too occupied staring wistfully at the House of the Unknown God to notice. To Rosie's surprise, its appearance had changed. The wall was much taller now, with massive double doors and a series of tiled rooftops gleaming with starlight beyond, a veritable palace.

"Lidojozháis Mäkherkis Ödamika." The warden took him by the upper arms and said firmly, but not unkindly, "Your brother is supposed to be there, but not you, not yet. Do not make the same mistake twice."

With that, he left them at the dock, walked to the huge double doors in the wall, and let himself in without needing a knob or a handle.

"I wonder what would happen if we fell in," Rosie mused as she watched Adam work the oars, admiring his innate athleticism, this man who'd fired an explosive arrow with deadly aim into the maw of a war dragon.

"Let's not find out," he said, his steady rhythm on the oars never wavering.

"I wonder what would happen if we fell in and a shark ate us."

"Please, by all means, force me to relive one of the more traumatic moments of my long life."

"Sorry, tiger. That was thoughtless of me."

"You are forgiven. Should I add Tiger to my list of names?"

"Yes, obviously, you should add Tiger to your repertoire. Why don't you let me take a turn at the oars for a bit while you're at it. You've been rowing for a long time now."

"We have both been rowing for a long time now," he said, but he switched places with her and let Rosie take her second turn in the unending night.

"The Briar Thief story I read when I was a kid talked about how everything seemed to take longer than it should," she recalled as she rowed. "Is that right?"

"Yes and no. Some things move quickly, while others slow down to a snail's pace. And, as you know, many years passed on Earth before I returned."

"I wonder how much time will have passed when we get back."

She didn't say *if.* She decided to treat their return like a foregone conclusion. If Adam noticed her word choice, he wasn't inclined to correct her.

A large wave billowed the boat, making it rise and fall steeply. Rosie's stomach lurched with the abrupt shift in height.

"Does the water seem choppier to you all of a sudden?" she asked Adam.

"Yes."

"Was it like this the last time you were here?"

"No. I had calm waters the entire journey."

A much bigger wave lifted them uncomfortably high in the air before dropping them again.

"I was kidding about falling in," said Rosie, white-knuckling the oars.

Again, the Salt Sea rose beneath them and sent them hurtling from the dizzying crest of the wave. An oar broke free of its mooring, nearly knocking Rosie off the bench.

Adam was reaching for her when she saw a wall of water coming at them. She had only enough time to scream "Adam!" before it struck, plucking him from the boat like a hand grasping a coin and pulling him under the water.

Rosie didn't think; she acted, abandoning the boat to dive in after him. She should not have been able to see anything in the dark waters of the Salt Sea, and yet a dim light glowed far below, illuminating the outline of Adam's body as the ocean pulled him deeper.

Rosie followed, pumping her arms and legs as hard as she could. Her lungs burned, and she knew that she would die soon, that she would revive and die and revive and die over and over. But still she kicked, still she dove farther and farther into the unknown, and all the while the light beneath her grew brighter and brighter.

At last, her lungs gave out, and she drew in water with a great heaving of her lungs, and...

She did not die.

She was very much alive as she stopped swimming and sank like a rock into the sea, breathing water as if it were air.

An ocean current took hold of her, drawing her downward toward the growing blue light below.

And then she was on the ocean floor, curled like a snail's shell on the gritty surface. Adam crouched beside her, his hair floating in the water, his shirt puffing around him, his vine swaying. She uncurled and launched herself at him, throwing her arms around his neck and holding on with no intention of ever letting go.

"I thought I lost you!" she cried, and it wasn't until the words left her mouth that she realized she could speak as well as breathe.

"You will have to work harder than that to lose me," he told her as he brushed aside a lock of coppery hair that had drifted into her face.

"Not funny!"

"Not intended to be funny. I would wipe away your tears, but..." He gestured to the Salt Sea.

They were surrounded on all sides by a breathtakingly beautiful luminescent coral reef. There was such order to it, such deliberation, that it almost appeared to be a sort of city under the sea.

"How am I breathing water and not dying?" Rosie wondered.

"You can't die in the land of the dead" came a withering voice from behind them.

Rosie and Adam turned to find a man seated above them on a throne of pink coral, although the term *man* wasn't entirely accurate. He had the face and arms and torso of a human being, but he was blue from the top of his coral-like hair to the tips of his fish tail, with the occasional violet scale thrown in for variety.

"Salt fucking Sea," uttered Rosie as her brain struggled to comprehend the sheer size and scope of the god looking down on them.

Either he didn't hear her f-bomb addition to his name or he didn't care. He stared daggers at Adam.

"Well, well, well. If it isn't everybody's favorite thief. Enjoying your shrines and mortal admiration on Earth, are we?"

Adam put on his coldest face. "Not particularly."

"Why do I find that difficult to believe, Ödamika? Tell me, what have you come to steal this time? A cup of the Salt Sea? One of Grandfather Bones's metatarsals? The Warden's door knocker? Do you think you can steal your brother from us next? I know that you believe the rules don't apply to you."

"What is this guy's problem?" Rosie murmured to Adam.

It was the god who answered her, his tone acerbic, his coral-pink eyes full of malice. "What problem could I possibly have with the mortal who dared to sneak into the land of the dead to steal the plant that destroyed my happiness?"

"It was the Trickster who created the plant in the first place. He was the one who lured Adam here during the War of the Gods. Take it up with him."

"Don't you mean 'Daddy'?"

Adam put a hand on Rosie's arm to stay her sharp retort. "We're not here to steal anything. We wish to return what was taken."

"Why should I believe you?"

"Does he look like he hasn't learned his lesson?" snapped Rosie. She'd had it with the Salt Sea's unthinking disdain. God or not, this guy was not going to stand between Adam and what he wanted—what he needed—not when they'd come this far and risked so much. "You called him a thief, but what did he take? He didn't steal the briar for himself; he was trying to give humanity a fighting chance while you and all the other gods duked it out. Who died in that war? Who was hurt? Who paid the consequences? What did it cost *you*? Nothing, that's what."

Rosie flung her hand toward Adam.

"But he lost his brother. And in the end, he lost everything, not because he was conniving, but because he cared about other people. He hung on that thorn for the gods know how long. He's lived two millennia longer than any human being should and racked up all the pain and losses that come with so many years. You, of all the gods, should understand what that has meant for him."

The Salt Sea seemed to turn to a hardened coral reef. He did not move. He said nothing. Only his burning pink gaze proved he was living.

"Why did you pull the vine out of your lover?" she asked him, and when he did not answer, she answered for him. "Because immortality made his precious life miserable, and you loved him enough to let him go. Well, I love Adam, and I don't want him to be miserable anymore. Please, don't stop us. Help us."

The Salt Sea remained silent, but the fire had gone out of his glowing gaze. All that remained was undisguised heartbreak.

"It's the same story. And a story is only complete when it comes to an end. Let us end it."

The god looked beside her to where Adam stood, small and alone in the infinite ocean. Rosie took his hand in hers; she didn't want him to be alone anymore.

"Fine," the god intoned with a dismissive wave of his hand.

"Thank y——" began Adam, but his gratitude was cut short by the arrival of a squid.

An incomprehensibly enormous squid.

A literal giant squid.

Its monstrous bulk blotted out the faint glow of the Salt Sea's underwater kingdom.

"Adam?" Rosie said feebly as the squid fanned out its staggeringly long tentacles around them, its huge mouth gaping wide before it drew them in and swallowed them both into the lightless cavern of its stomach.

Chapter Twenty-Nine

Rosie was on her hands and knees in the belly of the squid, the constant motion of the creature making it impossible to stand.

She heard Adam's stuttering cry somewhere ahead of her. Unable to see, she reached her hand out into the darkness, crawling toward the sound until she made contact, her fingers smushing into his torso. He made the sound again, and Rosie realized he was laughing, not crying.

"So, as it turns out, there are giants squids in the afterlife," she said, snorting with hilarity. "Good to know."

"Every day with you is an adventure. Every minute of every day."

She sat beside him, her butt squelching against the spongy texture of the squid's stomach.

"How in Old Hell are we going to get out of here?"

"I suspect that this is the Salt Sea's idea of assistance."

"That guy needs to get a sense of humor."

"Perhaps, but I can say with confidence that being eaten by a squid is better than being eaten by a shark."

"You can't drop that fact on me without explaining how you come back from being a shark's lunch."

"I can, actually," said Adam, and the little turd had the audacity to chuckle at Rosie's indignation.

He was still laughing when the squid disgorged them both

onto dry land, the force of the heaving stomach sending them tumbling across a chalky beach that glowed in the starlit night.

Adam staggered over to Rosie as she did her best to shake the squid's stomach slime off her arms. The dim light leached all the color out of him so that he appeared to Rosie as an animated black-and-white photo of himself, his hair slicked by fishy squid gloop; his shirt sticking to his skin in odd patches; his vine, weighed down by slime, hanging out of his open collar; his glasses obscured by a sheen of ick.

"Are you all right?" he asked her.

"Never been better. Can you see?"

He reached into his pocket and pulled out Rosie's handkerchief, which appeared to have survived the squid's belly unscathed.

"I just washed that. You stole it off the clothesline, you thief," she told him as he wiped clean the lenses of his glasses.

"The heart wants what the heart wants, my ruzhkel, and this handkerchief is as miraculous as the woman who gave it to me." He pocketed the linen and hooked his glasses behind his ears as Rosie took in their surroundings.

To their back was the Salt Sea, and the ghostly beach stretched for miles to either side of them. Before them were the strangest ruins Rosie had ever seen. The nearest structure sprawled across the land like a stone octopus, its tentacles broken, its bulbous head crumbling. Another building appeared to have broken in half, but when it was whole, it must have towered higher than any building Rosie had ever seen, higher than a dragon could fly.

Exactly as the story she had read as a child described it.

"Did you tell people what this place looked like when you came back?" she asked Adam.

"No, I told no one my story."

"Then how do we know all the details? How does anyone know what you did? How does anyone know you exist?"

"I..." He blinked at her. "I've never considered that before."

"In two thousand years, you never thought to wonder how the entire world knows what you did?"

Adam blinked some more, clearly stymied.

"Wow, you are allergic to attention. 'I tried to save the world, but don't mind me.' Maybe that's why I love the shit out of you; you're the polar opposite of my father. You're like the anti-Trickster."

The second she said it aloud, realization dawned on her.

"The Trickster," she said. "The Trickster told your story. Of course! That narcissist blabbed it all, probably trying to make himself look like the good guy. I bet he's been stewing over this for centuries, crying into his dry martini about how everyone blames him for tricking you when he was just a wonderful, humble god trying to do humanity a solid. Barf."

"I would defend him, but I don't want to," said Adam, drier than an old newspaper.

"Good. You shouldn't."

She put her arm over his shoulder, and he wrapped his arm around her waist, and together, they set off toward the garden of the Old Gods.

As the stories said, they seemed to walk for a long, long time without making much progress. The farther they got from the sea, the more oppressive was the eerie silence of the place, the sheer lifelessness of it, every inch of the island depressing and unwelcoming. What few houses remained standing were oddly shaped and ugly. It almost made her pity the Trickster, to have lived somewhere so utterly without comfort.

But then she remembered that he'd been living in Fairport on the west coast of Vinland in an ostentatious luxury estate—a swanky house that he'd had built while Jocelyn tried to make one package of noodles and a half stick of butter feed Rosie and herself for a week. And then Rosie didn't pity him in the slightest.

"It's so odd," she said, taking in the deterioration of the ancient homes. "You think of gods as being permanent, but nothing is permanent, is it?"

"Nothing but the stars."

They both gazed upward at the pinpricks of light on the altar of the night sky, at the gods who had come and gone eons ago, and the Old Gods who had surrendered at last when they didn't want to be stuck inside Tanria anymore. For the first time since their arrival on the strange island, Rosie sensed the sanctity of the place. It was like walking through an enormous shipyard, the dead reminding the living that there were things in the universe so much larger than oneself.

They moved on in silence, passing through a narrow, misshapen archway between two twisting structures before coming to an open courtyard on the other side. And there, rambling in all directions, was the briar, the Thorn of Eternal Life. It was mind-bogglingly enormous, the lowest stems as large around as oak trees, the uppermost tendrils as delicate as lacework, all of it gnarled and colorless and covered in barbs.

"It has grown," Adam observed, his words dwarfed by the enormity of the plant. Rosie had never felt so small in her life.

A *crunch* underfoot brought their attention to the ground. There, beside the pointy toe of Rosie's boot, was a broken terracotta pot, a small amount of powdery dirt covering the shards.

They stopped and stared at the pot that Adam had once filled with his own two hands, a metaphor for the fragility of all things in the face of time. Rosie pulled Adam in closer, and for a moment more, they held each other in that dark, sad place.

And then Adam said, "It's time, my ruzhkel."

Rosie forced herself to let go of him, because that was what you did when you loved someone whose end had come: you let them go. She nodded, willing herself not to cry. But as she reached for the vine twining around his neck, Adam grabbed her hand and pressed it to his beating heart.

"Thank you. For everything."

His unshed tears glistened in the dim light. Rosie's throat ached with the urge to break down sobbing, but she wouldn't. The last thing Adam Lee needed to see at the end of his life was Rosie's crying face.

"Thank you for everything, too," she told him, relishing his body's heat and the pulsing of his life beneath her palm. "Are you ready?"

"Yes."

He wasn't ready. Neither was she. But they were going to do this anyway, because it had to be done.

She took her steady hand from Adam's heart and wrapped the vine around it.

"I love you," she said.

"I love you, too."

"On the count of three?"

He nodded.

"One. Two. Three."

She pulled, cautiously this time, no tugging, but it hurt him no matter how gentle she was. She continued to pull anyway, because this was what he wanted her to do. She pulled when she would rather yank out her own fingernails.

Adam held his ground. He clenched his jaw, but cries of pain escaped through his teeth. The vine unspooled from his body, inch by inch. Feet turned into yards as Rosie hauled on the unnatural life that had taken root deep inside the last person she wanted to lose.

Time crawled between them, stretching as long as the straining vine. Rosie felt like this torment would never end, that they would go on this way for all eternity.

And then, all at once, it was over, like the ending of a tug-of-war game. Adam barked one last shout of agony as the plant gave way, sending Rosie tumbling to the ground with the vine slack in her hands while Adam collapsed where he stood. The bloody root ball landed on the ground with a wet splat. Rosie dropped her end and went tearing across the distance between them—a good ten yards—before crouching beside Adam's crumpled form.

He's dead, she thought. *I killed him. I did this to him.*

But then he moaned and rolled onto his back, his lungs heaving beneath the bloodstain spreading across his chest. She yanked open his shirt, popping buttons left and right, with a mind toward stanching the flow. Only, he wasn't bleeding at all. There was no blood to stanch, no wound to speak of, save a puckered white scar to the left of his heart.

Adam sat up. His hand fluttered tentatively over the spot where the vine had exited his body.

"I'm alive," he said, mystified.

Rosie grasped him by the shoulders. "Don't you ever make me do that again!"

"I'm sorry."

"Take your sorry and shove it up your ass!"

He cupped her face in his hands. "It's all right now."

"It's not all right! That was the worst!"

Rosie pulled him into a bone-crunching hug and burst into tears.

Adam stroked her back, murmuring, "It's over now. And we're together. It will be all right."

He waited until her breathing settled and the tears stopped pouring down her face before he added, "But I do wonder..."

"You wonder?"

He touched his chest. "Am I really living? How do you know you're alive in the land of the dead?"

"You will have to find that out for yourself, the same as all mortals must," someone answered from above.

"Gah! These gods have got to stop sneaking up on us like this!" exclaimed Rosie. She scanned the vast briar until she discovered a human-shaped smudge sitting on a thorn several feet above them. It bowed its head in apology—if the oblong shape at the top of its shadowy body could be called a head.

"Who are you?" asked Adam.

The being answered in an uncanny polyphony, as if each word was uttered by many people at once. "I am nothing and everything, nowhere and everywhere, at all times and in no time."

Rosie addressed Adam out of the side of her mouth. "Are you following this?"

"Not exactly." Adam stared in awe at the incomprehensible entity sitting in the briar. "Are we addressing the Unknown God?"

"If I am unknowable, how can I have a name?"

Taking this as a confirmation, Rosie and Adam gaped up at the oldest and most powerful of all the gods, the one who was utterly and completely unfathomable to the human mind.

"Perhaps this will help you understand me better." Slowly, the shadowy form took shape. Adam grasped Rosie's arm and squeezed as the blur became a man in his midthirties, dressed in an old-fashioned blue robe. A stylized tiger was emblazoned across his chest in silver thread. Atop his black hair, he wore a crown of laurel leaves in hammered silver. He didn't look much like Adam, and yet the resemblance was there. And based on Adam's reaction, it was easy to figure out which human form the Unknown God had taken.

Adam's brother—or, more specifically, the god wearing his likeness—descended from the Thorn of Eternal Life, floating unnaturally downward until they came to stand before Rosie and

Adam. They placed their human hands on Adam's shoulders and said, "You have done well, my brother—so well—but the story is not yet finished."

The god spoke in Eshilese, and yet Rosie understood them.

"The briar continues to grow where it does not belong—here and there—when it never belonged anywhere."

All three looked at the vine that Rosie had extricated from Adam. The roots sank into the ground, and the vine snaked toward the rest of the plant to join with it.

"You mean that the briar continues to grow in Tanria?" asked Adam.

The god inclined their head in affirmation.

"So what we did here—everything we've been through—none of it mattered?" said Rosie.

"I would not say that." They looked to the vine that Rosie had pulled from Adam's body, their face a mask of tragedy. "My child planted this life. He meant well, but consequences care little for intentions."

They spoke with fondness, but Rosie understood that *my child* meant the Trickster, and she couldn't bring herself to sympathize with the father who'd brought them to this moment.

Adam's shoulders sagged under the weight of the god's hands—his brother's hands. "You said the story is not yet finished. Can we end it?"

"Yes. That is why I am here and now, to tell you that you must reach the end."

Great. Cryptic Book of the New Gods *speak*, thought Rosie before addressing the Unknown God. "How?"

"How does any mortal reach the end?"

Adam and Rosie shot each other a look, both of them ready to put this adventure into the afterlife behind them.

"Through death," said Adam.

Again, the Unknown God inclined their head, their hands falling to their sides.

"But we can't die," said Rosie.

"Are you certain of that?"

Once more, the god turned their head to gaze at the vine that had lived inside Adam for two thousand years. It sprouted thorns once more as it wrapped itself around a larger stem.

"Am I . . . mortal now?" asked Adam.

"Yes."

Rosie had scarcely three seconds to celebrate the good news before Adam spoke and crushed her joy.

"So I must end my life in order to bring an end to the briar."

"What?" she exclaimed. "No. Hard no."

To her surprise and gratitude, the Unknown God seemed to take her side. "Your end is already certain. What good could it do now?"

The god considered Adam, their eyes the same shape as his but completely black, like cut obsidian. And yet those eyes were not menacing. They were not unkind. "You have mourned your brother, your friends, your mother, so many preceding you before your end. They are home now. Everyone comes home eventually, even you. Even gods. All except the Void—the unknowable."

The Unknown God returned their attention to the briar running riot over the courtyard.

"There were once many flowers on this tree, when it stood tall and straight and lovely on the banks of a clear lake. A mortal picked a blossom, and the tree gave him a thousand thousand years. Someone will need to give back those years to bring this to a close. All life must come full circle. But my children tell me that they are not ready to end, that ending is a job for mortals. Or perhaps an immortal mortal, if such a one exists."

The god pointed at a single red flower on a stem high above.

They looked at Rosie when they said, "Only one bloom remains now. I wonder who will pick it?"

Those boundless eyes transfixed her, nailing her feet to the spot as understanding poured into her. And then the god was gone—simply gone—though neither she nor Adam saw them leave.

An oddly familiar buzzing sounded in the distance, but Rosie's focus was on the matter at hand: killing the plant—here and in Tanria—once and for all. Adam must have read her intention, because he clutched her shirtsleeve.

"Tell me you are not considering climbing this plant and picking that flower."

"Of course I'm going to climb this plant and pick that flower. What other option do we have?"

She tore her sleeve free of Adam's grasp and strode toward the briar. Adam chased after her as the buzzing grew louder, more insistent. She knew that sound. Why did she know that sound?

"We have many options," said Adam, struggling to keep up with her long-legged stride.

"Name one."

He listed them on his fingers as he trotted beside her. "The Salt Sea, the Warden, Grandfather Bones, any of the Three Mothers—"

"I don't think we can expect the gods of life and death to sacrifice themselves. That might throw off the entire balance of the universe."

Adam lost his cool. He took her by the arm in a bruising grip. "Any immortal other than you could pick that flower!"

"And yet they haven't. In two thousand years, not one of them has climbed the Thorn of Eternal Life to pick the bloom and give their life to kill this sucker."

Somewhere in the back of her mind, Rosie noticed that the buzzing had stopped, but it wasn't important now.

"I am begging you," said Adam, clinging to her, panicked. "Don't do this."

"It's not your choice to make."

"Rosie, please. You can't."

She could swear she heard the door of an autoduck open, then slam closed, but obviously that was impossible.

And Adam was crying.

She took him into her arms, and he held on tight to her, his tears soaking into her shirt.

"I know from personal experience that it's much shittier to be left than to do the leaving. But you heard the Unknown God. They said everyone comes home in the end. It won't be long, and I'll be waiting for you when you come home to me."

"No. Don't leave."

Rosie held him away from her so that he was forced to look her in the eye. "When you wanted me to pull the vine out of your body, I asked you if you would do the same for me. Do you remember what you said?"

He glared at her, and since he wouldn't answer, she answered for him.

"You said, *I think I would. I hope I would.* Well, now I'm asking you to let me go."

"This is different."

"How is it different?"

"Because it is!"

Behind Adam, Rosie saw a strange man step out from between the buildings and into the courtyard. He wore the sort of old-timey suit that Jocelyn's gentlemen callers had favored, with a garish waistcoat, a pair of spats covering his shoes, and a brown bowler hat on his head.

"I can't believe I'm saying this, but I agree with the thief." He jerked his chin in greeting at Adam. "Hey, chump."

"Khäsh," Adam spat, so apparently Rosie's father needed no introduction.

"What are you doing here?" she fumed.

"The better question is what are *you* doing here? This is the last place you're supposed to be. I wouldn't have been able to find you at all except you said my name aloud. Well, don't you worry, kiddo. Daddy has come to the rescue."

He threw open his arms to her. She stayed where she was.

"No hug?" he asked.

"Go. Away."

"Oh no, young lady, I'm not putting up with your sass this time. Do you have any idea what you have put me through for the past couple of weeks? I have been worried sick! I couldn't see you! I couldn't get to you! And then, when I tried to open the door between the planes, I finally saw what the problem was, but I couldn't get into Tanria to do anything about it! You cannot begin to fathom how hard this has been for me!"

Rosie wanted to stamp her foot and scream. Amazing how this giant man-baby of a god could turn her into a petulant child in mere seconds. "Unbelievable. It's not about you!"

"I hate to tell you this, kiddo, but all of this is about me. There would be no *this* without yours truly." He gestured at the plant like a conjurer at a magic show.

"I know. Way to make the world shittier."

"Is it so difficult to believe that I was trying to do the right thing when I created this plant?"

"It's not difficult to believe. It's *impossible* to believe."

The Trickster huffed in offended disbelief. "This is so typical. Every time I do something nice, it blows up in my face. No good deed goes unpunished."

"Who punished you? Adam is the one who suffered for what you did."

"Right, poor Ödamika, the asshole who got my kid trapped inside Tanria." The Trickster turned his grievance on Adam. "Friendly reminder, princeling: *I* was the god who answered your prayers. I chose you, you little prick. Lidojozháis Mäkherkis Ödamika. Ooooh. Even the gods spoke of your great brain and greater bravery. How was I supposed to know you'd screw it all up?"

"It was a joke to you," spat Adam. "You never wanted me to succeed."

"No, chump, I didn't think you would fail."

Adam flinched as if the god had slapped him. This story differed from the tale that Rosie and Adam himself had always understood to be the truth. As if to pound the last nail into the narrative funeral boat, the Trickster added, "At least I tried to give humanity a choice."

"It's a shitty choice if people don't know what they're getting into," said Rosie.

"Of course they don't know what they're getting into. That's what having a choice is all about. It's better than not having a choice to begin with."

Rosie spluttered. She knew he was wrong, yet he didn't sound wrong. She didn't know how to argue with him on this, and it infuriated her even more.

"I'm taking you home, and I'll be nice and take your friend along for the ride, even though he's not good enough for you. Let's go."

He jangled his autoduck keys and made to leave, but Rosie didn't budge. The Trickster had the audacity to give her the stern father treatment. "Now, young lady."

"No. You don't get to play the daddy card on me. You're not

my father in any meaningful way. My whole life, you've wanted my love and adoration without having to put in any of the work that would actually earn you my undying devotion. And now you waltz in here to play the hero?"

He pocketed the keys. "Fine. I get it. I screwed up. I should have been there for you more than I was. But what you need to understand is that a god's love is different from a mortal's love."

"Is that why you let Jocelyn die without a copper to her name? Is that why you left me to fend for myself when I needed you most? Is that why you couldn't be bothered to rise to the occasion for either one of us ever? Because your love was so different and special?"

The Trickster scrubbed his face with both hands in frustration. "How can I explain this? For you and your mom, love was always attached to a clock and a calendar and the turning of the world around the sun. You wanted me at lunchtime. You wanted me on a certain Saltsday in the Month of Waters. That's what love looked like to Jocelyn, and that's what it looks like to you now. But a god's love doesn't work that way. A god's love simply *is*."

"Good to know. You and your amazing, ubiquitous love can leave now."

"Rosie," he said warningly, but she wasn't having it.

"I mean it. Leave. You weren't there for me in my life, so you don't get to be here at the end."

The Trickster went pale in his human skin. "End? What end?"

"That end," answered Adam. He stepped forward, a fire lit beneath him as he jerked his head at the single bloom high up in the briar. "You claimed that you wanted to help, that you cared about the people forsaken by the gods. If you still want to play the hero, do it now."

Rosie gaped at him. "Whose side are you on?"

"Yours. Always yours."

"Did you hit your head? Have you forgotten? He's the one who ruined your life! This—all of this—is his fault."

"Which is why he should be the one to fix it, not you. And he did not ruin my life. I never would have met you if it had not been for the Trickster."

"Finally, I get a little credit," the god said to the stars on the altar of the sky before leveling an authoritative finger at his daughter. "You're not picking that flower. It gives a thousand thousand years to a mortal, which means it *takes* a thousand thousand years from an immortal."

"I know."

"Which means you will die."

"I understand that."

"Then don't do it," he told Rosie, his voice dripping with condescension.

"I have to do it."

"Why?"

"Because everything in Tanria will die if I don't."

"So what?"

A deep sense of peace filled Rosie then. She understood that there was no point in arguing with her father. There never had been. If these were the last moments of her life, she didn't want to spend them in anger or resentment.

"I'm not mad at you anymore, but I'm doing this," she told the Trickster, and she repeated herself more lovingly to Adam. "I'm doing this."

"No. Let the god do it."

He was Stony Adam—Intractable Adam—when she needed him to be Understanding Adam.

"You and I both know what he is. He's not going to sacrifice himself. He has never put himself out a day in his long-ass life."

"That was uncalled for," the Trickster protested, but Rosie's attention was for Adam now.

"And even if he was willing to pick that flower, I'd still do it, because immortality sucks."

She stroked his cheek, grateful that this was how her own funeral was playing out.

"You know how the story goes. 'While everlasting life may appear tempting, it comes with pain and tribulation. And that is why death is as precious as life.' I don't want to leave you, but I also don't want to go on living forever. I know you get that."

His stony face cracked, the facade crumbling away to reveal the raw pain beneath. But he understood, and he couldn't deny it.

"Let me go," she said gently.

He shook his head, even as his eyes burned with the knowledge that this was a losing battle. He'd already made her argument for her when their roles were reversed.

She bent down, her face level with his. "Kiss me."

He did, a soft, sweet kiss that felt like the goodbye it was.

"Let me go," she said against his lips.

He released a shaking breath and echoed the benediction that they had both spoken at countless funerals throughout their long lives. "May the Warden welcome you home."

Rosie kissed him one last time before she turned away from him and began to climb, retracing his journey, thorn by thorn.

"Get down from there!" the Trickster shouted at her, but she paid him no heed. She felt strong as she pulled herself up, hand over hand, finding one foothold after another, climbing higher and higher until the thorns grew small enough to snag in her hair and clothes and cut her skin.

"Rosie!" yelled the Trickster, speaking in his god voice now, an alien sound unlike any voice he'd ever used with her.

She did not look down. There was only one way to go, and that was up.

In Adam's story, everything seemed to take forever, but Rosie's story was different. She wasn't reaching for a new beginning; she was careening toward the end, and time spun away from her.

The hateful barbs pierced her hands. The flower came closer, red as the blood dripping down her arms, red as garnets, red as a demigod's eyes.

She was nearly there when a shadow fell over her. A god flew between her and her goal and came to roost on the briar between Rosie and the last bloom. She had never seen him before, but there was no mistaking a god, not like this one. She had never beheld anything or anyone so beautiful yet so terrifying.

He resembled a man from the waist up, though his skin was pale as chalk, and his eyes were pure white and hard, as if he were carved out of marble beneath his exterior. Iridescent scales the color of midnight covered his legs, each of which ended in a claw with golden talons. Long feathers draped from his shoulders and arms in a shade of violet so dark they were practically black in the starlight, and a crest of feathers ringed his face, ending in two horns protruding from the top of his head.

"Still no hug?" he asked her in a strange hiss that seemed to speak at her from every direction.

It was so disorienting to hear his true voice and to behold him in his true body. He had always come to her in human form, as the sort of man who looked fatherly, at least to his own mind. He had been a nuisance to her for her whole life, never the partner Jocelyn deserved—or so she had assumed—nor the father Rosie had needed. She had never thought of him as divine until this moment, and now she found herself awestruck to see him exactly as he was for the first time: a god, older than all the gods save the Unknown God theirself.

But also a father who had tried in his own fallible way.

Here at the end, wasn't that what mattered?

"How can you think that I would watch my daughter die and do nothing?" he chided her in that haunting susurrus.

"I didn't ask you to help." Her words sounded small to her ears, a child's words. She looked at her hands clinging to the vines—a child's hands. Her knees were knobby and scabbed—a child's knees. Her hair hung on either side of her face in two messy braids. This was how her father saw her, a sweet and fragile child in a large and uncertain world.

He put his hand on her head, and his feathers lightly brushed her shoulders. "Kiddo, you never have to ask me for anything. The whole world is yours if you want it. I'm not like the Warden—that sanctimonious twerp. What, like he's winning Dad of the Year? When his own kid had to clean up his mess? Well, that's not going to be me. You're not fixing what I fucked up. And you and I both know I've stuck around long past my expiration date."

"No!" she cried, protesting an ending that she had never seen coming.

"Your mom always said I knew how to make a good exit."

"But, Dad—" she began, a million questions she had never bothered to ask him buried in her child's voice, never to be answered.

"This is what a god's love looks like, Rosa-loo."

He reached for the flower, but before he picked it, he turned to her and gave her a lopsided smile, one that made even his marble eyes seem warm.

"Be sure to tell them your old man saved Tanria."

With that, he plucked the red bloom. It was impossibly small in his enormous divine hand, and yet that flower was all it took to bring down an ancient god.

Powerless, Rosie watched as the life within the Trickster burned so brightly that it hurt her eyes to look at him. She refused to turn away as the light grew and subsumed his body. He shot upward and arced across the night sky like a comet, his light so much lovelier than Rosie could have imagined, until he came to rest on the altar, a star fixed forever in the cosmos.

Chapter Thirty

The briar withered, collapsing in on itself and taking Rosie with it. She climbed down as quickly as she could, trying to outpace the larger thorns and branches before they crumbled beneath her feet.

"Rosie, jump!" Adam shouted, but she was too high up, and she didn't relish the idea of breaking both her legs. Then again, she also didn't relish the idea of landing on a pile of dried-out thorns, and the plant was falling apart so quickly that she had ridden it downward several feet in the minuscule amount of time it took her to think through her options.

She jumped, doing her best to launch herself away from the collapsing remains of the briar. A barb caught her on the way down, cutting a gash on her upper arm. Rosie cried out in pain, and a second later, she hit the powdery dirt. A thick branch walloped her hip before she rolled away. She came to a stop at last, spread-eagled on the ground.

"Rosie!"

She held up a thumb as Adam came running to her. "I'm all good."

"You're hurt."

He shrugged out of his buttonless shirt to use it as a bandage on Rosie's bleeding arm.

"How many times do I have to tell you people: I. Can't. Die."

Except, she could, she thought. She didn't know how, but if the Trickster could die, no bets were off the table.

The Trickster.

He'd finally done a decent dad thing for her, and he'd gone and broken her heart all over again. She wanted to curl onto her side and howl and weep and have Adam hold her until she was done howling and weeping. But they were stuck in the afterlife, so for the time being, mourning a complicated father would have to wait.

Adam helped Rosie sit up. To her surprise, her hip twinged sharply. It continued to throb as Adam tore away the sleeve of her shirt in order to examine her wound. His face might have appeared passive to anyone else, but Rosie had become fluent in the Subtlety of Adam. She read everything in the tenseness of his now-naked shoulders, in the quick and efficient movements of his hands.

"You're mad at me," she surmised.

"I'm livid."

He didn't sound livid, but she chose to believe him.

"Payback's a bitch, huh?"

His lips thinned as he ripped a sleeve off his once-luxurious shirt—a crime if Rosie had ever seen one—and proceeded to wrap it snugly around her arm, which was still seeping blood. She watched him as he worked, her heart going softer and softer as she took in his disheveled appearance. The squid slime had long since dried, gelling his hair and forming pale crusty lines on his dark navy pants. His glasses were smudged and filthy.

She touched the puckered scar on his chest with her good hand. "I know you're upset, but you did the same thing to me, so we're even now, right?"

"No, and as soon as I've finished binding your wound, I'm going to kiss you until you pass out for lack of air."

"Is that supposed to be a punishment?"

"There," he said as he tied off the ends of the makeshift binding. Then he took Rosie's face in his hands and made good on his threat, kissing her until she couldn't draw breath. Not that she needed air, but she was, in fact, getting a bit lightheaded. She brought the kiss to an end and drew him into her arms.

"I'm sorry about your father," he told her, his raspy baritone a comforting blanket over her raw feelings.

"You know what? Me, too. Who would've thought?"

Adam examined her arm again. A bloodstain was beginning to dot the outer bandage. "How long do you think it will take for this to heal?"

"An hour, maybe."

"We can wait."

"Let's not. Let's get out of here."

Adam stood and helped Rosie up. Her hip twinged again as she got to her feet. That branch must have hit her harder than she'd thought.

"First things first: How are we getting off this island? We lost the Warden's boat, and I'm not champing at the bit to travel by giant squid again."

To her amazement, Adam held up a set of autoduck keys.

Her autoduck keys.

"Where did you get those?"

"The Trickster tossed them to me before he..." Adam's gaze drifted upward, to the now-blank space where Rosie's father had perched on a briar and picked a red blossom and, higher still, to a bright new star on the altar of the sky.

"He stole my duck to rescue us?" she asked as Adam handed her the keys and put on his buttonless one-sleeved shirt.

"To rescue *you*, and yes, it appears that he did."

"How did he get it here?"

"He's a god," said Adam, as if that were adequate explanation.

"He was."

Her hip and her heart and her everything twinged.

Adam rubbed her back. "Let's go find your pistachio on wheels."

They retraced their steps in search of her Gratton Parker series 7 coupe. She was glad to have Adam's support as she leaned on his shoulders; her hip continued to ache.

"I miss Duckers and Zeddie," she said to distract herself from the pain.

"So do I."

"And Zeddie's food. Hey, there are four of us. When we get back, we should hang out and play Gods and Heroes."

Adam groaned.

"You can yell 'It's me!' every time you play the Briar Thief card," she said, delighting in goading him.

"Yes, you know how much I enjoy attention."

"I know how much I enjoy Adam at his driest."

That earned her his gruff laugh. She would never tire of that sound, not if she lived until all the stars in the sky winked out.

Their journey to the shore seemed brief in comparison to the time it had taken them to reach the garden of the Old Gods. They quickly put the strange houses behind them and walked once more along the chalky beach. There, outlined by the starlit sky above and the midnight Salt Sea beyond, were the pleasing curves of a familiar silhouette. Rosie limped toward it as fast as she could.

"My baby!"

"I'll drive since your arm is injured."

"You just want to test out my fabulous duck."

"Correct."

He flashed her a smile, his ever-so-slightly crooked teeth on display as he ran his hand along the hood. "This drives beautifully on the open sea, doesn't it?"

"You're about to find out."

She handed the keys to him before getting into the passenger side, grimacing as she sat. *Not cool*, she thought at her bruised hip and aching arm.

"The fact that I'm letting you drive my darling child is a sign of my love and devotion. I hope you are aware of that."

Adam took his place behind the wheel and adjusted the seat. His hand grazed the dashboard with appreciation before he grasped the steering wheel, turned the key, and drove them in an arc around the beach until they were facing the Salt Sea.

"I invented the autoduck, but Gratton Parker Motors perfected it. They don't make them like this anymore."

"You do realize that the words coming out of your mouth constitute foreplay, right?"

"I could make you a sandwich, and that would constitute foreplay," he replied as he futzed with the rearview mirror, not that he'd need it. Rosie couldn't imagine there'd be much traffic on the Salt Sea.

"Meaning?"

He put the duck in park and leaned over to nuzzle her behind her ear. "You require very little of me, my rosebud."

Rosie fanned herself. "Mm, take me home, handsome."

"That's the goal." He scanned the vast ocean in front of them and pointed to his left. "I think we should go that way."

"Isn't the House of the Unknown God that way?" asked Rosie, pointing to the right, where welcoming lights seemed to be shining from the windows of... "Is that the Dragon's Lair? Are you seeing that, too?"

"Yes. That makes sense, actually."

"How so?"

"It's home," he said, and he was right. Over the course of one week, a restaurant had become the place where Rosie and Adam and Duckers and Zeddie had made a home for themselves.

"I wonder if the restaurant will let us live there when we get back."

"I would prefer a place with a real bed."

"I have a nice big bed in my apartment. I think you'll fit nicely."

"Then let's go home."

"Let's go home," Rosie agreed, reaching over to give his knee a squeeze with her good hand. Oddly, the cut on her arm was growing more painful rather than less, and her hip wasn't her best friend right now either.

"So you think we should head for Grandfather Bones?" she asked. "Not the Warden?"

"The House of the Unknown God is for the dead. The opposite direction is for the living."

"Which is us." Rosie pushed away the niggling reminder that Adam was mortal now. She suddenly had a lot more sympathy for the Salt Sea.

Adam put the duck in gear, the engine humming with its lovable buzz as he hit the gas and set them rolling across the beach toward the sea. As soon as they hit the ocean, the Gratton Parker showed what it was made of, a true work of art on the open water, cutting through the waves like butter as Adam steered them in the direction of where the Salt Sea met the shores of the living world.

Time lost all meaning as they drove across the water. They might have traveled for a few minutes or a few hours, or it might have been several days. Everything seemed to pass by them in a haze before Rosie spotted a mesmerizing light in the distance, and the world around them came into focus once more.

"Do you see that?"

Adam drove toward the light, a moth to a flame. "It's the lantern of Grandfather Bones. It calls to the soul."

"Just make sure Grandfather Bones doesn't call your soul out of your body. I'd like to keep you alive as long as I can."

"That makes two of us."

A dock came into view with the silhouette of a man standing on the wooden planks. As they motored closer, Rosie could see him more clearly. To say that he was old was putting it mildly. He was practically a fossil, his flesh withered to the bone, his gray skin wrinkled and papery. His cheeks and eyes were so deeply sunken into his face that they were nothing more than dark shadows, as black as the cloak he wore about his shoulders.

Adam pulled up to the dock, rolling down the window as Grandfather Bones approached the coupe. The god peered into the exterior and seemed mystified by the appearance of an auto-duck on his shores.

"Is this one of them newfangled boats?" he asked them. Rosie had never known her grandpa, and yet if she had to describe anyone as being grandfatherly, it would be the god holding a lantern on this dock.

"Yes," replied Adam. "You can use it to travel on land and water."

Grandfather Bones beamed, revealing two rows of ancient brown teeth. "Well, hot dang! What won't they think of next?"

Rosie couldn't help but laugh along with him. His delight belied his terrifying appearance.

"Not sure where you came from or how you got here, but just so's you know, you two are going the wrong way."

"Yoo-hoo!" cried a woman who was running down the gangway toward the dock, her high heels click-clacking a frenetic rhythm on the weathered wood. She held tight to her cloche hat as she ran so that it wouldn't blow off in her self-generated breeze.

"Don't worry, Gramps," she told the death god. "I'll take it from here."

She opened the driver's-side door of the Gratton Parker and told Adam to "Scoot" before worming her way into the tiny cab. Fitting three adults onto the front bench of the pistachio on wheels was next to impossible. Poor Adam found himself with one butt cheek on Rosie's thigh.

"Is a god hijacking my autoduck right now?" Rosie asked him as the mysterious woman situated herself behind the wheel.

"Yes, but I think the better question is, which one?" Adam replied under his breath.

The newcomer turned on the duck's interior dome light and pulled down the visor to look in the mirror. She studied her reflection as she smoothed down a glossy brown curl peeking out from the narrow brim of her hat. Still dissatisfied, she opened a brocade clutch—which appeared out of nowhere—took out a tube of red lipstick, and applied it generously to her pouting lips. She tossed lipstick and clutch unceremoniously into the back seat and trilled "Hang on to your hats, cats!" as she put the autoduck into gear and pressed the pedal to the metal.

Rosie and Adam were thrown against each other as the Gratton Parker took off like a bolt from a pistol crossbow.

"Say, this bucket really moves!" said the woman.

Obviously, Rosie had never met this god. Before her journey into the afterlife, she had only ever met the Trickster. But this one seemed familiar to her in a way none of the others had. In her cloche hat and short bias-cut dress and purple T-strap pumps, she reminded Rosie of Jocelyn. Maybe that was why she didn't mind the god's commandeering of her autoduck. That, along with the fact that she had encountered one iconic deity after another in dizzying succession, had worn down her resistance.

"We're getting close now," the god shouted over the zippy buzz of the engine. She turned sharply, driving onto dry land and sending Adam careening into Rosie once more.

The shore quickly gave way to a meadow, though it was difficult to say how and when that had happened, and soon they were zooming across a plain of short grass dotted with wildflowers. The sun began to rise before them, bringing the landscape to life in shades of yellow and pink and violet.

The god hit the brakes with a squeal of tires and a throwing of dirt behind the wheels, hurling her passengers into the dashboard.

"Here we are. Everyone out." The god clapped her hands twice and exited the duck.

Rosie and Adam staggered out of the cab. It felt like an eternity since either of them had had to walk on their own two feet.

Already, the god was on the move, effortlessly sashaying across the irregular ground in four-inch heels.

"Where are you taking us?" asked Rosie, trying not to limp as she and Adam caught up.

"Home, darling."

"Which home?"

"Whichever one you want."

Adam met Rosie's eyes and mouthed, *Bride of Fortune?*

"No, Rosie told her to go fuck herself," said the god, even though she could not possibly have seen Adam mouth his guess. She gave Rosie a saucy wink. "You might want to leave treats on Bridey's altar. For the rest of your life."

She came to an abrupt halt, cocked her hip, and winked at Adam. "I'm the Mother of Sorrows, darling. Surprised?"

"Somewhat."

"Not all moms bake cookies and behave themselves. Doesn't mean we're not good mothers, am I right, my darling rose?" She tugged playfully on the less unraveled of Rosie's braids, as Jocelyn used to do.

"Right," said Rosie. It had been so long since anyone had mothered her the way Jocelyn had, and she found herself tearing up at the god's innate warmth.

"It's not far now. Try to keep up, kids."

For the next few minutes, the Mother of Sorrows led them on

a bizarre, zigzagging path through the grass and flowers until she stopped and declared "Ah, here it is" in the middle of nowhere. She pulled up a key from around her neck and unlocked a free-standing door that had not been there a moment ago.

"Just when I think things can't get weirder," said Rosie.

"A few details before you go." The Mother of Sorrows put the chain over Adam's head so that the key now hung from his neck, landing over his heart. "You, take this. A mortal should have a birth key to pass on to any offspring they might have."

"But I can't have children."

"Correction: you *couldn't* have children, not while you were immortal. Now? I'd invest in a big box of condoms if I were you. Unless you want to start a family right away, in which case, go to town."

Adam's face went dark with mortification as the Mother of Sorrows booped his nose with one manicured fingertip.

"No worries," said Rosie, coming to Adam's rescue. "Even if he can have kids now, I can't, so—"

"You sure about that, Rosa-loo?"

"Yeah."

"How's your arm?"

"Crappy."

"And your bruised hip?"

"It's . . . How did you know about that?"

"I'm a god, darling. Comes with the territory. Speaking of which, I can't help but notice that you're not healing as quickly as you used to. I wonder why?" The Mother of Sorrows put a finger to her red lips and made a theatrical *I'm thinking* face.

Adam snapped to attention. "Is Rosie mortal now?"

"Well, her immortal life came from a god, and that god is no longer with us. It seems to me that he took her immortality with him." The Mother of Sorrows brushed her hands affectionately down Rosie's arms. "My condolences, by the way. He was a hard god to love, but we loved him all the same, didn't we? I'd tell you tough luck on being able to die now, but I suspect mortality isn't such a bad thing for a human."

"I can die now?" asked Rosie, reeling.

"Yes."

"I'm going to die?"

"You bet." Again, the Mother of Sorrows affectionately tugged on Rosie's unraveling braid. "All right, you two, scoot along, and have a nice life. Toodle-oo!"

She opened the door. Nothing but a white blankness waited for them beyond the threshold, but before Rosie or Adam had the opportunity to ask any more questions, the Mother of Sorrows ushered them both into the great unknown.

Chapter Thirty-One

Rosie and Adam stepped out onto a paved walkway bordered by garden beds full of brightly colored annuals as the door swung shut behind them. They turned toward the sound to see that they were staring at the front door of the Dragon's Lair. Rosie tried the handle, but it was locked, which was odd since they definitely had not locked up when they left.

"It must be Sorrowsday," said Adam, tapping the sign next to the door that listed the Dragon's Lair's hours of operation. Next to "Sorrowsday" it said "CLOSED."

"But—" Rosie stared at the front door, lost and confused.

"I suspect some time has passed since we left," Adam told her gently. "Look around you."

Rosie surveyed their surroundings—the yellow-leafed willows, the lake, the buildings of the Tanrian Dragon Preserve...and not a single invasive vine in sight.

"It worked." A wide grin overtook her face as the good news sank in. "We did it!"

"And we lived," he said, coming as close to an exclamation as he was likely to get.

"We're alive! And we're going to die someday!" cheered Rosie, dancing Adam in a circle to celebrate, making him laugh. She stopped suddenly, a realization deflating her joy. "My duck."

"It was a masterpiece. Can you blame a god for stealing it?"

"No, but ugh! Rude!"

He held her around her waist. "I'll buy you another, which should be easy. It appears that we've been away long enough for someone to fix the portals."

Rosie surveyed the changes in their surroundings: paved roads and what appeared to be a parking lot, non-Tanrian flowers in window boxes, a potager garden, and a restaurant that seemed to be in functioning order. "Gods, I hope you're right."

Two dragons flew overhead, greeting them with friendly *meep-meeps*.

"Eloise! Mary Georgina! Good to see you, too," Rosie called as she and Adam waved at them.

It was a ten-minute walk to the nearest barracks, even with Rosie's bum hip, but when they arrived, it was to find that the original building had been renovated and expanded, and there was a fairly new sign hanging over the door that read "Dragon Preserve Rangers' Station." Most bizarre of all, there was a parking lot beside the building with two all-terrain autoducks parked in it. The stable was gone, but an equimaris lingered where one had once stood. The stallion tossed his huge head and snorted menacingly at them. He was much older now, his scales the palest of lilac, but Rosie knew this jerk well.

"Saltlicker?"

He gave her a surly gurgle before cantering over to sniff Adam's neck with affection.

"How long have we been gone?" Rosie wondered. Based on the blanching of the stallion's scales, it had definitely been longer than a few weeks.

"There are gaslights on inside the station, so why don't we go in and find out?" suggested Adam.

"Gaslights in Tanria? I can't believe this."

They stepped up to the freshly painted front door of the former barracks / current "rangers' station," whatever that meant.

"I almost don't want to know," Rosie told Adam before sucking it up and stepping inside.

Where the barracks had once been was now a lobby with a front desk, a wall-sized map of Tanria, a seating area, a public restroom, and a display of brochures and maps. A bored-looking marshal in his dorky Tanrian Marshals Service uniform glanced up from the desk and sat up straight when he noticed their outlandish appearance.

It wasn't until this moment that Rosie registered how bizarre they must look, covered in dried squid stomach goop, each of them missing one sleeve, and Adam walking around with his shirt open since he no longer had any buttons.

"Are you folks okay?" the marshal asked doubtfully. He reminded Rosie of Duckers when they'd first partnered up, so young he was hardly old enough to buy beer legally.

"Define 'okay,'" said Rosie.

"Um." The befuddled young ranger's hair was a brassier shade of not-red than Rosie's, and his pale skin went pink in a not-red blush.

"Do you have a first aid kit?" Adam asked proactively, indicating Rosie's arm and the blood that was seeping through the half-assed bandage.

"Oh! Yeah. Um." The marshal fumbled around beneath the desk, while Rosie limped around the room, taking in all the shiny New Gods technology that absolutely should not work inside the Mist.

"He-e-ey, mail delivery" came the extremely chill call of a postal dik-dik before the nimkilim stepped into the lobby. Gobbo had changed up his style since they last saw him and was now sporting a tie-dyed T-shirt and a pair of denim cutoffs that showed off his knobby dik-dik knees. His general demeanor, however, had not changed in the slightest.

"Whoooooooa," he said when he saw Rosie and Adam, his circular sunglasses sliding down his nose. He opened his satchel, pulled out a parcel of letters tied together with twine, read the direction, and repeated, more dramatically, "Whoooooooa."

"Hi, Gobbo. Are those for me?" asked Rosie, holding out her good hand.

"Yeah, from, like, seven years ago," he answered, handing over her yellowed mail. "Good to see you again, Rock On or Fuck Off!"

"Seven years?" asked Adam. "Is that all?"

"What do you mean, is that all? We lost *seven years*!" cried Rosie.

"Seven years is not long."

"Says you."

"I lost considerably more last time."

"Found it!" the young marshal cried in triumph, setting the first aid kit on the counter. It seemed awfully small to Rosie, but Adam went about digging around for new bandages. They were both frowning at the slim pickings, so they didn't notice when another marshal came through the front door until the rookie said, "Hey, sir, we have a situation here."

A far more mature and seasoned marshal with an impressive black mustache stood in the lobby that was once a shitty barracks. When his eyes landed on Rosie and Adam, they went so wide Rosie could see the whites all the way around the brown irises.

Gobbo gestured to the returned castaways. "Check it, dude! Look who I found!"

"Rosie? Adam?" Penrose Duckers uttered in disbelief.

"Penny-D!" squealed Rosie. She hobbled over to him as quickly as her sore hip would let her and flung her one good arm around his neck.

"Salt Sea! RoFo!"

He wrapped her in a bear hug, and she hissed in pain as he accidentally jostled her arm.

"Shit, you're hurt."

"I got out the first aid kit, sir," the young marshal volunteered helpfully.

"Jablonski, that shit's for little kids with boo-boos on their knees. The real deal is in the closet."

"Yes, sir!"

Gods, Duckers has turned into Hart Ralston, thought Rosie as she watched this mind-boggling scenario play out. *And that poor kid is like wee baby Duckers when he first joined up.*

Pen tackled Adam next, consuming the smaller man in a bruising hug that startled a pleased laugh out of him. Once Duckers released him, he looked back and forth between the two people he thought he'd lost forever, laughing as he wiped tears off his face with the heel of his hand. "What happened to you? Where have you been?"

"It's a long story," said Rosie.

"I want to hear all of it."

"Is this it, sir?" asked Jablonski as he hefted a much larger kit onto the counter.

"That's it. Thanks, J." To Rosie and Adam, Duckers said, "I don't know what the fuck is all over you, but maybe you should both take a shower while I track down some clean clothes you can wear."

"There's indoor plumbing in Tanria?" marveled Rosie, longing to be clean again.

"There's everything in Tanria now. Try not to get that bandage wet. I feel like that's a thing. Come on, I'll show you around."

Duckers took them through a door marked "Staff Only" and showed off the marshals' updated quarters, featuring decent beds, a working kitchen with a gas stove and an icebox, and state-of-the-art showers. Rosie did her best to de-squid herself with one hand, and by the time she stepped out of the stall, she found a neat stack of folded clothes waiting for her on the other side of the curtain.

A Tanrian Marshals Service uniform.

"Are you kidding me right now?" she hollered, and was answered with Duckers's snickering from out in the hallway.

"Want me to find you a hat, too?"

"I will have my vengeance," she told him as she put on the unflattering uniform. The shirt erased her curves, and the pants heralded the coming of floodwaters, but at least she was clean.

By the time she joined Duckers in the hall, her hair dampening the shoulders of her khaki shirt, Adam was showered and dressed and looking neat as a pin in an oversized uniform.

"Have a seat in the lobby, and I'll see what I can do about that bandage," said Duckers. He ushered them to the seating area where the marshals' cots used to be, and went about redressing Rosie's wound, talking all the while.

"Do I even want to know how you did this? I know it'll heal by morning, but you should probably go to the infirmary anyway. Oh my gods, Zeddie! Wait till he finds out you came back! He's going to lose his shit."

"How is he?" Rosie asked, sidestepping the healing issue.

"Great! He's still at the Dragon's Lair. Won all sorts of awards. Newspaper write-ups. The whole works."

"Are you two a thing?"

Duckers flashed her a smile. "We got married five years ago."

"Ahhh!" Rosie screamed at him before hugging him with her good arm. "I love this for you! I bet Hart and Mercy were thrilled."

"Fuck yeah, they were!"

"Congratulations," said Adam, offering a far more socially acceptable handshake.

Duckers beamed at him before looking to Rosie. "Stone-cold classy. I love this guy."

"So do I. Up top!"

Duckers laughed and high-fived her. "L-O-V-E. You are in lo-o-ove with Dr. Hot Suits, and I totally called it," he sang, treating them to a few dance moves.

"You haven't changed a bit."

"I don't know about that." He patted his stomach before turning to Adam and jerking his head toward Rosie. "You really want to be stuck with this for all eternity?"

"Yes, but a lifetime is also acceptable." A hint of a smile played across his mortal face.

Duckers tied off the bandage. "That'll do for now, but it's deep enough that you might want to get stitches until your immortality kicks in."

Rosie and Adam glanced at each other, a mutual agreement passing between them. It was too new, too raw, to say any of it out loud yet. Rosie felt a pang of guilt for keeping the truth from her friend, but she needed time to adjust to mortality herself before she let anyone else know about it, even Duckers.

He retrieved a set of autoduck keys from behind the counter. "Come on, I'll give you a lift to the station. Jablonski, hold down the fort for me. I'm taking the rest of the day off."

"Yes, sir." The kid actually saluted, and Rosie couldn't help but snort.

"What's with all the New Gods technology?" she asked once she was situated in the passenger seat of the all-terrain duck. It was an open-top vehicle, so the wind whipped her hair around her face as they zoomed away from the marshals' station. "How are we driving inside the Mist?"

"The Mist is gone," Duckers yelled over the motor so that Adam could hear him from the back seat.

"What do you mean, gone?"

"I mean it's *gone*. A week after Zeddie and I got out, the whole thing came down. There hasn't been anything separating Tanria from the rest of the world in seven years."

Rosie looked to Adam. They silently passed between them the realization that their actions in the garden of the Old Gods hadn't simply killed the briar invading Tanria; they had, in many ways, ended Tanria altogether.

It was a lot to take in.

"We looked everywhere for you," continued Duckers, "the entire force of the Tanrian Marshals plus hundreds of volunteers. We couldn't find you anywhere. It was awful. Where were you?"

"We'll get to that. First, tell us everything that's happened since we've been gone."

"Where to start? Annie Ellis got married a few years ago. She's got twins now."

"Shut the front door!"

He went on, giving updates on Lu Ellis (chief marshal of Tanria National Park's Education Division), Frank Ellis and Twyla Banneker (retired to an equimaris ranch off the coast of Bushong), Hart Ralston and Mercy Birdsall (still sheriff of Eternity and owner of Mercy's Undertakings, respectively), their kids (growing up way too fast), and Duckers's own family (his mom enjoying more grandchildren than Duckers could count, his brother remaining forever and always a punk).

"Has Tanria kept its national park status now that the Mist has come down?" asked Adam.

"Yep. The dragon preserve keeps on keeping on, and the Dragon's Lair is hopping. We get a lot more tourism now that it's easier to get in and out and travel around. You can see a campsite over there." Duckers motioned toward a cluster of tents and recreational ducks in the distance. "The big difference is that the flora and fauna of Bushong has started to infiltrate the park, and vice versa."

"So graps are hopping around the border towns now?" asked Rosie.

"Not just graps. Dragons fly overhead from time to time, too. It used to freak people out, but everyone's used to it these days. Zeddie and I had an adolescent take up residence in our backyard swimming pool for a while. We had to trap her and take her to the preserve. Gods, I can't believe you're here. We all thought you were..." Duckers choked up, unable to finish his sentence.

Rosie put a hand on his arm as he drove. "I'm sorry, Penny-D. I didn't mean to worry you like that."

"Who are you kidding? Your middle name is Lacks Restraint." Rosie opened her mouth to defend herself, but Duckers waved her away. "So obviously you're staying with me and Zeddie until you get settled."

"I don't want to put you guys out. We can stay at the hotel."

"Shut your mouth. My house is your house. I know Zeddie feels the same way. We are always home to you. Both of you."

The West Station came into view ahead. Rosie's muscles tensed as they approached the Mist at speed, until she remembered the Mist was no longer there. Her mind was blown anew as they drove right through what had once been the impenetrable border between Tanria and the rest of Bushong, and parked in a new paved lot behind the station.

As soon as Adam and Duckers had helped Rosie out of the duck, Adam walked to where the portal stood, a doorway to nowhere. Rosie came up behind him, wincing as her hip continued to irritate her, and draped her arm over his shoulder. A sign stood in front of the archway now, outlining a truncated history of Tanria and the marshals and the end of an era when the Mist came down.

Adam reached out a hand to brush his fingers against the

frame before turning to Rosie and hugging her. She clung to him fiercely as the heady realization of being unstuck at last washed over them.

"We can go anywhere we want," she said into his hair.

"The only place I want to go is wherever you are."

"You say the nicest shit."

"I know." He pulled away but held her hand as he asked Duckers, "What happened to my autoduck? I left it in the parking lot."

"About that . . . Probably best if you see it for yourself."

He led them around the corner of the station to the old parking lot, which had become weedy with disuse. There, exactly where he'd left it, was Adam's panther of an autoduck.

Which was now a shrine.

There were bouquets of flowers covering it, some dried out with age, others bright and fresh. There were offerings of wine and beer and fruit and pastries around the tires. There were notes tucked into the doors and under the windshield wipers. Some of the letters had been blown away by the hot Bushong wind and were now making their way across the scrubby landscape alongside the tumbleweeds.

"Salt Sea, people sure like to worship your ass," Rosie told Adam.

He took a note from under the windshield and held it up for her inspection, her name clearly legible on the envelope. "Apparently, they also like to worship your ass."

Duckers came to stand with them. "Zeddie and I never told anyone who you are, Adam. It didn't seem like our story to tell. But people took it hard when we weren't able to find either one of you. You've become legends around here. We keep asking people to stop leaving food, because it attracts rodents, but we've given up on that."

"I don't suppose my Gratton Parker has turned up anywhere?" Rosie asked him hopefully.

"No, it disappeared around the same time the Mist came down. I think someone stole it. I'm sorry. I know how much you loved your little pistachio."

"Mother of fucking Sorrows."

Duckers put a hand on her shoulder in commiseration. "You're bleeding through your bandage. Let's have Dr. Levinson stitch you up until you can heal on your own."

"Okay, but you know she is not in the Rosie Fan Club."

"I think you might be surprised."

He escorted them into the station, which remained relatively unchanged and blessedly familiar. "Wait till Maguire gets a load of you two."

"Maguire's still around?"

"We call her Maguire-Won't-Retire these days. We'll have to bury her in her office whenever she sails the Salt Sea. I'll probably retire before she does."

By now, they had reached the infirmary, where Dr. Levinson was eating a sandwich at her desk. She stopped chewing and stared at Rosie and then at Adam and then at Rosie again.

"Got a patient for you, if you have a sec," Duckers informed her, clearly enjoying her astonishment.

Without a word, she set down her lunch, crossed the room, and hugged Rosie. "What did you do to yourself this time, Fox?" she asked tearfully.

The doctor's unexpected affection made Rosie's throat throb with the sudden urge to cry.

"I cut my arm, and my hip's janky."

"Hop up and let's take a look."

Rosie sat on the exam table as Dr. Levinson undid Duckers's work, cleaned the wound (which hurt), and put in stitches (which hurt even more). The doctor was examining Rosie's bruised hip when the door burst open, the hinge as squeaky as ever. There stood Alma Maguire, shaking her head, unfailingly exasperated. "Holy Three Mothers."

"Hi, Chief."

"Don't 'Hi, Chief' me, Foxy. Where under the altar of the sky have you been for"—she consulted her watch—"the past *seven years?*"

"Not here?"

"I gathered that." To Rosie's shock, she went misty-eyed. "I sure am glad to see you again, Marshal."

"Thanks, Chief. Same to you," Rosie said, a little misty-eyed herself.

Maguire softened more when she saw Adam. "I'm so sorry, Dr. Lee. You would not have been caught up in that mess if I hadn't called you in."

"Please, don't apologize. It was the best thing to happen to me in a long time." He took Rosie's hand in his and regarded her with a face that was no longer inscrutable to anyone.

Maguire raised her eyebrows. "I assume you two have an interesting story to tell."

" 'Interesting' doesn't cover it," said Rosie, grinning at Adam.

"I don't suppose you'd be willing to write up a report about everything once you've had time to adjust?"

"Sure thing, Chief."

"It's good to have you back with us, Foxy. You, too, Dr. Lee. Take care of yourselves."

"That's the plan," said Rosie, giving Adam's hand a squeeze. "Because you only live once."

All along the two-lane highway to Eternity, Rosie noticed many odd, subtle changes—patches of pink grass poking up here and there on the side of the road, the occasional Tanrian gray tuft flower tucked into a clump of bachelor's buttons, even a flock of Tanrian turkeys yodeling in a farmer's wheat field.

Driving down Main Street felt surreally mundane. There was city hall. There was the Salt and Key. There was the Sunny Hill Hotel. There was Banneker's Auto Repair. There was Mercy's Undertakings.

And there was a pink dragon circling high overhead.

Totally normal.

"That's Hart and Mercy's house," Rosie said as Duckers pulled into the driveway next door on Walnut Street.

"Yeah, when this house went on the market, Zeddie and I snatched it up. I can't wait to see his face when he gets a load of you."

A remarkably chunky gray-and-black cat crossed the lawns between the two Birdsall houses and *rowr*ed at Rosie.

"Blammo Tinky Fartface!" She abandoned the ice pack Dr. Levinson had given her for her hip and launched herself at the cat, picking him up and rubbing her face in his fur. He scratched her shoulder, so she set him down. "I love that little asshole," she said fondly.

"So do Bea and Lottie, but Hart's about ready to turn that thing into a hat. Speaking of my darling nieces."

Rosie followed Duckers's line of sight to a bespectacled teen-aged girl bordering on adulthood and a gawky brunette hanging up wet laundry on the clothesline in the backyard next door.

Duckers cupped his hands around his mouth and yelled, "Bea! Lottie!"

They looked up and waved at him. Lottie gave a quizzical look at the astoundingly tall red-eyed demigod whooping and waving at them while Bea tilted her head, trying to remember where and when she'd seen this bizarre person before.

"Go get your parents," Duckers called to them before ushering Rosie and Adam inside. "Oh, Zeddie!" he sang.

"Hey, what are you doing home?" came Zeddie's voice from

what Rosie presumed was the kitchen, sounding pleased by his husband's unexpected arrival.

"We have company."

"What?" There was a cacophony of noise, the sound of a baking tray clattering onto a cooling rack. "Please tell me you're joking."

"Nope, not joking."

"Ducky, the house is a wreck! You're killing me! At least let me—" Zeddie appeared in the parlor, an oven mitt on each hand. He froze when he saw who was standing in his entry hall.

Duckers wore his most mischievous grin. "I didn't think you'd mind if they stayed in our guest room for a bit."

Zeddie said nothing. He simply stepped forward and enveloped Rosie and Adam in his arms, his oven mitts making his hug extra cozy.

Mercy appeared in the open doorway, her brown curls lightly salted now. "What's going—holy Three Mothers. Hart!" she called over her shoulder before surging forward to join in the group hug.

"It's nice to meet you, Dr. Lee," she said as she leaned her cheek on his head.

Adam glanced questioningly at Rosie from underneath Zeddie's armpit. She mouthed *Mercy* at him.

"Lovely to meet you, too, Mercy."

"Salt fucking Sea." Hart Ralston stood in the doorway, unmoving, staring in wonder. His hair was more gray than blond now.

Rosie disentangled herself from the knot of her friends' arms. "Your door worked. And your dad says hi and he loves you and Mercy and the grandkids."

Hart stalked across the room and crushed her in his arms.

"Can't breathe. You're squeezing the life out of me," Rosie managed, surprised all over again that she now had a life that could be squeezed out of existence.

It was wonderful.

And kind of terrifying.

Hart gave her a searching look, as if he could read her the way he read all those boring nonfiction books he liked to check out from the library.

"Are you—" he began, but Rosie cut him off.

"Later. Please."

He nodded in understanding. He always understood her.

"Why don't you all come over for dinner tonight?" Zeddie asked Hart and Mercy before turning to Rosie and Adam. "If you're up for it."

"That'd be great," said Rosie.

Mercy clapped her hands. "I'll pick up some wine. The sparkling kind. Maybe I'll nick a bottle of Horatio's Veuf Didier. Don't tell the sheriff."

The sheriff let his wife's thievery pass. He was too busy gazing at Rosie with tears in his eyes.

"Don't you dare make me cry, Ralston," Rosie told him.

He gave her his understated smile. "See you tonight."

Zeddie saw Hart and Mercy out while Duckers ushered Rosie and Adam down the hall to the guest room, but he hesitated beside the door. "The thing is, we couldn't bring ourselves to get rid of your stuff, so we furnished the guest room with it."

"What?" Rosie reached past him and threw open the door. There, crammed into the room beyond, were the contents of her apartment: her worn velvet sofa, her comfy bed with the paisley coverlet, her lamps, even her silk scarves that went over the lampshades. The walls were covered with all the artwork she had amassed over the course of decades. Neither she nor Adam had a home to call their own yet, but their friends' guest room felt like a homecoming.

"This is perfect," she told Duckers, hugging him for the millionth time since they'd been reunited.

"We boxed up what you left at the Dragon's Lair. It's in the closet. There's a bathroom down the hall. I'm going to help Z with dinner and let you two settle in."

With that, he left them, closing the door behind him.

Rosie turned to Adam, gesturing to her earthly belongings. "What do you think?"

"It looks like your intimate apparel decorated this room."

"You love my intimate apparel."

"Exactly."

He tilted his head as something caught his attention across the room, and he navigated around the furniture to get a better look. Rosie came up behind him as he studied the velvet painting of the Briar Thief hanging on the wall between a bas-relief of the Mother of Sorrows holding a key and a collage frame of black-and-white stage photos of Jocelyn.

"This looks nothing like me," he said. He meant it as a joke, but the callback to her father shot a pang of grief through her heart. Along with the grief came a grace she had not had for the Trickster before now, and that was a comfort to her.

Adam took her in his arms. "Dinner will be nice, but sleeping beside you in a real bed will be far nicer."

"If I never sleep on a pile of tablecloths again, it will be too soon."

They swayed, falling into an impromptu dance of the truly fatigued, rocking to the rhythm of their own heartbeats. Rosie heard a crinkle of paper and remembered the packet of letters Gobbo had delivered to her, the small stack she had slipped into the pocket of the ugly uniform pants Duckers had given her. She pulled them out, untied the twine, and sifted through them— one from Hart and Mercy, one from Lu, a few from her fellow marshals, several from complete strangers.

And one from her father.

She dropped the rest, sending them spilling to the floor like snow as she stared at the letters of her name in the Trickster's oversized handwriting on the envelope.

"Would you like to read that in private? I can leave," Adam offered softly.

"No, please stay with me."

She sank onto her perfect old sofa, and Adam sat beside her, his arm around her shoulders as she read.

Hey, kiddo,
As of the writing of this letter, you have been out of my reach for two weeks. Normally, I would say that two weeks is nothing. Chump change. I've blinked, and more time has passed than two weeks. But today, two weeks may as well be an eternity. You are trapped inside the Mist, and I can't get to you or help you, and I'm beside myself.

I know I haven't always been around in the way that you wanted, but now I can't be there, and it feels lousy, to be honest. It feels like being left behind, and I'm starting to wonder if this is how you've felt for the past one hundred and fifty-seven years: left behind by your old man. Someday, I hope I can set the record straight, but until then, please know I have always been here for you, even if it didn't feel that way.

Maybe you know by now that time gets away from you, the longer you live. And, honey, I have been alive for a ludicrous amount of time. One minute you were a baby, and the next you were a teenager who hated me, and then all of a sudden, you were a century old (and you still hated me). All I can tell you is that I don't know where the time went. It's no excuse, but it's also the truth. I'm so sorry. You have no idea how sorry I am.

You're my smart girl—my resourceful girl—so I know you'll find a way to come back home. When you do, will you give me

*one last shot at this whole parenting thing? We have all the time
in the world, don't we? I don't have to be a shit father forever.
Even gods can change.*

*I guess what I'm asking here is, will you let me be there for
you? I swear, I won't miss the big things or the little things.
Whenever you want me around, I'll be there.*

*Just please come home to me. Or come home in general.
Come home.*

*Love,
Dad*

Rosie was ugly crying by the time she realized she was crying
at all. Adam held her, rocking her in his arms, his quiet strength
anchoring her.

"Hold on, ruzhkel," he told her before getting up and leaving the room. He returned a moment later with a box of those
scratchy paper tissues people kept in their bathrooms these days.

"Our handkerchiefs are better," she said as he dabbed at her
face with a wadded tissue.

"Our handkerchiefs are disgusting now. We should probably
burn them."

"Probably."

She took the damp wad of shitty tissues from him and was
blotting her nose when she bolted upright with a gasp.

"What is it?" Adam asked.

In answer, she hobbled to the closet. As promised, there were
several neat stacks of boxes inside, but she was looking for one
in particular. She frowned at her bandaged arm, and before she
could think to ask for Adam's help, he was there at her side.

"What do you need?"

"I need to look through these boxes."

Requiring no explanation, he took them out of the closet, one by one, and lined them up on the floor so that Rosie could pull off the lids and check the contents.

"Nope," she said to the first box. "Nope. Nope. Oh, this one's yours." She brushed her fingertips over the cover of the book he had been reading at the Dragon's Lair before moving on to the next box.

The right box.

Here was the lingerie Mercy had sent her, the copy of *Blandishment* she had borrowed from Adam, her extra clothes, the letters she had wanted to keep, and the Trickster's second-to-last letter, crumpled around an envelope. This she took from the box with the greatest care. She opened the envelope and cupped the contents in her palms—a cat figurine with two broken legs. But she had all the pieces. It could be mended.

Adam knelt beside her. She looked at him and asked, "Do you think Duckers and Zeddie have glue?"

"Would you like for me to find out?"

She nodded.

"I'll be right back."

He did come right back, and he helped her glue two tiny legs onto a corny cat figurine.

Epilogue

The evening before Rosie and Adam left, they had dinner with Duckers and Zeddie on the terrace of the Dragon's Lair. Rosie wore a sundress with an ivy print on it, and Adam traced the scar on her arm with his finger. He tended to do that after the second glass of white these days, and Rosie blushed, which she tended to do after her second glass of red. Eloise flew by to say hello before she returned to her nest for the night, and Adam played the lute after the restaurant closed. It was a nice way to say goodbye-for-now.

Late morning sunlight filtered in through the lace curtains as Rosie touched salt water to her mother's birth key and to the cat figurine with two legs glued on, both of which sat on the altar by the front door. They were the last two things left in the rent-by-the-month apartment Rosie and Adam had been sharing for the past six months.

And what a six months it had been.

At first, they were hounded by reporters and stared at by children and adults alike, whose filters were even flimsier than Rosie's. They gave their story, again and again, leaving out the parts they didn't feel like forking over to the rest of the world.

They made sure people knew that the Trickster had saved

Tanria, and that his star shone brightly in the night sky. Rosie knew exactly which one it was.

They had spent six months with friends, six months with aches and pains and scratches that didn't heal as quickly as they were used to, six months going through several boxes of condoms, per the Mother of Sorrows's advice. Six months of figuring out how to live with Grandfather Bones's lantern in the distance, both of them knowing the death god would call first one and then the other of them someday.

Eventually, things settled down. Rosie and Adam became old news, as unremarkable as the occasional dragon landing on someone's roof. They thought and talked and planned, and today, they were putting the plan into action. Their things were safely stowed away in storage, and what little they needed was packed into the hold of their new autoduck, a bright yellow Gratton Parker series 10 convertible.

"Safe travels in the banana-mobile," Duckers had wished them last night.

Rosie emptied the dish of salt water into the sink and placed it inside the foldable, portable altar Adam had made for her with his clever hands. She reverently set Jocelyn's key and the Trickster's cat inside as well, swathed in the soft velvet lining that would keep them safe on the long journey.

Adam appeared in the open doorway in a clean white shirt, the sleeves rolled up, the top two buttons undone. He had traded his wool suit pants for cotton trousers. They'd be easier to wash on the road.

"I think that's everything, if you're ready," he said.

"I'm ready."

He held out his hand to her, and she took it, weaving her fingers with his. The skirt of her emerald-green cotton dress swished over the tops of her ostrich leather boots. She'd decided that dresses were more comfortable to wear for hours in the banana-mobile, but nothing would tempt her to give up her boots or her ludicrously expensive luxury intimates. She had invested in many new pieces since her return, but today she wore her peacock feathers underneath her dress for luck.

They carefully placed the altar on top of their luggage in the hold of the duck before Rosie got behind the wheel and Adam strapped himself into the passenger side. They had the top down, so Rosie's messy not-red bun and Adam's jet-black, un-silvered hair were about to be whipped by the wind, but in a good way.

Rosie steered them onto the two-lane highway that took them past the shipyard where the dead of Eternity were buried, cutting a meandering route through desert scrub until the landscape grew greener as they got closer to the Bushong coast.

Eventually, they planned to visit Twyla Banneker and Frank Ellis at their equimaris ranch and slowly make their way through the Federated Islands of Cadmus and on to the Pritean continent and, one of these days, to Eshil Craia. And then, when they felt like it, they'd come home to Duckers and Zeddie and Hart and Mercy and everyone else they called a friend. They'd come home to Eternity.

But for now, the Great Western Sea opened up before them, and they were free to go wherever they liked.

"Which way?" Rosie asked Adam as they sped toward the ocean.

"Wherever you want, my ruzhkel," he told her. "We can go wherever you want to go."

And they did.

Acknowledgments

As I bid a fond farewell to the bonkers world of Tanria and Eternity, I find myself composing acknowledgments that are as unhinged as the setting of these books. Prepare yourselves for a fairly ridiculous cavalcade of gratitude.

The most staggeringly enormous of thanks goes to my editor, Angelica Chong, who jumped into the third book of this series with grace, good humor, and magnificent communication skills. And three cheers for Nadia Saward, my UK editor, who has stuck with me through all three books!

Thank you to everyone at Orbit US and Orbit UK for shepherding this series from page to shelf. Special thanks to Lisa Marie Pompilio for designing the three best book covers a quirky fantasy author could hope for. (Thy lady asked for furry frogs, and furry frogs she did get. Bless.) Also, thank you to Angela Man for being an absolute delight to work with. And as always, thank you to my copyeditor, Janice Lee, for rescuing me from myself.

All the warm fuzzies to Mother of (glitter-breathing) Dragons and first of her eponymous shingle Holly Root for encouraging me and my weirdness every step of the way. Air fives to everyone at Root Literary as well.

To my fellow Nebulous Dread Cloud band members, Amanda Sellet and Miranda Asebedo: Thank you for your brilliant insight and for scraping me off the floor on a daily basis.

Acknowledgments

I would be nothing—NOTHING—without Jenny Mendez. (Hi, Kathee!)

Thank you to my sisters, Susan and Katy, who helped me understand that, no really, calling a character "Little Miss Hot for Teacher" is way too Van Halen for a secondary-world fantasy novel.

To my friends and family, especially Mike, Hank, Gus, Mom, and Dad: Thank you for the support and love as well as the tacos and the bibimbap and all the meals I didn't have to cook.

Thank you to hormone replacement therapy for giving at least 60 percent of my words back to me. I couldn't have done it without you, HRT! (You think I jest. I do not.)

Most of all, thank you to the readers who have embraced this banana-pants series. I have been blown away time and again that so many people have picked up these books and thought, "Yeah, I'm totally down with this." I cannot tell you how grateful I am to each and every one of you.

extras

orbit

meet the author

Brian Paulette

MEGAN BANNEN is a former public librarian and an award-winning author of speculative fiction. Her work has been selected for the RUSA Reading List, the Indies Introduce list, and the Kids' Indie Next List, along with numerous best-of-the-year compilations. While most of her professional career has been spent behind a reference desk, she has also sold luggage, written grants, collected a few graduate degrees from various Kansas universities, and taught English at home and abroad. She lives in the Kansas City area with her family and more pets than is reasonable.

Find out more about Megan Bannen and other Orbit authors by registering for the free monthly newsletter at orbitbooks.net.

if you enjoyed
THE UNDERCUTTING OF ROSIE AND ADAM

look out for

HOW TO SUMMON A FAIRY GODMOTHER
Fairies and Familiars: Book One

by

Laura J. Mayo

Lady Theodosia Balfour has certainly gotten the short end of the stick—her stepsister, the newly crowned Princess Beatrice, is telling everyone in polite society that Theo, her sister, and their mother are evil, wicked, and horrid people who treated her like a slave. Though Theo knows this isn't exactly true, it seems her life is thoroughly ruined by the rumor. With the Balfour family estate on the verge of bankruptcy, Theo's only path forward is a forced betrothal to the Duke of Snowbell, a foul-tempered geezer who wishes only to use her as a broodmare for spare heirs.

Desperate for help and with no one on her side, Theo clings to the only thing that might save her: the rumor of a fairy godmother, one that supposedly helped her stepsister secure a prince. After all, if a fairy can get someone into a marriage, getting someone out of one should be easy....

Chapter 1

WHERE GLASS SLIPPERS ARE NOT EXCLUSIVELY USED FOR FOOTWEAR

Theodosia Balfour's ball gown was made of fine white silk, and that's where the compliments ended. The bodice was fitted, but it reached all the way up to her throat. Her mother always found it necessary to say that a lady needed to leave some things to the imagination when dressing, but Theo had seen nuns with less restrictive necklines. The sleeves found their inspiration from marshmallows, excelling in both fluff and volume. Not to be outdone, the skirt took up the poofiness challenge and asserted dominance. In the unlikely event of anyone at the ball wanting to dance with her, they'd have to do it from the next room, just to make space for its circumference. And yet, none of those horrifying qualities could compare to the fabric pattern. Twisting down and around the entire ensemble were stripes of green and red, making Theo look like a giant walking peppermint candy. If she was to get noticed, it would only be for looking like she had lost a fight to a confectioner with a vendetta.

"Theodosia, if you're waiting for me to tell you that you look beautiful, you'll be here awhile," her mother, Lady Balfour, said when Theo expressed her apparently outlandish desire to not want to feel hideous. "I did not select that gown because I thought it would help you be attractive. I selected it because you will need to stand out if you want the prince to pay any attention to you. Which, I'm sure I do not have to remind you, is not a talent you possess on your own."

Theo's sister, Florentia, wore a mint-green dress with a tight fit of boning in the waist, the skirt flaring out around her in an explosion of matching bows and ribbons. When Flo came downstairs after putting it on, she twirled around the drawing room, caressing the fabric as she envisioned herself dancing with the prince. All Theo saw was a spinning green cake topper.

However, Theo knew it didn't matter what they wore. The odds of Prince Duncan noticing the Balfour sisters were slimmer than their mother's own corseted waistline. If he were forced at gunpoint to pick Flo or Theo from a line of three women, the kingdom would need a new prince. He'd met them before at various royal functions over the years, but if he'd bothered to spare more than a brief nod at their curtsies, Theo couldn't remember it.

But that pesky detail was not going to spoil Flo's excitement. Ever since their stepsister, Beatrice, stopped attending events and stealing the spotlight, Flo could finally shine, and she was determined to capture Prince Duncan's attention this time. Even though it had been years since Flo and her stepsister were at an event together, competing with Beatrice had left its mark, carving a brutal gouge of jealousy through her already thorny nature. She would have young men admiring her, asking her to dance, bringing her drinks, only to be dropped like a corn husk doll the instant that porcelain beauty, Beatrice, showed up.

If Flo and Beatrice were dolls, Theo was a rock some child had drawn a face on, such was the romantic interest she inspired in potential suitors. But while she didn't have the same level of enthusiasm for the ball as her sister, it was hard not to get sucked up into Flo's excitement. Theo, even in her silly dress, was hoping that maybe this ball would be the one to buck tradition. She was a titled lady just like her sister. Why couldn't she also fantasize? Maybe not about becoming a princess, but there were going to be plenty of other available men there. With any luck, one of them might be interested in her.

With those fantasies dancing handsomely around their heads, they went to the ball.

———————————— • ————————————

It was going just as well as every other ball before. The kingdom's royalty had turned out in full, each level of nobility presenting their eligible daughters to a very unimpressed Prince Duncan. With every passing minute, he was becoming dangerously close to slumping right off his chair and onto the floor.

The invite-only ball's sole purpose was an attempt by the king to find his son a bride. The previous few galas had not resulted in any love matches at all, though that did not deter His Highness, who kept throwing more and more lavish parties in the hopes that maybe his son just needed to see the same eligible ladies more than once to decide that one of them might be good enough. But this ball was set to be the last one. The prince had had enough. The king had finally had enough. If Duncan didn't find his bride this time, then they would have to take the search elsewhere.

On the guest list was, of course, the royal house of the Earldom of Merrifall, headed by the twice-widowed countess, Lady Martha Balfour.

Her first marriage had been to a wealthy merchant, with whom she had two daughters. It lasted for just a short while until his untimely death, a sickness of his lungs coming to claim him.

Because of her first husband's affluence, she had been a part of a number of high-society circles, which was where she met the widowed Earl of Merrifall. It was another sign of good fortune that their daughters were so close in age, Florentia being ten when they were married, Beatrice, nine, and Theodosia, eight. But only five years later, Lady Balfour was left with two husbands pushing daisies and three daughters to look after.

And while technically all three girls were of society age, only two were ever allowed to attend any royal function: Florentia and Theodosia. The reasoning was simple: Lady Balfour didn't want Beatrice stealing the eye of Prince Duncan away from her own children. And since this was the last chance for Florentia and Theodosia to make a good impression, she would ensure her little blond stepbrat stayed far away from the palace.

Unfortunately for the Balfours, the order of presentation was not alphabetical, so before either of the sisters had the opportunity to curtsy to the prince, *she* arrived.

When the herald standing at the door asked for her name so she could be announced, she didn't give one, choosing instead to make an understated entrance. But in no way was she able to fade into the background. She glowed with light, like a star that had fallen to earth. From her sunshine blond hair, to her resplendent dress, to her magnificent if not impractical glass shoes that tinkled like icicles when she walked, there would be no blending in for Lady Beatrice Balfour, daughter of the late Earl of Merrifall.

It was as if Prince Duncan's heart stopped the moment he saw her. The party, the people, and the palace all melted away as he walked toward the shimmering newcomer. And when he finally reached her, the entire ball came to a standstill. Even the music stopped, the string ensemble too mesmerized to remember that they were supposed to play their instruments. So every person in the grand ballroom saw him take her hand and heard him ask if this was a dream, such was her ethereal beauty.

Whispers of "*Who is she?*" whipped through the grand hall, everyone speculating as to the identity of this woman. Some were even saying she was a visiting foreign princess. How humble she must have been to not want to be heralded into the ball.

Of course they had all forgotten her true identity. Due to the fickleness of noble attention spans, she had completely fallen out of their collective memory the second she stopped showing up to events. Beatrice had not been seen in public since her father died four years prior.

But that didn't matter to anyone at the moment. Not when this gorgeous enigma and the prince danced the night away, falling more in love with every step.

The three other Balfours did not recognize her at first. After all, it couldn't possibly be Beatrice—she was locked in her room, still in her dirty clothes, ashes under her fingernails, with no way to even get to the ball.

But somehow, it was Beatrice.

And when that realization danced past them on glass slippers, their hatred for their already detested stepsister and stepdaughter swelled like a river in a storm.

Taking his cues in manners from Beatrice, Prince Duncan

waltzed her right out of his own party, leaving everyone else behind with the now-slimy cheese platter and room temperature punch.

Flo, jealousy eating her alive, was close to losing any semblance of ladylike behavior. She was only just able to stop herself from shrieking, and instead was emitting a high-pitched squeal like a possessed teakettle.

If the king could weaponize the look of pure malice on Lady Balfour's face, he would no longer need a standing army. Theo could almost feel the heat pouring off her as she twitched in anger. If Theo hadn't been so shocked at the situation, she might have grabbed an extra glass of water, just in case she needed to splash it on her mother before her head popped off and lava spewed out.

But before Lady Balfour had a chance to fully ignite, a guard approached.

"Excuse me, Lady Balfour?"

Her mother took a deep breath, nostrils flaring, straining to regain composure. "Yes?"

"Follow me." He walked off without waiting to see if she was behind him.

The three Balfours were led to a small courtyard. Little seating areas dotted the walking paths that wove like a maze between flower bushes. It was a perfect, private garden for a romantic walk. Which was probably why Beatrice was there. However, instead of being on an intimate interlude with Prince Duncan, she was standing between two guards.

Beatrice's eyes widened when she saw who was approaching, but Theo could not read her expression. For a moment, she almost looked relieved.

The guard who had escorted them to the garden cleared his throat and once again asked, "You are Lady Balfour, Countess of Merrifall, is that correct?"

"Yes."

"This young woman claims to be Lady Beatrice Balfour, daughter of the Earl of Merrifall." He gestured to Beatrice, whose hands were clutched to her chest, her head moving in an almost imperceptible nod.

Lady Balfour's confusion warped into a cruel smile. "Lady Beatrice Balfour? Why, that would be impossible. Lady Beatrice is at the manor in her room, right where I left her."

Beatrice was vibrating with shock and anguish. "No. *No!* Tell them the truth! Tell them who I am! Theo, Flo, tell them!"

Lady Balfour glared at her daughters, that earlier madness shimmering in her eyes, silencing them without a word.

"Well, that settles that. Let's go." One of the guards took Beatrice's arm.

She shrugged out of his grasp. "Wait. Just wait. Duncan will be back any moment. He will tell you who I am. Please, just wait for him."

Lady Balfour gasped dramatically, her hand on her chest. "How *dare* you! First you impersonate a member of an esteemed royal household and then show such disrespect! That is *His Highness, Prince Duncan*, to you! Guards, take this impostor away at once!"

Theo watched as Beatrice took a small step backward. She looked like a trapped rabbit as her eyes, wide and frantic, darted between the guards as they closed in. And curiously, she halted, shrinking by a few inches as she did so. Suddenly, Beatrice dropped to the ground. At first, Theo thought she had fallen, but as quick as she had gone down, she popped up. And in each hand was a glass slipper.

She did not have size on her side, but what she did have was the element of surprise and the guards' underestimation of just how desperate she had become. Because, like a cornered prey animal when fleeing was no longer an option, Beatrice chose to fight. Faster than blinking, she threw a shoe at the guard in front of her. Her aim was perfect, the glass resounding with a *ping!* as it bounced off the guard's head. He fell to the ground, clutching his face and repeatedly shouting, "*My eye!*"

But Beatrice hadn't watched the trajectory of that shoe. She was too busy using the other one to club the second guard next to her. With a little yelp of a battle cry, the tiny warrior swung, striking him in the throat. It was a sloppy attack, Beatrice not known for her fighting skills, but it was effective. He coughed and sputtered, backing up until his legs hit a bench and he toppled headfirst into a rosebush. Still gripping one shoe but leaving the other where it landed in the garden path, Beatrice ran straight for Lady Balfour.

Stunned into inaction by the crazed and flailing Beatrice, she was completely unprepared when Beatrice rammed in between her and Flo. Lady Balfour crashed into the remaining guard with such force it was all he could do to remain standing. Flo was thrown into Theo and they both went tumbling down onto the pebbled path. It was the first and only time Theo was thankful for her ridiculous dress, the sleeves preventing her head from directly hitting the hard ground. However, it made her hate Flo's dress even more, as she was now buried in mint fabric and getting elbowed in the gut repeatedly by her sister, who was trying to stand.

By the time Flo had found her way out of her own skirts and Theo was saved from a tragic death by fabric asphyxiation, Beatrice had sprinted out of the garden.

The guard who hadn't been accosted by ladies' footwear sprinted after her.

"She's getting away!" Lady Balfour was screaming and gesturing at the two injured guards.

The first guard tried to give chase, but his progress was

severely hindered by his new lack of depth perception, a chair proving to be a formidable obstacle as he ran full speed into it. In a dazzling display of acrobatics, the chair and the guard both somersaulted into the hedge. The other had managed to extract himself from the guard-eating shrubbery, but that could only be considered a small victory. Still wheezing and coughing, he was now covered in dozens of bloody, thorny scratches. He, too, tried to run after Beatrice, but breathing being essential to running, his progress was slower than it might have otherwise been had he not been sucker punched with a glass shoe.

Lady Balfour picked up her skirts and joined the chase, her daughters finally upright and hot on her heels. When they reached the front courtyard, some guards were already on horseback racing down the drive, presumably chasing after a pumpkin-shaped carriage.

After waking their old driver by smacking him with his whip, Lady Balfour shoved her daughters into their carriage. "Home! Now!"

Theo and Flo sat quietly in their seats, hands in their laps with the hope that if they stayed still enough, their mother might forget they were there. Because with every mile, Lady Balfour seemed to be coming more and more unglued from her normally well-regulated, near-emotionless composure. Every few minutes, her eyes would widen and a vein on her forehead would twitch as a fresh wave of anger rolled over her. Then she would huff and sputter, talking to herself in a muddled mess of language usually reserved for sailors.

When they reached Merrifall hours later, Theo suspected Beatrice might not have returned at all. They had been only a few minutes behind her, and there was only one driveway leading to the manor, but there was no trace of Beatrice's carriage turned getaway vehicle.

However, when Theo looked up at the otherwise-dark manor, there in the west wing was a faint, flickering glow coming from Beatrice's window.

Lady Balfour must have spotted it, too, given the fervor at which she vaulted from their carriage and sprinted inside. By the time Theo and Flo had made it through the door, their mother was already at the top of the staircase. But instead of heading straight for Beatrice's room, Lady Balfour went the opposite way toward her own suite.

Theo thought she and Flo were also moving at quite a clip, but their mother was putting both them and prize-winning racehorses to shame. Before they had even made it halfway up the stairs, Lady Balfour bolted past the landing and to the west wing. Not knowing what else to do, the sisters scurried after her.

They halted at Beatrice's room. Beatrice, no longer in her fancy dress, was backing into the hallway with her hands in the air, tears streaming down her face. Lady Balfour stepped out after, arm outstretched, pointing a flintlock pistol at Beatrice.

Flo grabbed onto Theo's arm with a vise grip.

Theo slammed her hand over her mouth to stifle the shriek that was threatening to burst out, the terror of seeing the earl's gun pointed at anyone again almost more than she could bear.

"Mother?" Flo dared to ask, her voice no louder than a scampering mouse.

"*Quiet,*" Lady Balfour whispered. With her eyes nearly bulging out of her head and her lips pursed so tight they had lost all color, she motioned for Beatrice to keep walking. "*I am fixing this. She will not ruin us.*"

Beatrice continued walking backward, her hands still raised, leading the strange procession to the tower. From the bottom of the tower stairs, Theo and Flo watched as Beatrice climbed the wrought iron steps and went into the room. Lady Balfour slammed the door shut after her, fished a key out of her pocket, and locked the door.

With the key in one hand and the pistol in the other, she closed her eyes, took a deep breath, and sighed to the ceiling in relief, as though a great weight had been lifted. Then, without even a glance at her daughters, she went to her rooms.

Without knowing what else to do, Theo and Flo went to their rooms as well.

Unfortunately, their lady's maid had gone home for the night. Having no other way to get herself out of the silk monstrosity, Theo grabbed the fabric at her shoulders and pulled forward with all her strength until the buttons on the back popped free and she could shimmy out of it. She looked at it sitting on the floor like a plop of cake frosting and thought about destroying it further, but that would take energy she just did not have. She left it in a pile instead, making it the maid's problem.

Theo crawled into her bed, wishing the whole evening had not happened.

———————————— • ————————————

When Prince Duncan showed up the next day to whisk Beatrice away, turning her into a princess, Theo *really* wished the whole evening had not happened.

Almost as soon as the royal carriage left the estate, Beatrice's fantastical story exploded throughout the kingdom: Wanting to go to the ball but having no means to do so, poor, angelic Beatrice sat alone covered in soot next to the fireplace she was forced to clean and cried. To her surprise, *poof*, out of nowhere her fairy godmother appeared, asking if she would like to attend the ball. Of course Beatrice said yes. But, alas, she had no dress, and no way to get there. Not a problem for her benevolent patroness—the fairy said she would gladly help Beatrice, because Beatrice was pure of heart and deserved to go.

First, the fairy godmother solved the problem of transportation by finding a pumpkin and converting it into a carriage. Then, spying two mice running through the grass, she turned them into horses. A dog was transformed into a liveried footman. Last but not least, the fairy godmother turned her attention to Beatrice, dressing her in a gown so splendid it was said to have been made of spun silver.

However, Beatrice was not given free rein to party the night away. Most certainly not. Like many proper ladies before her, she was given a curfew, and it came with consequences for not adhering to it. Unlike everyone else, though, her repercussions for a lapse in responsibility and time management were magical. She only had until midnight to have a grand time at the ball. For once the clock struck twelve, her dress would vanish, and every other part of her enchanted facade would revert back to what it had been (except the shoes, naturally). But since she was the pinnacle of trustworthiness, she made it home just in time. It would have wrecked the whole evening if the grand finale was Beatrice sitting on a pumpkin in nothing but her underwear and fancy glass slippers surrounded by rodents and a stray farm dog in the royal courtyard.

Prince Duncan, dismayed that his mysterious true love had fled the palace, immediately set out to find her. He'd been dancing with her for hours, so of course there had been no time to ask even the most basic of conversation starters such as *What is your name?* or *Where are you from?* And certainly no time for more in-depth questions like *Is that your natural hair color—so if I'm asked to describe you later I can say "blond" with confidence?*

His only clue as to her identity was one glass shoe left behind in her haste. But, women's shoe sizes being as individual as fingerprints, he had all he needed to positively identify her. So he scoured the countryside searching for his bride, shoe in hand, hoping to find the foot to whom it belonged, and thus, the perfect woman attached to that foot. When he found her, locked in a high tower by her horrible, awful, evil, despicable, poorly dressed, and mirror-shatteringly ugly stepmother and stepsisters, he whisked her off to his palace, where they instantly became engaged to be married, to the delight of the kingdom.

A magical fairy tale for the ages.

A cartload of horseshit was what it was.

if you enjoyed

THE UNDERCUTTING OF ROSIE AND ADAM

look out for

THE LAST HOUR BETWEEN WORLDS

The Echo Archives: Book One

by

Melissa Caruso

In the Deep Echoes, no one can save you.

Star investigator Kembral Thorne has a few hours away from her newborn, and she just wants to relax and enjoy the year-turning party. But when people start dropping dead, she's got to get to work. Especially when she finds that mysterious forces are plunging the whole party down through layers of reality and into nightmare.

One layer down: It's no big deal. Stay alert, and you'll be fine.

Two, three layers down: Natural laws are negotiable, and things get very strange.

Four layers down: There are creatures with eyes in their teeth and walls that drip blood. Most people who fall this far never return.

Luckily, Kem isn't most people. But as cosmic powers align and the hour grows late, she'll have to work with her awfully compelling nemesis, notorious cat burglar Rika Nonesuch, for a chance to save her city—though not her night off.

REST WHEN YOU CAN

It's easy to fall into the wrong world.

It happens most often to children. Their grip on reality is loose to begin with, and when their imaginations wander, sometimes body and soul will follow. I've seen it happen. One minute the kid is there, playing in the dirt and whispering to themselves, and the next they've slipped down into an Echo. You have a tiny window, maybe five seconds, where they go a little transparent around the edges; if you spot it in time and you're fast, you can catch them. Otherwise someone like me has to go in after them, and that's dangerous work.

Adults can fall between worlds, too, though it's rarer. If you stumble into a spot where the Veil is frayed or torn, you may suddenly find that all the familiar things around you have gone strange and wonderful. Since Echoes are confusing, you might not be sure when it happened or how to get back.

Echo retrievals were always my favorite part of the job. In my years as a Hound, I'd rescued dozens of lost kids and a good handful of adults. I was the only active guild member with a perfect success record. When I brought them back home through the Veil between worlds, they all got this same dazed look at first—as if wandering through bizarre reflections of reality had changed them, and it seemed impossible that the world they'd left behind was still the same.

I felt a bit like that now. Two months at home with a new-born wasn't *quite* like falling into another world, but I'd had almost as little contact with my old life. Being out in public at a party surrounded by people felt strange as a half-remembered dream.

I haunted the buffet like a ghost of myself, stuffing candy-sweet grapes into my mouth more out of nervous reflex than hunger. I only had a few hours of freedom, so I had to make them count—but blood on the Moon, I'd forgotten how to talk to people.

It would be easier if Marjorie's year-turning party wasn't so . . . stuffy. Dona Marjorie Swift was on the Council of Elders, and her social peers packed the ballroom: the solid, serious merchants and bankers of the class that ruled the great city-state of Acantis, dressed in elegant tailed jackets or pale puffy gowns, all of them striving to impress. One of their pocket handkerchiefs probably cost more than my entire outfit, even counting my Damn Good Boots (a precious find, knee high in soft leather, practical *and* stylish). This was the first time I'd been able to squeeze back into them after my feet had swelled up so much while I was pregnant.

I searched the room for familiar faces, but it was hard to pick them out from the sea of muted colors. You'd think everyone would dress more festively to greet the New Year, but it was still the Sickle Moon for a few more hours, and that meant sober restraint was fashionable—so, drab colors and under-seasoned food. Not that I could complain; I'd been eating odd scavenged scraps since the baby came, with no time to cook or go to the market. I could hope Marjorie would break out more interesting fare after midnight. Some of the more fashionable partygoers would have brought a sparkling white Snow Moon gown to slip into when the year turned, or a jacket that reversed to flash silver and crystal in the lamplight. I might get about one hour of a livelier party before I had to go home.

Still. It was a party, and I was here. Without the baby. Which felt more than a little like magic.

I'd hoped to see some of my friends from the Hounds, but the one Hound I glimpsed was Pearson, who only talked to me when he had a mission to assign. There were a few members of other guilds around; they might be my best bet. The guilds didn't care how much money you had or what quarter of the city you hailed from, only what you could do. I spotted a couple of Butterflies—a well-known actor in a silky cape talking to a friend who defied stodgy Sickle Moon fashion with his vivid iridescent eye makeup—and a vaguely familiar shaggy-haired youth with some kind of guild tattoo on their hand, maybe a Raven.

And...shit. There was Rika.

She'd cut her black hair along her jawline, but I'd recognize her anywhere. I'd seen that wiry back disappearing through windows or over walls too often. Been too late to stop those slender fingers from plucking some priceless object from its protections one time too many. Her gown was all smoke and silver, draping around her like she'd only just formed in this layer of reality from one of the Deep Echoes.

Rika was no Hound, sworn to guard and protect and seek and find. She was a Cat, light and nimble, velvet and hidden steel, and she was trouble.

She'd been chatting with an older woman in a violet gown, but she broke off, rubbed her arms, and glanced around as if she felt someone watching. Before I could look away, her grey eyes caught mine across half the ballroom.

Once she might have slipped me a wink or a wicked smile— but it was the first time we'd seen each other since the Echo Key affair. The usually mischievous bow of her lips flattened, and she turned back to her conversation.

The slice of cheese I'd just grabbed crumbled in my fingers. I wasn't ready for this. Not now, when I was a sleepless mess of underbaked feelings. There was too much I'd been trying not to think about before I went on leave to take care of Emmi, and Rika was at the thick of it.

Why was she here? Rika would never come to a party this rarefied for fun. She must be on business. And that meant she was here to spy, or to steal something, or maybe even to kill someone, though I'd never heard of her doing blood work. I had to tell Pearson. I had to figure out what she was up to. I had to—

No. I was on leave.

I'll take Emmi, my sister had said. *Go to the party. You need to get out of the house. But I'd better not hear about you doing a lick of work, or I swear to the Moon I'll put hot pepper powder in all your tea.*

I was here to have fun. To talk to people. Right.

It would be nice if I had any idea how to do that anymore. Socializing was a mysterious activity that Past Kem had done, irrelevant to Present Kem, who primarily existed to make milk and desperate soothing noises. Sure, a few of my friends from the Hounds had come by in the first week or two to meet the baby, some of them bringing gifts of varying appropriateness (my old mentor, Almarah, had been excessively pleased to give Emmi her first dagger, never mind that it'd be years before she could use it), but after that...well, it had been pretty lonely.

Apparently my sister had been right when she said I needed to get out of the house. It was unfair; no one that bossy should be right so much of the time.

I nibbled my cheese and wished I could drink. But my sister said the wine would get into my milk and be bad for Emmi, so that was out. I'd have to remember how to make words *and* say them to people all on my own.

"Kem. Hey, Kem. Didn't expect to see you here."

It was Pearson. He had a rumpled, worried look, all stubble and shadows. There was only one thing that ever meant.

"I'm not working." I gave it a bit of emphasis in case he'd forgotten. "I'm allowed to go to parties."

"Right, right." He laughed, as if I'd made a joke, and took a sip from his wineglass. "Listen, do you want a drink? Can I get you something?"

"Can't," I said shortly. "Nursing."

He blinked at me like some sad owl, and I relented a bit. "How are the Hounds doing?"

Pearson leaped on the opening. "It's not the same without you. We've got lots of good people, everyone's great, but nobody like you."

I grunted. "No one who can blink step, you mean."

"Well, yes, but also not much experience on hand at the moment. A lot of our best are on assignment outside the city." He licked his lips. "So, you know, I was wondering—"

"Did you see me on the active roster, Pearson? No. Because I have a baby, remember? Small, potato-shaped human."

"Right, of course, of course." He said it in the vague way you might acknowledge the existence of hippogriffs, or some other animal found in distant lands you'd only seen in wood-cuts. "Motherhood. Splendid. Only we've run into something that looks like it might be big—just hints, but maybe some kind of power game stirring in the Deep Echoes—and we've got no one available with much Echo experience, so of course I thought of you." He flashed a tentative smile.

I gave him a flat stare. "It can't be urgent, or you wouldn't be at a party."

"Probably not, no," he agreed quickly. "So you could look into it in your spare time."

"My spare time." I rubbed my forehead. "You're not a father, are you."

"No, no." He seemed alarmed at the thought. "A bit damp, babies. And loud, I'm told. Not really my area of expertise."

"All right then, let me explain to you in four small words." I raised four fingers and then folded them down, one after another. "I. Am. On. *Leave.*"

He sighed, and his shoulders drooped. "Can't blame me for trying."

"I suppose not." I lowered my voice. "Did you know that Rika Nonesuch is here?"

"Really?" He was good enough not to peer around openly, but his eyes darted about the room. "She's bound to be up to no good."

I shouldn't ask. It was too much like work. But I couldn't help myself. "Any idea what she might be after?"

Pearson scratched his chin thoughtfully. "Could be looking to rob Dona Swift. Or to spy on the other City Elders—I think there are three of them here. Or she could be after the clock."

"Clock?"

He tipped his head toward the far end of the ballroom. "This supposed antique grandfather clock Dona Swift bought off a sketchy dealer. You only have to look at it to know it's not from *this* layer of reality. Could be a good fake, but I'd bet cold money it's from an Echo."

"That's just what we need." I shook my head. "Well, good luck. I'm not going to go finding things out on purpose, because I'm not working, but if I hear anything useful, I'll let you know."

Pearson nodded. "Thanks. Can't wait to have you back, Kem."

I grunted noncommittally as he moved off. There was no sense letting him know how comments like that currently plunged me into a whole inner crisis. Of course I wanted to go back to work; I missed the Hounds, missed seeing my friends, missed the excitement of a challenging mission and the satisfaction of a job done well. Stars, I missed just getting to walk around the city without a fussy baby strapped to me. But I also couldn't imagine leaving Emmi. I hadn't been away from her for an hour and it already felt *weird* to have my arms empty, as if part of my body were missing. I missed her funny little face, her wide wondering eyes, her tiny grasping fingers.

At the same time, damn. *Damn.* I could do what I wanted, and nobody was depending on me for every single little thing. I was just myself again, existing only for myself, for these few hours at least. I felt light and giddy, as if someone had untied heavy weights from my arms and legs.

Now, if only I knew what to *do* with all this freedom.

Dona Marjorie swept toward me with the inevitable momentum and grace of a galleon in full sail. Acres of suitably subdued forest-green skirts puffed around her, sleeves and bodice trimmed with modest ivory lace; emeralds winked with a splash of cheeky color in the tower of elaborately coiled and woven braids of her iron-grey hair. Her round brown cheeks beamed, dark eyes sparkling. She always seemed so genuinely happy to see me, and I never could tell for sure if that was because I'd saved her son's life or because she was just an absolutely delightful sugar puff who loved everyone. Probably both.

"Signa Kembral!" She threw her arms wide; I accepted her hug, a little embarrassed, as her voluminous skirts enfolded me. "I'm so glad you came. How's little Emmelaine? Is she sleeping?"

"No," I said, letting two months of despair come through a bit. "Not so you'd notice."

Marjorie shook her head. "Oh dear. Do you want me to send someone over to take her for a while so you can rest?"

"She screams like she's on fire every time I leave the room, and I doubt I could sleep through that, but thanks for the offer."

"Well, you just relax and enjoy the party, then." She patted my arm, then dropped her voice nearly to a whisper. "I'm glad you're here tonight. Just in case."

"What does *that* mean?"

Marjorie laughed, lifting her painted nails to her lips as if I'd made a slightly off-color joke. "Oh, you know, politics always get a little intense at the year-turning, that's all. Everyone's all fired up to charge out the gate with new legislation and new alliances as soon as it turns from a Sickle Moon to a Snow Moon, and the knives are out. It's good to have level heads like yours around. Don't you worry about it—focus on having a lovely night!"

My smile slipped from my face as she moved on to greet her next guest, her voice rising in welcome. *Great.* My first time in public in two months, and I'd picked a night when Dona Marjorie expected "politics" to get so wild my skills might be needed—and I doubted it was because she wanted a third at tiles. Maybe I should have worn my swords.

Suddenly a low, harsh, brassy music jarred the ballroom. It shook deep into my bones, reverberating in my teeth, seeming to come from the air itself. Just a handful of notes, each a deep *bong* like a punch to the stomach—and then silence.

A hush fell over the gathering, the kind that comes when a large number of people all hold their breath at once.

The clock. That had been the simple melody the city bells played before tolling the hour; it must be the grandfather clock Pearson had mentioned. He wasn't kidding about it being from an Echo, with a chime like that.

The whole party waited, but no hour rang. The room's other and more mundane clock, a marble antique on the mantel, still showed about ten minutes shy of nine o'clock in the evening.

A smattering of nervous laughter rose up, like a handful of pigeons taking flight to the ballroom's high ceiling. The murmur of conversation swelled back into its usual busy clamor, everyone no doubt telling one another *Oh, it's just the clock.*

I resisted the urge to go look at it. That would be too much like work. If it were dangerous, I'd feel obliged to do something about it; if it presented a puzzle, I couldn't resist trying to solve it. No, I absolutely should not cross the ballroom, weaving between partygoers with one muttered *Excuse me* after another, waving away a servant offering a tray of drinks, nudging an errant chair aside with a swish of my peacock-tail scarlet coat.

The last thing I wanted to do was lurk around waiting for the crowd drawn by its disconcerting chime to dissipate, giving me a clear view of it at last. And under no circumstances should I approach it so close that my breath misted on its glass face, staring at it in fascination.

Fine. *Fine.*

I could see what Pearson had meant. The basic shape of it was dignified enough, a grandfather clock with a cabinet of shining dark wood, its round face gleaming. But the carvings surrounding the face were twisted and phantasmagorical, with staring eyes and strange creatures climbing and writhing up into a spiked crown. Each number was in a different style and size, some of them crazily elaborate or tilted off-kilter. The three hands formed wickedly sharp spears of shining steel that patrolled the numbers menacingly, threatening them with impalement.

A single fine crack marred the face, running from top to bottom, starting at the number twelve and snaking down like a bolt of lightning. Iridescent colors showed in the silvery ribbon of broken edge embedded in the glass. I reached out, curious, and ran a finger down its length to see if I could feel it.

The glass felt slick and unbroken. But I pulled away a bloody finger.

I cursed and sucked it. *That was stupid, Kem.* What did I think would happen, petting broken glass?

"Well, well. If it isn't Kembral Thorne, in the flesh."

That was the last voice I wanted to hear right now. She'd come up behind me without making a sound, and it was too late to escape.

I forced myself to turn slowly, as if I wasn't surprised, to face my nemesis, Rika Nonesuch.

Follow us:

/orbitbooksUS

/orbitbooks

/orbitbooks

Join our mailing list
to receive alerts on our
latest releases and deals.

orbitbooks.net

Enter our monthly
giveaway for the chance
to win some epic prizes.

orbitloot.com